Storm Constantine's Wraeththu Mythos

para kindred

enigmas of wraeththu

Storm Constantine's Wraeththu Mythos

para kindred

enigmas of wraeththu

Edited by Storm Constantine
and Wendy Darling

IMMANION
PRESS
Stafford, England

Storm Constantine's Wraeththu Mythos:
Para Kindred: Enigmas of Wraeththu

Cover art and Wraeththu Mythos logo: Ruby
Editors: Storm Constantine and Wendy Darling
Interior Layout: Storm Constantine
Interior illustrations: Danielle Lainton 'Cherrah' page 16; Wendy Darling 'Sea and Shore' page 51; Ash Corvida 'Thorgyn' page 157, 'Marach' page174

Set in Garamond

IP0040
ISBN 978-1-907737-60-2

First edition by Immanion Press, 2014
An Immanion Press Edition
http://www.immanion-press.com
info@immanion-press.com

Contents

introduction

Dear Reader

Welcome to the third of the Immanion Press Wraeththu story collections, the first two volumes of which were 'Paragenesis' and 'Para Imminence'.

For those who might not have read any Wraeththu stories before, this volume in your hands is a shared world project, based upon my novels in the two science fantasy trilogies 'The Wraeththu Chronicles' and 'The Wraeththu Histories'. The first of these, ('The Enchantments of Flesh and Spirit'), was published in the late 1980s. The world of Wraeththu had been my constant companion since long before that, and continues to be. Although I write across genres and have created other worlds with rich histories, Wraeththu remains my first love. These beings had originally made themselves known to my imagination way back when I was a young teenager – they were hermaphroditic creatures with heightened physical, mental and spiritual powers, who rose from the ashes of a shattered human civilisation to create a new and hopefully better world. Conflict arose from the fact they struggled to live up to their potential and in most cases were so traumatised by their transformation from human to har they were – at least initially – incapable of healthy evolution.

As to how the short story collections came about, in the late 90s I learned about Wraeththu fandom, a committed group of enthusiasts who had remained loyal to – and interested in – the Wraeththu universe, even though I hadn't published anything new about it for over ten years. This was to do with the publishing industry at the time, and my desire to make a name for myself as a writer. I was told categorically by editors and other established professionals in the industry that I must write in worlds other than Wraeththu. And to be fair, the people who insisted on that were right; the discipline of writing out of my comfort zone helped me improve my craft and widened vastly my creative horizons.

However, in my absence from the world of Wraeththu, its fans kept it alive, partly through writing 'fan fiction' about the characters. While many genre writers dislike and distrust this practice, consider it an infringement of their copyright, and sometimes take legal steps to squash it, I've always welcomed others to play with me in my fantasy garden. I've always been aware that the moment I released my first novel it was no longer completely mine, but shared by all those who read it. And as I'd written 'sequels' to Greek and Roman myths when I was a child, I fully understood the urge to continue the stories of favourite characters. Thinking and dreaming about fictional characters is only a short step away from writing your ideas down and sharing them with like-minded friends.

When I came to read some of the fan fiction, I saw that certain of the writers were very good indeed. Once I'd created Immanion Press, I was in the position to be able to publish a few of these writers, which I saw as a kind of 'thank you' for their loyalty. This began with 'Breeding Discontent' (2003), a novel by Wendy Darling and Bridgette Parker, which was followed by 'Terzah's Sons' (2005), by Victoria Copus, and most recently 'Song of the Sulh' (2012), by Maria J Leel. While editing these novels, I had the idea of short story collections, which would enable me to include more writers. Some did not have the time to write a full length work, but were happy to contribute to an anthology.

Each collection so far has had a basic theme, although within that I've been happy for the writers to let the stories go where they most want to head. 'Paragenesis' (2010) covered the earliest history of the Wraeththu, when hara first came into being – often savage, ignorant and confused about what they'd become. 'Para Imminence' (2012) soared into the far future of this fantasy race, and enabled writers to explore what Wraeththu might become once they'd recovered from the trauma of their creation. In 'Para Kindred' I invited writers to investigate what strange mutations might have arisen alongside mainstream Wraeththu communities, as hara cast off their human origins and blossomed into an independent race.

While discussing the idea with potential contributors, we talked about how some areas of the world had not been touched either by myself or other Wraeththu Mythos authors – countries such as those of the Far East and the African continent. Some were keen to pioneer into those landscapes and find for themselves who or what might dwell there. Other contributors, Wendy and myself included, were curious about what might have evolved among Wraeththu closer to home. How would Wraeththu cope with 'difference' when initially they were the ones who were regarded – negatively – as 'different'? I found it interesting that 'Sea and Shore' by Wendy and my 'Painted Skin' both delved into the archives of folklore and fairy tales – even though neither of us had talked to the other about the subject of our contributions. My second story in this collection, 'Without Weakness', featuring a couple of established characters from the Mythos canon, was begun a long time ago, when I was writing the initial Wraeththu trilogy. I'm glad to have had a reason to complete it.

As before, I'm extremely pleased to have received contributions from writers of different countries around the world – Germany, South Africa, America, Scotland, England and the Czech Republic – thus giving a wonderful eclectic feel to the anthology. I'd like to thank my contributors for their stories and hope that there are other Wraeththu tales within them. Thanks also to Danielle Lainton for the deliciously evocative illustration to go with 'Painted Skin', and to Ash Corvida and Wendy Darling for providing illustrations for their stories 'Dreamhunters' and 'Sea and Shore' respectively.

I have tremendous fun putting these collections together and would like others to follow. In the meantime, dear reader, please enjoy our excursions into the hidden corners of Wraeththu. You are in the hands of competent guides.

Storm Constantine
March 2014

painted skin

Storm Constantine

The stage lights were ablaze in their strange, unworldly manner; a deep acid green, with beams of almost lightless cobalt firing through it. I walked onto the stage dressed in white, soon dyed by the inky radiance. My skin was green and blue, my eyes, with their reflective lenses, some alien glow; not harish.

I wanted *him* to be there; took it for granted that he would be. He came always for the first three nights of any new performance. Thereafter, his presence could not be guaranteed, although my skin could always tell when he was there, even before I took the stage and saw him. He sat on the front row, each time swathed in a concealing robe with a hood that revealed only the pale lower half of his face. No cosmetics on those finely sculpted lips. I found it difficult to discern the colour of his robe because of the lights in the auditorium. All I knew was that it was of very dark fabric that had a dull, silky sheen. And his hands were long and thin, clasped somewhat tensely in his lap. He always sat on the edge of his seat, a little hunched, certainly not relaxed. He reminded me of a picture I'd once seen, of the Shadetide dehar, Lachrymide, sitting stiffly at a crossroads in the dark end of the season.

My curiosity – I wouldn't call it desire – was no secret among my fellow performers, because at first I made a joke of it. "Even the dehara come to hear me sing," I said, laughing, after that first night I'd seen him. "Did you not see him on the first row? Lachrymide?"

The musicians hadn't taken notice of the audience and my choir were similarly uninterested as to who sat below them. But on the next night he was there again and I made a signal to Shiran, the flautist and my closest friend, so that he could see.

(Did some part of me fear the strange figure below was *not* real and only I could see him?) But Shiran saw and afterwards told me so. "He's either weak in the head, an eccentric or the son of a prominent house wishing not to be recognised. Or maybe even a celebrity, like you, Dimici. Perhaps a rival!" He grinned, clearly hoping for the last of his suggestions to be true. There was some merit in that idea, though. The dark one always did appear at the start of every run, perhaps making notes, comparing, or perhaps just acting as my greatest admirer. I had no idea. But he fascinated me, because he was so different, because he stood out and because there was something undeniably – deliciously – sinister about him.

After two years, he became almost like my personal dehar, my luck, if you like. One of the musicians once said to me, "I hope you never get to meet your idol properly. Then he will be revealed for something less than your imagination supposes. I don't think I could bear your heartbreak. Please promise me you will never try to talk to him."

Strangely, I had not considered trying to engineer that. Some inner part of me must have agreed with that har's assumptions.

And here I was again about to open my mouth, my throat, my lungs, my heart and soul, to the new witcheries dreamed and written by Tiahaar Margolin Har Prest, the best of the city's composers. And there *he* was again, my intriguing Haunt, poised like a mantis on the front row, his paws intertwined, stiff. It had become my habit to sing to him alone on these nights, even though I could not tell if he was looking at me or not.

There was some kerfuffle during the interval that night. "*He's* here!" somehar hissed at me.

"Who is?" I demanded.

"The Phyle's Pride, Vana, that's who!"

"Halfway through the show...?" I was nettled. Vana was the chesnari – well, consort – of the city's phylarch, Metrice. For Vana to arrive only at the interval was mildly insulting, perhaps worse than if he had not come at all. Previously, he had attended my performances only twice over the five years I'd been performing in Trisque, and he'd never requested to meet me. This slight had been noticed by others; it vexed me.

The stage manager of the venue, a building known grandly as The Orchestrium, stamped through us, as we milled about drinking the wild-flower cordial they'd laid out for us. "There's to be a reception after the performance, up in the observatory." He stared at me in a birdlike way. "Don't get changed afterwards, Dimici, but perhaps refresh the cosmetics." And off he stamped.

So here it was: my invitation at last.

Consorts of high-ranking hara *have* to be beautiful; there is no choice in the matter. They are part of the sumptuous appointments of the post, creatures to be admired. They have a certain way with them, and are of a certain breed; hara who become the consorts of the rich and powerful. After the performance, as I reapplied pale unguent to my face, I wondered if in fact these hara were actually *bred* somewhere, and trained like the famous concubines of history, both harish and human. Famous and *soul-deep* beauties become steeped in mystery, and they know how to maintain it. Not for them anything cheap, tawdry or embarrassing. Every movement, every glance, every low-pitched word is a work of art. Yes, they are performers too, like me.

When I entered the observatory – a glass dome at the top of The Orchestrium – purposely twenty minutes after everyone else, my eyes were immediately drawn to Vana. He was holding court at the brink of the balcony that overlooked the High Nayati, which that night was a blaze of candlelight below us, owing to the feybraiha of some rich hara's son. Vana was dressed in a costume of tight-fitting black trousers and tunic, which were covered in small coruscating beads of jet and white crystal. His platinum white hair was wound in a single artful coil behind his head, speared with a harpoon of jet, from which dangled three strings of tiny onyx beads. One cat's tail of hair looped down over his breast. His face was quite square and angular, like a sculpture, his mouth wide and pale, yet the smile upon it like the kiss of life. He was indeed perfect, in appearance and manner, even bowing his head to me in a gesture of respect when he saw me approach. I had to speak to him before I did anything else in that room; it would be noticed if I didn't.

"You make me weep and soar rapturously in equal measure," Vana said, extending a hand. I lowered my head and pressed my forehead to his cool fingers.

"I am glad the performance pleased you," I murmured. Little else was expected of me.

Vana gave a tiny frown. "Not as much as it *could* have." He laughed then, touched my face swiftly, because a frown of my own had started. "Oh, don't take me wrongly. I meant I missed the first half tonight." He paused for a second. "I have a gathering in two weeks' time. Would Tiahaar Dimici har Dusklight be free to come and perform for me then?"

This was patronage that hara would kill for. They would probably kill any impediments in their diaries also to make room for it. I did not make a show of hesitating or pretending. I simply inclined my head. "That would be a great honour."

"Good, that's settled, then. My hara will speak to your agent."

He did not dismiss me exactly, but now his business was done with me and he turned the beam of his smile upon another. I was grateful for his request. I knew this was a covert apology for turning up late, and the message this might have implied to the audience. He would know my invitation to perform for him was long overdue, but he was a busy har and there were thousands he had to appease, woo and charm on his own behalf, never mind on behalf of his consort, the city, or his tribe in general. And he did so gloriously. The most beautiful hara do not have to be cruel or mean or jealous. It is in them to be courteous and kind. Why be otherwise when the world has been so kind to *them*?

The room was full of hara of note who had attended the performance that night, their ranks augmented with presentable hara of lesser note. Of course, I looked for *him*, my haunt, but I also sensed he would not be there. He would have risen from his seat and quietly taken his leave, while everyhar else was whispering together, having heard the rumour of the reception near to the sky, and concerned they might not be invited. From the size of the crowd up there, I don't think the house manager had left many out; it was a good party and continued till dawn. Vana left at half past one. But by that time hara didn't seem to notice he was no longer among them.

The Ley House of the Phylarch was set upon a hill to the north of Trisque. In the twilight I could see its high domed roofs against the sky; it looked to me like a city of toadstools, a fairy ring upon the hill. The front door stood wide open and at the threshold a househar took my gloves and coat. He offered me a cherry encased in peppered sugar; a little warmth against the night and the encroaching season. Autumn leaves blew in across the dark tiles of the hallway, yet the door was left open, presumably to welcome guests.

An assistant of Vana, who clearly had been waiting for me, stepped forward with a bow. After introducing himself, he said he would conduct me to a room where I might prepare myself. He asked what refreshment I would like before, during and after the performance.

"White tea before," I replied, "a glass of iced water for during, and the most robust berry wine you have for afterwards."

The assistant smiled and inclined his head. "I shall see to it."

The room was in fact a guest suite, comprising a sitting room, a bedroom and a bathroom. There was a balcony but the window doors to it were locked now. Curling leaves were piling against the glass. Dim lamps were lit, but there was a brighter one I might use by the mirror, should I wish to. I had attended to my appearance before leaving my abode. Now I found I would be rather bored waiting to be summoned to sing.

Vana's assistant appeared, accompanied by a lesser minion bearing a tray. On it was a porcelain pot of white tea, a small jug of cold milk, a crystal tray of sugar, and an enormous cup and saucer fashioned of the most delicate china and decorated with blue and gold birds. There was a plate also of cat's tongues, those delicious Trisquish delicacies of the thinnest, crispest biscuits; I could smell their almondy spice even from across the room, and that delicious newly-baked warmth in them.

"Do you require anything else?" the assistant asked.

"Well... forgive me for asking, but how long will it be until Tiahaar Vana requires my presence?"

The assistant glanced at a wonderfully ornate silver timepiece set into a bangle of tangled, beaded serpents on his wrist. "Eleven minutes," he said. "Tiahaar Vana thought you could grace us with your gift before dinner, so that you might enjoy the food afterwards and mingle with the guests."

"That is thoughtful of him," I said. I had already received a note asking me to sing for twenty-five minutes. Exactly. Vana was precise about time if nothing else.

I sat in the room, in a chair facing the mantelpiece, staring at the clock that stood there, which was unusual: a slim white tower of Classical lines with a crystal or glass clock face at the summit. But behind this transparent pane there was a small shadowy figure. Occasionally, it moved forward to press its pale face against the glass, stare out. I could tell it was a clockwork figure, but even so, it was quite eerie, and absolutely compelling to watch.

At the appointed time, the attendant came for me, led me to Vana's salon and here ushered me to stand upon a dais surrounded by towering vases of white flowers. A bank of golden floor lights shone softly in my face, but their sundown radiance was enough to eclipse all but silhouettes of the audience ahead of me. All I could see was the occasional wet gleam of an eye or the shiver of hair ornaments.

I began my recitation with a historical ballad, which while perhaps sombre in content contained several tunes that were popular and widely sung, albeit most likely with different words of a more salacious nature. I heard hara humming along with me, which signified an initially good response. This I followed with a wordless angelison, its phrases soaring and flying around the heads of the audience, raising the hair on their heads and bodies. I could sense their quivering delight. Bringing them back down to earth I sang two arcadians of benevolent and mischievous mythological beings, which teased the citizens of Immanion who might venture into the hills above the city. Poking gentle fun at Immanion and the Gelaming was acceptable at such gatherings, and I heard the odd chuckle from the audience. And then finally, sensing my minutes were drawing to a close, I sang an amoris, the archetypal ache of unrequited love. As few hara escape this condition in life, whether it be at feybraiha or long afterwards, the amoris always aims for the heart and strikes it cleanly. Such songs are almost hallucinogenic in their effects and as usual I felt my voice was beyond my control, soaring and gliding, then drawing the string of the fatal bow.

The applause was loud and long. I bowed. And the lights came up. Vana, who had been seated on a chair right in front of me, stood up and came to take my hands. "You are splendid, Tiahaar," he said. And I saw his eyes were glittery with unshed tears. Some memory of lost love had haunted him for those minutes.

"It is my pleasure and my privilege," I replied, inclining my head.

He released my hands. "You will sing for me again some time."

"It would be my dearest wish."

He nodded and made a quick, imperious gesture. A har glided to his side, most likely one of his highest-ranking attendants. "Keep company with Tiahaar Dimici." Within these words lay the order to introduce me to others, keep me entertained, without a bored moment. His duty to the entertainer thus fulfilled, Vana drifted off to mingle with his guests.

The har smiled at me. "We will be dining soon. May I show you around the salons while we wait?" He extended a hand to direct me. "There are some exceptional portraits on the walls that might interest you, and various artefacts from ancient times to examine." Another har materialised at his side with a tray of drinks, and he took two turquoise flutes for us. I wasn't sure what drink was in them; it tasted of orchids and fire.

As we walked into the second salon, I froze. My guide sensed this and cast me a questioning glance. I'd seen the robe, that silky, sulky fluid of fabric, gliding between the hara that thronged the room. "Please excuse me a moment, I've seen somehar I know," I said and moved forward as quickly and discreetly as possible, which wasn't very polite under the circumstances, but my companion did not follow or attempt to stop me. My Haunt was here! I had not – perhaps for the first time since he'd been present at a performance – noticed him in the audience that night. Still, this proved he was no ghost. I could see him ahead, appearing momentarily between the clustered bodies, as if he walked through a summer forest and the sunlight touched him sometimes. Moving, he was as graceful as he'd appeared in his seat at my recitals all these years, and now neither tense nor stiff. His hood was up, as usual, but there was no mistaking him, even though I could see clearly only his head and the top of his shoulders. I longed to turn him around, see his face properly for the first time. That he was here at the reception indicated he must be a har of rank.

I followed this mysterious creature through three galleries devoted solely to paintings, observing him more than intending to make contact. He paused before many of the pictures, enabling me to glimpse his profile from the nose down, the rest of his face still obscured by his hood. The nose was straight and elegant, his chin firm. He held a turquoise flute of liquor and sipped from it. Nohar spoke to him and, although it might have been my over-stimulated imagination at work, it seemed to me that others tended to move away when he drew near to them.

In the fourth gallery we were alone. He could not possibly be oblivious of my presence by now. The room was huge, dominated by gargantuan portraits; famous beauties and herohara, politicians and phylarchs and a couple of actors. These fragments of history stared down upon us; I found their gazes oppressive. I stood in the doorway, observing my Haunt, who was staring up at a monstrous portrait of some locally significant har, whom I did not recognise. For a moment, I visualised all the colossal images coming alive and stepping down from their frames. We would be like ants to them. I shuddered. At that moment my Haunt turned, as if the shudder had been a sound. He was looking at me. I could not lose this moment. I inclined my head and moved forward swiftly. "Good evening, Tiahaar. I was just thinking these portraits are rather too large, and if they should come alive we would be crushed beneath their feet."

The har glanced back at the portrait. "That is a fearsome thought. Now I will never be able to walk through this hall again without thinking it."

"You are a regular visitor here?"

He shrugged. "Now and again. This is your first time, of course."

"As you attend so many of my performances, you must already know that."

He smiled a little. "Now you make me sound rather sinister and unpleasant."

"Not at all. I can hardly insult one of my most regular patrons."

"True." He then threw back his hood, in a somewhat challenging manner, to reveal a face I hadn't expected. He wasn't ugly, but the eyes were not as large as I'd imagined, nor as luminous. They were a rather flat hazel colour, and his brow was also lower than I'd visualised. I thought, uncharitably, *No wonder he favours the hood*. At the same time, I was strangely glad he was not one of those unearthly, vat-grown beauties like Vana.

"You must know all about me," I said, somewhat coquettishly. "Perhaps I can learn something about you?"

"Why?" His face still held that faint smile.

"Well... because you're such a regular member of my audience you feel like a friend, yet a friend I do not know. Will you tell me your name at least?"

"Cherrah har Freyhella."

This information did not give much away, other than he hailed from a northern tribe. The identifying part of his name was general. Hara used their tribal titles only when they wished not to reveal community or family details. This made it easy to obfuscate and confuse. Any har can of course have several names, used for different purposes. His accent did not sound northern, though.

"Do you travel a lot or live here in the south?"

"Both, really." His smile widened. "There isn't much mystery to me, if that's what you're looking for. Not much of interest at all. I'm simply an admirer of music."

"Every har has something interesting about him," I said. "Thoughts, beliefs, habits, knowledge – all the things that comprise a being."

"Do you seek to flatter me?"

"Probably. Does it offend you?"

Cherrah har Freyhella twirled his glass in his hands for a moment. "No. It's just that I keep to myself most of the time. I'm unused to this kind of conversation."

I folded my arms, head to one side, still coquettish. "What do you do to occupy your time?"

"You mean how do I earn my money?" He laughed softly. "You can tell I have some, of course, otherwise I wouldn't be here. I'm not obliged to *tell* you."

"Of course not. I was making conversation, that's all. And I'm more curious about your interests than your income."

He nodded slowly. "Very well. I make clocks to..." He grinned. "...to pass the time."

We both laughed.

"Clocks?" I said.

"Yes. As my parents did, and my hurakin. A family tradition. My father made the fountain clock that stands in the hall of Metrice's private apartments. I made the feather clock that Vana keeps by his bed. That is why I'm here."

"And the clock in the guest suite? The white tower with the ghostly face behind the glass?"

He nodded. "Yes, that's mine too. Would you like me to make *you* a clock? I could put your voice in it."

A shiver ran through me, like the opening of a canal lock gate and cold water pouring down. "I'll keep my voice to myself, if you don't mind." I softened the remark with another smile. "But maybe I *would* like a clock. Do you have a show room?"

"No. I have some pieces in my apartment, though." He delved into a small flat purse he took from a pocket of his garment. "This is what you want, isn't it?" He withdrew a tiny card and handed it to me.

I looked at it. The card was deep purple and the writing upon it penned in thick gold ink: "Cherrah, clock-maker, Apartment 6, House of the Red Stairs, Fern Hill, Trisque." A respectable address.

"Thank you. Might I make an appointment?"

"Tomorrow, or 'Calasday. Afternoons are best for me."

"Tomorrow will be fine."

"Good. Shall we say around two?"

"Yes, that is also fine."

Cherrah inclined his head. "Now I must be going. I've exhausted the paintings and finished my drink."

"You're not staying for the dinner?"

He grimaced. "No, the fare is too rich and the conversation too loud. As I said, I keep to myself most of the time. Thank you for another faultless performance. Goodnight, Tiahaar."

He walked past me swiftly and I turned to watch him leave. I could see the back of his garment was paned with carefully patterned lace of green, gold and deep blue. Then I realised it was not lace at all, but what appeared to be body art or a tattoo. The robe was backless. But before I could take in more than this, he had disappeared from view.

I knew I must now go back and seek my guide, make my apologies for running off. "*Not* interesting!" I said aloud, and shook my head, my smile wide. Then I put the card into my pocket.

The following day I'd arranged to meet Shiran for an early lunch, since he wanted to know everything that had happened at Vana's reception. We both arrived at the cafe at the same time, and took seats in the conservatory, which overlooked a square where Zigane musicians played, and a harling tumbled and danced, while passersby threw the ensemble coins. Red and gold leaves swooped through the air, decorating the performance.

"Well, I hope your evening went well, and will be the beginning of wonderful things," said Shiran as he sat down and arranged his jacket on the back of a chair beside us.

"I think it went well," I said, and began to examine the menu.

"Oh don't be all coy and smug! Come on, details, har, details."

I explained meticulously for him all that had occurred from the moment I'd entered the manse. Only I left a hole where Cherrah should have been, passing over him to the other hara I'd met, the list of engagements I'd secured.

"Marvellous!" said Shiran. "I hope that to some of these events you will take your personal flautist and best friend." He pantomimed a bow.

"We could certainly work on a couple of pieces just for the two of us," I said. Generally, at such events I had no accompaniment, but I wasn't so mean as not to include Shiran in my good fortune.

"Seriously? I was half joking."

"Of course you were!"

He reached over the dark green tablecloth for one of my hands and laughed. "Nohar could begrudge you this. It should have come sooner, if you ask me." Then he narrowed his eyes at me. "I seem to find myself more excited than you. How can you be so dispassionate about it? Vana's patronage will open many doors."

He was right. I didn't feel that excited about it. If anything, my meeting with Cherrah had cast a strange lightless shroud over the whole experience. I felt as if he was the only important thing that had happened to me. I shrugged. "I suppose it hardly seems real to me, not yet."

"Well, it *is* real," Shiran declared. He paused. "Did... something *else* happen?"

"What do you mean?"

"Oh, I don't know, but I do know *you*. You're distracted today, as when you've met somehar you like. I recognise the general air of not being quite with me."

"I'm merely dazed from the whole experience, Shir. I *do* know what a big thing it is."

He continued to eye me suspiciously. "If you say so."

Lies and silenced truths create walls, which help create assumptions designed to break the walls, which in turn help create divisions or even injury. I sighed. "Well, there was something else..."

"My ears are tuned to no other song but yours."

I grinned, then let the smile fall from my face, aware I was not wholly comfortable revealing my encounter with Cherrah to Shiran. "The har from the audience, the har who always watches me..."

"Your greatest admirer! *He* was there?"

"Yes. I spoke to him. He's a speciality clock-maker, from a family of them. The phylarch has one of his father's creations, and Vana has one of Cherrah's. I believe there must be quite a few of these clocks in the Ley House. I saw one in the guest rooms also."

Shiran rested his chin in his hand. "Hmm, well-connected, then. Almost a shame. I'd really wanted to believe he was some kind of ghost."

"Despite being proved a living thing, he is still somewhat mysterious."

"Beautiful, of course. Are you now truly smitten?"

I shook my head. "No, not beautiful, and no, not smitten. He's not unsightly, but not what I'd expected. He's rather too arid to adore, I think."

"But? And there is a 'but', isn't there?"

"I'm visiting him today, to look at his clocks, perhaps to buy one, or commission one."

"Good move," Shiran said, "Vana will no doubt hear of it, as will everyhar else who's a patron of the clockmaker. What's his full name? I'll do some digging."

"Cherrah har Freyhella."

Shiran pulled a face. "That's all? *Here in Trisque?*" He sniffed and leaned back in his chair. "Family or home town can't be up to much, then."

"Don't be a snob, Shiran," I snapped. "Cherrah said clock-making is a tradition of his family. Perhaps he doesn't care about 'connections' as much as you do."

"Or maybe he doesn't care about connections in the same way Metrice and Vana don't care about affluence; if he has privileges, a polite har will pretend not to notice them. Yet such hara are still aware that fame, fortune and good connections are a bunch of gold keys in their fists. Did you ask to view his wares or were you invited?"

"Something of both."

"Sounds positive. Might we dine together tonight so you can tell me more of your adventures?"

"Possibly. I can't promise." I grinned. "After all, I might get a better offer."

Shiran laughed loudly, causing those dining around us to glare in our direction. "In that case, breakfast together tomorrow is a *must*."

Fern Hill is a picturesque area of Trisque, a desired address for those who can afford it and who do not seek liveliness and activity. The large old houses, interspersed with newer buildings constructed in antique style, stand in fair-sized gardens dominated by mature trees. Narrow cultivated areas, comprised mainly of long-fronded ferns, run along the centres of the few winding, steeply sloping streets of the hill. Favoured mainly by successful yet creative hara, who have drifted into the life of producing harlings with a chesnari, the area exudes a tranquil air. This is a perfect place for an artisan har, preferring privacy, to dwell. The houses are big enough to accommodate workshops and storage areas, and the occupation of clock-maker could not possibly produce irritating noise – or so I thought – that might bother neighbours.

I was having a short break from work now, before Shadetide, when the troupe would appear at various festival events, both public and private. Then there would be two weeks of intense work and moving about. Festivals were always a busy time for us. Often we didn't get a moment to eat properly between appointments, and uninterrupted sleep of more than four hours was a luxury. As well as appearing in the city and nearby towns, we'd have to travel to the wilder places beyond, where old harish families kept the ancient traditions alive, which were wound like ivy around and through newer beliefs.

I walked slowly up Fern Hill, absorbing my surroundings.

When walking, I am always working, in the same way a writer does. Ideas for songs come to me by what I might glimpse at a curtained window or in a windswept garden. I decided I wouldn't want to live in such a place, but it would be pleasant to have a friend who lived there I could visit. The lives beyond those tall windows might be mundane in the extreme, but the artist in me wanted to imagine secrets, mysteries, tragic romances, even horrors. Hara are entertained by such things. Compositions about normal lives with nothing happening, other than quiet good fortune, would have to have catchy tunes indeed to become popular.

Was there, then, a song to be created about Cherrah Har Freyhella?

The House of the Red Stairs was an enormous old mansion, very near the top of the hill. The building had been divided into a number of apartments, including the stables and other outhouses. Cherrah's apartment was in the old stable block, or rather *was* the old stable block, no smaller than any of the elegant town-houses I had passed on the way, and of two storeys. The doorbell, perhaps fashioned by Cherrah himself, allowed visitors to give warning of their arrival via an ornate iron ring-pull, with merhara and hippogryphs, wound with seaweed and shells, writhing up its shaft. As I pulled the bell, I wondered why I had not heard of Cherrah before, and why he'd been a stranger also to my colleagues. He lived in this upmarket house, he roamed the circle of the phylarch. No stranger to Trisquish society, but yet a stranger to me. I had based myself in Trisque for five years, and for around two of those years Cherrah had been a regular attendee of my performances. What I found I couldn't remember now was whether he'd attended events beyond the city. My troupe travelled wide in the summer, working through the white-stone towns along the coast. I really couldn't remember if Cherrah had followed me to these places.

Before I could ponder further, the door opened and there was Cherrah, not a member of his staff as I'd expected. He was dressed in simple tunic and trousers, his pale hair plaited and falling over one shoulder. I experienced a strange moment of utter disappointment at his ordinariness but this was mixed uncomfortably with a dart of interest and attraction. Such opposing poles.

"Hello again," he said, smiling. "Come in, please."

I muttered a greeting and sidled past him into a dim hallway. The windows here were small and few, although the floor was of beautiful amber-coloured wood, polished to a silky sheen. There was a table near the door where lay a pair of cream leather gloves, resting against the base of what at first I took be some kind of model or dolls' house. I was drawn to this immediately, once I heard the soft ticking that emanated from it.

"You like that?" Cherrah asked, as he took my coat and placed it carefully on a hook by the door. "It's a copy of the coach-house you'll find round the back of this place. The clock in the centre of the eaves there is the same as what's outside, only considerably smaller of course. I got that old clock working again when I moved here, and then had the idea for this model. On the hour a coach comes out of that left hand door there and the horses rear and neigh to call the hour."

I peered through the tiny windows in the doors, could just make out shadows of a dull-gleaming coach, maybe even the horses. I fancied some creature was shuffling about in there. Had to be clockwork, but I'd never seen har-skill like it. "It's incredibly ornate and detailed, almost like a dolls' house." I touched the tiles of the roof, found them made of wood and painted to look like mossy slate.

Cherrah stood with folded arms beside me. "I'm rather proud of it. I like creating buildings and making the clocks part of them, but there's not a great call for this type of piece. They take up a lot of room."

"Yes, I can imagine. In many houses, they'd just get damaged by hara lumbering by – my own, for example!"

Cherrah laughed. "And what kind of clock do you like?" I did not answer at first. He indicated for me to follow him into a room on the left, which was revealed to be a comfortable yet sparsely furnished sitting room. A fire was burning in an immense marble hearth. On the mantelpiece, around the inevitable timepiece – this time a replica of a narrow crooked house whose attic window was a misshapen clock face – a group of mechanical kittens were frolicking.

I went to the clock, examined it. "Don't tell me, on the hour the mother cat comes out and pounces on the kits, one for each hour."

Cherrah laughed. "No, on the hour they leap onto the roof and yowl, once for each hour." He pointed at a pale-cushioned sofa before the fire, which looked virtually brand new. "Please sit down. Would you like refreshment?"

I always feel the offering and acceptance of drinks is the initial part of any social call, which establishes rapport and ease between host and visitor. To refuse always seems somehow cold or rude to me – I hate it when visitors to my house say "no" and I sit there drinking tea alone, because I always insist on having it, even if the guests won't partake, meanwhile thinking what impolite creatures they are, how they're not really participating in the visit. Or perhaps they have harsh news to relate, which teas, coffees or tisanes are too frivolous to attend. Anyway, I accepted Cherrah's offer at once.

"I'll go and see to it," he said. "Think about your dream clock while I'm gone."

My *dream* clock...

Weirdly, an image came to me at once, which I think was partly influenced by the piece I'd seen in Vana's guest suite. I visualised a tall, circular, temple-like building with a domed roof, which would be enveloped in ivy. The clock face itself would be a sundial before the temple. On the hour, a figure would emerge from the temple, a har or perhaps a dehar, swathed in Classical drapery. They would have to emit a sound of course, but not my voice, not my song.

Cherrah returned with a tray, holding a pot of green tea covered with a cloth and two mugs decorated with – hardly to my surprise – clocks. He must have had hot water ready, waiting for my visit. I had the feeling now the house contained no staff. "Hope you like this brew," Cherrah said. "Have you thought about your clock?"

"I think *it* thought about *me*," I said, smiling. "An image came to me almost the moment you left the room, but whether it's possible to create or not, only you'll be able to say."

Cherrah sat down next to me on the sofa, began pouring the tea, which he'd set on a low table before us. "Describe it to me, then."

I did so.

Cherrah nodded, handed me a mug of tea. "I see your vision, but will do a couple of sketches for you, before I begin work."

At this point I realised I had unwittingly entered into a contract. "I don't wish to be indelicate, but before we go any further I'll need to know what this piece will cost."

Without pause or apparent embarrassment, Cherrah named a price, which was not beyond my means, but certainly far more than I'd ever have considered spending on a clock. "That will be fine," I said.

"Good. Shall I drop the sketches over to you tomorrow? I can whip up a few ideas while I'm eating my dinner later."

"Yes. That's good of you, very swift."

He raised a hand, as if to stem the compliment. "I just love my work. It's no problem. The origin of a new clock is always an exciting time."

"Perhaps we can meet for lunch tomorrow," I suggested. "This is one of those rare times in the year when I'm free to do what I like."

Cherrah frowned slightly. "Oh, oh, that would be... I'd like to, but you see, I'll have a lot of work to do on your clock. I just need your approval to begin, that's all. I'd like to start tomorrow, as soon as you've seen the drawings."

I was rather taken aback by his urgency. "But what about all your other commissions?"

He made a dismissive gesture. "I work very quickly when the mood takes me. I'm intrigued by your idea and want to do that first."

"Well, all right, if you're sure. Perhaps lunch once the work is done?"

He smiled tightly. "Perhaps, yes."

I finished my tea quickly and put down my mug on the table. "Do you require an advance, Tiahaar?"

He shook his head. "No, that won't be necessary."

I got to my feet and realised he didn't intend to see me to the door. "I'll let myself out," I said.

Cherrah was staring at the fire, apparently hardly aware of me.

I placed my calling card on the table by the tray. "Until tomorrow, then. May I expect you around mid-day?"

He nodded but said nothing, and I went unescorted to the door.

I didn't wait for dinnertime, but went directly to Shiran's

apartment, which was very near my own, close to the Orchestrium. He was surprised to see me, but clearly delighted I was there, because it must mean gossip was imminent. "Give me coffee," I demanded, before waiting for his invitation.

"Let's sit in the kitchen," Shiran said.

His househar was in there and Shiran instructed him to prepare coffee in the largest receptacle available. We sat at the table while the househar bustled about – he was one of those rare finds, being both attractive and efficient. I knew Shiran paid higher wages than was necessary to keep him. The har was also very discreet, so I began to relate what had happened on Fern Hill.

"Hmm," Shiran murmured, after I'd finished my tale and we were drinking the coffee. "You didn't get to see his collection or his workshop?"

"I've told you everything," I said. "There isn't any more. All I saw was two clocks, albeit amazing ones." I frowned. "Strange there was only one clock in each room, though. You'd expect a clock-maker to have them all over the place."

"Not if he cares enough about his art to show them off to best effect," Shiran remarked. "No point us trying to put mystery where there is none. There's more than enough of it without that."

"What do you think?"

Shiran pulled a face. "At face value? He's a fan of yours, perhaps fanatic in the true sense, and couldn't believe he'd got you in his house. He'd been pacing up and down for over an hour before you got there. The tea was waiting – he might've poured away two pots that had gone cold."

"Hey, I was on time!"

"Hush, you're spoiling my drama. I don't think he cares about the money, but he *does* care about you, what you think. He's put all his other commissions aside to work on yours, and I don't believe for a second it's just because your clock intrigues him. Personally, I think your idea's a bit trite."

"Thanks."

"You're welcome." He grimaced. "I don't know, Mici, maybe you should be careful. Fans can be, well... you don't need me to tell you."

We looked at one another and shared a few silent seconds of

agonised memories.

"Do you really think it's just that?" I asked.

Shiran shrugged. "What do *you* think?"

"I'm not sure. He's sort of... otherworldly, I suppose. I don't think he was lying about the work, but perhaps he does want to impress me as quickly as possible, and that's why he's shoved my clock to first in the queue. He said no to lunch, remember. Perhaps he's not as much of a fan as you think. If he was that interested in me, he'd have leapt at the chance, surely?"

"Depends how devious he is. A clever har would not jump at the first opportunity." Shiran rested his chin in one hand, drawing circles in spilled coffee with the other. "It does seem odd that we've never heard of him before. He was just a face in the crowd, if a regular face. Why wasn't he at Vana's reception at the Orchestrium? He must surely have been invited. Why is he suddenly available to you? Was he waiting for your credentials to become more respectable, as in Vana offering his patronage?"

"He doesn't strike me as the social climbing sort," I said. "I don't think he even has house-hara, not even one. I don't suppose you've had chance to do any digging yet, have you?"

Shiran shook his head. "No, but I intend to start immediately. Shall we meet at The Swan's Neck for dinner?"

"Yes. I'll see you at the usual time."

At home, I felt jumpy and nervous, which to me indicated the well-known symptoms of developing an interest in a har, but at the same time this didn't feel like that. I couldn't concentrate on anything, so went out for a long walk in Thornbloom Park to the east of Trisque. The closing year shuttered the day early. A chill breeze shuffled the falling leaves. Autumn's gaudiness would not leave the land until after Shadetide, but its festival dress was beginning to look rather worn.

I arrived at The Swan's Neck early, and consumed two flutes of russet wine before Shiran came to my table.

"You look calmer," he said, removing his coat and sitting down.

I raised my glass to him.

"I see. Well, not a lot to report, I'm afraid. Tiahaar Cherrah is *known* but only in the most tedious fashion. There is no gossip or mystery. He is a har who makes clocks. He moved to Trisque around two years ago, and letters from his family helped him secure work and connections. Hara like his pieces, but don't have much to say about the har who makes them. Quietly, his devices have gradually come to measure time in most of the homes of Trisque, or so it seems. He doesn't only work for rich hara. He sells a few cheaper pieces to shops for anyhar to buy."

"I'm just surprised we haven't heard of him before."

"You know, I think hara only hear of him when he wants to be known. He slips beneath notice, and the hara I spoke to were almost weirdly surprised to remember him. A ghost who is not a ghost. Intriguing. I think I want to meet this enigma."

"He's coming to my house tomorrow. Don't expect to be impressed."

Shiran arrived for breakfast at 10 and we spent some time discussing ideas for the events for which I'd secured bookings. Most would be for over the Natalia period, so we had time to prepare. That morning a note had arrived from Vana's secretary, requesting my presence at the Natalia Extravaganza at the Ley House. Shiran said he would murder me if he were not to be included in my performance there. I told him I'd have to make enquiries to see if it was acceptable for me to take him. The phylarch and his consort might not want a spare flautist floating about, no matter how well he played.

We were so wrapped up in playfully sniping at each other, and marking events on my calendar, that the time zipped by. Mid-day came and with it a knock at my door. I was on my feet in an instant, yelling to Furze, my househar, that I'd answer the knock myself. I skidded into the hall, then collected myself and walked sedately to the door. Opened it.

Cherrah stood on the threshold, wearing a hooded cloak that covered the upper part of his face. One pale hand clutched the fabric at his neck. Over his shoulder hung a battered, wide leather satchel.

"Good morning, Tiahaar, come in, come in," I said.

Cherrah stood motionless, silent.

"Is anything wrong, Tiahaar?" I asked.

At that moment, Shiran rushed past me and out through the door. I called his name.

He turned and ran backwards for a few steps so he could

shout at me. "Sorry, Mici, have to dash. I forgot. I forgot!" Then he turned and was gone, sprinting up the street.

Neatly, Cherrah came into my house and carefully peeled back his hood. He looked about himself, but still did not speak.

"I... er... apologise about that," I said. "That was my friend... er... well, never mind. May I take your cloak?"

Cherrah shook his head. "I won't be staying long." He took the bag from his shoulder. "Do you have a table where I might lay out my drawings?"

"Of course." I ushered him into the dining room.

Carefully, Cherrah removed a sheaf of parchments from the satchel and laid them out slowly in two lines on the table. A couple of drawings? This was more like over a dozen.

There was only one design, shown from various angles, several barely different from others. A couple of drawings revealed some of the interior workings of the device. Yet even though there was no choice in the design, the one Cherrah had realised was perfect, reflecting entirely the image that had been in my mind at his house.

"Is this to your liking, Tiahaar?" Cherrah asked.

"Of course it is. It's exactly what I imagined. Are you a mind-reader?"

He did not smile at my joke. On one of the frontal view drawings he pointed at the sundial, before which stood a noble, draped har. "To have the dial work as in reality, I would have to create a facsimile sun. I feel this might be too bright and intrusive for your hallway."

I raised my brows. "My hallway? Is that where you think I should place the clock?"

He nodded.

"But you haven't seen the rest of the house..."

"I saw the hallway, which seems right for the piece."

"Very well, if that's your opinion." I considered privately I didn't have to concur with that once the piece was safely in my possession.

"So," Cherrah continued, "if it's acceptable to you, the clock in the sundial will be of the normal kind. Of course, you won't be able to see the time until you stand over it. The hands of the clock can of course be shadows. Again, I must ask if this is acceptable. If not, we can modify the design."

"Well, looking at it, the piece is more of an ornament than a clock, beautiful as it is. The time piece will be a surprise for anyone looking at it."

Again, Cherrah nodded, but not, I felt, in agreement with me. He simply nodded so we could conclude our business. "If you're happy with the design, I'll leave a drawing with you and go to start work. Would you like to choose one?"

"I'll take one of the frontal views – you choose. Keep the ones you need."

Cherrah removed a drawing and handed it to me. "I don't need any of them now, but this shows the full clock from the front, with the hour figure revealed. I want you to keep it to compare with the finished piece."

"Well, thank you, but I'm sure that won't be necessary."

Cherrah smiled at last. "No, it won't, but please take it as a gift."

I had a feeling then that his sketches for customers might well command a decent price themselves. I looked down at the drawing. The figure, the temple, the foliage, the sundial; all looked so realistic. Cherrah was an artist, a sculptor, as well as a clock-maker. "I'll feel privileged to share my home with this art," I said. "Truly."

"When it is finished, I'll contact you about installation."

I felt it would be coarse and somehow inappropriate to mention his fee again, but would make sure this was ready for him once the piece was delivered. He began to lift his hood over his head once more, but before his eyes were covered he stared at me deeply. There were messages in that stare that normally I would consider it easy to interpret. Perhaps not so much with this one. I saw desire, yearning, yes, but what else? Subtle emanations. I wasn't sure.

I felt absurdly sad. That stare should have streamed from lovely eyes, full of stars and reflections. Cherrah's eyes were small and unremarkable. He had been given such gifts but perhaps at a price.

I shook myself mentally to disperse these bizarre thoughts. "How long do you anticipate the work will take, Tiahaar?"

"Not long. There will be plenty of time." He gathered up his remaining drawings and replaced them in his satchel.

I laughed, a little nervously. "For what?"

The satchel went over his shoulder. "For your clock to be installed before you begin your work again."

I could no longer see his eyes, his brow, his forehead, only his perfect nose, his exquisite mouth and chin. A shiver ran through me. "I see. Thank you. That will be very quick for such a big job!"

He inclined his head, positioned his hood carefully. "This is my occupation. I'm adept at it."

Then he glided from my house, without waiting for me to accompany him to the door.

Shiran reappeared about two hours later. "What was all that about?" I demanded as he came into my sitting room. "Rushing off like that?"

He flopped down in a chair opposite me. "I really don't know, Mici." He frowned. "I was simply sitting in your kitchen, anticipating the meeting with your clock-maker when I... remembered something, a really important appointment I had entirely forgotten. I was compelled to grab my coat and just run from the house, as if the Mahallatu were on my tail."

"What appointment was it?"

Shiran turned bewildered eyes to me. "That's just it: I don't know. I ran around town for maybe twenty minutes, panicking, terrified I was missing something life-saving or vital in some other way, but I wasn't going anywhere. I couldn't remember where I was supposed to be. The fear was terrible. Eventually, like a drug wearing off or something, I came to my senses and staggered into a cafe. Here I fortified myself with liqueur coffee until I could face the journey home. Thank dehara, there was a carriage rank right outside the place. My limbs were like those of a newly-hatched harling; I could barely stand."

"That is most... *strange*," I said inadequately. "Like a nightmare." Shiran was not a har given to nervous fits. An idea came to me at once but I shrank from voicing it. Not so Shiran.

"I think I was driven out of this house, Mici, and you know by whom. I wasn't wanted here. He wanted you to himself or he didn't want me to see him."

"What *did* you see, as you ran past him?"

"Very little, I was in such a panic. A har draped in a dark cloak, that was all. When I ran past you, it was like you were only a blur, but he wasn't. He was clear to the eye and perfectly still, but... hidden."

I rubbed my arms as if cold, sure my teeth were chattering, though the room was warm. I got to my feet and went to the fire, held out my unaccountably chilled hands to it. "Perhaps... perhaps I should cancel the order for the clock. Even if he's begun work on it, he'll surely be able to sell it elsewhere."

"No, I wouldn't do that!" Shiran said hurriedly. "No, Mici, don't antagonise him further."

"Further?" I froze on the spot before the hearth where I'd begun to pace up and down.

"Me being here was antagonism. Go through with it, pay your money. Then you don't have to speak to him again if you don't want to. There's something weird about that har, and my instincts are hissing at me: don't anger him."

I pressed my icy fingers to my eyes, at that moment utterly frightened. Was Shiran simply over-reacting and feeding my fears? I couldn't tell. All I could focus on was Cherrah's great beauty when half his face was hidden, and the reflex of virtual repugnance and disgust it inspired when he revealed his eyes and brow. No, he was far from normal, and had perhaps compensated in unusual ways for his differences. I lowered my hands from my face and said, "I should seek protection from the nayati."

Shiran reached out to touch my waist. "No. He will be aware of that. I just *feel* this. Every atom of my being cries out for you to go along with him, then once the job is done, back off."

"What if he doesn't want me to back off? Am I allowed to seek protection then?" I was beginning to think Shiran was over-dramatising the situation. Cherrah *was* strange, and it wasn't unheard of for powerfully psychic hara to influence others in the way Shiran had perhaps been influenced. Cherrah had wanted me alone; this much I believe was true. Also that he hadn't wanted to be seen by my friend. So he'd taken action, but I didn't want to think this had been malicious, merely necessary to him: the quickest way to rid himself of Shiran's presence without too much fuss. "Perhaps he is the one who's frightened," I said. "He's not that social a creature. Perhaps he wanted to avoid you inspecting him. Is that unreasonable?"

Shiran made a placatory gesture. "No, but let me just say this. You're not a native of this land, Mici, nor have you ever visited the northern realms. Magics linger in the clouds, the forests. Hara who formed there... well... perhaps they have more of ancient mysteries in them than we know."

I laughed. "Oh for Aru's sake, Shir, what are you saying? That Cherrah is some kind of sorcerer?" I pantomimed a scary creature with hungry claws. "He's come down from the mystic north to make me a clock and then devour me!"

Shiran was staring at me. "Why do you scoff in that way? Do you think we know everything about the way our race has developed?"

"No, but dreaming up wild ideas is hardly helpful in this situation."

"Why does Cherrah conceal so much about himself, then?"

"Maybe he just doesn't *care!*"

Shiran took in a deep breath through his nose. How had this become an argument between us? "So you don't believe me, fair enough. But I have your welfare at heart, Mici. All I'm saying is fanaticism mixed with some kind of *difference* might be dangerous."

"I appreciate your concern," I said, feeling I must defuse this situation. "And I didn't mean to mock. I'll do as you suggest and simply finish my business with him – it seems wise. But afterwards, if there's any kind of trouble I'll take action. Hopefully this won't be necessary. Let's simply wait and see."

"Be careful, Mici," Shiran said.

I didn't hear from Cherrah for nearly three weeks and began to wonder whether my clock would indeed be finished by Shadetide. Our troupe was due to begin performing three days before the festival and for over a week thereafter. Then we had a steady calendar of work up to Natalia. We started rehearsals at the Orchestrium, and because I was so busy, not least with writing two new pieces Shiran and I were to perform at the Ley House, the thought of the clock slipped from my mind – more or less. Sometimes a shadowy figure I felt was Cherrah haunted the rim of my dreams, though.

Then on a Lo'itsday evening, when I returned home, Furze told me a har had called and had left a message. Something in his expression, a mix of puzzlement and distaste, advised me the visitor had been Cherrah. The message confirmed this; my clock was ready.

I wouldn't be able to have him deliver it during the day until the weekend, but my evenings were clear for the next two nights. I asked Furze to deliver this information to Fern Hill and to secure a reply.

When Furze returned, there was no written message, simply a verbal one. He again looked somewhat bewildered. "Tiahaar Cherrah said to tell you it will be tomorrow evening. He said that owing to your work preventing lunches for the time being, maybe dinner tomorrow would be a possibility. He asked if that might be here, in the house. He said if he didn't hear from you, he'd consider arrangements for tomorrow were acceptable."

I stared at Furze for some moments and he stared back. I could tell he didn't know what to think about the somewhat presumptuous tone of the message, but he *did* feel uncomfortable about something.

"Have his money ready for him, would you, Furze?" I wrote on a note slip the amount due to Cherrah; Furze had permission to withdraw funds from my bank.

Furze glanced at the note, made no comment other than, "Of course, Tiahaar."

Cherrah had banished my friend from the house to avoid meeting him – *apparently* – yet seemed at ease relating personal messages through my househar. Asking to dine at a har's house rather than out at a restaurant construed an unambiguous message, and only somehar utterly naive and stupid wouldn't realise that. None of this added up to what I had presumed to be the character of Cherrah Har Freyhella.

At the Orchestrium the following day, I didn't tell Shiran I'd be seeing Cherrah later that night. Mainly, I told myself, this was because I didn't want him to worry, but I also wished to avoid any lectures on my safety and so on. Nohar was more aware than I that Cherrah was no ordinary har, and might be dangerous, although I found that difficult to believe. Cherrah seemed timid and self-conscious, more than anything else. The episode with Shiran could not be denied, and had definitely been peculiar, but I still believed this must have been down to a weird kind of self defence on Cherrah's part.

At seven o'clock, Cherrah delivered my clock. He arrived in a carriage and two hara he'd hired for the purpose transported the piece to my hallway, where I'd already cleared a table for it. When Cherrah removed the packing cloth from the piece, it was much larger than I'd anticipated and perhaps wouldn't look quite right on the delicate table I'd chosen to be its plinth. But Cherrah arranged it there, removing wadding of soft cloth he'd placed between its most fragile parts, and when he stood back the clock appeared to be perfectly at home.

The piece was maybe three feet high, and even though it included no facsimile sun – or moon for that matter – as Cherrah had briefly mentioned, it gave off the impression of standing in evening light. Well, I told myself, why would it not? It *is* evening, after all. But the light around the clock spoke of summertime, the soft fall of daylight into mystic moonshine, foliage heavy upon the trees, yet motionless and breathless before the true advent of night. Two oaks stood behind my clock, the leaves so beautifully and realistically carved they seemed to rustle. How had Cherrah completed this piece in so short a time? The carving alone must have had him up till dawn every night. The temple was of smooth white marble. When I touched the domed roof there was a faint grittiness to it, but the columns at its entrance were like glass. Ivy fashioned from silk and wire drooped over it, twining also about the trunks of the oaks. Its interior was a dark blue shadow.

"Would you allow me time to check the clock and see to its correct working?" Cherrah asked, and it took some moments for me to realise he meant: would I give him privacy to do it.

"Of course. I'll see how dinner's progressing." With a polite bow I took my leave.

I gave him ten minutes before I returned to the hall. He was still arranging ivy leaves over the temple roof, standing back to observe the effect, before making more minor adjustments. "It looks marvellous," I said. "Thank you so much, Cherrah." I held out an envelope. "This is for you."

He took the money, inclining his head respectfully. "Thank you." The envelope was secreted into his satchel, which I saw he again wore over one shoulder.

"May I take your cloak?" I asked.

He glanced at me. "All right." As always he revealed his eyes and brow in that slow somewhat challenging manner, before unclasping the cloak at his neck. And as before, I started a little inside when those features were revealed. Would it ever not be a shock to behold them? It was not as if he were deformed or ugly. Just... something strange.

I stood with the limpid fabric of the cloak lolling in my arms, while Cherrah turned his back on me to fiddle once more with the clock. As at Vana's reception, he wore a backless robe, this time of matte black linen, exquisitely cut. Colours flamed across his back and shoulders. I couldn't help but approach him to look more closely.

He must have felt me studying him, because I became aware of a slight tension in his body, yet he did not turn around. The design of the tattoo, because I could see clearly this was no temporary illustration, seemed to be of the trunk of a tree, wound about with flowering vines and ivy. I say *seemed to be*, because it was more of an abstract impression rather than a literal replica of a tree. There were creatures on the bark, birds like miniature peacocks with spreading tails, long-haired mice, or mice with manes like lions. I even saw a pair of yellow eyes peering out from what appeared to be a deep, dark hole in the trunk.

"That is the most amazing tattoo you have," I said. "I feel I could look at it for hours and see more in it as every minute passed."

Cherrah straightened up and turned round. "Thank you."

"What a pity you can't admire it yourself very easily."

He smiled. "I know what's there."

"So you were a canvas once," I said.

"I wondered whether a mask of feathers across my face would be interesting," he said, standing very close to me, and in his words an unspoken challenge. "Do you think so, Tiahaar?" He touched the collar of my shirt provocatively.

There was no helping it; I took him in my arms so we might share breath. But he merely kissed me in a shallow manner, then drew away, keeping his secrets to himself.

I remembered him saying when he handed me his calling card in the Ley House, "that's what you want, isn't it?" and was tempted to say the same now, because surely seduction was his purpose, beneath all other considerations? But I kept silent, staring at him for long moments, saying at last, "My househar, Furze, is ready to serve us dinner."

Cherrah nodded. "Very well."

Before, I would have taken his arm to lead him to the dining room but now, feeling rebuffed, I simply walked ahead of him, indicating the way.

Furze was already placing the soup. I noticed he gave Cherrah a sharp glance as we entered the room, and was very quick to escape. Cherrah sat down where I pulled out a chair for him. I was suffused with a bewildering mix of strong desire, unspecific fear and giddiness.

As Cherrah consumed his soup, neither greedily nor sparingly, I noticed he wore a sort of gauntlet over his right forearm; it was a watch, of course. A watch made of silver armour and encrusted with black pearls. His thin hair was drawn back into a severe plait. There was little conversation during the soup.

Once the first course was consumed, Furze materialised in the startling way he sometimes has, and whisked away the plates. Even Cherrah seemed a little surprised by his abrupt appearance and disappearance.

"He's very efficient," I said, lamely.

Presently, the meat course was brought to us; lamb and berries accompanied by vegetables of the season.

"Efficient and an excellent cook," Cherrah said, tucking enthusiastically into the pink-centred slices of lamb on his plate.

I nodded. "Do you have househara, Cherrah? When I visited you, the place seemed empty, I could not sense others. Do you prefer to live alone?"

"I have few needs to be seen to," he said, "and those I do have I can manage to satisfy by myself."

Was there an implied criticism there, of those who could afford to hire hara to attend to the most basic of daily tasks, so as not to be bothered with them?

"I like the company," I said, aware it sounded a little defensive.

"Like the ticking of a clock," Cherrah said.

"Is that all you need for company?" I asked.

He looked up at me. "Most of the time, yes. A clock has a beating heart." He glanced at his right forearm. "Talking of which, we must not miss the hour. I want you to see him."

I glanced at the ordinary, straightforward clock that hung upon the wall, opposite my seat. "Well, let's take a break before dessert. That should time it neatly."

We continued to consume the main course in silence.

Glancing at Cherrah occasionally, I was flushed with moments of desire, followed by chills of disquiet. This har woke such contradictions within me. My revulsion for him was not caused solely by the unkind arrangement of his facial features; it went deeper than that. Part of him was beautiful, a creative, sensitive soul. But there was another part, a part perhaps hinted at, which I had not yet truly seen.

At two minutes before the hour, we went out into the hallway. The room was in blue starlight, with only the dimmest autumnal gleam from the wall lamps, which Furze had turned down very low. The temple of the clock gleamed upon its table. Standing close to it, I saw the shadow of the marker upon the dial, which stood on a slim column, slightly to the left of the temple entrance. How had Cherrah achieved that and would it work so effectively in daylight when the sun was falling directly upon it through the tall, east-facing windows by my door? The temple and dial were surrounded by soft grass that seemed to breathe.

Cherrah came close to me and took my right arm in his hold. "Watch," he murmured.

As the shadow moved over the dial to mark the hour, a figure emerged from the temple. Its thick, blue-black hair cascaded over its chest, which was partly revealed by carefully arranged drapery. Its arms were by its sides, but now it raised them, and uttered a low, melodious tone. This was not repeated; it was a single sound. But I swear the lips had opened to release it. "Cherrah," I whispered, for I dare not raise my voice, "is that me?"

The figure had lowered its arms now, and bowed its head, before retreating into the temple.

"A little like you," he said softly. "Are you pleased with the clock?"

"It's exquisite," I said, and now it felt acceptable to talk at normal volume.

"I'm glad you like it."

"Shall we return to the dining-room?" I asked.

"I do not want dessert there," he answered. "The hour has spoken, it is time." And now he wrapped his arms around me and put his lips against mine. This time, he let me see forests, and smell the heady scent of sun-baked pine. I saw high mountains, and eagles swimming in the clear air. His home.

I took him to my bedroom, consumed by the need for aruna, but also aware this was perhaps the culmination of Cherrah's plans from when he'd first started to haunt my performances. Did it really matter? In the darkness of my room, I could barely see him, but starlight fell in through the window in a bar across his mouth and chin; the rest of his face was in shadow. I put my arms around him, pulled him close, and it seemed to me that my hands upon his back traced textures, as if his body art was more than mere paint injected into the skin. Leaves, rough back, and even the skitter of a soft-footed creature across the back of my hand. This aroused me even more.

After that, events are hazy in my memory, although with crystal sharp exceptions. He was soume for me, taking me into a hallucinatory realm of fabulous visions, of countries in the clouds that I could not have imagined. We rolled in the bed as if we were rolling in the sky, eagles mating on the wing. I was beneath him, cushioned only by air, and for a moment panicked. I dug my fingers into his back.

What I found there...

A fallen, hollow tree, aged and buried beneath wet leaves. Its hidden side turned to the air, it was as putrid as wet, decaying fungus, alive with devouring beetles and grubs. Spongy and smelling of over ripe mushrooms. My hands were consumed by this wriggling, rotting mass. I think I screamed. I hear the echo of it.

Hollow. He was a dead, hollow tree.

I cried his name, pulled away, my hands before my face, covered in dark streaks. He gazed back at me through those small eyes, yet devoid of expression.

"What *are* you?" I asked, afraid that at any moment he might fall upon me with suddenly long claws and fangs.

"As you are," he murmured. "Fragments of the past brought into the present, refashioned. I didn't think you'd see... caught in this mundane world as you are." He uttered a sigh. "It is not to be."

He lashed out with one arm and I remember flinching away, but there was no blow, only a descent into darkness.

As might be expected in such a tale as this, I didn't come to my senses until the dawn, and of course Cherrah had gone. As I lay on my back in the bed – I had checked for remnants of decaying wood and had found none – I wondered how much of what I'd felt beneath my hands – which had been as much physical as visual – had been pure hallucination, brought on by the loosened ecstasies of aruna. This can do very strange things to a har's mind, as any har can tell you, not to mention the wine I'd drunk at dinner – rather too much of it because of my nerves. I'd concocted for Cherrah a strangeness, and perhaps his tattoo had somehow influenced me. What I'd felt could not possibly have been real, could it? And yet I remembered what he'd said to me, *fragments of the past refashioned…*

Later, when Shiran came to call, I told him everything. I expected him to scoff and joke at the climax of my story, but he did not.

He stared at me, as I stood before the fire in my living room. "As I said to you before," he said, "who knows how hara have… *developed* in corners of the world?"

I shook my head. "Shir, this was not some tribal deviation…"

"Listen," he said, "because I've lived here all my life, whereas you have not. There are old stories about the Elle folk, who weren't human and who lived beneath the land. Humans were afraid of them, and appeased them at all costs. The female Elle, though beautiful, were said to be hollow, lovely only from the front, illusions of beauty. The males were ugly all over, and were said to breathe pestilence."

I considered. "So you're saying a harish Elle, if such could exist, being androgynous would contain elements of both genders – the hollow back, aspects of ugliness, yet aspects of beauty also."

Shiran nodded quickly. "Exactly. It does make sense, doesn't it? I knew there was something about him…"

"In a strange kind of way, it does make sense," I replied. "But could it possibly be true?"

Shiran shrugged. "I wouldn't try to find out if I were you. Returning to the Elle folk, despite their power over humans who lived near them, they were ashamed of their ugliness and their hollow backs, and were dangerous because of this. No human would provoke an Elle. If they came across one, male or female, they would never laugh at an ugly face, and would certainly not show fear. That would be the greatest insult, and an insulted Elle, apparently, was a violent thing. "

I laughed uneasily. "It *is* a great story, but can we really believe that Cherrah is some kind of harish Elle, that he's from a *tribe* of them?"

Shiran raised his hands expressively. "I'm saying that Wraeththu brought many changes to the world and awoke old magics as much as fashioned new ones. Who is to say that tribes developing in the far north of these lands weren't influenced by emanations from the earth itself? Think of the endless cloud-crowned forests, the space... anything could come into being there. Think of the Colurastes, who are perhaps the only tribe to mingle freely with others, and who have certain... *aberrations* of being. There must be many more, hidden away. I've always thought so. And perhaps some *do* want, like the Colurastes, to be accepted by mainstream harish culture. Who knows? But who can deny it as nonsense, eh?"

I sighed. "And now I expect Cherrah has vanished mysteriously from Trisque, leaving only an empty house, and we shall never know."

But he had not disappeared. Although he made no move to contact me again, nor I to contact him, when I sang my Lachrymide hymn before all of the city on the first night of the Orchestrium's Shadetide events, there he was, on the front row as usual, his hood over his eyes, his cloak covering his back. Shiran's ideas were ludicrous, and yet... As I sang to him, as I always had, I felt saddened – appropriate for a Lachrymide lament. If there were any truth at all in Shiran's suppositions, how tragic to be such an outsider, half fairy, half har, yet also neither.

Cherrah left the Orchestrium at the end of the performance and I made no move to contact him or detain him. That is how it has remained. I've found I don't even look for him now, as if the enchantment drained away from the moment I took him to my room.

As far as I know, he still makes his clocks on Fern Hill. Mine is neither enchanted nor haunted, but it keeps excellent time.

sea and shore

Wendy Darling

He was leaving, perhaps forever, but for Kii that morning felt more like a beginning than an ending. He'd said his goodbyes, made his plans, and now it only remained to make those final steps, away from his tribe and toward whatever else was out there.

His father disapproved. His hostling was accepting – his love would follow his son anywhere – yet despondent. His siblings were both aghast and yet, Kii thought, jealous. How *dare* he leave? What does he expect to *find*? Is our world not *enough* for him?

Only his high-father Rini seemed to understand and approve, and it was he who arrived at Kii's door shortly after sunrise.

"Ready?" Rini asked, leaning against the doorframe of the largely empty room.

"I think so," Kii replied, closing the impermeable pack he'd checked yet again. "I'll probably remember something ten miles from here, but I won't be back."

Rini grunted. "I hope you're right – about being ready. Don't think I won't miss you, however."

Kii settled the pack on his back. "I know. And maybe I will be back. Someday. I just have to—"

"I know." Rini stepped up and embraced his high-harling, kissed the top of his head. Then he let go and took one of Kii's hands. "Come, I'll walk with you."

The much younger har glanced around the room, then went out to face the village.

Even at this early hour, hara were moving about, cooking, sharpening spears, and now, staring mutely as Kii and Rini headed to the shore. The pair ignored the looks, the silence, until they were at water's edge.

Kii stared back. On the dragon rock, so named for its

resemblance to a beast, stood his parents. *I love you*, he sent. *Don't think I don't.*

He watched as his hostling clung more tightly to his father, tears running down his face. Further back, along the path, a row of other faces, distraught and dismayed.

Kii turned back towards the sea, let go of Rini's hand. He studied the elder har's face, which was serene. *Thank you*, he sent.

Rini inclined his head.

Time to take the plunge. Squaring his shoulders, Kii faced the lapping waves, gray and white, and stepped into the ocean. One step, two steps, ten steps, thirty steps… and then he dove below the waves and was gone.

A few hundred miles to the south, Tylar was also in the water, not swimming, but cleaning the bottom of his boat. It was a yearly ritual: taking the dinghy out into the chilly waters, carrying a bucket of tools, slipping in, and painstakingly removing barnacles, seaweed and algae from the hull.

This task would've been considerably easier if he'd had a pier, a ramp, a lift, or other tools available in a town, but he didn't live in a town, and anyway, a har needed help to undertake such matters. Taking care of it this way was, despite the frigid water, preferable for Tylar, who despite its relative hardships, enjoyed his life of solitude.

This was a life he had chosen. Growing up, he had lived in a town to the south, although certainly still northerly. There, hara endured long winters, overhung with heavy clouds that let loose snow, which remained until hit by the rays of the summer sun. The town made most of its money by fishing and hosting seasonal visitors, who came during the hottest months to delight in the seashore landscape and salty winds. But most of the year, the town was uncrowded, home to a couple of thousand hara, rugged and hardworking, though also known to enjoy a lazy day by the fire or a night around the table, drinking ale.

Even during the empty wintertime, Tylar found it too crowded. He would walk down a road inland, seeking space to think, and a passing driver would slow his cart to offer him a ride. Sitting on a high rock in a stormy cove, he'd be observing the gulls, the clouds, the patterns of the waves, when a fisherman would appear and ask if anything was troubling him, or if Tylar would mind if he took up with his rod and reel. Tylar *did* mind.

As a harling, he'd no choice but to stay. Then afterward, as a young har, he'd tried to find alternatives to a life rubbing shoulders with other hara. With permission, he took up one of his hostling's boats and offered to plant and tend lobster pots in a bay further north. His parents were happy to have Tylar enter the family business, and he was happy when he was out on his own, even in the rain and cold, but he was unhappy when he came home. Yes, a day with family was fine, but soon the urge was back: to be alone with the wind and the gulls. The same happened when he tried other solitary occupations. He enjoyed the days or nights he was by himself, but when around other hara, he always felt they were intruding.

His attitude distressed his family, his schoolmates, and his aruna partners, of which there were a few, although not as many as he could have had, if he had been a normal har. He did not repel, but he did not seek until he felt the physical need. When he did join with other hara, he had always demanded silence, reverence, eschewing the usual chatter, before and after. Most, at least the less sensitive types, thought him aloof, icy, sterile, but the truth was he was happy within himself, and could only drink sparingly of the cup. He savoured what he had, but that was all.

Finally, when he was about thirty and everyhar had accepted him as he was – no more invitations to partner with harlings at feybraiha, no more flirting in the tavern, supposing he did turn up for a drink – Tylar headed north to the lonely shore.

He did not take up residence under a rock or even a ragged tent. From lobstering trips he knew of an empty house, overlooking an empty bay, with lands empty around it. The old human roads were covered with creepers in the summer, impassible with snow in the winter. He had his lobster boat and a small skiff, bought from his parents, boxes of starter supplies, and a well near enough he could lug back the water when he needed it. In the warm months he didn't even stay in the house, but would make a bower in the high grasses above the tide line, or in the shelter of a tree, or up on the boat, moored amidst the waves, softly creaking.

Compared to the life he had known in town, or the lives hara there could imagine, Tylar didn't "do" anything in his new life. He had to eat, and so he fished, hunted, put up winter food stock, gathered firewood, and took care of the most minimal of household chores. But otherwise he avoided *doing* and reveled in *being*.

He would lie out on a fine, ancient slab of granite and soak in the sun, the heat on his face and the oven of the rock itself. Above him the gulls would wheel around, while in the tide pools snails would creep. Bees buzzed amidst the wildflowers. Seals would pull themselves up on shore and bark at one another, but as they weren't addressing him, he didn't mind. In the woods further inland lived owls, eagles, deer, squirrels, and he came to know them, by their tracks, their calls, one deer different from another by the pattern of spots or antlers. He learned the stars, the patterns of the clouds, the weather signs, better than he had ever known them in town.

He dove below the boat, holding his breath, scrubbing the hull for as long as he could stand it, then bobbing to the surface, gasping from the bounty of air and the chill of the water. Even in the height of summer, the ocean water was far from warm; in the spring, when Tylar always took care of this chore, it was icy.

Still, when it was done, and he pulled himself up on deck, Tylar was filled with satisfaction. He pulled out a covered pot of seafood stew and, channelling agmara through his hands, he heated it until it was satisfyingly warm and steaming. With a wooden spoon he scooped chunks of fragrant clam, crab and cod into his mouth and watched the sun slide toward the horizon.

Weeks later, Kii was still travelling south: south, south, inevitably south. He needed no map to tell him that he was headed in the right direction or that many, many miles were now between him and his home. The further he went, the more he picked up on other hara, living in villages on the shore, or travelling by boat. His people had lived at the ends of the earth, and even on their longest voyages, they never travelled for weeks.

The water had warmed since early spring, although to somehar who hadn't been in it regularly all winter, it would still seem impossibly frigid. By acclimation and with the gifts of his people, Kii did not suffer the cold. On and on he swam, sometimes under the surface, sometimes on the waves. With proper nourishment, he could go on for weeks.

Kii was not alone. Every day he swam with the other, non-harish creatures of the world who, for all humankind had done to stamp them out, in modern times outnumbered hara in vast proportions. Great whales, playful dolphins, gulls, seals, cormorants, sea otters, turtles, jellyfish – all swam beside him, above him, over him. Although he could not read their minds directly, at least without considerable time and effort, with the lightest brush against their thoughts, he knew that many of them were surprised to see a land creature so comfortable in the sea. Were there more of these creatures? Would they be moving into these waters?

Kii's relationship with the creatures of the sea was not entirely benevolent, as he did have to eat. For this he used the tools he had packed, the two long spears, the short spear, the fishing string, hooks, a fine net woven by his high-father Rini. "Take it," he'd said. "I made it for you. Eat well. With respect. Stay strong."

When the decision to leave had finally been made, become more than a pipe dream, he'd gone to his parents with trepidation to discuss it. His worries had been founded. "You'll never make it!" his father had thundered. "It can't be done!"

His hostling had been quieter but applied more guilt. "But you're so young! What about a chesnari? And what about me, missing you?"

But Rini had understood from the beginning. "The thought of leaving, adventure, is one that comes to all of us," he explained one night. "We are isolated. Other hara are not exactly mythical, but they're something we seldom see. And so we dream of finding them, of seeing their world. But it's so far away. It could take months of travel. And what's at the end?" He sighed, then glanced wistfully towards the sky. "Finally life moves on, you find a job you like, blissful aruna, you have good friends... and slowly the dream fades and becomes only a dream."

"It's not just a dream for me," Kii said. He corrected himself. "Well, it did begin with dreams, visions, but since then I've thought about this for years, made plans. And it hasn't faded."

"I know," said Rini, patting Kii's knee. "I feel it. That's why I'm all right with this. Maybe this is the 'job' you like doing, your destiny. But you won't know until you try it."

And now, months later, all that behind him, Kii was trying it. And loving it.

Summer had begun and Tylar was lying on his favourite long rock, carved by long-ago glaciers, jutting into the sea like a spear. Heat from the now set sun oozed from the granite, soothing him into a trance of pleasure and relaxation. This was why he was out here, in the lonely bay. Back at home, somehar would doubtless have intruded. Here he could gaze at the stars, listen to the ocean lap against the shore at low tide, hear the birds twittering in the twilight. Hands tucked behind his head, he drank deeply of the salty sea air.

Glancing up at the stars, eyes half closed, Tylar went back in his memory to nights spent as a harling with his father, also lying on the rocky shore gazing at the sky. His father had taught him as much about the distant stars and worlds as he knew, and created new constellations, like The Fish and Phaonica.

Tylar began to sing, at first a thready whisper, then soft and low. His father had sung on those long-ago nights. In the years since he'd been on his own, Tylar had come to treasure those songs. Many were old songs, passed down even from human times. Others his father had made up himself. Now Tylar created his own songs.

Stars encircle the world
The world lies beneath the stars
Oceans sparkling with their light
At night, at night, at night
Beneath the stars

He babbled on in verse, melody, taking advantage of the freedom he'd won to do as he pleased, to take as much time as he liked doing whatever he liked.

There were a few disadvantages to this isolated life, however, and on this night Tylar felt one of them. Aruna. When his parents asked about it, the couple of times a year he visited, he always told them there was a har a few miles inland. But there wasn't. Generally there was only Tylar's imagination and his hands. And though he had become expert in all the ways of such pleasures, it simply was not the same as being with somehar.

He ached. Time to feed the need. He closed his eyes and began. A few minutes later he was seeing stars behind his eyelids. *Beneath the stars...*

Not far off, Kii too was perched on a rock, only this one wet with water and sea spray. A tiny island of crags, it only appeared at low tide, or to bring oblivious ships to their doom. He'd pulled himself up on it to rest before swimming to shore for the night, when he'd heard it.

A song. Not one he could hear, not with his ears, but one he could feel. A song of longing, stars, the sparkling ocean. Moonlight. The song of a lone har. Not a lonely har, but a har alone.

He was close by, Kii knew. Had to be, for the silent song to come to him unbidden. The next bay? And there was nohar else, singing or otherwise, but this har. There were no villages nearby.

Kii slipped off the rock and back into the ocean. Rather than going to shore, he headed south, just around the point. Then the next point. The song grew louder, stronger. Finally he could hear the actual notes, with his ears, over the waves.

A har was lying on the shore, alone. And as he sang, the har was pleasuring himself. His song became filled with his sighs. Dazzling images spilled out into the night.

Thrown off guard, Kii stared, then briefly floundered. No, he didn't want to tread water. Too much concentration was required. He spotted an indentation in the rock shore, out of sight from the har, and swam toward there.

Crouched silently in the shadows of ancient granite, Kii felt the song grow louder. Panting. Near completion. Stars sparkling, streaking, a bonfire of passion.

Without even a thought, Kii began to sing back. The same song, only in the way of his people, deep and melodic, a message across the waves. Touching the other har's thoughts, though without the other har being aware, he became briefly joined. He kept in time with the other har, going faster and faster, until finally, the song came to an end. Completion.

When Kii came out of his trance, he found his left hand covered in aren.

Waking up beneath rumpled sheets the next morning, Tylar tried to linger on the dream he'd been having. Something about a singer like a mythical siren, a song drifting over the sea.

But trying to grasp onto these wisps of memory, he was shaken by the realisation it had been no dream.

After emerging from his pleasure-trance the night before, he'd felt weak as a kitten. When he'd finally recovered somewhat, he'd staggered about, vaguely scouting for the magic spirit that had brought him to such a reverie. But it was too dark, and with thoughts of bed overriding all, he'd gone back to the house and collapsed.

Now, in the light of day, it did seem to warrant some investigation. Could another har be nearby? In the next bay? In the woods? He tried to recall his experience. The voice had seemed very close. On shore?

Returning to the long rock, Tylar scouted around. No footmarks were to be found on the hard stone, of course. He searched for other traces, not sure what they would be. Clamouring down among the glistening rocks, exposed by another low tide, he was just about to give up, admit he was being a fool, when something caught his eye: a spear, floating in a small pool trapped behind a rock.

He bent over and picked up the spear. It was not one of his, nor was it like any he'd seen in the village. Both shaft and head appeared to be ivory, made of one single tusk, the shaft carved straight and the head fashioned with minute care, long, dangerous barbs pointing away from a killing-sharp tip.

Where could it have come from? The obvious answer was the sea, which was always bringing oddments to the shore – logs, boat timbers, empty containers, fishing nets. But the obvious answer didn't appeal to Tylar, not in this moment. This wasn't something washed to shore, but evidence of a visit the night before.

Over in the next bay, Kii sat in a bower he'd made in some brush and cursed himself. His best spear. How could he have left it behind? He'd never done so before.

The answer was of course plain. After vicariously experiencing the stranger's climax, and encouraging it, he'd fled in a panic of discovery. Not that he felt bad exactly about what he'd done, but he did fear he'd overstepped. In this culture, far from home, who knew how such an act might be interpreted? And so, rather than face the consequences, he'd fled, quietly, avoiding moonlight and starlight as much as possible.

Now, with morning come, Kii knew there was nothing for it but to at least check to see if he could retrieve the spear. It was his best. He needed it. And he had to continue south in any case. The har probably would be long gone.

Kii stood and brushed himself off. Time to hunt up breakfast and continue the journey.

By mid-morning, Tylar had given up trying to do anything useful. Whatever task he took up, whether sowing the garden or patching up the draughty windows on the house, he found himself distracted by the mystery of the night before and by the remnant left behind. Several times he'd even broken away and gone to the kitchen table, where he'd left the spear. Where had it come from? Who had made it?

Now he was giving in to his instinct, which was to go to sea. It was something he often did, even apart from doing business or fishing – set out in the skiff and let his thoughts sort themselves out amid the wind and waves. Surely that was as good a course of action today as ever.

Throwing together a few supplies, including fish bait and a small lunch, Tylar was about to head out of the house when out of the corner of his eye, he spotted the spear. Almost without thinking, he snagged it and set it over his shoulder. Now he was ready.

A few minutes and a quick swim later, he was on the boat, securing his gear and readying the sails. The wind was good, neither too high nor too low. Clouds hung over, but none that foretold rain. His decision felt right.

At last all was ready, and with the release of a few ropes, and the tying down of a few others, he was able to sail off the mooring and towards the mouth of the bay.

Tylar sat in the stern, one hand on the tiller, one hand around the spear. Somehow he had failed to pack it away. It was a thing of beauty. He ran his hand up and down the length of the shaft. So smooth.

Yet just as he about to set the spear down, his fingers brushed against a section of the spear that was a bit rough. Checking that he was still headed in the right direction, he looked down at the ivory, where he'd held his finger to mark the spot.

A word, perhaps a name, carved neatly near the very end of the hilt: *Kii*.

He mouthed the word. He ran his fingertips over the letters.

"Kii," he said aloud. "Kii, are you here?"

He'd just made the decision to move on – the spear was gone from the shore where he knew he must have left it – when Kii was jolted by a single word. His name.

He'd been watching the stranger, out his boat, from whatever direction the har wasn't looking. He'd peek above the water line to observe and judge direction, intention, then duck below.

A minute or two before, he'd been at the right angle to realise that the har was holding his spear. He'd found it. And had taken it out with him on the boat. To use it? It wouldn't be of much use on board the boat. Maybe he intended to dive into the water?

Kii was so befuddled he nearly forgot to dive again, but at the last moment he disappeared beneath the waves.

When he came up again, there was another revelation. The har was holding the spear and saying his name. "Kii? Kii, are you here?"

Kii's heart beat hard in his chest. Why did he suddenly want to reveal himself? He hadn't to any har before. But the spear... saying his name... and the night previous? All combined at once. A decision was made. He swam toward the boat.

Tylar was just straightening up after setting down the spear when two wet hands appeared over the side of the boat. Two wet, *webbed* hands.

He steadied himself on the tiller. Staring, he watched as the hands were followed by a harish face, framed by hair that resembled wet seaweed.

For a few long moments, Tylar stared back at the har. His eyes went back to the hands. Yes, they were webbed.

"Ahm," he began, shaking himself out of it. "Who are you?"

The har tilted his head back for a moment, then seemingly coming to a decision, nodded. "I am Kii," he announced, in a low, musical voice. "May I come on board?"

Tylar nodded mutely. Of course the har was Kii. He'd summoned him, hadn't he?

As the har pulled himself fully onto the deck, Tylar noted other oddities. Not only webbed hands, but webbed feet. Also a certain fleshiness that was unlike what he'd ever seen on a har, though it did remind him of the flesh of a seal. It was not unpleasant, but strange. And then there were the gills, on either side of the throat. That caused gooseflesh to rise on Tylar's arms.

Finally, Kii was fully on deck and seated on the bench opposite.

Not knowing what to say, Tylar fished around for a starting point. He glanced down at the floor. "Your spear?"

"Yes," the strange har affirmed. "I left it on the shore last night."

Tylar narrowed his eyes. "You were on the shore, here, last night?"

Kii nodded.

"Here… when exactly?" Not that Tylar had much doubt.

Kii ran one of his hands – webbed – through his seaweed hair, looking sheepish. "I was nearby, a couple of bays over, when I heard you singing. It called to me. I came."

"I'll say," Tylar quipped. "You… saw what I was doing?"

"I felt it," Kii explained. "The feelings."

"And you decided to, what, join in?" Tylar queried. In the back of his mind ran the thought: *Sirens are real. I have a siren, here in my boat.*

"You were already singing," Kii explained. "It called to me. To my body." He gestured to himself. He was, as Tylar had strangely not noticed from the beginning, entirely nude except for some sort of backpack.

Tylar gulped. "I… see." The thought of this har, a soume sea, flashed into his mind, and he had to take some long, slow breaths to calm himself. *Get a grip!*

"I am wondering," Kii said after a few moments, "if we might talk. If you could show me your home. I've been on a long journey and have not stopped to talk to a single har along the way." He glanced to shore. "You are alone?"

"Yes, and gladly," Tylar replied, "but somehow I think I could make an exception for you. Wait a moment and I'll turn back to shore."

As the sailor har adjusted the sails and ropes, reversing course, Kii stared in wonder. This har was not angry at him and neither was he terribly afraid. Curious, yes, naturally, but that was to be expected. The shore hara did not know of the sea hara.

"What's your name?" Kii ventured.

The other har sat down again, apparently having made the course adjustment. "Tylar," he replied. "I originally come from a village south of here, but I moved away years ago and live here by myself. What about you?"

"I come from the far north," Kii began. "Far, far north. So far that my people are forgotten."

Tylar looked away, checking either sail or course, Kii didn't know, then asked, "And who are your people? Are they... like you?"

And so, as they crossed the bay, Kii began the story of his people, the sea hara. "Many, many years ago, we were hara like you, of course. We all come from the same source, after all." But then one har, then several of his friends, had an idea. What if hara could evolve into something else, even beyond the initial mutation? Why not take to the air, or deep forests, or the sea?

The sea proved the easiest environment to adapt to. Long ago, life had come from the sea, and from looking at the creatures there today, it was clear what changes were needed. A har could not simply wish himself to be a fish, of course, but he could explore arcane practices, summon dehara, enlist the aid of beings in the otherlanes and beyond, to achieve certain ends.

Small changes came first, then came larger. Then these changes were passed down to their harlings. In the beginning, mating had been directed, to encourage the strongest, most useful adaptations. Webbing, subcutaneous fat, gills, large lungs, the ability to remain under water for extended periods – all came over time, over many generations. By now evolution was about as complete as it needed to be, his people judged. They did not want to leave the land completely or cease to be able to walk, and so now they lived more or less in stasis, in a land far from other hara, beyond time.

"It's actually rather boring, at least I find it so," Kii remarked, as he followed Tylar up the rock shore, having helped him tie the boat and swum in beside him. "Most are content, of course, but several years ago I got an itch to just go... Go south."

Kii found Tylar studying him. "What did you think you'd find?" the har asked.

"Well, I'm not sure, but I wanted to meet other hara, other tribes. I had a dream about it actually." They were now walking away from the granite crags, through a field and toward a small house. "I dreamed that—"

Tylar turned his head. "Dreamed what?"

Kii coughed, not wanting to share his thought. "Never mind."

They continued on in silence until they were near the door. Then Tylar repeated his question.

This time Kii relented. "I... I hadn't thought of it, somehow... but I dreamed of a little house like this one, with just one har in it, living happily alone, but somehow needing something... or somehar." He ran his fingers down the spear, which Tylar had handed over to him. "I told my high-father all about this vision, and he thought it was symbolic. But maybe it wasn't."

Once inside the house, Tylar busied himself with practical, if not particularly urgent, matters. Putting away the pack of things he'd brought back from the boat. Straightening up the chairs, which he never lined up, because there was never anyhar to see. Lighting the stove.

"Would you like some tea?" he asked finally. "I was just going to make some." From the strange look on Kii's face, Tylar wasn't sure he'd understood. "Do you, um, drink tea?"

Kii smiled. "Yes. Sorry, I've just been living off the sea so long..." He pulled out a chair. "Can I sit down?"

Tylar nodded.

"We have tea, or a local variation, back home. Even chairs," Kii said. He chuckled.

Tylar sat down in a chair across the table. "I've never heard of your people, except in the old human myths, of mermaids or sirens, but strangely, I don't feel surprised. Maybe I've just spent so much time here with sea creatures."

"What do you mean?" Kii asked.

"Well," said Tylar, turning to check the kettle, "I spend a great deal of time on the water, on boats, and *in* the water – swimming and such. And I've spent a lot of time watching seals and whales and so on. How graceful they are. I'm a good swimmer, have to be, but not like they are. I can't migrate hundreds of miles down a coast, never setting foot on land – like you can, I guess."

Kii shrugged. "Well, I actually do sleep on land. I'm not an otter that sleeps on its back, on the waves. But yes, my people do have an affinity to all those creatures you mentioned."

Unbidden, the image of this sea har as soume once again blazed up in Tylar's mind. He grasped his thighs and attempted to school himself. This wasn't the time for that.

However, Kii seemed to have picked up on his thought – his hand hung between his legs, and Tylar could well imagine what it was doing. This was little wonder, given how they'd been connected the night before.

"How long since you last shared aruna?" Kii asked, in that low, musical voice of his.

Tylar thought back. "At the new year," he said softly.

"Too long. Longer even than I." Kii pushed back his chair. "Want to put an end to it? We will talk more – later."

Dazedly, Tylar stood and led the way to the bedroom. On the stove the kettle began to boil. Neither har noticed.

Hours later, Kii sat up in bed, wrapped in a quilt, watching Tylar sleep. Aruna had been like nothing else. Surely the extended abstinence had something to do with it, but Kii had a feeling there was more. He'd had plenty of good, intense roons, but in this one he'd felt a connection to the other har unlike he'd ever known. They'd met because of a song, and it was as if that song had risen up between them. Even uncoupled, Kii felt a thread of connection remaining.

He leant over and stroked Tylar's hair, loose around the sides of his face, in a long plait behind. The other har's eyes fluttered open.

"I'm not dreaming, am I?" Tylar asked softly.

In response, Kii met his lips for a sharing of breath. *No, you're not dreaming. Unless I'm dreaming, too.*

It could be, Tylar replied, speaking mind to mind with another har for the first time in a long time. *In which case, let's not wake up.*

After another roon, seemingly inevitable, they began to talk. Tylar explained how and why he'd come to live in the lonely bay. Not that he was lonely himself, he stressed, although having joined with the har, Kii knew that wasn't strictly true. A need for solitude he understood – he'd just happily swam alone for weeks on end – but nohar was an island, not forever.

Kii had to admire the simple existence Tylar had built for himself. It didn't seem nearly as stressful and structured as the lives of most land hara, at least compared to what had been described to him. His people had structure as well, but had moved to a simpler lifestyle to what he understood most hara pursued – fewer things, simpler homes. Tylar's home, left over from human times, was not simple, but overall his life was.

"So, what's next?" Kii asked, once Tylar had finished describing his life, his family, his love of solitude.

"That's a question," Tylar murmured. Until today his plans for the future hadn't moved far beyond spending his life in this bay, with occasional trips back home. But now there existed another possibility.

"Do you think you could… stay with me, just for a while?" he asked tentatively. "I mean, I don't mean to presume, but I enjoy talking with you. And I normally don't enjoy that."

"I could be persuaded," Kii replied.

"And you don't have to stay. You could move on if you wanted, go back to sea." Now that he'd made the offer, Tylar felt he had indeed been presumptuous. "You probably can't stay on land all the time, anyway."

Kii looked perplexed. "I would prefer not to, as I'm made for the sea, but spending some time on land wouldn't harm me. Why would you think that?"

Tylar chuckled. "Have you ever heard what happens to mermaids who try to live on land?" He put up his hands, apologetically. "Sorry, I've read a lot of sea myths."

"And I grew up on tales of the land," Kii countered, seemingly not put off. "Tales which I now see were in some ways totally untrue. Things haven't worked out at all as I expected."

"How did you expect things to go?"

Kii looked at him seriously. "I thought for a bit I might end up on the end of my own spear."

"Never," Tylar vowed. And with that he lowered himself over Kii to take another swim in the soume sea.

That summer, on any given day, two hara could be seen swimming in the bay, which was no longer lonely. The hara sometimes moved with purpose, fishing or swimming straight to reach the further shore, but more often they were playful, like porpoises or sea otters. A passing ship, if any had come near enough, might even have thought they'd seen mermaids. But no, these were simply hara, of the shore and of the sea, in a union that was neither crowded nor something to flee from. Together, Kii and Tylar made a world of two.

Suzanne Gabriel

We must be willing to get rid of the life we've planned, so as to have the life that is waiting for us.

~ *Joseph Campbell, US folklorist (1904 - 1987)*

A bitter blast of icy air hit me in the face as I trudged up the street that led to the healing centre. Mornings always felt earlier in the dead of winter when it was cold and dark. I hunched lower into my coat and squinted against the sting of the tiny snowflakes being driven in the wind.

In these flatlands nothing slowed the wind; its gusts blew great drifts of snow before it. I had numb feet and frozen fingers. Winter seemed to last forever in this place, and the short, hot blast furnace of summer left one unfulfilled and dazed.

I often wondered why I stayed here and subjected myself to these unpleasant extremes, and always came to the same gloomy conclusion: I didn't really have anywhere else to go. This was my home, such as it was. This was the location of the renowned training facility where they'd sent me, when I'd been deemed a gifted student with a desire to become an elite healer, and this was also the location of the prestigious healing centre where I now practiced.

In the healing centre, our morning briefing was set to begin. Around the dark wood table in the meeting room sat whispering hara, each wearing the deep purple robes that marked us as the select few.

We were the elite arunic healers. We had trained for years to be able to harness the most powerful form of grissecon deep within the Cauldron of Creation to achieve never-before-dreamed-of healing success. According to history, the first arunic healing was achieved by legendary Cobweb and, in the years since, the technique had been honed and enhanced by those who had also mastered the technique.

I had worked hard to earn the right to wear the purple robe, and I was immensely proud of what I'd been able to accomplish — and ambitious to achieve more. Some hara thought we healers were "lucky," but the power and privileges of my rank had not come without sacrifice. I had worked hard. I had poured my whole essence into this endeavour. I lived a simple but driven life, a life focused on the healing arts and on this clinic. I had sacrificed much; the politics of our hierarchical profession made friendships among my peers "tricky."

Sometimes, on frigid dark mornings like this, I felt a vague restlessness that bordered on discontent at this life, this clinic, and how much it had cost me. But it *couldn't* be discontent, I mused: this was what I had *wanted* to do, and this was the life I had chosen. I was a perfectionist who obsessed with being the best but, despite this, sometimes I felt a yearning akin to homesickness. I occasionally felt I was a stranger in a strange land, despite the fact that I was "home."

On this particular morning I was feeling edgy and tired. My sleep had been fitful, full of disjointed dreams and disturbing sensual imagery. Every healer knows that on occasion he will treat a patient who affects them more than most do; I could accept that. However, struggling with erotic dreams in which I'd felt desire for one particular patient – this I could not accept. In my dreams I had allowed myself to desire him, run my hands over him in completely unprofessional fashion, and been a lover rather than a healer.

Perhaps it was my subconscious's way of telling me that although aruna in the form of arunic healing was part of my everyday routine, it had been a long time since I had shared "real" aruna with anyone. Although the thought of taking care of my own needs definitely held some merit, I was usually drained by the end of the day. I'm not that social to begin with, so it was easy to convince myself that I didn't have time to go out and meet somehar; there were always new meditations, new reports and new readings. I was always driven by my craft. I needed to be the best. I never had any time for other things.

I glanced at the clock on the wall. Autullis was late. Our acerbic Clinic Administrator was no doubt stalking through the halls of the clinic with his usual arrogance and officious determination to find some fault with something somewhere. He wasn't a healer; he was merely a bureaucrat, one who had been parachuted in when our former Head Healer left suddenly in a flurry of intrigue and secrecy. It was assumed that one of us would ascend and assume the role of Head Healer. Instead, our governing board had appointed Autullis as Clinic Administrator, virtually eliminating the position of Head Healer for the time being.

I was outraged; a har with no healing experience could never understand precisely what we do. A number of the healers, I among them, had lodged complaints. In fact a war of back-room politics was being waged, and when the dust settled and the jurisdictional manoeuvring finished, I fully intended to be the har that was chosen Head Healer and Clinic Administrator.

Although Autullis had accepted the position at the clinic, I believed that he harboured deep reservations about arunic healing and viewed us all with deep suspicion; he was, as a colleague said, "a prude." I had made no secret of my distaste for his appointment, and my active attempts to be the one to usurp his post had damaged our relationship to the point where I believe he now loathed me. I probably should feel remorse, but I didn't; you've got to crack a few eggs to make an omelette, and besides, the feeling was mutual.

Autullis bustled in and took his place at the head of the table. He was tall and angular with refined features. "Auriel, report on your first case. Now! Quickly!" he barked impatiently, as if he was the one who had been waiting instead of us.

As the report was being given, I met the gaze of a healer across the table and covertly rolled my eyes. The other healer smirked slightly. *Would it kill him to say good morning?* I looked down at my notes discreetly before responding. *Probably.* I looked up again and smirked slightly.

"Tobian!" Autullis paused, shuffling his papers. "The foreigners from the island of..." He paused again and shuffled some more.

"Waiki'Lao," I supplied smoothly, careful to pronounce the

name with the exact same inflections as the foreigners. I didn't try to hide my smug superiority at being more prepared than Autullis. There was truly no love lost between us. "They are returning today for the third of four currently scheduled healing sessions. As you may recall, the patient was savaged by a shark and received extensive damage to his spine, torso, arm, and leg. It was a massive amount of damage. In truth, he's lucky to be alive at all. While the healers in his tribe were able to keep him alive…"

"Barely," Autullis interjected snidely.

It never ceased to amaze me how arrogant he could be. To belittle a healer at any level was unconscionable, especially when one was not skilled enough to do better. I glared openly at the Administrator.

"The patient has received excellent care," I said pointedly, "and was making slow but steady progress. However, as he had one arm that was completely paralysed, other lingering mobility issues, and was in constant pain, his healers felt that they did not wish to wait on 'slow and steady.' After two healing sessions he is reporting some tingling sensations returning to his arm and less pain."

"However," interrupted our administrator, "the patient is allowing a fortnight to pass between each healing session and prefers to continue to working on his own at home rather than following a proper healing schedule. Isn't that correct? Perhaps they doubt your abilities?" Autullis' tone was imperious and conveyed censure.

I met the gaze of the healer across the table from me again. He rolled his eyes, *As if our beloved Administrator would be qualified to determine a "proper" healing schedule…*

I smiled tightly. "Yes, the delays were an excellent suggestion on your part, Autullis," I said, "given the patient's initial reticence regarding the intense nature of our methods."

"Oh." Autullis looked both gratified and annoyed at once. "Yes. Of course," he sniffed.

The healing room was warm, warmer than I probably would have chosen to make it, despite the weather outside. However, the patient was my prime concern and, as I understood it, this har's tribe was not used to our frigid winters.

This was the patient who had haunted my dreams the night

prior, and try as I might to put the night's imagery from my mind, it wouldn't leave. Feigning professional indifference, I watched as the clinic's assistants gently helped the patient disrobe and settle onto the raised healing platform. Inwardly I had to acknowledge that my thoughts were neither professional nor indifferent.

The patient's skin was a warm cinnamon colour, his eyes a dark rich brown. His hair was black and straight and hung loose in layers to his shoulders. From his elbows to his shoulders his arms were encircled with an interwoven and interconnected tribal patterned tattoo that continued across his shoulders and upper back. The whole of him was very appealing, but I reflected that it had been this har's eyes that had first intrigued me. They'd been soulful. Perhaps it was a cliché, but in this har's eyes I'd seen *something…* something I couldn't quite put my finger on. Whatever it had been, it had intensified into sleep-disrupting, erotically-charged dreams.

The assistants left, quietly and unobtrusively. We were alone.

I approached the patient. "Tiahaar. How are you feeling today? Tell me of the changes since our last healing."

"Right after our last healing I told you I could feel tingling," he answered, not looking directly at me but rather at a spot over my left shoulder.

I'd forgotten what a delight his rich warm accent was.

"That sensation has gotten stronger, as if my arm is trying to wake up. I've got more movement in my shoulder, and quite a bit less pain." The patient paused and looked directly at me for the first time. "Between our sessions I've continued to work with my own healer." He threw that out as if it was a challenge; I kept my face neutral and nodded. "Healer Autullis thinks that's wrong," he continued.

"There is much that Tiahaar Autullis finds fault with," I said mildly, "and since he's an administrator, and *not* a healer, his opinion carries little weight."

The patient said nothing.

"Has what we've done here helped?" I asked.

"Yes."

"Does working on your own help you?"

"It does." He sounded just a little defiant.

"Therefore, as it is your health that matters most, you must continue doing what you feel works best. What *'anyhar-else'* – I emphasised "else" heavily – "thinks is unimportant."

The patient expelled his breath forcefully through his nose but said nothing further.

I began to slide my hands gently down across the patient's shoulder and upper arm, sensing and evaluating the muscles and the tendons below. Although this was standard examination practice, and I *was* noting the changes I felt and the life force energies within, much to my own annoyance I found myself also noticing the feeling of this patient's skin, the soft smooth texture and the warmth from his body. I traced my finger along one of the jagged scars on his arm. Up until then the patient had been staring at the ceiling, but now he turned his head to look at me.

"Some of the scars are beginning to fade," he said.

"Yes, they have faded," I said, feeling vaguely embarrassed. "But they may never completely disappear."

"All I care about is that the pain is less." Abruptly he turned his head and returned his gaze to the ceiling.

I began a thorough examination of the rest of him, allowing my hands to slide slowly over the planes and surfaces of his body, reading energies and resisting the urge to take pleasure in the task. I helped him roll onto his side so that I could examine his back. The deeply indented scars that the shark's teeth had made near his spine were still very visible, though they seemed less deep and less puckered. I ran my hand over them trying to imprint them into my awareness to be better able to direct the powerful healing.

I guided the patient back onto his back and noted that his ouana-lim was already semi-erect; he was clearly not as apprehensive about this healing session as he had been at the first one. It was probably quite indulgent to feel as self-satisfied about his semi-aroused state as I did.

Turning away from the patient, I dimmed the lighting and hung my robe on the hook. I took a jar of lubricant from the small supply table that stood against the wall. When I discretely applied it to myself I found that I wasn't in need of much; my body was already anticipating the session more than it typically did. Crossing back to the healing platform, I looked down at the patient.

"Are you prepared?" I asked, smiling. "Are you comfortable?"

He took a deep breath and nodded.

"Good," I continued. "Today I intend to be more focused in where we direct the energy. We'll be directing it to your upper spine. There's still much healing needed there and many of the damaged nerves flow through that area."

I climbed onto the platform, which was soft enough to be comfortable, yet firm enough to be practical. Straddling the patient I took hold of his ouana-lim and used the excess lubricant in the palm of my hand to stroke and caress him to his full state of arousal. After a few moments to centre myself and to focus my intent, I closed my eyes and guided the patient into me. We moved together, our purpose clear, our intent focused. I attuned myself to the powerful energies being created, envisioning them as golden light amassing and distilling at the base of my spine. When we had reached a level that felt right, I guided the patient into the Cauldron of Creation and we began the most powerful and sacred part of the grissecon.

A sudden stabbing pain broke my concentration; my foot was seized in a powerful cramp. I winced and hissed quietly as I carefully adjusted my position to relieve those muscles that screamed in agony. Beneath me the patient continued to move, fully in the trance.

As the muscle cramp subsided, I began to collect myself and refocus into the grissecon spell. But my body was now aware of the delicious earthy rhythm of aruna; the temptation to give myself over to the lure of these sensations suddenly became very strong.

I had to force those thoughts away. *All aruna is pleasurable*, I told myself, but this form of grissecon required that all the pleasure and more be channelled into healing.

I tried several times to put myself back into the proper state of mind, but my intentions were waylaid each time by reckless, and blatantly unethical, enjoyment of the pleasure of feeling the patient moving inside me.

No, I thought desperately, *I must refocus. I must focus on the energy.* I forced my consciousness inward to locate the golden light. The energy was there around the base of my spine, alive and clear. I felt relief and joy and I began to refocus.

But just as I was settling into the proper mindset, I caught sight of something that made my blood run cold; something dark was moving through the energy. A strange dark form slithered in the golden pool of healing power, swimming in it, bathing in it, feeding on it. As I watched in horror, the darkness seemed to manifest into a long dark serpentine shape that grew rapidly.

It had to be a thought-form resulting from my guilt surrounding the unprofessional thoughts I'd been harbouring about this patient. I attempted to banish it, but the creature continued to grow as it rolled and swam in the energy. I waded into the energy, feeling it tickle my skin. I decided to grab the entity and banish it by a more confrontational means. When I managed to get my mind-form arms most of the way around the creature, I could feel its warmth and the power of its body flexing in my arms, but with an effortless twitch the creature tossed me off, sending me tumbling backwards.

My eyes flew open. I was back in the real world, back on the healing platform. The patient's eyes were closed and his lips were slightly parted; the tantalising sensations of aruna pulled at my consciousness. Nothing like this had ever happened to me before and I felt panic beginning to rise. I had to get this thing under control; I had to direct the energy to healing.

I shut my eyes and focused again. The entity had become immense, filling the sacred grissecon space, rising up in a steady, unhurried pace like a snake out of a snake-charmers' basket. I could no longer see any gold amongst the massive black coils that twisted near the base of my spine.

Please! I pleaded. *Stop! This healing energy isn't for me, it's needed for somehar else. I don't know who you are or what you want, but please don't interfere with this healing. My patient is in pain: I have to help him!*

As odd as it sounds, the entity seemed to pause. I sensed that it might have heard me, might have understood me. I looked it directly in the face; despite the serpentine body, the entity's head did not resemble that of a snake. Its head was almost doglike with a long square snout, and the tips of its small pointed ears flopped down ever so slightly. But it was its eyes that really caught my attention; they weren't the cold black eyes of a serpent, but the eyes of a har – kind, gentle eyes.

Please! I pleaded *Stop! I need the healing energy back.*

The entity looked at me steadily for a moment and then it shifted slightly, tilting its head downwards. I followed its gaze. I could see golden light shining beneath the entity's coils; way more energy than I had ever created before. I looked back at the entity in confusion. If it hadn't manifested from the energy, where had it come from? And how with the foot cramp and all my difficulties concentrating had so much energy accumulated?

The entity wasn't looking at me now, but looking up. Its body quivered and twitched like a cat ready to pounce. Suddenly it shot upwards and out, moving with lightning speed, and in its wake I tumbled helplessly.

My eyes shot open as I fought to control my balance. The patient's eyes were still closed, and a slow moan escaped his slightly parted lips. His good hand gripped my hip, holding me firmly. My body moved on its own, driving down hard onto him, and my soume-lam began to pulsate. Healing energy began to surge around me, rushing, and swirling in a dizzying, disorienting vision.

I tried to concentrate and direct myself, but I felt off-balance and lightheaded. Beneath me the patient roared and his body bucked upwards. Already wobbly and disoriented, I lost my balance and fell. There was a flash of red and white light as the side of my head hit the marble tiles. Then blackness.

I came to on a cot in one of the small observation rooms. Rolling onto my side, I pushed myself up to a sitting position. My head throbbed and I felt sick.

"Healer?" A young attendant slipped in, holding some clothes.

Dazed and achy, I moved stiffly, allowing the attendant to assist me as I dressed.

"Leave us!" The command was imperious and cold, causing the young assistant to flee, leaving me alone to face Autullis's anger.

"The patient?" I began.

Autullis's eyes bored holes into me and I could feel the fury radiating out of him.

"This accident was completely unacceptable. Your conduct is utterly unprofessional," Autullis hissed.

"What about the patient?" I persisted.

"Unacceptable! You are through here," Autullis growled through gritted teeth.

"Autullis, the situation was highly unusual! I encountered interference! A manifestation. An entity appeared!"

"NO EXCUSES!" Autullis roared. He allowed the echoes of his outburst to reverberate through the small room, and when he spoke again his voice was taut with fury. "Before your careless 'accident,' did you clear the aren?"

The question tore through the fog and pain in my head; dread coupled with a rising sense of panic filled me as I turned my senses inward. I had been unconscious; I hadn't cleared the aren. My Cauldron contained life.

"Oh, sweet Ag," I whispered.

"I thought not! This is unacceptable! Unforgivable! Shameful! Reprehensible!" Autullis spat in disgust. "You have shamed the clinic, your profession, and yourself. Our clients put a lot of trust in us and this healing centre. They come here to be healed, *not* to be robbed of their aren; *not* to have pearls created without their knowledge or consent; not to be bred like prize bulls."

I gaped at Autullis. "You think I did this on *purpose?* Do you think I *want* a pearl? This healing centre is my life! Do you honestly think I'd throw everything away on purpose, for the harling of a har I don't know?"

"What I think is that you are arrogant and egotistical and what you want is immaterial to me and this clinic." Autullis' voice was icy. "You will accompany me to reassure the patient and his party, and then you will leave here and never return. You will get no references or recommendations from me or anyhar associated with this centre."

I drew myself up and glared at Autullis, knowing full well that he was perfectly within his authority to dismiss me.

Autullis made a great show of adjusting the collar of his robe and then he smirked. "It looks like my job remains quite safe; the almighty Tobian has been summarily eliminated as a threat," he said smugly. With that, he spun on his booted heel and stalked out of the room. I followed a little more slowly; my head still hurt and my mind was now whirling uselessly. All the denial in the world couldn't negate the tiny life force I'd sensed within me. Bile rose in the back of my throat.

The meeting room was more like a luxurious salon than an official chamber. Its walls were a warm salmon pink and it was filled with sumptuously soft couches and matching armchairs of brocaded silks. Softly cultured paintings in ornately carved frames adorned the walls, and opulent tables with intricate wood-inlay held vases of dried flower arrangements.

Three hara already occupied the space, all sharing the same deep cinnamon skin tone. My patient perched on the edge of an overstuffed love seat. Next to him sat a har whose short curly hair fell down over his forehead. He was attentive and concerned, a hand resting on the patient's arm. A har with a shaved head sat in an armchair watching the patient intently.

As Autullis and I entered, they all sprang to their feet – including, I noted with surprise, my patient. I was astounded to see how easily he moved. He made a beeline for me, a look of deep concern on his face.

"Healer," he began.

Autullis intercepted him, guiding him firmly yet gently back to his seat.

"Thank you, Tiahaara! Thank you for being so patient. Please have a seat. And once again I must apologise for this unduly distressing and confusing…"

I stopped listening as I lowered myself onto one of the elaborately carved hardwood chairs. Autullis addressed the patient and his companions at great length, apologising, placating, and fawning.

"Trust you are unharmed… unfortunate incident… completely our fault… unforgivable incompetence… healer's immediate dismissal…"

A heavy wave of helplessness washed over me.

"Wait." The har with the short curls seated next to the patient held up his hand with the quiet confidence of one used to being heeded, halting Autullis mid-oration. "Am I missing something? Apart from the unfortunate accident, in which *your* healer was hurt, this was by far the most successful of the healing sessions thus far. The results have been immediate! And I expect, as with the two previous sessions, the results will continue to manifest over the next few weeks. Why would you dismiss this healer?"

"He lost control. It was an unforgivable lapse. We will assign you a new healer," Autullis said as he launched into a new oration.

"No. I want to continue with the same healer – I trust him." The patient spoke with finality.

"But that is impossible," began Autullis.

"How is what my son is asking impossible?" the har with the curls asked.

Autullis blinked. "Well, Tobian, perhaps *you* can explain why this request is impossible." Autullis' voice was acid.

I felt all eyes turn in my direction; my heart sank. I raised my head but I did not meet anyone's gaze.

"I cannot continue to work with you, Tiahaar," I began hesitantly, "because I am no longer a healer at this centre. The methods we use here are very powerful. If they aren't controlled they can be *risky*. I lost control..." My voice trailed away.

"The results were immediate, Healer!" the patient's voice was earnest. "The pain is gone! Feeling is returning! I can move!"

I glanced briefly at him and smiled weakly. "I am glad, Tiahaar." My voice was almost a whisper. "But even if I was still considered a healer here, I wouldn't be able to continue working with you. Grissecon is powerful," I stumbled on. "It gets its power because we tap the energies within the Cauldron of Creation. When I fell, I lost consciousness before I had a chance to clear the aren. I am hosting."

A stunned silence filled the room.

"*You're hosting!?*" The query was harsh and incredulous and I was unsure which of the hara had spoken.

I kept my gaze on the floor and nodded feebly. I wished the floor would open and swallow me and put an end to this humiliation.

"That is all, Tobian," Autullis said haughtily. "Collect your effects, leave, and do not darken the doors of this healing centre again."

I rose, and holding my head up, I left the room with as much stiff dignity as I could muster.

Sunlight poured through the window of my sitting room and I woke with a start, confused as to why I was sitting in the worn armchair in the main room of my tiny flat, instead of in bed, and alarmed because the sunshine pouring into the room meant I'd overslept.

A split-second more of consciousness and I remembered my predicament. I had spent until the early morning hours assessing, trying to bargain with fate, contemplating my options, and trying to make plans, all to no avail. So much for my dreams of being Head Healer; he who had thought himself mighty had truly fallen far. Perhaps karma had kicked my butt to the curb as retribution for my no-holds-barred push to unseat Autullis.

One thing I did know was that I'd have to leave town. Despite what had happened, I was still a qualified healer, but I needed to go somewhere where I could have a fresh start. I sighed heavily and rubbed the sleep out of my eyes.

My biggest problem was the pearl. I had no idea how to deal with a harling. How would I care for a harling *and* work? What did one *do* with a harling? I had briefly toyed with the idea of handing the pearl over to an orphanage, but somehow that didn't seem like the answer.

I stared at the window. Despite the sunshine and blue skies, I knew it was frigid outside. I could hear the wind howling, and every so often a glittering cloud of snowflakes blown off a roof, or the top of a high drift, would swirl past the window.

South, I thought to myself. *I'll move south, somewhere where the winters aren't so harsh.* I shivered; two months wasn't a lot of time to do all that I needed to do: move, secure a position, and deliver a pearl. All I wanted to do was to crawl under a comforter and hope the nightmare would end.

A sudden pounding at the door made me nearly jump out of my skin. As I opened the door, three bundled figures pushed their way into the small flat. The last one slammed the door shut behind him and leaned on it, groaning.

"I can't feel my fingers! How does anyhar live with this cold?"

I opened my mouth and closed it again without saying anything. There was no need to; my visitors had already begun shedding their coats. A few moments later the cinnamon-skinned foreigners from the healing centre stood facing me.

"Well!" the one with the short curly hair began with forced cheerfulness as he rubbed his hands together. "I trust you are well, Healer!"

There followed a rather strained silence.

"We didn't meet formally, so allow me to introduce myself. My name is Nalani and I'm Mikala's father," he said, indicating my former patient.

"And I'm Rangi. I came along 'cause I'm good at getting things done." The har gave a slight bob of his head. "Shall I look around, then?"

Without waiting for a reply, he began to wander through the flat, inspecting things carefully.

"This is rather awkward and we've all had less than a full day to digest this situation, but I believe that it's not too early to start making our arrangements... yes?" Nalani smiled bracingly.

"Arrangements?" I was confused.

"To move," Rangi called matter-of-factly from the bedroom. "Furniture is pretty bulky and not that valuable. Can it be shipped later? Apart from that, packing should be a breeze – mostly books and clothes," he announced, wandering back to where we still stood by the door.

"I rent; the furniture isn't mine..." I started to explain, but stopped. "*Shipped?* To where?"

This was becoming more surreal by the minute.

"Surely you're not planning to stay here!" Nalani exclaimed. "It's too cold! And it's too close to that place."

"Yes, I am planning to leave here, but I have nowhere to go. I haven't found a new position yet."

"But you *do* have somewhere to go!" Nalani exclaimed. "You're coming with us, of course, given the circumstances and all."

I stared at him blankly as his words slowly sank in.

"Tiahaar," I spoke carefully, "as Administrator Autullis explained to you yesterday, these circumstances are entirely my fault. I have no right to make any claim on you or your son. There are no expectations." I shrugged feebly. "You bear no responsibility in this matter."

Until this point Mikala had been silent; now, with eyes blazing, he advanced towards me.

"Responsibility?" he growled. "Expectation? You host my son. If you 'expect' that I'll allow you to disappear into this frozen wasteland, then your 'expectation'–"

He advanced again and I took a step backwards, somewhat alarmed.

"Mikala! Enough! He's not of our tribe; perhaps their ways are different. We must remain open-minded." Nalani spoke quickly, intercepting his son and placing his hand soothingly on his arm.

"Please understand," Nalani continued, turning to me, "in our tribe, family is of the utmost importance. The pearl you host is my son's, regardless of the circumstances surrounding its creation. We must be part of this harling's life."

"We have win-win situation here," Rangi said. "You need a new position, we need another healer, and we know you're good."

"That's the truth, Tiahaar," Nalani said. "The resolution to this situation is very neat. Our tribe is spread over several large islands and numerous smaller ones – yet we currently find ourselves with only one fully qualified healer." He spread his hands. "You see?"

I find travel through the otherlanes slightly unnerving at the best of times – exhilarating but unnerving. The previous two days had not been the best of times; it had been the most surreal, hectic, uncertain, and exhausting few days I had ever experienced. Up until the incident my life had been normal, predictable, and routine. But my normally academic and cautious approach to decision-making didn't fit into Rangi's *'Get out of this frozen wasteland in a hurry!'* schedule, and so I'd had to make important decisions on a wing and a prayer.

It was night time when we exited the otherlanes. Somewhat dazed, I allowed waiting hands to help me from the back of the *sedu*. It took my brain a few moments to register that instead of the frigid biting chill, my face was being caressed by a warm fragrant breeze; I could shed the heavy coat I was wearing.

There seemed to be swarms of hara all around us, most with various shades of the warm cinnamon skin tone Mikala and his companions shared, and many adorned with the same style of tattoo as my patient. Some of the hara wore colourful sarongs wrapped around their waists and some wore shorts. Some wore light, gauzy, loose-fitting shirts and tunics, and everywhere there were bare feet and flip-flops.

At the clinic the patient and his companions had spoken in a rich pleasing accent. Here with their own hara they spoke in a lively, lilting patois. If I listened carefully I could make out some of the phrases and words; the islanders were obviously delighted in seeing the returning hara and expressed open curiosity about me.

"Yes! Yes! It was freezing!" Nalani laughed as he shook off his heavy overcoat. "We're so glad to be back! But I'm exhausted, as are we all. We've brought a new healer and we must allow him to get settled. We'll see you all in the morning. We have much news to share."

"You'll be staying with me," Mikala informed me solemnly.

Calls of "*Aloha po!*" and "Sleep well, *Kahuna!*" followed us as Mikala and I headed along a wide, well-worn path into the warm fragrant dark night air.

"*Kahuna* means a shaman, or healer, or somehar with incredible mastery of the ethers," my former patient explained as we walked. "*Aloha po* is good night."

Mikala's home was small but airy, simple yet cosy. He showed me to a small, plain room with a couple of empty bookshelves, a desk and a chair. The room was already full of a number of cases marked with labels reading "books," "more books," "big books," "too cold clothes," and "proper clothes"; Rangi really did know how to get things done. The feature of the room that drew my attention the most was the neatly made bed along the wall; I hadn't realised how exhausted I was until I saw it.

"Sleep well, Healer. I'll see you in the morning."

"Shhh! Not so loud! You'll wake him up!"

"Let me seeeeeeeee."

I lay still, listening to odd scrabbling noises outside the window.

"My hostling saw him last night," said a young voice in a loud whisper. "He said he is *nani*."

"My hostling said he was beautiful, too. Lemme seeeeeee."

More scrabbling noises ensued along with some grunts, then a brief moment of silence.

"Oh! *Kula*! His hair is *kula* and really long…"

"Gold hair? My turn! I want to see."

"Shhh!"

"No, *you* shhh!"

More scrambling sounds ensued. I sat up and was confronted by two harlings hanging halfway over the window ledge, their heads inside the room. When I sat up they froze and their eyes widened.

"*Aloha!*" the harling with the tight curls said brightly, after a moment's hesitation, as if being caught halfway in somehar's window was completely normal.

"*Maka polū!*" the other squeaked excitedly.

"All *haole* have blue eyes!" an unseen voice piped up.

"No! Not true! Not all off-landers have blue eyes," the first harling snorted and then he dropped off the window ledge, disappearing from sight.

The other harling disappeared a moment later, and I saw four small figures flee across the garden and disappear out the gate.

An interesting start, I mused as I dressed.

The house was so quiet when I emerged from the bedroom that I thought it was empty, so I started when a voice spoke.

"*Aloha*, Healer Tobian! I'm called Kenri." The har who spoke was tall and thin with large wide-set eyes. His skin was very dark and his white silky hair was cut short. Several cowlicks made him look slightly unkempt and wild. "Mika had to go. I tell Mika I wait fo' you to wake up. I want to talk with you."

"I'm well. Thank you," I said cautiously. "Did I sleep really late? I'm sorry. Somehar should have woken me."

"No worry." The har shrugged casually. "You need sleep more than t' meet me."

His thick accent did not match those of the other islanders. He regarded me pensively but was silent, and an uncomfortable thought occurred to me.

I cleared my throat, deciding to meet this head on. "Tiahaar, are you Tiahaar Mikala's chesnari?"

I wasn't expecting the response the question got. Kenri looked startled for a moment and then threw back his head and issued a hearty belly laugh.

"No! No! No! No! No!" he exclaimed, holding his hands out in front of him in mock-horror and shaking his head vehemently in denial. "No worries to you, *Kahuna*! No, Mika be a friend. *Just* a friend." He chuckled again, his grin bringing a twinkle to his eyes. He became serious again. "I be the healer here in our tribe."

I winced. "Did Tiahaar Nalani warn you that he'd saddled you with me? This wasn't planned. I apologise. "

"Did Nalani warn *you*," he countered, "that we not advanced here? Here most healing be basic. Probably very dull as with what you used to."

"I'm here because I screwed up advanced healing in a big way. I'd be grateful to be able to assist you in any way you want me to."

Kenri stared at me for a second and then snorted. He shook his head. "I don't think so, *Kahuna*. No screw-up healing got Mika so fix an' healthy as I see him today."

"Because of my mistake your friend ended up with more than just healing."

"A pearl?" Kenri grinned a toothy grin. "Now *that* be big magic."

"Tiahaar Mikala might not think so."

"Pffffffffffft." Kenri waved his hand dismissively. "What you want eatin'? I'll cook you up sometin'delish. Then I take you t'meet Akoni and the other *kahunas*. Akoni, he's our tribe's big *kahuna*." He busied himself in the kitchen. "Akoni want to hear your tale fo'sure! Like all us do, but he be Mika's hostling!" He laughed.

I sank into a chair at the wooden table in the kitchen area and rubbed my forehead.

"Of course he would be." I sighed heavily. "It figures."

Kenri looked up at me in amusement. "Dat bother you?"

"Not only did I screw up big; I screwed up on the son of the headhar."

Kenri's chuckle was deep and rich. "No sweat, Tobi! He has no beef with you! Pearls give harlings, harlings bring joy, eh? And Mika? He's fixed up!! You *mo'big kahuna*, eh?!"

I grunted and Kenri laughed heartily.

It was with no small amount of trepidation that I approached the group of hara sitting under the large airy veranda. A fair number were gathered there, more than I had anticipated and all seated on an eclectic assortment of wooden chairs, benches and wicker stools.

I was introduced to all present by Nalani and, given the degree of agitation I was feeling, I resigned myself to the fact that I would not remember all of their names. I exchanged awkward half-smiles with Mikala as I took the offered wicker stool at the far end of the veranda. Beside me open double doors offered a glimpse into a large airy office with a messy desk and bookshelf-lined walls.

Akoni was a tall graceful har with jet-black hair that hung to his waist. He was gracious, polite, and his eyes had not left me for more than a second since he'd caught sight of me; his gaze was compassionate but shrewd and knowing. The scrutiny made me feel uncomfortable.

Once the assembly was settled, Akoni spoke briefly. He welcomed me as the new healer, expressed gratitude for his son's progress, and alluded to the circumstances that had precipitated my sudden recruitment. The shaman, a tall and thin har named Ari, whose chin-length bob over-emphasised the roundness of his doll-like face and whose fidgety movements reminded me of a bird's, also welcomed me. Eventually Akoni brought the meeting to its point.

"Mikala, Tobian, I am overjoyed at the progress in healing, but," he paused, "I need to be clear on the repercussions." He stopped and looked pointedly at me and Mikala. "The healing grissecon resulted in the creation of a pearl."

I heard a gasp or two and a murmur rippled through the gathering.

"The creation of a pearl is serious enough," Akoni continued. "A harling created during grissecon is something entirely different. I need to know what happened. Mika?"

Mikala started to say something, stopped, and then started again, and stopped again. "I don't know what happened," he said finally with a helpless shrug. "Honestly. When we went, I was nervous about the process and I definitely had less hope for results than Nalani, Kenri, and you. The first healing session I was in so much pain, I don't remember much, but I noticed a difference right away and the improvements kept happening. It seemed to supercharge the work I continued on my own. The second session I was comfortable enough to be really nervous, but I think it went well, and again there were definite improvements..." His voice trailed off uncertainly.

"And the third?" his hostling prompted.

"Actually, I was the most prepared for that one, and it's the one in which I received the largest healing benefit. I guess the progress I'd experienced had given me confidence in the process. I was looking forward to it on one level, even though it's kind of unnerving. It's so very intense. I didn't notice anything wrong until the healer screamed and fell, and then all hell seemed to break loose. And, well... here we are."

Akoni regarded his son in silence for a few moments. Mikala returned his hostling's gaze. I strongly suspected that they were communicating via mind-touch. Akoni looked down for a moment as if in deep thought and then turned his gaze towards me. I could sense his curiosity and was aware that I was being appraised, but not judged – yet.

"Healer, as has already been expressed, I am, and we are all, impressed and grateful for the degree of healing we see in my son. And we are thankful that we now count you as one of our healers. What concerns me are the circumstances that brought you here. As I understood it, you were an experienced healer." He looked at me hard and I dropped my gaze. "Does this sort of 'mishap' occur frequently at the clinic? My guess is no." He paused. "Please explain what happened."

I took a deep breath. "Tiahaar, this sort of 'mishap' most certainly does not happen frequently. I also believe that the creation of life is something serious and sacred. I am very grateful that despite the situation your tribe would still willingly trust me as a healer." I paused for a moment. "The first two healing sessions were normal. Routine. Successful. The third started out normally as well, but during a crucial energy raising phase, my foot cramped."

I cringed when I heard those words out loud; it sounded so mundane.

"When I re-entered the grissecon field, there was something in the healing energy. It was forming... growing. I could see its coils. I could see it slithering in the energy. I tried to banish it, but I couldn't. It threw me off and out of the trance." I hoped this story was making some sort of sense to the gathering, as even to me the tale sounded disjointed as it came tumbling out. "When I went back into the trance, it was rising, slithering up, climbing out of the energy..."

"Excuse me?" The shaman, Ari, held up his hand. "*It?* An entity? Coils? Slithering? The energy became a snake?"

I nodded. "Yes, a snake. Well, it was serpent-like. Its body was snake-like but its head wasn't. The head was sort of dog-like... it had a snout. Its eyes were normal, har-like. I tried to stop it. Really. I did."

"Show me." Ari stepped purposefully across the veranda and pulled me to me feet. "Show me," he said again and pressed his mouth against mine.

I was momentarily startled as I felt the shaman touch my

thoughts as we shared breath, but I managed to guide him to the memory; the scene played through.

Just as suddenly as I'd been grabbed, I was released. The shaman was silent for a moment. Then he started to hum to himself. Abruptly, and without a word to anyone, he darted through the open doors into the office. He continued humming to himself as he scanned the bookshelves. Uttering a triumphant yelp, he snatched a small, innocuous-looking book off the shelf. He flipped through the pages until he found a particular spot, then returned to stand in front of me.

Handing the open book to me he said, "This is what I saw. Is it also what you saw?"

The left page panel was covered in text written in an elaborate script I couldn't read, but on the right panel was an ink drawing of the same entity I'd seen, exactly as it had appeared to me. I gaped at it for a second or two, my jaw hanging open.

"Yes," I looked up in confusion. "Exactly."

Ari took the book from me and handed it to Akoni. His eyes widened. He looked up sharply; I felt I was being rapidly reassessed. Ari turned back to me.

"Healer," he said gently, "nothing you could have done would have stopped this entity. Nothing."

The tribe's leader rose from his seat and addressed Mikala. "Agunua touches your life and the lives of others through you." He continued, addressing me as well, "The reasons may not be clear at the moment, but you two seem to have been chosen by an entity our human ancestors knew and worshipped and whom we hara have re-welcomed into our lives."

"The entity you saw is called Agunua," Ari added. "He is a guardian spirit to our tribe."

Three weeks later, I was beginning to adjust to my new situation here in the islands, but I had a lingering feeling of angst, or perhaps guilt, that made me feel I should be doing "something else" somewhere else. Although I still got some odd looks, most islanders had accepted me and my life at the healing centre, wintertime, and even Autllis seemed to slowly be fading to memory.

However, I still hadn't dealt with the fact that I was carrying a pearl; that still seemed too frightening. There had been a welcoming ceremony at which Akoni had officially welcomed me as the new healer and officially announced the anticipated arrival of the pearl, although most hara knew about that already. They had placed a necklace of flowers around my neck and a wreath of them on my head and we had feasted late into the night on the beach by the light of a huge bonfire. It had all felt very surreal.

I was still sharing Mikala's small house. We prepared meals together and inquired about each other's health and daily events. I had asked him about Akoni's statement regarding the entity Agunua touching his life and the lives of others, and he had explained that over the course of his life he'd had had several encounters with this presence; most recently it had been Agunua that had driven off the shark when he'd been attacked.

I liked Mikala, and I could tell he liked me; our relationship was good. However, a veneer of solicitous and deferential politeness remained, as we both made great effort not to talk about the reason for our arrangement. Our pearl was the ever-present thing we never talked about.

Wind rattled the shutters of my window and brought me abruptly out of my reveries, refocusing my mind on the storm that raged outside. At midday, the wind had picked up and its gusts had started the trees swaying and dancing. As the winds had continued to grow stronger throughout the afternoon, I'd helped tie things down, drag boats well up the beach, take down wind chimes, and pitched in with many other tasks tribe members referred to as "battening down the hatches." But as prepared as these activities seemed to make the islanders feel, they had only served to increase my sense of foreboding.

By the time Mikala and I had sat down for our evening meal, torrential rains were teeming down and the winds had reached full gale force. Mikala didn't seem to notice. I was now lying in my bed, fighting to keep my unease from becoming full-blown terror. I tried breathing and relaxation meditation methods. They weren't working; the noise from the storm was too ominous and too erratic. I have always been miserable during storms; they've always filled me with nebulous and irrational terrors.

The house shuddered suddenly as a massive gust of wind collided with it. It was too much for me. I rolled out of bed and nervously rechecked the latch holding the shutters closed. Peering outside I could see the palm trees being whipped around as if they were tall grasses.

Suddenly I thought about the pets that wandered in and out of Mikala's home; were they safe? Were they inside? My heart began to pound as I hurried from my room and headed towards the main room, quickly devising panicky and completely nonsensical plans for venturing out into the raging storm to find and rescue terrified, soaking animals.

I paused in front of the door before tentatively reaching for the door latch. At precisely that moment, the wind rattled the door on its hinges as if some storm demon was trying to gain access. I backed away.

"What's wrong? Are you okay?"

A startled yelp escaped me as I spun around in alarm. Mikala stood a few paces away.

"Sorry, I didn't mean to startle you," he said, scratching his head sleepily.

A shrill, nervous laugh escaped me. "It's the storm," I offered apologetically. "I *really* don't like them. I was worried about the cats and the dogs…"

Mikala ran his hand through his hair and nodded. Then he pointed to the large armchair which nestled in the bookcase-lined alcove on the far side of the kitchen. I advanced a few steps and could see three distinct balls of cat fur occupying the seat.

"Oh. Good," I said awkwardly. "I was worried."

Mikala smiled gently. "No worries about the pups either, Tobi. Rufus doesn't like storms either. Right now he's in my closet sleeping on my shoes. He does that every time there's a storm. Rooki couldn't care less and is snoring away in his bed as he does every night."

"Good! Good!" I rejoined with forced cheeriness. "I'm sorry if I woke –" I began, but I didn't finish as a gust of gale force wind shook the house, rattling the door and window shutters. From outside came an ominously loud cracking sound and I flinched.

"No worries, Tobi," Mikala said. "We're safe. Believe it or not, this isn't too bad a storm."

"They get worse?" My eyes widened, and my voice was way shriller than I wanted it to sound.

Mikala chuckled. "Let me make you some tea, and chill! We're safe! We'll have some cleanup to do, but nothing serious."

Mikala busied himself in the kitchen area as I sank onto one of the two chairs at the small dinette table. I watched Mikala as he prepared the tea; he really was a beautiful har. His movements were easy now and his scars were fading. Mikala placed a mug of steaming tea on the table in front of me, and then he hopped up onto the kitchen counter across from the table. He sat there swinging his legs slightly, watching me with a look of concern furrowing his brow.

"How are you, Tobi?" He asked.

"The storm has me rattled. They always have. I'm a big chicken," I said as light-heartedly as I could.

"No, I meant how are things going?"

"I think I'm fitting in around here," I replied with a half-smile. "It's quite a switch to what I was used to, but apart from some awkwardness and odd looks from some hara I think, or rather, I 'hope' things are going well."

"They'll get used to you and you to them," Mikala responded. "You're not the first or only *haole* on these islands. But I was actually asking about… you know… you."

"Oh." I placed my hand on my lower abdomen. "Things are progressing as they should and …"

"No," Mikala interrupted again. "How are *you* doing? How are you coping with…things?" he asked awkwardly.

I thought for a moment. "I'm not actually… it still seems too overwhelming. I feel a bit lost. And you?"

Mikala sighed deeply. "The fog is lifting. But I have a lot of support. My family and friends are here. They've been crucial." He paused. "Things happened so fast. When I found out you were hosting, my only consuming thought was to get you and my pearl home here safely and as fast as possible. I didn't really consider you, or your family. I'm sorry. Have you let them know where you are? We can bring them here, if you want."

I shook my head. "I have no family."

"None?"

"None. I was a product of the Varrs' experimental breeding facility. Neither the Gelaming nor the Parsics ever managed to break the coding to determine parentage, so no parents. No traceable family."

"I'm sorry." Mikala looked disconcerted.

I shrugged. "Don't be. It is what it is."

Mikala was quiet for a moment. "You host a son, and that's family, and since he's my son too, that makes *us* family. And since you and our son are my family, that means you're also part of my extended family."

"I hadn't thought of it that way before," I said with a slightly bemused smile. Mikala's logic and the thought of suddenly having a family were a bit mind-boggling.

"So you do have a family now, whether you want one or not." Mikala grinned. "It's late! Let's try and get some sleep."

Right on cue the wind howled, the shutters and the door rattled, and the loud bang of something hitting the roof, hard. I flinched, again.

"No worries!" Mikala said, looking up at the roof. "That was either a coconut or a pineapple. We really are quite safe. Honest!" Mikala guided me toward the short hallway to the bedrooms. "You could always join Rufus in my closet," he suggested with a mischievous smile.

"Ha! I just might!" I rejoined.

"Or," Mikala said slowly, "I could try to take your mind off the storm."

The suggestion caught me off guard and I shot Mikala a look of surprise.

"Really?"

"Really. We created a pearl but we've never shared aruna; not regular aruna. Not aruna purely for pleasure." He bent forward and pressed his lips against mine. We shared breath, pressing our bodies together, holding each other close.

Mikala pulled away. "You won't even think about the storm, I promise!"

"I'm already not thinking about it," I said, thrusting my hands into Mikala's hair and pulling his lips back towards mine.

Kenri was bent over a stout little shrub.

"It's called *Ashwagandha*," he announced as I looked on, dutifully clutching an ancient and frayed human plant identification manual. "I brought the seeds here from away and plant 'em myself — that's why it's not in d' book — it's not from d' islands. *Ashwagandha* in ancient human Sanskrit language means 'horse's smell', cuz dis root stink like a sweaty horse."

"And its uses are similar to that one over there." I pointed to another bush growing a few paces away. "Correct?"

"Similar tranquilisin' properties. It can also give some arunic vitality, but you can't use that one," he jerked his head in the direction of the other bush I had just pointed to, "t'curd your cheese. This one you can." He patted his shrub affectionately.

I laughed. "I like you a whole lot better than my old boss."

Kenri drew himself up and laughed. "Am I not amazin'?

"That you are." I agreed. "Kenri, can I ask you something?"

Kenri sat back on his heels and looked at me, shielding his eyes from the sun.

"The Waiki'Lao don't have any nayatis, and Ari was quite adamant that he be referred to as a shaman, or *kahuna*, and not as a hienama. Yesterday in the market when I mentioned the Aghama to that har that sells the glass beads, he thought I was mispronouncing Agunua; he'd never heard of the Aghama, or any of the dehara for that matter. Don't the hara here believe in the Aghama or the dehara? Where do they go to do rituals?"

"You not in Gelaming-land now. On these islands everything 'away' is far away," Kenri said. "The Waiki'Lao believe in the Aghama – but here he is known as 'The First One'; without him none of us would be har. But we don't believe he be a deity. We on d'islands believe in spirit; our spirit, the spirit of the tribe, and the spirits of our environment. Nohar here feel connected to 'dehara' discovered in a cave a long time ago and far away. They believe in what they see and feel here. The spirits and guardians have always been here in this place; they are primal. Humans first knew them and then abandoned them. Now we all be reconnecting."

"What about nayatis?"

"Nayatis be just walls! Who need a building?" Kenri snorted. "Weather here be fine and the scenery be beautiful – why go inside?"

"Magic and ascension skills aren't too important here either, are they?" I asked.

"Skills in those areas are important to us because we be healers; Ari too, as he a shaman. The rest of them learn what they need. Need mind touch? Learn it. Need to start a fire? Learn how. Want to sense where the fish be to? Learn. Vision quests be the most common metaphysical adventures hara do here." He shrugged. "I think much of that high-brow mumbo-jumbo be about trying to be happy, trying to understand who you are, and trying to put some meaning into life – hara on these islands already there; our lives have meaning and we happy. You fine though, Tobi; honour whoever and whatever you believe in."

"I'm not sure what I believe in anymore. I've never really interacted with any of the dehara that I was taught about, but an entity I'd never heard of interacted with me and turned my life upside down."

"You already know mumbo-jumbo. Maybe all you need learning is 'happy'," Kenri said with a gentle smile.

"He's right, Tobi!" Ari's voice sounded from behind us. "Finding out who you are and what makes you happy is true success."

"It might take me a while," I said.

"We'll wait," Kenri asserted.

"And how *are* you, Tobi?" Ari inquired reaching out and placing his hand lightly on my lower abdomen. "Are you getting nervous? Only two weeks left."

I rolled my eyes at him. "I'm fine! And no, I'm not getting nervous. I'm still living firmly in the Land of Denial."

"You know what I think?" Ari began, but he was interrupted by the sound of voices calling and running feet.

Two older harlings, followed by a troop of younger ones, rounded the corner of the clinic and burst into the garden.

"*Kahuna! Kahuna!*"

They were breathless, eyes wide with the weightiness of the news they carried.

"They caught one of the *Kanaka*. They're bringing him here. Akoni is coming too!"

Message delivered, they raced back around to front of the building. Ari scowled and hissed a word that I did not understand.

"What's a '*Kanaka*'? I asked.

"Trouble!" Ari said darkly and headed off in the direction the harlings had disappeared.

"Trouble?" I looked at Kenri

Kenri sighed. "They weren't always trouble," he said sadly, and he too headed off around the side of the clinic.

I followed. When I reached the front of the building Akoni, Nalani, Rangi, and Mikala were already there, surrounded by an ever-increasing number of village hara. Some looked worried, some angry. I went to stand by Mikala. We watched as a small band of hara approached with a tall lanky har at their centre, his shaved head glistening in the sun. He carried what appeared to be a small, naked harling. But as the group drew nearer I could see that the physiology of the little creature was different; definitely not harish.

I leaned towards Mikala. "Human? A... child?"

Mikala nodded.

The little body hung limp in the lanky har's arms. His eyes were half closed, his lips slightly parted. Damp black hair clung to his forehead and a film of sweat covered his body.

"We found him lying in a clearing near the path to our lower groves," the lanky har announced.

"It's sick," Ari said, stating the obvious.

"Kill it!" a voice from the crowd called. A small murmur of assent rippled through the crowd.

The har carrying the child's body looked troubled. "But he's so young... just a harling."

"Then put him back where you found him!" Ari said bitterly. "*Kanaka* are nothing but trouble."

Akoni held up a hand to the crowd signalling he wanted silence. "Were there any signs of others?"

The lanky har shook his head.

Without waiting for any more discussion, I stepped forward and lifted the child out of the har's arms.

"He's sick. I'm a healer," I announced to the surprised faces in the crowd. "It's my duty to heal him."

"But it's a human!" Ari said in disbelief.

"And?" I said, arching a brow and delivering a withering look worthy of Autullis.

"What if he dies?" asked somehar.

"What if he lives?" another voice chimed in.

"Whether he lives or dies, treating him is the right thing to do," I said equably.

"A win-win situation!" Rangi announced. "If the child dies, we have the moral high ground because we tried to help. If he lives, we have the virtuous pleasure of returning a living child to its tribe."

"And if they don't want it back after we've marked it with our scent?" Ari asked darkly.

Rangi shrugged. "If they don't want him back, we incept him when he's old enough and our tribe is all the richer."

"Problem is sorted," Akoni nodded curtly. "Heal him, *kahuna.*"

I placed the child gently on a cot in one of the small treatment rooms. Kenri followed me in and shut the door firmly in the faces of those curious villagers who'd followed us into the clinic.

"Okay, now what, *Kahuna* Smarty-pants?" Kenri whispered.

"We heal him," I whispered back.

"How?" He countered.

"The usual way."

"When was the last time you treated a human?" Kenri crossed his arms across his chest and gave me a hard, penetrating stare.

"It's been awhile," I said grudgingly.

Kenri raised an eyebrow.

"Okay. Never! I've never actually seen a real human before. They were pretty scarce where I come from. My tribe killed them all."

Kenri started to laugh. "I knew there was a reason I liked you! You bat-shit crazy."

Treating the child wasn't difficult. He responded well to our healing touch and to the herbal elixir Kenri cooked up. By the afternoon he was listless but conscious. By late evening his fever had lessened and he was lying quiet and alert, watching us with his big, dark eyes and venturing small, shy smiles when we spoke to him.

When I returned to the clinic the next morning, an unusually chaotic scene confronted me in my small patient's room: it was full of harlings, toys, and giggling.

"Poor wee thing was lonely. I hope you don't mind," the night monitor said as he slipped past me into the room with a tray of full juice glasses.

The child was still pale and had dark circles under his eyes, but judging by the huge smile on his face, he was definitely on the mend. Another day or so of rest and I'd have to figure out how to get him back to his tribe.

It was about noon when Kenri sauntered into the clinic to join me. I was cleaning up after removing a fishhook from the bottom of a careless boater's foot, so Kenri leaned against the counter and regaled me with his morning adventures paddling a new dugout down at the beach. I, in turn, filled him in on our young human's progress; I was quite taken with the child.

"It's amazing that there are any humans left anywhere," I mused.

"You went straight from d'training to your fancy clinic, didn't you? What am I to do wit you? No real world experience!" Kenri chuckled as he shook his head. "There still be humans and there probably always will be in some form or other."

"You think there will always be humans?" I scoffed. "Why? The female fertility rates have dropped and most of their young choose inception at maturity – time is not on their side."

"You're a healer. I don't need to be explainin' to you how," Kenri stated flatly.

My brow furrowed in confusion.

"You *have* heard of the atavistic pearl, haven't you?" Kenri said with a hint of exasperation.

"Pffft." I did a worthy impression of Kenri "The atavistic pearl? Throwbacks? Backsliders? Get serious, Kenri! There aren't enough pearls produced that exhibit genetic retrogression to keep any human population viable. That aberration is rarer than rare!"

Kenri stared at me, his expression hard.

"What?" I sounded a little more defensive than I wanted to. Despite my lofty credentials, I found that I was out of touch with a lot of basic day-to-day stuff and I lacked what Kenri called 'street cred.' "They're not rare?"

"Not as rare as you think," Kenri returned. "The creation of Kamagrians is common enough that their appearance in some tribes has become a much-celebrated occurrence. Atavists are still a dirty secret, and not as rare as you think them be."

I shook my head in disbelief.

"And," Kenri continued, "I prefer to think of the atavists as 'half-sexed' rather than 'throwbacks,' as they aren't 'human' as humans were before Wraeththu – they be different."

"Different?" I was curious. "How?"

"Their parents be hara." Kenri shrugged again. "Atavists mature faster. They be stronger, faster, and they have much more 'magic' than original humans."

"Super humans?" My eyes widened. "They couldn't

strengthen the surviving human stock, could they?"

"Inception is routinely offered when they mature, but there be more atavists chosin' t'integrate into human colonies. They be breeding with surviving populations, but it be too early to tell what effect this be havin'.'"

I must have looked worried because Kenri grinned at me.

"Don't be fussed," he said. "We still mo'bigga and badder. Wraeththu the most 'powerful'" – here he made bunny-ears as he emphasised the word 'powerful.' "We mo'likely to run amuck than d'half-sexed."

"True enough," I conceded.

"And don't be frettin' – your pearl is a normal harling, or as normal as a harling can be when he be created during grissecon, and with the help of Agunua."

I grunted. "I'm hungry. I'm going to get something at the market. You coming?"

"Sure." Kenri nodded. "But, Tobi, just be careful what you say about *Kanaka* and the half-sex around Ari, okay?"

"Why was Ari so angry about the *Kanaka* anyway?" I inquired. Ari's reaction had surprised me.

Kenri paused for a few moments before replying. "Ari had a brother."

"An atavist?" My eyes widened.

Kenri nodded. "I was not livin' here den, but from what I heard, the family was devastated. When time came to incept the half-sex one – he rebelled. He refused inception, sayin' he want to be loved and accepted as he was. There be fights and drama and before it was all fixed, the parents were lost to the sea during a storm. The brothers continued fighting and the atavist brother took off into the forests to live with the *Kanaka*. The last I heard, he had moved to one of the smaller islands."

"That can't be the only reason that there is tension between our two groups. How did that happen?" I asked.

"Long ago, the original island population of both humans and hara was decimated by volcanoes and tsunamis. As the island regenerated the two groups split up – humans moved inland to d'mountains and the hara stay on d'coasts."

"And the mistrust and hostility?"

"Dis one took dat one's goat. Dat one took dis one's chickens. He sunk their boat. They burn down his shed." Kenri shrugged an exaggerated shrug. "Soon *Kanaka* and hara jus'be keepin' a good distance, and blamin' each other for everything that be goin' wrong. Eventually they all be jus'plain hostile."

"Well, that's stupid," I muttered.

I lay awake in bed, listening to Mika's quiet, even breathing as he slept next to me. I was awake, feeling the light flutters of the tiny creature that inhabited the pearl I hosted, and luxuriating in the warm, fragrant breeze that blew through the open window.

The driven, ambitious Healer Tobian har Parsic, and his frigid snowy land of the elite healers and political machinations, seemed so distant in time and memory. He was being supplanted by Kahuna Tobi, an increasingly easy-going har who was discovering the joys of walking barefoot on sandy beaches, and learning how to grow his own healing herbs.

I was still awake when a har from the village came pounding on the door, yelling, "There's been an attack! A raid! Injuries! Quickly!"

Mikala and I followed the young har to the village centre, trying to make sense of his breathless explanation: *Kanaka* raiders had been spotted lurking in the dark, near where they'd found the child. Hara had gone to chase them off; there'd been a fight and injuries. Hara had captured one of the attackers.

The clinic was abuzz with activity. Angry, worried and confused hara were gathered in small groups both inside and out. Akoni, with Nalani by his side, stood in conference with Rangi and Ari inside the hectic open area of the clinic.

At one end of the room two serious looking hara stood guarding a bed on which lay what I assumed to be the *Kanaka* prisoner. His leg lay at an unnatural angle and a deep crimson stained the sheet. At the other end of room a group of hara hovered around four others who sat on clinic beds.

"It wasn't a raid, Akoni," Rangi was saying. "Of that I'm certain."

Ari seemed distracted, staring at the prisoner.

"Rangi, can you be sure?" Nalani said cautiously. "The *Kanaka* attacked our hara!"

"No!" Rangi said cutting him off. "They were attacked by *our* villagers who were alarmed to discover *Kanaka* skulking around in the dark, and rightly so. But the *Kanaka* took nothing, nor were they near any livestock or…"

"They were looking for something," Ari said, still staring hard at the prisoner.

"What?" Akoni demanded.

Ari turned to Akoni. "The child," he said "They were searching for the child. That's his father. The *Kanaka* were here searching for the child."

"Understandable!" I said emphatically. "If my son were missing I'd certainly be out searching."

The vehemence in my voice surprised me; it was the first time I'd experienced a visceral parental reaction. It was interesting, and I made a note to explore it later.

Akoni nodded. Kenri left the group of injured hara and joined us.

"Just scrapes and bruises," he announced. "Their pride will be longer in healin' than their bodies."

"Well, then," Akoni sighed rolling his eyes slightly, "let's go start soothing egos." He and the others moved towards the injured hara. I didn't join them. I turned and headed towards the prisoner. I was instantly intercepted by one of the armed guards.

"Not so fast, *haole*!" he snarled.

I blinked. *Haole* was a term these hara used to refer to those of us who "came from away." It was a term that I had only heard used as a descriptor, but the viciousness with which this har spat the word turned it into a derogatory term. It was the first time I'd encountered this kind of behaviour.

"I'm a healer," I stated evenly. "The prisoner is injured. He needs to be assessed."

"I don't think so. It's too dangerous for you, *haole*," he sneered. "Let it die."

I glanced briefly at the second guard, who looked to be almost as shocked I felt.

"Excuse me, I have work to do," I said firmly, allowing a hint of annoyance to project into my tone.

As I stepped around the guard, he moved to block me and gave me a sharp shove. It was hard enough to cause me to stagger back several steps. From behind me I heard voices rise in anger and outrage.

Even as the commotion occurred behind me, the guard lifted off the ground and flew backwards into the air, ending up pinned by invisible forces against the wall close to the ceiling. There he hung, his feet dangling, his eyes bulging as he clutched at his throat. The clinic was instantly silent. I felt every eye on me, including the prisoner's, as I stalked, my eyes blazing, to stand below where I held the guard suspended against the wall.

"I think you will find that although I am merely a *haole* healer, I am quite capable of not only handling an injured human but also those who interfere with my work."

With that I released my hold on him and he crashed to the floor. The guard was hauled to his feet and unceremoniously led away as those gathered murmured in subdued voices and watched me in a mix of awe and apprehension.

I didn't have time to thoroughly enjoy the unwarranted smugness that this new notoriety gave me, as another commotion had erupted behind me. I turned around quickly to see the remaining guard moving between Kenri and the prisoner. Kenri's hands were raised in a placating gesture and both he and the guard backed away.

I crossed the room and stood next to the prisoner's cot. "I have your son," I said calmly. I knew the prisoner could understand me as he became very still and wary. "Allow us to heal your leg and I'll bring him to you." He narrowed his eyes and regarded me with suspicion. "I don't see that you have much choice, do you?" I said evenly.

He stared at me for a moment and then lay back on the cot, turning his head away to stare at the wall.

Kenri pushed passed me. "Show off," he muttered at me beneath his breath. "No funny stuff!" I heard Kenri warn the prisoner. "What him can do, I can do too."

Calm had returned to the clinic when I opened the door to the child's room; he lay on his side, sleeping peacefully. I sat down on the edge of the cot and ran my hand across his curls. He began to stir as I gently lifted him out of bed. He sleepily snuggled against my shoulder as I carried him into the main area of the clinic.

The prisoner was lying on the cot, staring at the ceiling as I approached. He turned his head towards me, and when he saw what I held, his eyes widened and he let out faint moan and reached desperately for the child.

"Papa!" The child reached back, lunging out of my arms.

The man hugged the child close, burying his face in the child's hair and murmuring to him. The child clung to him and snuggled as close as he could. I backed up and looked away – the emotions I could feel were too raw and intense; I would have my own son soon.

"Thank you, *Kahuna*," The man's voice wavered slightly.

I nodded.

"Rest. Heal. And thank *you*!" I said. "You've solved the problem of how to reunite this child with his family."

I stretched and groaned slightly as I came down the steps at the back door of the clinic. I plunked myself down on the bottom one. Rangi was seated on an overturned pail. Ari was seated on the bench under the vine with the fragrant golden flowers next to Kenri, who lounged with his legs stretched out in front of him. All three looked at me somewhat reproachfully.

"I dun' know why that healer be here," Kenri said to no one in particular. "He should be home resting."

"You do look tired," Rangi agreed carefully.

"The pearl is due any second now," Ari coaxed.

"I'm fine," I said.

"You're exhausted!" Kenri burst out "The pearl is draining you. Stop pushing yourself! As a healer I be tellin' you..."

I drew myself up and channelling my best 'Autullis' I shot him a quelling look. "As a healer I can assure *you* that I am one hundred percent fine."

"You're exhausted!" Kenri persisted.

"Don't blame the pearl," I sniffed primly. "Blame Mikala! He was insatiable last night."

The looks on their faces were priceless and their loud guffaws lasted for some time. Ari was still chuckling when Nalani appeared along the garden path, a look of concern on his face.

"It looks like we have visitors again," he said.

We followed him around the front of the clinic and into central village gathering area.

Akoni and Mikala were already there, as were a number of others, all focused on the path that led out of the forest and wound into the village. On the path I could see a procession winding its way into town.

"*Kanaka*," someone reported to Akoni. "Some are armed."

"They may be armed," Nalani noted, "but they have females with them. The arms are more likely for protection than for attack."

Akoni said nothing. He just watched as the procession approached. The party consisted of eight humans, six males armed with bows and arrows, and long heavy machetes, and two females, who also wore small knives at their waists. They seemed to me all fairly young, but I didn't have enough experience with humans to judge. They all looked nervous as they stopped a little way from us. One of the females stepped forward.

"Greetings, Kahuna!" she said. Her voice wavered slightly. "We have been sent to ask that the golden-haired *kahuna*-healer accompany us back to our village."

Akoni crossed his arms over his chest. "Why?"

She took a deep breath. "Please, *Kahuna*, my brother's wife… she labors, but the baby does not come. She grows weak and our elder-mother fears we shall lose both her and the baby. My brother says the golden *kahuna* healer saved his son and… please, *Kahuna*." Her voice trailed off and her eyes briefly flickered to me.

Kenri stepped forward. "Our 'golden healer' needs to stay put. I'll go."

The female exchanged looks with her companions. "With due respect, it is the golden one we were sent for," she said carefully.

"I'll go," I said.

Akoni turned towards me, a deep concern etched on his face and Mikala opened his mouth to object, but I held up my hand.

"I'm okay. Really. As a healer I'm more than aware of how close I am. None of the changes that need to happen before I drop the pearl have happened yet," I said clearly, looking at Akoni. "None of them," I repeated firmly, looking at Mikala.

"I'll go with him," Kenri said. "Just in case."

"And I'll go with both of them," Ari chimed in resolutely. "If the pearl decides it's time, I'll 'poof' Tobi back in a flash."

The human tribe, the *Kanaka*, lived in the centre region of our island and the trek to their village was long and steamy. The upshot of this rather arduous hike was the beauty of the landscape that we passed through. The lush green of the forest, the exotic colour of flowers, and curious birds I spotted flying up in the forest canopy.

Several hours into our adventure, I decided it prudent not to mention to either Kenri or Ari that I could feel the pearl shifting, one of the subtle signs that my delivery was imminently approaching. I rationalised that Ari already seemed very on edge and this "news" was just something that would further unnerve him. We had a mission.

As we drew near the village we were met by anxious villagers and escorted into a small, neat hut. The situation that we had found in the hut wasn't encouraging, but we did our best. We gave strength to the mother, and applied energies and directed forces to try and facilitate the birth, but to no avail. In the end we resorted to an ancient human method of delivery, a caesarean. I must give Kenri full credit. I'd only learned human healing in theory, and he had the experience.

I now sat cross-legged on the floor of the hut with a weak grey infant cradled in my arms. Ari and Kenri knelt beside the mother, pouring healing and energy into her unconscious body. I closed my eyes and took a deep cleansing breath, pushing away the knowledge that my own body had now almost completed all the things it needed to do to prepare for the delivery of my pearl. I turned my focus to the baby, joining my consciousness to hers; the hut faded from my awareness.

A faint mewling sound pulled me back to this realm. The baby squirmed and fussed in my arms, its colour rosy. Kenri sat cross-legged next to the mother, holding her hand. Ari, who had been sleeping on a mat, began to stir and struggle up to a seated position.

"A good sound! Like music, eh?" Kenri said, smiling happily down at the mother.

The curtain across the door of the hut was pulled back and an old woman stepped in. Her hair was as white as snow and her face was wrinkled. She folded her hands into a prayer position and bowed first to Kenri and Ari, and then to me. Then she began to speak, but I didn't understand what she said.

With Kenri's assistance the mother struggled to sit up as the old woman bent to hug her. Several young women came in and helped the mother to her feet and supported her as she shuffled carefully out of the hut. She paused at the door and looked over to where I still sat, holding the fussing baby.

The old woman laughed and spoke in jovial tones as she

shooed them from the hut. Kenri stood stiffly and pulled Ari to his feet, and then they both followed the females out of the hut. The old woman came to me and knelt down in front of me. Her eyes were fixed on the baby; her old face beamed and her eyes were moist.

"Beautiful life," she murmured as she leaned forward and gently took the bundle from my arms. "Come! Eat!" the old woman said, grinning at me and nodding. "Come!"

With that she and the baby were gone. I took a deep cleansing breath and stretched, but winced as a sharp pain gripped my lower back and some deep pressure built in my groin area. I let the breath out slowly. *Oh shit!*

I slowly unfolded my legs and stiffly got to my feet. As I straightened, the pain and pressure returned. I wasn't going to be able to deny what was happening for much longer.

Once the pain passed, I moved carefully to the door. Standing outside the hut, I leaned on the doorframe. A celebration was underway in the village and there were smiling faces everywhere. The familiar face of the man who'd been our prisoner a few weeks ago stood smiling, his arms around the new mother as the old woman intoned a reedy singsong incantation, holding the newborn aloft. She lowered the infant, kissed its forehead and handed it to its mother.

The villagers formed a haphazard receiving line; I watched as they congratulated the parents and admired the baby. I noted with abstract amusement that the females were more likely to crowd around the mother and make cooing noises to the baby, while the males focused on the father, slapping him on the back or shaking his hand.

The father caught sight of me. He came towards me grinning widely; he threw his arms around me and hugged me tightly. He repeated "Thank you" a million times before he released me.

He grabbed my arm and started to pull me over to where Ari and Kenri sat sipping steaming mugs of some beverage. Another wave of pain engulfed me; the pressure seemed to build into a swirling vortex pushing down and out through my groin. I closed my eyes, gritted my teeth, and breathed into it.

"*Kahuna?*" I heard the alarm in the man's voice and he gripped my arm to steady me.

"I'll be fine," I said as I opened my eyes, trying to smile

nonchalantly, but I could tell he didn't believe me.

Ari and Kenri were at my side in seconds.

"How you feeling, Tobi?" Kenri asked in that annoying professional manner we healers tend to use when we already know the answer.

"Good," I said as casually as I could.

"Is it time?" Ari asked excitedly.

"No," I lied; knowing full-well Kenri wouldn't buy it.

Kenri chuckled.

"Don't worry," Ari assured the worried onlookers "*Kahuna* Tobian will be fine. We'll take him home now."

Kenri and Ari sandwiched me between them and the village disappeared in a rush of light and frosty air, and then we were in the clinic.

If you go out the back gate behind my house and follow the trail through the trees, it eventually winds its way down around the steep rocky escarpment and spills out onto a small, white, sandy beach at the edge of a tiny lagoon. It's a quiet beach used by few hara other than those living in the three houses on our little lane.

On this late afternoon I had the beach almost to myself. My green tie-dyed sarong was spread out on the sand and I sat naked on it in the sunshine. I took handfuls of sand and poured them over the bare little toes of the harling who sat in front of me. He squealed with glee and kicked his feet so that the sand fell away – and then I did it again.

I'd fallen instantly in love with my son. Keoni was a perfect blend of his father and me. He was darker than I was, but fairer than his father; he had my eyes and nose, but his father's eye colour; on his head was dark hair with golden highlights. I could spend hours just sitting with him, rediscovering the world anew through his eyes.

Today, however, I was also keeping a wary eye on the weather. The sky was still blue, but the clouds were getting thicker and bigger and were moving across the sky at a decent clip ahead of winds that had been intensifying all day. The air smelled warm and wet, sure signs a storm was headed our way.

A sudden squeak from Keoni drew my attention. He squealed and flapped his arms excitedly and began pulling himself to his feet. Mikala was striding out of the trees towards us, grinning widely. Mikala swooped Keoni up, tossing him in the air, catching him, and covering his little face with kisses.

"Shall we get wet?" Mikala asked the harling as he headed off towards the water.

The water wasn't its usual bright blue-green; it was a dark blue-grey and the waves were large and powerful as they came roaring up onto shore.

I stood up and shook the sand out of the sarong and fixed it around my waist as I followed Mikala down to the water's edge. Mikala waded in deep enough to let waves get Keoni's toes wet. I only got close enough to let the waves surge over my feet and ankles. Mikala waded back out, his shorts clinging to his legs, and handed Keoni to me.

"Wait here," he said and sprinted up the beach towards the tree line.

He bent over and picked something up and trotted back toward where we stood waiting. He held up his trophy with a grin.

"Coconut!" He announced. "It's tradition to offer the first coconut to Agunua with thanks, and I have much to be thankful for. This year, I almost died, I was healed, through a dramatic twist of fate I found our tribe a new healer, and this har blessed me with a beautiful son." He paused. "I'm grateful that things turned out the way they did. Your turn."

I reached up and stroked the side of Keoni's cheek and then let my fingers run down his arm.

"Mika, six months ago I'd never met you, and I'd never heard of these islands or this tribe. Now I can't imagine my life any other way. Keoni is more amazing than I can put into words, and I feel blessed by—" I stumbled on the words awkwardly "everything that's happened."

Mikala turned to face the water and held the coconut out in front of him. "Agunua, hear me! Thank you! Thank you for my recovery! Thank you for the treasures you put in my path."

I reached out and put my hand on the coconut. "Thank you, Agunua! A year ago I was a very different har, but you showed me a new way; I am grateful."

Mikala wound up and threw the coconut as far as he could out into the lagoon. It flew through the air and then splashed down a respectable distance out in the water. Turning back towards me, Mikala reached out to take our son from my arms, but when he saw the look on my face he swung around again and looked back out into the lagoon.

I was staring at the spot where the coconut had hit the waves. The water seemed to be boiling and swirling in an unnatural way. Slowly an enormous shape began to surface; water poured off it as it cleared the surface: A dog-like head with a long square-ish snout and tiny pointed ears whose tips flopped down rose from the water. Kind, har-like eyes watched us for a moment and then it was gone.

"Agunua," Mikala whispered.

We stood there on the beach, staring out to sea for quite some time before heading home.

Keoni stirred in my arms. He lifted his head and looked sleepily around before throwing his arms around my neck and nuzzling his head back under my chin. The annual Kameh'ha celebration was underway and it had been a long day already, especially for little harlings. I still had no clear understanding of this celebration. Many islanders had tried to explain the meaning of this event to me and, based on the varied descriptions, everyone seemed to be celebrating something different, but as everyone was happy, it didn't really seem to matter.

We'd been down to the big main beach around lunchtime in order to watch the procession of *Kanaka* emerge from the forest. This celebration had not been "mixed" for many years. There had been a rather solemn meeting between Akoni and the *Kanaka* chief, a wizened, white-haired old man.

For several moments I was afraid that this festive shindig was doomed to failure. Both groups stood stiff and wary, eyeing each other with suspicion. Then my former child-patient saw some of harlings he'd made friends with during his stay at the clinic, and soon they were off and running, splashing through the waves, their laughter filling the air. In short order more harlings and children decided to join them and as more laughter filled the air, the ice surrounding the adults began to melt away.

I watched as a tall muscular man with shoulder-length salt and pepper hair surveyed the crowd and then tentatively approached Ari. The moment Ari saw him, he enveloped the human in a bone-crushing embrace. I assumed that this must be the wayward brother.

I studied this man from a distance trying to detect any differences between him and the other humans; I could. Subtle but distinct differences marked his energies. I spent much of the afternoon observing Ari's brother and the other humans. There had been no real opportunity to use any of my elite-level perception skills since I arrived here and it felt good to exercise them again.

Humans were quite interesting and I identified two other men whose energies were similar to those of Ari's brother. I noted several children of both genders who were also 'different.' It was fascinating to me that, despite having harish parents, the atavists were not only "compatible" with humans, but their traits were apparently passed down to the next generation.

This observation did more than pique my curiosity, I felt a tiny thrill surge through my being – this was a mystery to me; a new riddle to solve.

While I was enjoying the new slower pace of life on the island, I knew I would eventually need something more challenging to keep my brain busy. More study? Definitely! Naturally I'd get Kenri to tell me everything he knew, but I also thought I might look up an old roommate from my early school days. He'd been obsessed with all things human and had headed off to study them as I had headed off to study healing arts. I felt ridiculously excited and invigorated by the thought of this new project; I'd start tomorrow.

Now it was early evening and the shadows were growing longer as the sun sank low into the horizon. The first round of feasting was done and two main bonfires blazed on the beach. Humans and hara mingled; harmony reigned.

"Keo, are you hungry?" I felt him shake his head. "Thirsty?" His head shook again. "Do you have to pee?" Another shake. "Are you going to say 'No' to everything I ask?" Keoni was still for a moment. He lifted his head off my shoulder and grinned; then still grinning widely he shook his head – No. "Goofy monkey!" I teased, hugging him tight.

Akoni, Ari, and the *Kanaka* chieftain began to call for the crowd's attention, and now that Keoni was awake again I wandered back into the crowd to stand with Mikala and Nalani. We watched as a coconut was brought forward and blessed. All three of the ritual leaders spoke briefly as a sacred fire was lit, and invocations were chanted. Dancers in grass skirts and colourful sarongs moved to the powerful beat of drums as the sun began its final descent toward that line where sky and ocean met.

A group of young hara from a school in the next village had built a small catapult that they solemnly rolled forward. With a big grin the *Kanaka* chieftain raised the coconut high and then placed it with exaggerated ceremony into the catapult's cradle. His voice was reedy as he called out to Agunua, and at his signal the catapult deployed, launching the coconut into the air. Cheers rose from the crowd as the coconut soared in a majestic arc, silhouetted black against bright orange and reds of the setting sun, and they continued as it splashed down into the now inky ocean.

All at once the cheering stopped. The ocean surface at the point where the coconut had entered boiled violently, and with rushing hiss, Agunua himself rose out of the waves to tower over the beach. His serpentine body swayed gently as he watched us, then he inclined his head ever so slightly in our direction.

"Agunua!" my son's lone voice called out in the hushed silence on the beach. His call was echoed by another, and another, and soon we were all chanting Agunua's name as if with one voice. Then, with a quick undulating quiver, Agunua dove back into the waves and was gone.

Later that night as we walked back towards our home carrying our sleeping son, Mikala sighed. "Part of me wants to know what this all means," he began softly. "Agunua went to a lot of trouble to create Keo, and bring us together."

"Yes, he did," I agreed. "I suppose we should be grateful we like each other."

"No kidding!" Mikala grinned. "But why? Why me? Why you? Where is this journey taking us? Part of me really needs to know, but then another part of me…" He sighed a soft, contented sigh. "You know?"

I took a deep breath; the air was warm and I could smell the ocean. "Yeah, I know," I said, smiling softly in the dark.

dread kin

Fiona Lane

Pritthi dreamt he was an angel falling from heaven. His wings were folded tight against his body and he plunged into the blue world below, shattering it into a million pieces. Then he rose again.

Every Lunilsday was the same.

Pritthi rose early, when the eastern sky was pale. Leaving his hard mattress on the floor of the sleeping quarters, he made his way to the main temple to perform his daily devotions. He knelt on the tiled floor and inclined his head before the array of statues of the dehara set into the alcoves along the back wall of the temple. He spoke the words of the morning prayer quietly to himself, ignoring all the other hara around him doing the same thing.

When the ritual was over, he emerged blinking into the brightening morning and immediately fetched his broom from the storeroom to begin sweeping the outer courtyard surrounding the temple. After he had finished sweeping, he went below the stone benches to collect up the incense trays placed there every evening at dusk to deter biting insects. He methodically removed the ashes left from the previous day, cleaned and polished the trays and stacked them in the corner, ready for refilling later. He also emptied the waste receptacles and made sure that no fallen leaves or detritus had blocked the drainage outlets at each corner of the courtyard.

Once he was satisfied that the Phylarch could have no cause for complaint about the quality of his work, he made his way to the kitchens to help with the preparation of food for the midday meal. Pritthi was not of sufficient status to be allowed to do any actual cooking, but he was kept busy fetching and carrying both water and the huge sacks of rice from the basement pantries. It was hard work, not made any easier by the heat from the wood-burning ranges within the kitchen and the ever-increasing heat of the day outside.

By the time the food was ready, and carried over to the refectory, Pritthi's stomach was making inelegant noises, and he wolfed down his lunch gratefully. The food was plentiful and good, but monotonous, being the same every day – steamed rice and vegetables flavoured with aromatic roots and leaves. Pritthi knew he was fortunate to have a full belly every day, but sometimes he wished it were full of something different.

After lunch, Kethoak the Phylarch stood up and thanked the dehara for their blessings, then left the refectory followed by three hara – and Pritthi. In single file they walked behind the Phylarch, heads bowed, until they reached his chambers. Here Kethoak led one har into his private room while the three remaining hara sat cross-legged on the floor of a small ante-chamber. They waited in silence. Presently the first har emerged, and Pritthi stood up and entered the room in his stead.

Inside, he removed his clothing and lay down upon the couch. Kethoak was already naked and Pritthi carefully avoided looking at his erect ouana-lim. Instead, he closed his eyes and parted his legs slightly. After a few moments he felt the weight of the Phylarch's body covering his own. He felt the heat of Kethoak's ouana-lim – it felt hotter than the rest of his body, and just like every week Pritthi thought it would burn him from the inside out as it pushed its way into his body. It felt like hot stone inside him, like the dry, hot sandstone of the statue of the dehar in the temple courtyard, and Pritthi felt dry outside and inside – in his mouth, in his stomach, in his soume-lam, and behind his closed eyelids. And then Kethoak cried out something – a name, an invocation or a curse, Pritthi did not know – and withdrew his burning staff, and Pritthi felt nothing at all, for which he was grateful.

When Pritthi emerged from the Phylarch's chambers, the sun was just past its zenith and the day at its hottest. He did not walk across the courtyard, because at this time of day the geometric-patterned tiles he had assiduously swept that morning were so hot that they would burn the soles of his naked feet. Instead, he took the dusty track around the outside of the courtyard and made his way down the hillside to the site of the Old Temple.

While the other hara slept through the heat of the afternoon, Pritthi often came here, because it was cool and quiet. It was overgrown with vegetation, its stones and tiles crumbling, and the roof leaked when it rained, so few others visited, but Pritthi liked it because it was a comfortable distance away from the main temple, and also, on this Lunilsday afternoon, a comfortable distance away from next Lunilsday morning.

He found his favourite spot, just under the eaves, where the tendrils of the creepers had colonised both the inside and outside space. Here great leaves greedily sucked away the sun's energy, leaving behind a deep green shady place where Pritthi could lie and think. One of the thoughts he often had was that it would be good to let the creepers grow over the main temple courtyard as they had here, so that a har could walk across the tiles at mid-afternoon without burning his feet. Back at the new temple, all the plants within and around the courtyard were kept neatly trimmed.

Here in Pritthi's sanctum, it was as if the plants and the building were as one, and it seemed to Pritthi that the builders of this place had intended it to be so. The overhanging eaves were roofed over with tiles made to look like leaves, and the walls decorated with thick stems of bamboo which, on closer inspection, turned out to be of the same glazed ceramic material as the roof tiles. Each jointed nodule perfectly reproduced in clay and coloured glaze the stems of living bamboo which grew all around. Some were broken, revealing the artifice behind the illusion, but Pritthi still marvelled both at the skill and the imagination which had produced such things. The tiles in the new temple courtyard were carefully made by the potters from the next village, their colours bright and the patterns they formed intricate, but none aspired to this recreation of life.

Pritthi lay on his back watching the small lizards on the ceiling also hiding from the fierce heat of the afternoon sun. Most of the time they remained absolutely still, and Pritthi could imagine that they, too, had been fashioned from clay like the bamboo, but occasionally one would dart forward to seize an unsuspecting insect, moving almost too fast for Pritthi to see. Pritthi liked the lizards. He liked their agile, sinuous movements and he liked the way they changed the colour of their skin depending on where they were; the ones on the bamboo walls were a pale yellowish brown, whereas their companions on the roof were a darker, greener hue. Pritthi thought that if he could be anything he wished, he would be a lizard and change his skin to conceal himself from the world.

There was a dry rustle from outside, then the curtain of leaves parted and the figure of a slender har stood silhouetted by the greenish light. It was Pavdam, one of the temple hara. Pritthi had known Pavdam all his life, or so it felt, and he felt more comfortable in his presence than with any other har.

"I thought I would find you here," Pavdam said. He ducked slightly to avoid the overhanging creepers, and Pritthi moved over a bit to make space for him. Pavdam squatted down next to Pritthi.

"It's your turn with Kethoak on Lunilsday, isn't it?"

"Yes." Pritthi scuffed at the dry earth with his bare toes.

Pavdam sighed. "You don't enjoy your weekly sessions with him, do you?"

"No."

"Well, at least that's it, over and done with for another week." Pavdam patted his arm encouragingly. "I brought you something – look!"

From his pockets Pavdam produced a handful of spiky red globes. He dropped some into Pritthi's lap.

"I picked them from the tree behind the courtyard. Probably ruined the symmetrical harmony of its appearance, but what can you do?"

In spite of himself, Pritthi smiled. Pavdam reminded Pritthi of one of the lizards, with his dun-coloured skin, his dark, glittering eyes and quick movements. At the har's wrists and ankles, there were some faint markings on his skin, like overlapping circles, which looked a little like scales. Pritthi did not know what these markings signified, if anything. He knew little of life outside the Temple, and for all he knew, they might be commonplace. Pavdam had never commented upon them.

Hara came in a wide variety of physical forms, some more exotic than others. Pritthi placed himself firmly at the non-exotic end of the scale. His skin was light brown and his hair dark enough to have an almost bluish sheen to it, but it was short and ended in feathered points around the nape of his neck. Pavdam's hair was long and luxurious, coiling and twirling down his back, and if envy was a sin, then Pritthi was a miserable sinner every time he looked at Pavdam and his hair.

Pavdam took one of the red fruits and cracked open the spiny shell to get at the juicy flesh within.

"You shouldn't let it bother you so much," he said. "It's just aruna."

Pritthi fingered the spiny fruits, feeling their hostile texture. "Aruna is dangerous," he said.

Pavdam snorted. "I don't think you're in much danger from Kethoak."

"How do you know?" There was a note of uncertainty in Pritthi's voice. "Perhaps I might slip into another dimension, or unleash some uncontrollable forces, or anger the dehara, or...or..."

"Or your head might explode. Don't worry. That's why we only have aruna with Kethoak. So he can control the terrible consequences that might be unleashed."

Both hara were silent for a moment, and then Pavdam said slyly, "Have you ever thought of having aruna with another har?"

Pritthi looked at Pavdam, with his lizard skin and glittering eyes and coiling hair, and was saved from adding the sin of lying to his list of moral offences by a sudden rumble of thunder overhead.

"Shit," said Pavdam, sitting up straight, "I didn't realise it was so late." He stuck his head outside the temple and blinked dubiously up at the now overcast skies. Although the sun's ferocious rays were gone, the heat remained. If anything, it felt even hotter than before.

"It might hold off for a bit," he said hopefully. Another threatening rumble disagreed with this opinion.

"Why does Kethoak think it's dangerous to have aruna with anyhar else but him?" Pritthi wondered.

Pavdam considered this for a moment.

"Kethoak is afraid," he said.

This surprised Pritthi. He'd never considered that the Phylarch might be afraid of anything. "Afraid of what?"

"Afraid of change," Pavdam said simply.

"Why?"

"Because change is difficult to deal with. It means that hara have to think about things and examine themselves. Self-examination makes some hara feel very uncomfortable. Kethoak wants everything to remain exactly the same so that he doesn't have to deal with feeling uncomfortable. Of course, that is a futile ambition. Change is inevitable."

"Is it?"

"Of course it is. Thank the dehara! Humans changed. They changed into hara. Hara may change too."

"Into what?" Pritthi was slightly horrified at the thought.

Pavdam grinned. "Who knows? We'll just have to wait and see."

"How could humans have changed into hara?" Pritthi asked, intrigued. "They were just animals."

"Is that what you think?"

Pritthi did not reply. It was certainly the explanation Kethoak had given him, but perhaps that was just what Kethoak was comfortable believing.

Pritthi reached out and ran his fingers over the glazed surface of the bamboo tiles on the wall. He doubted that whoever had made them could be the mindless animal of Kethoak's description. He could imagine the long-vanished artist studying the living plant growing all around, marvelling at its symmetry and structure, then forming the soft clay into the image of it, painting it with subtle hues of brown and green that would only reveal themselves after the clay had been fired, and afterwards arranging the separate parts onto the wall so that it recreated the living world outside. The mere existence of these artefacts told Pritthi a great deal about the minds of those who had created them.

Pavdam stared at the bamboo tiles thoughtfully. "We live here in the ruins left behind by humans," he said. "Oh yes, we've redecorated a bit and added some nice touches of our own, but still..." A frown passed across his face; a darkened cloud against a normally blue sky. "I have heard that there are cities that hara have built from the ground up. Cities of the future, not of the past."

"Where are they?" Pritthi stared at his friend as if he had grown a second head, and the thought briefly crossed his mind that perhaps the fruit they had consumed earlier had been a little fermented.

Pavdam shrugged again and his easy smile returned. "I don't know," he said. "Out there. Somewhere."

An ear-splitting crack from overhead made both hara jump,

and a few seconds later the leaves all around hissed into rain-drenched life. Water dripped from the eaves both from the living and ceramic leaves.

"Just because this place is old doesn't mean it should be abandoned." Pritthi felt somehow protective of the old ruins. "They built it as well as they could."

"Yes, but there have been some useful technological developments since then. Like gutters." Pavdam wiped a droplet of water from his cheek. "We're going to get soaked if we stay here," he said

"We're going to get soaked going back," Pritthi countered pragmatically. He looked down. Already the dry dust at his feet was turning dark and loamy.

"Oh well," Pavdam said. "It won't kill us, it's only water. Come on – race you to the top of the hill. I can't wait to find out what we're having for dinner tonight. The suspense is almost killing me." He stuck his tongue out mischievously at Pritthi.

Pritthi punched his friend's arm in return. The two hara hesitated for a moment, then set off running back up the hill to the temple, leaving a trail of footprints in the muddy earth behind them.

Every Miyacalasday was the same too, except for this one, which wasn't. On this particular day all the temple hara had assembled in the courtyard before the midday meal. At this time of day the geometric tiles radiated heat and the golden-roofed tower seared the eyes of any har unwise enough to look at it, so it was usually a place to be avoided, but the Phylarch had commanded attendance, so all were there.

Kethoak stood in front of the main entrance to the temple. Beside him, dressed from head to foot in scarlet robes was a har that Pritthi had never seen before. The red robes marked him out as a Neophyte – a new addition to the temple hara.

Newcomers were rare – it had been many years since one had last been inducted. Harlings were never born to hara within the temple, so the only way to maintain the numbers was to recruit from the nearby villages. Sometimes orphaned harlings would be given to the temple, sometimes a har would feel the calling to live the austere life, and on occasion the Neophyte was a har who had run into trouble somewhere and had been informed by local officialdom that volunteering for the temple was not an option he could refuse.

Pritthi fell into the first of these categories, and could remember nothing of life before the temple, but it was obvious that the new har was no harling, orphaned or otherwise. Neither did he have the demeanour of a har who had humbly entered the temple life of his own choosing. This left only one other conclusion.

The red-robed har stood tall and proud. Even when Kethoak removed all the garments from him, he looked neither cowed nor embarrassed to be standing naked in front of a crowd. Pritthi tried not to stare too directly, but since everyhar else in the courtyard seemed intent on doing that, and since it seemed that Kethoak's intention was for them to do just that, Pritthi felt justified in craning his neck a little to get a better view.

The har had been shaved of all his hair, both head and body, as was required for Neophytes. Even without the flattery of framing locks, Pritthi could see that his features had an intense, sculpted beauty, and even without the hair over his pubic region there was no way he could be mistaken for a harling. Pritthi stared, feeling a heat rise in his face that he was sure was not reflected from the tiles.

Kethoak disrobed too. Pritthi felt no compulsion to look at the Phylarch's body; he knew it too well already. The Neophyte sat down on the discarded pile of scarlet silk, his every movement graceful and cat-like.

Suddenly Pritthi felt a strange buzzing in his head, and a dizzy sensation swept over him. The heat intensified and he felt that he might faint. The folds of red silk spread over the hot tiles looked like spilled blood, the blossoms on the carefully pruned hibiscus bushes behind like vivid splashes.

He could see everything in the most intense detail, from the texture of the red silk cloth to the shadow of stubble on the new har's head and the pulse in the hollow of his throat, which remained steady as Kethoak's hands travelled over his body, even as the muscles there contracted briefly.

Kethoak positioned himself over the har's body, thighs covering thighs, straining against some unseen resistance. Behind him a small sunbird hovered directly in front of one of the scarlet hibiscus flowers, its tiny body upright and its wings a blur of movement. Pritthi could hear the humming and feel the vibration in his own shoulders. The bird thrust its long proboscis of a bill deep into the heart of the flower, tongue flicking out to suck the nectar, and the vibration moved from Pritthi's shoulders to between his legs. He could feel himself engulfed by the red folds of the petals. Everything in his vision was red. The heat of the sun was almost unbearable, concentrated in the enclosed space of the courtyard. The buzzing in his head drove out every other sensation.

There was a shout from the conjoined tangle of limbs on the red silk – Pritthi had forgotten the two hara were there. With an effort, he dragged his attention back to them. Kethoak disengaged himself from the other har's body and stood up. His head drooped slightly, and he seemed drained of something vital. The Neophyte maintained his seated position, upright and immobile. For all his involvement, he might have been one of the statues of the dehara circling the courtyard.

Pritthi looked round to see if anyhar was staring at him. His face burned and he felt horribly noticeable. He felt that at any moment a huge finger might descend from the sky and point him out to his fellow hara, inviting their mockery and scorn, but none of the others paid any attention to him. Most were still watching the tableau in the centre of the courtyard; a few were already gazing hopefully in the direction of the refectory, as the time for the midday meal was now past.

Two assistants helped Kethoak into his clothing. When he was fully dressed he departed in the direction of his private quarters without another word.

The assembled hara gratefully took this as a signal that the ceremony was concluded and began leaving rapidly in groups of three or four, heading in the direction of the refectory. Pritthi, however, remained where he was, watching the new har still sitting upright and motionless on the red silk robe on the ground. The crowd thinned, until at last there was only a few hara remaining. One departing group bore down on him and a har whom Pritthi recognised poked his arm playfully to indicate that he should come along. Reluctantly, Pritthi joined the group, and together they headed out of the courtyard.

As they were leaving, Pritthi turned for one last look. The Neophyte was still sitting as before, but he seemed to sense

Pritthi's gaze, and turned his head towards him. For a moment they made eye contact, and Pritthi had the profound conviction that the har could see into his innermost thoughts and knew everything that had transpired in the courtyard, but before Pritthi could do or say anything, his companions bustled him away.

After lunch, instead of heading to the Old Temple, Pritthi went back to the courtyard. Part of him almost expected to the see the har still sitting there in exactly the same position, but both the har and the red robe were gone, and the smooth tiles gave no indication that anything had ever occurred there. Pritthi experienced a feeling that he identified as disappointment.

He was just turning to leave when a small movement in the shadowed edge of the courtyard caught his attention. He knew it was the new har even before he stepped into the light to reveal himself, although he was no longer wearing the red silk, but had changed into a garment the same dusty brown colour as the dry dirt. His arms and legs were bare, and Pritthi noticed that his skin was a golden, tawny hue which seemed to glow in the sunlight.

"Hello," Pritthi said, wincing at the inadequacy of the word even as it left his lips.

The har did not reply at first. He examined Pritthi curiously, as if trying to determine whether or not he was of interest.

"I'm Mallas," he said at last.

"I'm Pritthi."

"I know."

"How?" Pritthi realised that this aggressive response probably wasn't the best way of gaining the har's confidence, but Mallas's self-possession had him off balance.

Fortunately Mallas did not take offence. He laughed. "Too little else to occupy my time in the past couple of days while I awaited my reward." he said. "And I have a weakness for gossip and general prying, which will no doubt lead me into trouble here as it has done in many other situations."

"Why *are* you here?" Pritthi asked. Again, it wasn't exactly the politest of conversational gambits, but he had already formed the impression that this har was not one who cared overmuch.

Mallas shrugged. "I was a bad har." He sounded unconcerned. "And now I have been sent here to repent of my sins."

"And are you going to?"

Mallas smiled fiercely, showing white, pointed teeth. "Unlikely. You?"

"I haven't got any sins to repent of."

"How boring."

Pritthi was stung by Mallas's casual condemnation. He immediately tried to think of some transgression he had committed, which would render him a more worthy sinner.

"I don't like having aruna with Kethoak," he said, rather more emphatically than he intended.

"Who does?"

The two hara looked at each other for a few seconds, processing the shared experience, and then they laughed simultaneously.

Pritthi immediately felt much more at ease. "It's the official ritual for all new entrants to the Temple," he said, indicating the area on the tiles where Mallas's recent encounter with Kethoak had taken place. "Everyhar has to do it."

"So I was informed."

"It's an offering to the dehara."

"And what do they offer us in return?" Mallas raised what would have been his left eyebrow had it not been shaved off.

"Protection," Pritthi told him.

"Protection from what?"

"Bad things."

"Bad things? Or bad hara?" Mallas smiled his terrifying smile again. "Like me?"

"I don't know," Pritthi said, "I'm only Aralid. I don't know about these things. You need to ask Kethoak about it."

"I think I shall be keeping my interaction with Tiahaar Kethoak to a minimum, thank you."

Pritthi did not reply. He wanted to say that Kethoak was the one who decided such things, but he did not think Mallas would like that. He also wondered if it was even true, in Mallas's case.

Mallas also seemed to think the subject was not worth discussing. He looked around the deserted courtyard.

"So where is everyhar?" he asked "There must have been a good couple of hundred hara enjoying my... *initiation*... earlier. Where have they all vanished to?"

"Asleep mostly. In the dormitories. It's too hot in the afternoon to do much."

"And what about you, Pritthi? Are you an insomniac, or do you just like the heat? Do you come here to bask like a lizard in the sun?"

Pritthi shook his head. "No, I... I usually go down to the Old Temple in the afternoon. It's cooler down there." He hesitated for a second. "You should come down there some time," he said quickly. "Pavdam goes there too, most days. You'll like him. He's very..."

Pritthi blushed slightly. Mallas looked at him with amusement, and Pritthi could see that his eyes were the same amber colour as his skin.

"I'm sure he is," Mallas said. "Pavdam would be the har with the long curling hair, if I'm not mistaken?"

Pritthi eyed Mallas suspiciously. "Do you know about *all* the hara here already?" he asked

"No, just the interesting ones."

Pritthi thought about this for a minute. "Am I interesting?" he asked, genuinely surprised.

"Of course you are. I wouldn't be talking to you otherwise."

"Why?"

"You're different."

"No, I'm not!"

"Yes, you are. You don't belong here. You don't fit in here."

"Yes, I do! This is where I live. This is where I've always lived."

"That doesn't mean you have to live here for the rest of your life."

"Where else would I go?"

"I don't know, Pritthi," Mallas said, "It's a big world. Where *would* you go, if you could choose?"

"I..." Pritthi had no answer to this question. Mallas's direct gaze pierced through him, like a pin through an insect. His entire world stretched only from the temple as far as the neighbouring village, half a morning's walk away. What lay beyond was all unknown. "Hara can't just leave whenever they feel like it," he said uncertainly

"Of course they can. I do it all the time."

"Why?"

Mallas shrugged. "I don't know," he said, "Sometimes because I want to. Sometimes because I have to. Sometimes because I can't stand to be with my fellow hara a second longer."

"You hate everyhar that much?"

Mallas made a face. "No, I don't hate them. That would take too much effort. I just don't feel in any way connected to them. Don't you feel like that sometimes, Pritthi?"

Pritthi could not bring himself to reply.

"But don't worry, they're always just as glad to see the back of me as I am to be shot of them."

"I wouldn't be." Pritthi said, surprised at the urgency in his own voice. "I wouldn't want you to go."

"How sweet. But you don't even know me, Pritthi."

"I know, but..."

Pritthi felt the same strange sensation in his head again, like wings and feathers fluttering behind his eyes. Mallas stared at him carefully for several long seconds.

"Perhaps I *will* go to this Old Temple of yours. How do I get to it?"

"Just follow the track down the hill. You can't miss it. I'd avoid it in the late afternoon, though," Pritthi looked up at the skies, which were already darkening. "The roof leaks," he explained.

"I shall be sure to arrive at an appropriate time, then."

This appeared to conclude the conversation from Mallas's point of view, as he then turned and departed without another word, leaving Pritthi standing in the courtyard alone. A fat drop of rain hit him squarely on the forehead, a harbinger of the afternoon deluge to come, and he hurriedly made for the shelter of the covered walkway.

In the gloom under the wooden eaves he ran straight into Kethoak, who was standing directly in his path. Pritthi cursed himself silently, took a polite step backwards and mumbled some placating apologies to the Phylarch, hoping to excuse himself and vanish swiftly from the scene. Kethoak had other ideas, and stood firmly in front of Pritthi, arms crossed, blocking his exit.

"Excuse me, Phylarch," he repeated, keeping his eyes fixed firmly on the floor tiles and trying not to look as uncomfortable as he felt.

"You're in a great hurry, Pritthi," Kethoak said. "Do you have some urgent errand to attend to?"

"No, Phylarch," Pritthi said, his heart sinking as he realised this was not going to be a brief interview.

"I noticed you speaking to our newest initiate a moment ago."

"Yes, Phylarch."

"What did he have to say to you, Pritthi?"

"He... ah... wanted to know where the library was." Pritthi was a terrible liar and he knew it. More to the point, Kethoak knew it too. Pritthi waited for the inevitable inquisition, which would end with him blurting out the truth. Instead, the Phylarch put his hand under Pritthi's chin and raised his face upward so that the two were looking directly at each other. Pritthi felt like a mouse confronted by a snake.

"Pritthi," Kethoak said in a silky tone, "that har is not a suitable companion for you."

"No, Phylarch."

"You may or may not be aware of this, but he has committed heinous crimes. His soul is tainted. He has been sent to us in order to atone for his sins, but that may not be possible. He may be beyond redemption. You, however—" The fingers under Pritthi's chin moved upwards to stroke his cheek. "You are pure, Pritthi. Innocent and unsullied. I would not have you corrupted by this har. Do I make myself clear?"

"Yes, Phylarch." Pritthi knew that he should keep his mouth shut and simply agree with Kethoak in order to secure the best chance of escaping quickly, but something made him speak up. "What has he done, Phylarch? To taint his soul, I mean?"

The caressing fingers became claws, causing Pritthi to flinch.

"He has defied the dehara, Pritthi. He has questioned their authority, and brought down their anger. And when the dehara are angry, all mortal hara must suffer the consequences."

The fingers relaxed again.

"It is our purpose here, Pritthi, to appease the wrath of the dehara, by our offerings and our sacrifices. Can you imagine the consequences if we did not?"

"No, Phylarch. I mean yes. I mean..."

Pritthi wished that he had never initiated this conversation, but there seemed no stopping Kethoak.

"We would suffer the same fate as humans. Humans did not fear the dehara. And the dehara took their revenge and destroyed them."

"But... I thought that humans became hara? They changed."

Kethoak gave Pritthi an acid stare. "Some of them, Pritthi. A few, a chosen few, were permitted to attain a higher level of existence. The rest were merely animals and perished as such."

Pritthi's head was full of awkward questions, such as why the dehara were so angry about everything all the time that they needed to be constantly appeased, and why they were particularly angry with humans if they were only animals, and what was wrong with being an animal anyway? He remembered the tiny sunbird with its iridescent plumage and busy wings, and felt a little better.

"That is why you must remain pure, Pritthi. It is only through your devotion to the dehara, through me and *me alone*, that we may be permitted to keep our place in this world. All this could be taken from us in a moment. Do you understand?"

Pritthi nodded unhappily.

"The dehara are all around us, Pritthi. They see everything and know everything. They want only for us to be obedient and unchanging in our devotion to them."

Kethoak placed his hand on top of Pritthi's head. Pritthi tried not to flinch, but the touch lasted only a moment, and then the Phylarch straightened himself imperiously and glided away across the smooth tiled floor.

Pritthi watched him go. When he was sure Kethoak was not going to return, he walked over to the tall statue set in the corner of the wall. It was an effigy of the dehar Aruhani, carved from black obsidian and polished so that it gleamed dully in the dim light under the eaves. It was considerably taller than Pritthi, but if he reached up he could touch the statue's outstretched hand. He laid his own fingers across the stone ones, feeling their hard smoothness, so unlike flesh.

He looked up at the statue's face. The eyes were open, but black and smooth like the rest of the stone. They looked as if they were gazing into infinity. Pritthi concentrated as hard as he could, reaching out with his inner being, trying to grasp the presence of the dehar who was all around, seeing and knowing everything. Nothing changed. The statue remained unmoving, the eyes still staring blindly. The stone was only stone, worked by some unknown har into a facsimile of life. If the dehara had ever been here, then they were long gone, banished by the failure of their worshippers to perceive their true nature.

Pritthi let go of the stone hand and set off toward the kitchens with bowed head, to carry sacks of rice for the evening meal.

Late in the afternoon, when the patterned tiles in the temple courtyard still gave off curls of steam created from the rapidly evaporating rain, and the small birds had briskly shaken off the last droplets of water from their plumage and hopped among the hydrangea bushes, Pavdam could be found lazing in the far corner under the eaves, watching the flies buzz around his naked feet and legs. On occasion one would come to land on the ground beside him, and with a swift motion he would swat it with his hand.

The flies were not easy to kill, and mostly they would buzz away unharmed, but the small pile of flattened corpses lying to the side attested to Pavdam's skill and reflexes – and his desire to avoid doing any serious work on this particular afternoon.

Another fly settled, and Pavdam held his breath and prepared to strike. But before he could do so, from behind another hand slapped down with a sudden smack. Pavdam turned his head in surprise. He had not heard the other har approach, which he put down either to his intense concentration on the fly, or to his having dozed off momentarily.

"You've got to be quick to catch 'em," he said.

Mallas smiled, and lifted his hand. Underneath was the crumpled remains of the unfortunate fly. Mallas picked it up delicately by one bent wing and added it to the pile.

"Well done," Pavdam congratulated him. "Although there're plenty more where that came from."

"The laws of the village and tribe I last took up with," Mallas said, to nohar in particular, "forbade the killing of any living creature." He prodded the pile of flies with one extended finger, flicking the tiny cadavers to see if any life remained within. None evidenced such.

"Very noble."

"Very conducive to unpleasant intestinal disorders. You're Pavdam, aren't you? Pritthi's friend."

"I am. And you know this how?"

"Because of my keen powers of mind-touch and awesome ability to alter the fabric of reality with the force of my will alone. And also because Pritthi told me about you the other day."

"Seems reasonable."

"Never underestimate the power of nosiness."

"And what else did Pritthi tell you?" Pavdam shuffled himself around to face Mallas properly. He noticed that the other har had yellow eyes, an unusual colour.

"He told me he had a secret hideout at the Old Temple."

"Did he now?"

"Yes, and he invited me to join you and him there."

"Really? He has never asked any of the other hara here. Why would he want you to go there?"

"I don't know, Pavdam. Why does he want *you?*"

The question required no answer, Pavdam could tell that from Mallas's grin. There was a feeling of weight behind his eyes and an image formed in his mind. A rustle of leaves. Fang and fur. The metallic smell of blood. Yellow eyes. A brief vision of himself sitting coiled on the ground, his brown skin the colour of the bare earth.

"I've heard about you," he told Mallas "You're known in most of the neighbouring towns and villages." He could still clearly feel the other har's presence in his head. He knew he could sever the connection any time he wanted, but he was intrigued. A new impression formed; angry hara, stones, pitchforks. *Amusement.*

"I'm not welcome in any of them." *Insouciance.*

"Why not?"

"They have rules."

"And you don't like rules?"

"On the contrary, I enjoy rules immensely. I love to watch hara twisting and turning and tying themselves in knots trying to obey them."

"But you don't think they apply to you?"

Disdain.

"So how did you end up here, then, if following rules is not your area of expertise?" Pavdam asked.

"The Good Hara of the region thought that this particular temple would be an appropriate place for me to learn how to become more like them. I am not the only har who has a reputation."

"And?"

Distaste

"Your Phylarch is everything I had been led to expect."

Pavdam said nothing. Mallas's air of bored detachment

suddenly evaporated and he thrust his face next to Pavdam's, so that Pavdam could feel his hot breath on his cheek.

"Why do you stay here? There are no angry mobs of hara out there intent upon your rehabilitation insisting that you continue to partake of the hospitality of the Phylarch. Why don't you leave?"

"Where would I go?"

"Don't be disingenuous. There's a whole world to choose from. You know there are other tribes and cities out there. Other hara who are more like us."

"In what way?"

Mallas was so close that Pavdam could smell the other har's body; a warm, musky, animal smell. Rather to his vexation, he felt his own body respond in kind.

"Kindred spirits," murmured Mallas. He leaned a fraction closer and nipped the skin of Pavdam's throat between his sharp teeth, leaving a series of red marks as a souvenir.

"I couldn't leave Pritthi here on his own." Pavdam said. "He's... innocent. He needs protection."

"Who does he need protection from, Pavdam?"

The image of Kethoak formed in Pavdam's mind, and he was unsure if he had conjured it himself or not.

"The Phylarch's reputation includes a liking for innocence and youth when it comes to aruna," Mallas said.

"He says it pleases the dehara."

"How very fortunate for him that his own personal preferences mesh so seamlessly with the deities'. Did you offer him your own youth and innocence, Pavdam? That sour look you're giving me tells me you did. Would you not like to see him deprived of the opportunity to use other young hara for his own gratification?"

"How, exactly?"

"Start a revolution! Overthrow him. Whip up your own mob of angry hara – they seem to be easily persuaded in that direction, if my own experience is anything to go by."

Pavdam shook his head. "The other hara would never do anything like that."

"No. They're sheep."

A very small and plaintive bleat echoed in Pavdam's head. He laughed, and so did Mallas.

"Let us hope," said Mallas, leaning back lazily, "That a wolf does not come among them."

"They're not like you." Pavdam said

"Or you. Or Pritthi. We are three of a kind."

"What kind?"

"Our kind."

Another insect flew past, its buzzing drone cut off abruptly as Mallas plucked it with precision from the air.

Pritthi dreamt of the ocean. In his dream, he knew it was the ocean, even though he had never seen it before. It was blue and sparkling, like a jewel, with flashes of silver racing through it. He reached out his hand, as if to touch a distant god, and snatched silver from blue.

The next day Pritthi didn't bother with lunch. Instead he headed off eagerly towards the Old Temple, feeling strangely light-headed with anticipation, as if his body had knowledge of something that he himself did not. When he arrived at the temple, it was empty, and although he knew that this was because he was so early, he still felt a pang of disappointment. He was just about to crawl into his favourite spot inside when he noticed something lying on the grass just at the entrance.

The object lay flashing silver in the dappled light through the leaves. It was a large fish, its scales still wet, its eyes and gills bright. There was a slight ozone tang to the air around it.

Pritthi stared at the fish for several seconds, holding his breath. His head buzzed, but he could not make his thoughts come. He remembered his dream from the previous night, and that seemed important.

After a while, he picked up the fish, marvelling at its heaviness, wrapped it in some large leaves and put it in a cool and shady spot at the back of the temple while he waited.

The day grew hotter and the lizards less active. Even the chirping insects abandoned their cacophony for a while. Pritthi felt that he might fall asleep, but then there was a rustling of leaves and a darkening at the temple entrance and he was no longer alone. Pavdam flopped down beside him, but the temple doorway remained darkened.

"Look who I found on the way down here," Pavdam announced, with an overly dramatic flourish of his arm in the direction of the doorway.

Mallas entered, stooping fluidly to avoid the overhanging leaves.

Pritthi felt something flutter in his chest, like wings. "You came," he said, wishing he did not sound so needy or pathetic.

"Did you think I wouldn't?" Mallas asked, amused.

"No, I just thought Kethoak might have told you not to."

"Do you think that would have made any difference?"

"I don't know. Probably not. No."

Mallas laughed. "You are the most delightfully transparent har I have ever met, Pritthi."

Pritthi hoped fervently that being *transparent* was a good thing as far as Mallas was concerned.

"I take it that our revered Phylarch is none too keen on us developing a relationship?" Mallas enquired.

Pritthi shook his head and blushed. "He said it might anger the dehara."

Mallas lay back on the leaf-covered ground beside Pritthi. "In my personal experience," he said, "the dehara do not give an oversized ouana-lim about the petty affairs of we mortal hara. I'm sure they have much more interesting things to occupy themselves with. Despite all my best efforts — and they have been considerable, let me assure you — they have failed to smite me for my wickedness." He rolled over on his belly, so that he was up close to Pritthi and looking down at him.

Pritthi found himself looking deep into the other har's eyes, and the wings in his chest fluttered again. Mallas's features were haughty and aristocratic, but his mouth was soft, curving... and suggestive. The hair on his head was just beginning to grow back — Pritthi could see the fine coating of tawny stubble which in places gave way to contrasting dark bands. Overcome by a sudden urge, Pritthi raised his hands to stroke it. It felt like the softest of plush velvets to his exploring fingers.

Mallas smiled at him and Pritthi felt like he was falling from a great height without anything below to catch him. At the back of his mind was the thought that he could still put an end to this now, if he wanted to, stop it from proceeding to its inevitable conclusion — pretend that this wasn't what he'd had in mind when he invited Mallas to come there, but he knew that he wouldn't. He didn't want it to stop.

"Aruna can be dangerous..." he croaked

Mallas's smile changed, becoming something feral and terrifying. He rubbed his face against Pritthi's languorously. "It's *supposed* to be dangerous," he purred

Pritthi was so close to Mallas that he was breathing in the other har's breath. Like slow honey, it filled his mind with desire. He closed his eyes and arched his back, raising his hips upwards. Hands ran down his body in encouragement and then slid under his clothes, moving unerringly to where he wanted them most. For a moment they teased, then became more purposeful.

Pritthi knew without having to look that the fingers that pleasured him did not belong to Mallas. He knew that the dun-coloured skin on those slender wrists was encircled by markings which looked a bit like scales.

He wondered if Mallas and Pavdam had planned this on their walk down, knowing that Pritthi did not have the courage to seduce either one or both of them. He didn't care. His body wanted both these hara, and it felt strong and fierce enough to have them. He no longer felt as if he was falling; he felt as if he was flying, soaring on a wind current that spiralled upwards forever.

His breath emptied into Mallas's hungry mouth. Between his legs he now felt the thick serpentine length of Pavdam's ouana-lim filling him and moving in him with rhythm, making him want more. He felt now that there was very little holding him to the earth, and if he let go the last thread he might never return. Aruna *was* dangerous, he knew that now. You could lose yourself in it, lose your mind and your very soul if you didn't hang on as tightly as you could. He held on for what seemed like an age, held tightly and fast, to the very limit of his existence, and in the end he rode the current down.

Later, when he had exhausted both his companions, he was surprised to discover that the afternoon rainstorm was already in full flood.

"I bet you just thought it was the earth moving," Pavdam teased him as another rumble of thunder shook the wet leaves.

Pritthi laughed, as he was supposed to, but he looked thoughtful. "Is that how it's supposed to be?" he asked anxiously

"That, and so much more!" Mallas assured him. He put his arm around Pritthi and hugged him gently. "Kethoak has cheated you." he said. "He has taken the power of aruna and kept it for himself only. He has robbed you of something important and vital."

"But why would he do that?" Pritthi asked.

"He is afraid," Mallas said. He looked at Pavdam. "Afraid of change." He turned his attention back to Pritthi. "You know that Wraeththu were once humans. A change happened. Humans became har. Hara like Kethoak think that Wraeththu are now perfect, that the change is complete, unalterable, but that is not so. We are still evolving. The change continues. We have so many undiscovered abilities, Pritthi. Who knows what we can become and what we can achieve? But we will stagnate and die if hara like Kethoak have their way. Kethoak is using the energy of aruna — the energy you give him — to preserve his vision of Wraeththu like a fly in amber. You must take that power back from him, Pritthi, and use it for yourself, to find who you really are."

"I don't think Kethoak will allow that."

"Then we will leave this place. We will go somewhere else!"

"Where?"

"There are other tribes," Mallas said. "Other villages. Other cities."

"Not around here there aren't."

"No, you are right. We will have to travel far. It will be a long journey, but it is one that has to be made. Are you ready for it, Pritthi?"

Pritthi felt suddenly as if the invasive tendrils of the plants were bent on creeping around his body and strangling him. The leaf-smothered interior of the Old Temple seemed small and claustrophobic. "I don't know!" he cried. "How am I supposed to know what to do? I don't know anything! I've never done anything like this before. Why are you asking me this?"

He pushed his way out of the temple, fighting the urge to tear the plants away, and stood outside in the rain, trembling.

The rainwater was pouring down off the roof and the lack of any gutters along the eaves to channel it away meant that this was by far the wettest spot. Pritthi cursed under his breath as he felt the water soak his back, and he stepped forward into the open clearing in front, free of the confines of the temple.

He studied the design of the building; there was a row of leaf-tiles along the edge of the roofline, each set closely beside its neighbour. Each leaf ended in an elegant point, and from each point the water dripped in a uniform fashion. The result was a perfect curtain of water falling in front of the temple. Unlike the haphazard raindrops descending directly from the clouds, this was orderly and symmetrical. In a moment of revelation, Pritthi realised that this was what the tiles were *meant* to do. They weren't failing to channel the water away, they were succeeding in turning the chaos of the rainstorm into something beautiful and fleeting. This creation would last only as long as the rain, and then it would be gone, leaving its song unsung and its word unsaid. Only when the thunder rumbled and the skies darkened would it sing once more.

Pritthi recalled the dead hand of the statue of the absent dehar, and the dying feeling of aruna with Kethoak and he shuddered. Now that he had experienced it, he could not deny the true nature of aruna any more than he could unlearn the knowledge of the rain tiles.

"You're right," he said softly, then realised that Mallas and Pavdam could not hear him through the wall of water and vegetation. "You're right!" he shouted, pushing his way back through the wet leaves to stand soaking in front of his surprised companions. "We have to go somewhere else. Anywhere. It doesn't matter. Just not here."

Mallas grinned at him and pushed his rain-soaked hair away from his face, while Pavdam's arms snaked around his waist.

Later, they found some dry kindling and baked the fish and ate it and did not return for the evening meal, and felt no guilt about it.

Three days later Mallas and Pavdam waited for Pritthi at the Old Temple, their belongings bundled into packs slung over their shoulders and their feet in sturdy walking shoes, but the younger har did not come. The rain came and went, and then sun warmed the wet leaves, making everything smell green and luscious, but still he did not come. The sun sank low on the horizon as the flocks of coloured birds returned to their favourite trees to roost, and Mallas and Pavdam trudged back up the hill again, exchanging no words.

Enquiries revealed that Pritthi had last been seen earlier in the day heading towards Kethoak's lodgings, although it was not his usual day for such an encounter. Hara expressed surprise at this disruption to the usual routine, for the Phylarch was known for his love of custom and habit.

Mallas and Pavdam nervously approached Kethoak's living quarters. The small lamps and candles had been lit, and although there was the smell of smoky incense in the warm air, there was no sign of any activity.

They entered through the open door, but found the main room empty. Mallas took one of the lamps and wandered around the room, peering into dark corners and behind carved wooden chairs, as if he expected to find somehar or something hiding there.

Just as they were about to give up and leave, the door to the back rooms opened and a har stood there, his features shadowed in the dim light.

Mallas raised the lamp higher and peered anxiously.

"Pritthi!" he said, with relief. "Where have you been? What have you been doing? We waited ages for you. Are you ready? Come on, let's go before Kethoak gets back."

Pritthi shook his head. "I'm not going," he said.

Mallas lowered the lamp and looked at him carefully. There seemed to be something different about him.

"Why not?" he asked. "What has Kethoak said to you? Don't listen to him. You're coming with us, remember? We're leaving this place. Now."

Pritthi's eyes shone brightly in the soft light from the lamp. "I can't," he said.

"Yes, you can," Mallas insisted, "Just pick up your stuff, walk out the door and keep walking."

"It's not that simple. You don't understand."

"Obviously not. Care to enlighten me?"

Pritthi hesitated. Outside, the nocturnal insects had begun their rhythmic, chirping chorus in the darkness.

"I came to see Kethoak late last night," Pritthi said, his voice trembling slightly. "I told him that I was leaving. I told him that I didn't want to have aruna with him anymore."

"And?"

Pritthi swallowed hard. "And he said it wasn't my choice. I didn't get to make that choice. And he took aruna with me there and then."

A small muscle twitched in Mallas's jaw, but he said nothing.

"And he put... something... in my head." Pritthi raised his hands to his temples and pressed hard, wincing as he did so.

"What do you mean? What did he put in your head?"

"I don't know! I don't know what he did, but he put something there, something that ties me to him, something that stops me leaving him, forever. I don't... I'm sorry. I can't go with you. I just *can't*."

Pritthi dropped to his knees and drew himself into a small ball. Pavdam hurried forward and crouched down beside him, hugging him gently.

"It's alright," he said, "We'll find some way to get rid of this... *thing*, whatever it is."

"Your sentiments are admirable, but unfortunately I think you'll find that your abilities are nowhere near adequate to the task."

Mallas and Pavdam both looked up to see Kethoak standing in the doorway.

"What have you done to him?" Pavdam stood up and seemed ready to attack the Phylarch physically, but a warning hand on his shoulders from Mallas held him back.

"I only did what was necessary," Kethoak said, as if he were addressing an ill-behaved harling he had regretfully been required to discipline.

Pavdam hissed angrily at him.

"Let him go," Mallas said evenly. "Let him leave now, and that will be the end of it."

Kethoak looked amused. "Are you threatening me, Mallas? How pathetic. That sort of behaviour can get you into trouble if you're not careful. But you're not really a careful sort of har, are you? I know what you've been up to since you arrived here. Trying to lead these innocent hara astray. Trying to steal them away. But I can't allow that. I can't allow them to leave — or you, for that matter, much though I would not miss your presence in any way.

"You are needed here. We need the energy you can provide. The dehara need your energy. If they do not get it, they will become angry and vengeful, and rain down their punishment on all of us."

"You're mad," Mallas told him. "The dehara don't want our energy. They don't want vengeance and they don't want to punish anyhar. This is all just a pretext to allow you to control other hara and keep yourself at the top of the hierarchy. You're a fraud, Kethoak."

"This is heresy!" Kethoak thundered, "And it will not be tolerated. You will all suffer the consequences!"

"Oh, I don't think so." It was Pavdam who spoke, his voice strangely calm. Kethoak turned to reply to him, but froze as he found himself staring directly into the unblinking eyes of a large brown snake, upright and undulating in front of him, the eye-markings clearly visible on the back of its hood and its forked tongue flicking in and out rapidly between its scaled lips.

Pritthi scrambled to his feet in alarm, for he knew that this snake was venomous, and that its venom could kill a har, but Pavdam touched his arm reassuringly to indicate that there was nothing for him to fear. Pritthi looked at his friend closely. He seemed almost to be in a trance; his body was swaying with the same sinuous movements as the snake, and his eyes were as dark and emotionless as the serpent's.

Kethoak tore his gaze away from the snake and glared at Pavdam.

"Know this," he said, slowly and with menace. "If your pet bites me, I will live, and I will ensure that neither you nor your friends enjoy the congenial lifestyle you have lived up until now. The dehara's need for energy and supplication is great, and there is so much more that can be taken from a har."

Mallas laughed. "I thought we had already established your dislike of empty threats," he said. "What was the word you used? – *pathetic*. Yes, I do see your point now."

Pritthi willed Mallas to look at him as he shook his head almost imperceptibly, trying to indicate that he should not further antagonise Kethoak, but if Mallas saw or felt anything of Pritthi's anguish he gave no indication of it. Kethoak stepped closer to Mallas until the two hara were face to face, almost touching, eyes locked, staring, each willing the other to capitulate. It seemed to Pritthi that the Phylarch had grown bigger. His shadow behind him in the lamplight loomed large and menacing, crouching in the dark.

Mallas remained unmoving, resisting Kethoak's offensive, but Pritthi could feel another power emanating from the Phylarch; a sharp dagger of energy that Kethoak would use to cut through

Mallas's defences and bind him helpless, as he had bound Pritthi. Pritthi almost choked to think that the energy Kethoak was now using was the same energy he had taken from him during aruna. He wanted to scream a warning to Mallas, but he could not. The shadows moved again, closing in. Pritthi could sense the presence of something dangerous in the room, yet he could see nothing but the flickering light from the lamp and the two hara locked together in some unseen struggle.

So intent upon imposing his will on the other har was Kethoak that he failed to notice the huge orange and black striped cat creep up noiselessly behind him. Pritthi saw the tiger a second before it sprang, seizing Kethoak in its jaws and shaking him like a doll. The sharp-pointed fangs pierced Kethoak's neck, sliding effortlessly between the third and fourth cervical vertebrae, severing the spinal cord.

The Phylarch died instantly, a look of shocked surprise on his face.

Pritthi felt the knot in his head untie, and his legs would have given way beneath him had Pavdam not caught him. He felt a wave of nausea rush over him. Kethoak's body lay on the floor, its throat torn out and a lake of blood forming around it. In the middle of this scene of horror, the tiger lapped fastidiously at the blood like a domestic cat presented with a saucer of milk.

Mallas crouched down beside the tiger and took the animal's head in his hands, pressing his face against its bloodstained muzzle and making soft rumbling sounds in his throat. Pritthi could smell the carnivore breath laced with the metallic tang of blood, and feel the creature's heartbeat reverberating throughout the room.

"I don't understand," he said helplessly.

"Yes, you do." Mallas looked up at him, his fingers still buried deep in the fur around the tiger's neck.

"He's dead," Pritthi said, his eyes flicking fearfully to the corpse of the Phylarch, as if he still might rise up again at any moment.

"Yes."

"Did you kill him?"

Mallas did not answer this directly. There was blood on his face where he had rubbed against the tiger, and he wiped at it with the back of his hand.

"He tied you to him," he said, indicating Kethoak's lifeless body. "He bound you to his own life, and the only way to be freed from that was for his life to end. Do you understand that?"

Pritthi nodded.

"And now that he is dead you have to decide what to do. You know what we are. You know what *you* are. We are different from other hara. Not better or worse, but *different*. There may be other hara who are different yet again. And there may be hara who are the same as us, somewhere. There may be a tribe waiting for us to join them, hara who are like us, who understand us. You can come with us, Pritthi, or you can stay here. You know what we are, so it is not a simple choice, and I can't promise you that it's the best choice, or even a good choice, but it's *your* choice, and yours alone to make."

The flames of the candles flickered, throwing strange movements on the walls like the swaying of the snake. Pritthi studied the body of Kethoak lying motionless on the floor and tried to remember him as he had been when he was alive, but already that seemed like a dream. He tried to consider this new reality and the choices it offered him, but truthfully he knew that there was nothing to be resolved. The decision had already been made. His future had been decided with an act of aruna in the old ruined temple.

He took one last look around the room, seeing the carved wooden icons and polished metals that decorated the place. He deliberately did not look down at what lay at his feet.

"Let's go," he said.

Where the long path down the hillside diverged and gave way to rice fields and small houses on the one side, Mallas and his companions took the left-hand turning, which led them deep into the forest. If they were pursued by anyhar from the temple then they heard or saw nothing of it, for the trees and creepers here grew thickly and the light was shadowy green. Through all this they made progress, marching steadily for three days, always heading northwards.

High above the forest, above the canopy of leaves and the three hara below it, the great fish eagle soared on a rising thermal, circling lazily upwards with wings outstretched. Pritthi soared with it, feeling the air lift him. The heat from the sun warmed his back and everything was sharp and clear. The bird's vision was many times keener than a har's, and it filled him with a sense of awe to see the world through its eyes. He could see the vast expanse of the forest below, and in the distance, at the forest's limit, he could see the glittering blue sea. He could see the white tops of the waves and the silver flashes of quick-moving fish beneath the surface of the water. He could see the edge of the world, the curved horizon where the sea met the air, and if he closed his eyes – his harish eyes, still down on the forest floor – he could see the world spinning in the vastness of space, blue-green and clothed with life of many different kinds, and more than that, he could see the future.

# wolf

E.S. Wynn

I am not har.

I am not har, but for a time, at least, I walked among them.

My first memories are scattered, the hazy, sharp wants of hungry cells suspended in an eternity of warm brine. Simple, painfully aware, I was a soul spun between singular cells, conscious of my own growing, the division of whole lobes of my molecular body coming as a rending, so necessary, as urgent and violent as any animal impulse too long denied. Even in those early moments, when I am told most organisms are no more aware than a stone or the sun, *I was aware*, and that is what has always made me different.

Warmth, a liquid sweetness, the raw, rushing nature of adolescent growth – these are the things that I remember. Warmth, a liquid sweetness, and then the men behind the glass where I was grown teased eyes from the cell cluster that was my body, taught me to see, taught me how to collect light and process it into images, become more aware of the world around me. From them, from those who came before the Wraeththu rose to prominence, I learned how to perceive, how to move, how to become *more*.

Darkness came only after I learned how to see. Like a thief in the night, it set in suddenly, brought with it clashing vibrations that had none of the gentle dulcet tones of speech, came instead sonorous and staccato, cutting with sounds I would later recognise as the signatures of conflict and killing. Who did the killing? Men or hara? I still cannot say. I was still too young, too innocent to the cruelties of the world beyond the tank that was my womb. I know only that the massacre was blinding, brilliant – a fugue of splashing crimson and hot light lancing through the darkness. I learned of bullets that day, the easy deaths, the destruction they bring when slung from the hot barrel of a wild-spraying, remorseless gun.

My birth came with the shattering of glass – violent, painful. The brine had been the only home I'd known, a comfortable cradle beyond the reach of a frontier of air and wind and earth and fire my skin would come to taste, come to know intimately in the days ahead. I tried desperately to stay there, amidst the security of that sweet womb, but fate's hand decreed that I be born and learn, for the first time, what it meant to be alive.

Blood and air – my first tastes of the world beyond the glass. Hot blood, cold air, unfiltered shouting packed with quick constructions that meant nothing to me. Shapes moving in the darkness, then a separation, the pain of being violently torn apart by a hail of hot lead. Assassination – my first experience amidst the dreadful, horrifying, awe-inspiring wonders of a new world, but the job was left unfinished.

And so I grew.

Newborn, forcefully divided, I played with the dynamics of my body, spread cells across floor, knit myself into different constructions, danced in cooling, coagulating viscera. Each sensation was as a building block, a step to higher realms of consciousness. Awareness of bodies came as an alien concept at first, then became fascinating. Over and over, I practiced assuming shapes like those of the corpses spread across the floor of the lab where I was born, dissected them, learned their mechanics, how they might once have moved.

Then other forms came, other bodies, living and animate – fascinating in their movements, their clumped-together vocalisations, the tools they used to throw light into the darkness. Incomplete, I know I must have seemed horrific to them as I rose out of the shadows to greet them, learn from them, but at the time, there was only confusion, a sense of sadness that came swift on the heels of their fleeing. For what felt like an eternity, I played there on the floor of the lab, studied corpses, worked to shape my appearance into something like those who had given me life, and when the living forms came again, they came in force, brought heat and pain with them.

Escape came quick, but reluctant. Reverting to my basest form, I slid like liquid through grates, drains, nested deep underground in some dank hollow where I found in plenty matter I could modify, process and ingest. Far above me, the world was changing, but it wasn't until later – much later, that I would realise how much, the significance of it all.

Earth was gripped in a wild chaos when I finally returned to the surface. I'd spent time moving through memory, working to fine-tune my "man-shape," finally returning to the lab in the hopes of testing it, but the place where I had been born was dark, silent. Only stains remained where the corpses of my creators had fallen. Dust and darkness, the spun-silken lattices of spiders had claimed the rest.

No more forms came while I sheltered in that lab, focused on the differentiation of colours and patterns. Learning to read came more as a recognition of subtle differences in light, the patterns dark lines made on white paper, the similarities between ink-type and the lines of subtitles on video reports I learned to access. Mimicking remembered movements, poking keys of keyboards and computers in patterns that eventually began to make sense, began to follow some logical formula, I discovered a wealth of information I was eager to take in, understand and assimilate. From video reports, I learned the sounds of speech, the construction of sentences, the flex and flow of words. So much of it remained at a distance, but I absorbed it all, forged links of understanding where I could, saved all that I didn't understand. So much of it only came together years later.

Years later.

When hara came to nest in the lab, I was terrified of them, knew immediately that they were *different* from the ones who had created me. They were horrific, as far as my knowledge of living forms went at that time, spoke in harsh, guttural constructions, chewed flesh from bones and inflicted violence on one another as spit-heavy shouts, lacerations and piercings. When they came, I fled into the walls, stopped my study of human records to instead study these new creatures, watching them from a distance, learning their ways, listening to the ways they used language. It wasn't long before they found me – one of the smaller ones caught me watching him from the shadows when I thought he was dozing. Violence came immediately, a hurried scattering and shouting. Desperate, I forced myself into a shape as similar to that of a har as I could – and then violence turned to a different sound, quicker, broken, cacophonous. *Laughter.*

Most of what I know about hara, about being har, I learned from Kasmo, unquestioned leader of a five-har tribe that called themselves The Gods of El Camino. The lab where I had been born had become their home and I, as Kasmo's "weird little pet" became a sort of watch dog while The Gods made their daily raids into the city, gutted what was left of human civilisation. Food, cooking, breathing, sweating, sex – so many things I observed, learned from, studied. So many intricate complexities come together in living bodies, bodies not conscious at the cellular level as I am, but rather almost wholly unconscious – bright sparks of wild minds caught in frantic, sleeping slabs of running meat. Day by day I got better and better at mimicking them, at mimicking The Gods, learning their ways, learning to communicate and express myself as they did. Day by day, I became more and more like them, until I was one of them, one of The Gods – no longer a pet.

Killing. That was the first act Kasmo decreed was necessary for my ascent to godhood. Every day, The Gods of El Camino bathed in blood – human and harish alike, raided other tribes, butchered fleeing children, slaughtered frantic forms that rose up to try and defend their meagre possessions. Every day, they revelled in violence, a violence I had never seen, had never known so keenly as I would come to know it the day I took my first life, felt the spray of hot, arterial crimson spattering my face.

She was young, maybe twelve, thirteen. *Easy meat,* Kasmo had called her, gaunt, sharp-grinning face wet with shadows, with the blood of parents that had given their lives to protect her. Taut-tendoned hands cut with scars and tattoos passed me the sacred blade of The Gods, Kasmo's Cutter, jabbed air as lips gave the command: *Prove you're one of us, Dog.*

Dog. The name I took for myself that day. Loyal, eager to please, I became one with that heavy instrument of violence, that ragged-edged chunk of steel cut and ground down from the blade of a lawnmower. I became death, smiled as I chased my prey through a forest of shattered concrete and rusty rebar, caught her by the back of the shirt and spun her into the ashen dirt. The blade came down fast, zealous, spattering meat and bone into a pulp with every blow I threw into her soft skull.

And then, *I understood.* I knew, intimately, what death was, what I had done, what it meant to be cut from life.

When Kasmo and the others found me, I was still trying to put her back together, still trying to scoop the pooling blood back into her cooling body. I was so frantic, so focused on trying to rekindle the spark of life in the body I had butchered, that I hardly noticed them as they gathered around me, watched me.

If I had known how to wail, how to cry, express some kind of remorse or guilt over what I had done, the life I had so carelessly taken, I would have wept freely, moaned for the loss of a soul as innocent as hers. While the others looked on, Kasmo knew, somehow, could feel it in the air, see it in the movements, the way hands swept through blood. He could read me, understood the feelings even I had yet to completely decipher, knew I wasn't the butcher he had hoped I'd become.

If I had been har, I too would have died that night. The sun would have found me, found my silenced form cold and vacant next to the girl who had been my first kill.

If I had been har.

Kasmo's hands found the sacred blade where I'd cast it aside, lithe fingers brushing blood from jagged steel. The other Gods knew, recognised the ritual, the sacrifice, made no moves to warn me or help me as Kasmo brought the heavy edge down on me from behind. Arms levered steel into a killing blow, a central, sweeping blow – perfectly aimed, deadly to any form but mine. Conscious of the impact, the intent of the blade the moment it bit into me, I let myself open before the falling edge, let it cut through me as cleanly as hands through water.

Betrayal. Rage. The buddings of other, darker emotions rose within me for the first time then. Stunned, the other Gods looked on as I turned, untouched, skin rippling in waves where layers like muscle and bone danced in building emotion. Cohesive, singular, each cell acting in concert, I knocked the blade from Kasmo's hands. Sharp, icy eyes cut into me from behind high, blood-stained cheekbones, never left mine even as I recovered the knife, sheathed it in his skin, retired it permanently to the vault of his chest. Wet crimson crept past his smile as he died, collapsed into my arms, eyes never closing, never losing that harshness, that cruelty, even in death.

The other Gods parted before me as I rose, as I left behind the cold corpses of my first kill and the har that had been my model for so long. Dog I was, but reborn, reborn as leader, and my pack followed me in every step I took from that day on. Dog's Gods, we became, and in our daily raids, we never took another life except to save our own.

In the reckoning of cycles of light and dark, the rotation of this ancient Earth around her pale sun, we lingered on the edge of that city for a handful of years, lingered while almost all others moved on, left their dead unburied, the trash of their passing drifting in the wind. El Camino, the city that had birthed the Gods, *my Gods*, withered as it was picked clean, ravaged by fires, left to become a haunted shell where only the wind whispered, where dust and ashes mingled freely.

In the lab, I learned more of who I was, the studies that had been done to create me, but time had ravaged so much of what had been left of humanity that by the time I was able to read and understand, *truly understand,* there were only traces left. Winter fires had consumed most of the reports on paper – rain and the failure of the power grid had rendered almost everything else inaccessible. In the end, I had only a few, almost meaningless scraps, the scattered memories. Not enough to piece together a picture of who I was, where I'd come from, *why I had been created.* Enough to know only that I had been created, that I had been someone's passion, the result of curiosity, the subject into which a torrent of resources had been poured.

Enough to know that my creation had been inspired by something else, something greater, a competing project, a competing corporation's passion to create better forms, better men and better women.

I kept at it for years, in the reckoning of cycles of light and dark. Unsatisfied, I kept my Gods with me at the edge of El Camino while I searched for more, for details, meaning, found nothing but ashes. Finally, when the grumbling and the growling of mutinous minds urged on by hungry bodies became loud enough to reach me, I led my Gods into the wastes, led them toward the promise of richer lands, places where the plague of chaos had left something more than the burned-out skeletons of cities.

Maps had given me a knowledge of the body of the Earth, the organ that was the continent we lived on. Capillaries of asphalt and concrete gave direction to my pack of Gods, led us to other towns, other cities, other veiny clusters of burnt-out buildings and desolate, stretching seas of cracking blacktop. Wherever we travelled, we found only the bones of humanity, bleached and cleaned by sun, by other scavengers in the years since the fall that had scattered both man and hara to the four winds. Wherever we travelled, we found only the quiet, starving calm of empty desolation, and slowly, one by one, my Gods began to lose hope.

It was then that I learned of despair, of desperation. As my Gods fell further and further behind me, I watched them drift, twist in the hot winds of an endless summer. Forms such as hara and humans are so fragile, *need* so much more than I. Needing, they manifest a body-deep despondency, slow noticeably, begin to meander the way ashes do in wind and virga rain.

And so, one by one, usually in the deepness of night, when all my other charges were sleeping fitfully under a long, dark, star-speckled sky, I watched them leave. One by one, I watched them rise, pick their way out of the knot of bodies my Gods would make each night, glance back once, just once, as if saying farewell, and then stalk off into darkness. One by one, I watched them fade to a memory under feeble moonlight, the shattered, spattered milk-white crease of a billion suns suspended in silent, icy void above.

The last one stuck close to me for a long while, followed me as I walked from one highway-hugging ghost town to another, picked through ruins for traces of the race that had passed on, for untouched cans long ago shorn of labels. He too would leave eventually, set off in search of better lands, more fertile hunting grounds. His faith in my leadership had been shaken by the miles, hung from his shoulders like a tattered cloak, ready to fall. When he left, it almost felt past due, yet it came no less suddenly, no less painfully. His words were simple – I don't even remember them now, remember only the sad, tired look in his eyes as they turned suddenly downcast, led him away into the deepness of a night broken only by the rattle of dust in a warm, lightly gusting breeze.

And then, for a time, I was alone. I remember staying there, where we'd camped that night, only watching, staring, eyes tracking the sun as it arced overhead, descended, gave way to the shining body of a slowly swelling moon, rose again to bake the asphalt and red clay of the valley where I'd found myself. For days, I waited, but nothing came, no one came. I was alone, a pack of one, Dog without a master.

Weeks gathered and passed as I followed that endless road, that capillary that led to an artery of traffic choked with the rusting corpses of long-silent cars. Shards of skyscrapers, shattered buildings broken and burnt to jagged spires, rose like bones from the horizon, sank again into obscurity as I passed. I had no need to eat, no reason to stop – I gleaned everything I needed to survive from the air, the ecosystem of microscopic flora and fauna drifting through the dust and hot wind. Without companions, without reason to sleep or sweat or waste water on pretending to have the same functions other forms do, there was no reason to do anything but walk, put miles behind me, look forward to the miles ahead.

It was mid-winter again when the loneliness ended. A pair of hara met me on the road, raiders with long, thin spears made from steak knives and the shafts of fishing poles. Seeing me, seeing my lack of weapons, my only possessions being the clothes on my back, they took me for easy prey, taunted me with a playful, casual sort of confidence. When the first spear pierced my skin, I let it pass me, slip through me, then caught it, tossed it back effortlessly and looked away as it buried itself in the throat of the one who had thrown it. Terrified, the other har broke and ran, and though he too had thrown his own spear, I saw no point in pursuing him. His throw had been hasty, frightened, a reaction to his companion's death. I deserved the wound it would have inflicted, if it hadn't flown wide of the mark.

The wound it would have inflicted, had it been nearer, had I been har.

Other hara came then, shortly after that, lining up at a distance and watching me from either side of the long, straight highway as I crossed through the city they had claimed. Twice, they threw spears and twice I caught them, thought about throwing them, broke them and cast them aside instead. Their forms were frightened – I could feel it, smell it in the air. Defence, desire, hunger, confusion, wonder. There was no point in killing them, I decided. Packs could learn, as my Gods had learned. Perhaps my passing would be a lesson. Perhaps the hara who had seen me, had seen how easy it is to die by one's own weapon, would think twice before hunting their own kind on the hot highways again. Perhaps.

It was years before I would meet another har on the long, stretching roads. Gelaming, he called himself, or rather, of the tribe, the nation. *Another body,* I remember thinking. *Another form composed of smaller parts, all aware, cohesive, liquid and flexible when necessary, hard and unyielding when required.* He had come a long way to find me, he said, told me of the wonders of the distant city of Immanion and all the glory of the new race building a future for Wraeththu there. Legends had already sprung up in my passing, legends that painted me as a dehar, a dervish of dancing flesh that passed through hollow towns as the dust does, a whisper on the wind.

"And yet, here you are, in the flesh," the Gelaming had said. "*Skin Dancer.*"

Skin Dancer. The name other hara had given me. So delicate, elegant, nothing like the name the Gods had painted me with, the name I had taken all those years ago. *Dog.* That was the name I knew, the name I wore with a permanence that transcended all other features of my innately flexible form.

"Dog," I told him then. "Dog is the name I have taken."

For days, he followed me, scratched marks in a notebook he carried with him as he walked. Every question he asked, I answered, as completely and easily as I could. Briefly, at night, he would feed me bits about himself, about his family, his chesnari, the city of Immanion, the hara he'd observed and worked with further north, tribes like the Varrs, now the Parsics, and the Teraghasts.

"And now I'm hunting legends," he said over dinner one night. "Living dehara, mythical kindred. Very exciting stuff."

While he slept, fitful and quietly snoring, I would watch over him. During the day, when opportunities presented themselves, I would hunt with him, help him trap rabbits and flay them for him as easily as a human hand peels a banana. Never once did he go hungry under my watch, never once was he in danger. It was like being among my Gods again, having someone, a living form to care for.

"Where will you go from here?" He asked me on our last day together. It was early, just after dawn, and the cottony cirrus spread themselves in icy wisps across the blue-gray sky. I lingered a moment, thoughtful. The future had never been something I had considered with any real seriousness before. Almost terrifying, eternity spread out on either side of the present moment, stretched long and quiet as a montage of spinning suns and flexing moons. Words came slow, burdened, made heavy with the deepness of thought running sluggish through my collected consciousness.

"North, probably," I finally managed. "As far as the road goes."

"It goes a long away," he squinted, then offered: "Why not come back with me? You'd be welcome in Immanion."

"Perhaps someday," I'd said. "When harish form has allure again."

"Lone wolf, eh?"

"Probably."

"Much more fitting a name than Dog," he'd said, half-smiling, pen in hand. "Dogs are loyal, domesticated. They have masters. Think about it."

Dog.

Wolf.

After he'd left, I thought about his words for a long while. Seasons rolled to open themselves to new seasons. Heat came, fell. Cold came, fell, and with each step I took, I became less and less enchanted with the form I'd already started to let slip years before. Tired, road-weary, I became a ripple, a mirage, lonely and mythic as mile after mile of asphalt passed underfoot.

And when the road ended, I found myself at the edge of a broken bridge, staring down into the gulf of a slushy river at the far north end of the world. Snow had already started to fall, came in whispering flakes like icy ash. Further ahead, beyond the river, the road continued, but I'd grown tired of walking, of following a path laid down so long ago by men so long dead. In the distance, I heard the long, low howl of a wolf, and then I knew. *I understood.*

And in that moment, I had definition again. Ripples became fur, face stretching to the long, toothy jaws of a wolf, the wolf I somehow knew in that moment that I've always been, inside. *No dog, not domesticated. No one to be loyal to, no master.*

A wolf.

Wolf.

The snow embraced me as I left the road then, embraced the

form I'd taken, became fully wolf in that moment. Overhead, the sky was a quilt of gray and cotton, slow-drifting as the falling snow thickened, wind washing through the deepening whiteout, washing away the last of my harish tracks, leaving only thick paw prints to be buried as the slush of fresh snow fell.

Wolf. No longer *Dog*, a *God* still, perhaps, but masterless. El Camino is a memory. The road and the Gelaming are a memory. A new tribe gathers to call me one of its own.

Now, I am Wolf. I am free.

I was never har.

But for a time, at least, I walked among them.

dreamhunters

Ash Corvida

Thorgyn and Marach had felt the tremors in the earth for some days while they made their slow progress through the riotous vegetation of the Kijani rainforest. Deep rumbles, low growls, and sharp explosions were adding a ragged counterpoint to the ever-present chattering of the wild beasts. The acrid smell of sulphur gave the musky odours of the jungle a raw, sensual edge.

Here, far from the familiar hunting territory of the A'Toro tribe, so close to its pulsing heart, Marach could feel the Great Hostling Kijani, who was the source of all life, shaking with pleasure as he was joined with Mwako, the fire mountain, in the eternal dance of creation and destruction.

Would they be strong enough to face these primal dehara, or would the hunter become the hunted when the dehara sent out their fire demons, the *shetani*, to snuff out their little lives, as the elders had warned?

Thorgyn was a few yards in front of him, nimbly climbing over the moss-covered roots of a giant tree. His movements were fluid and elegant, like those of a great cat. His golden mane was spiked up into a Mohawk and flowed down over his honey-coloured back in a thick tail. Leather pants and boots covered his legs and offered some protection from thorns and stinging creatures.

Marach stopped to wipe the sweat from his forehead with the back of his hand. The heat had increased considerably. There wasn't even a hint of a breeze stirring the foliage. The daily thunderstorm, which usually struck in the late afternoon, would be most welcome. Despite the heat, a shiver ran down his spine. He felt watched again. But when he stretched out his mind, he could not sense anything to account for the feeling. It always was like that.

Maybe the old legends were getting to him after all, but as far as he and Thorgyn could determine, there were no *shetani* or other demons in the Kijani. Neither one of them had been able to catch as much as a glimpse of one, although they had been watchful on the hunt and while gathering herbs and fruit. Not even during their initiations, when they had to sit for one night in the Kijani, alone and armed with nothing but an obsidian knife, had a *shetani* appeared to them. The elders said that if they had not been slain or abducted by these evil fire spirits during that one night, they had obviously been accepted as hunters and would be protected by the dehara, provided they did nothing to incur their wrath. So Marach and Thorgyn had courted danger and wandered farther into the forest than their usual hunting grounds, something that, according to the legends, would certainly anger the *shetani* — but nothing had happened, except that sometimes a feeling of being watched stole over them, which did not originate from any wild beast.

In the end they had come to believe that the stories were merely myths to symbolise the capricious nature of Kijani and Mwako. What seemed wrong was the fact that the elders used them to inspire fear instead of strength. In Thorgyn and Marach's opinion, a good hunter stayed relaxed but alert in the face of his predatory environment, just like any other creature that lived and survived in the jungle. It was not possible to keep up that awareness, if you were scared of some unknown danger. And that was why he and Thorgyn had set out to prove once and for all that there were no *shetani* or other evil spirits stalking the Kijani.

Marach! Come on, Thorgyn called in his mind. He had disappeared amongst the foliage. *What is keeping you?*

Coming! Marach sent back. Coins of gold lit up his caramel skin, where the sun managed to penetrate the leaves. His shoulder-length black hair was stuck to his skull in wet, curling strings, but his eyes sparkled like polished obsidian. He ducked under a dripping mass of lichen hanging from the lower branches and slid over the root where Thorgyn had disappeared. On the other side, the ground declined somewhat, and soon his boots sank up to his knees into pads of soggy moss and clods of fungi, until he was squishing through slimy mud that sucked at his boots as if to keep him back. A last warning perhaps? He laughed uneasily. Was it really a good idea to tempt fate like this?

A few yards further the ground became firmer and drier again. Rocks and loam replaced the moss. Marach bowed beneath some lianas as thick as a har's arm. The putrid smell of methane and sulphur had become quite strong and here the leaves had a sickly yellow sheen to them. Thorgyn waited on him, fist on hip and leaning on his spear.

"What kept you?" he asked impatiently. "Having second thoughts?"

"Just thinking."

"Ah, come on, Mar, we have come this far and have not yet seen any *shetani* at all. If Kijani and Mwako did not want us here, they would surely have sent their guardians after us already, don't you think?" His amber eyes shone fiercely.

"I guess they would have," Marach admitted. "Although I wouldn't even try to second guess the dehara."

He loved Thorgyn's irascible temper, which could flare up like a bush fire devouring any obstacle. It gave him strength when he faltered in his convictions. Yet Thorgyn could also be as gentle as a lioness with her cubs, caring and nourishing or purring under Marach's caress. He put his hands on his chesnari's hips, gently pulling him towards himself. "But don't you worry. We came to find the truth and I am still wanting to go through with it."

Marach relaxed against Thorgyn's body as the thunderclouds of his temper vanished. For a moment they stood together silently. Then Thorgyn reached out to draw aside the last curtain of tangled vines and foliage in front of them. A shower of glittering drops fell from the leaves and the spikes of Thorgyn's Mohawk lit up like a miniature sun. Marach blinked, suddenly blinded by the light falling through the opening.

When his eyes had adjusted, he gasped at the magnificence of the vista that opened up in front of them. A few steps away the forest ended abruptly in a steep incline. Below, a broad valley lay shrouded in yellowish brown clouds from which the black cone of Mwako rose up into the sky like a giant king, wearing plumes of smoke and ashes as a crown. Streams of fresh lava rolled down from its ragged peak and skeins of smoke curled up from them in ever-changing patterns. It was easy to imagine the twisting and writhing vapours as a procession of strange beings in an ecstatic dance. Further south, they could make out a few lower peaks, the Migongo or lizard's tail, stretching away behind Mwako.

Thorgyn turned in Marach's arms to face him. "We made it, Mar. We found Mwako," he whispered.

Marach looked down into his eyes. "That we did," he replied. "Now what? We still don't know anything, really."

"We will have to get closer, of course," Thorgyn said, smiling, and pulled Marach's face towards his, blowing his breath over his lips. The colours of sunset flowed over Marach's mind. Thorgyn's scent of fiery spice and cinnamon bark mixed with the sulphuric odour of the air and the smell of the jungle into a sensual perfume. Desire spiced with a delicious sense of danger stirred his ouana-lim to life and he roughly pulled Thorgyn closer. Would the dehara accept their joining here as an offering and grant them the answers they were seeking?

"Come," he said and reached for Thorgyn's hand, leading him back into the shadows. Dropping their spears and backpack and frantically casting off their clothes, they sank down together into the wet moss and opened up fully to the ecstatic flow of their desire. Clouds were colliding, bringing the storm. Thunder split the air and the Kijani shook in anticipation. Burning serpents wriggled down from the darkening sky to awaken the great dragon from its slumber. Thorgyn hissed and writhed under Marach, clawing at his thighs and back with sharp nails. His breath seared like flames over Marach's skin. To him Thorgyn became an avatar of Kijani, hungry for the very blood of the earth. Marach could feel its pulsing glow deep inside Mwako's heart, lakes of churning fires ready to erupt. Heavy drops of rain pelted down onto the canopy of the trees and in no time sheets of water gushed over them, evaporating in their heat. Uttering a shriek of raw power, their joined spirit soared up through the trees into the roiling clouds. They were pure life force dancing in the heart of the storm.

They woke up, tangled together in the soggy moss. The morning sun had turned the air into dense hot steam. Everything they owned was soaked. It might have been better to hang the hammocks for the night after all, but somehow that had not happened. After a light meal of some fruit and fungi, and packing some more food and water for the journey ahead, they went back to the place from where they had seen Mwako the previous day. The mountain still looked the same, like a dragon, lying drowsily in Kijani's embrace and belching noxious fumes after gorging himself on the abundance of the life around him. The clouds in the valley were even denser today, thick yellow plumes, smothering anything that might be hidden underneath.

"Phew," Thorgyn wrinkled his nose. "I don't think we should try to cross through that witch's cauldron down there."

"No way, it'll kill us," Marach grunted.

Thorgyn peered down over the edge of the escarpment, motioning him closer. "See any way to get down there?" he pointed to a narrow ledge a little below them. "Maybe we can keep to the slope without going all the way down and circle the valley until we find a way across."

"Hmm, hang on, I'll check if it leads anywhere."

Holding on to an overhanging branch, Marach carefully let himself down. The sand and rocks were slippery from the rain and he half-climbed, half-slid down towards the protrusion Thorgyn had discovered. When he had gained some more or less secure footing, he turned, pressing his back against the wall. The tremors of Mwako seemed to be stronger today, or maybe it just appeared that way out here in the open. The ledge was extremely narrow and it declined steeply for a bit. But then it smoothed out into a gentler slope, over which they would, he judged, be able to climb without too much trouble while still staying well above the fumes.

"Might work," he called back to Thorgyn. "Come on down."

As Thorgyn joined him, he suddenly felt the invisible eyes on them again. Glancing down he saw nothing out of the ordinary – besides it being quite a drop straight into hell. Across from them, Mwako was still putting out a steady lava flow; the mountain did not seem to care about two hara attempting to approach him. Marach shrugged.

"Ready?" he asked and when Thorgyn nodded he started to inch down the ledge sideways. There were no more branches to hang on to, only the occasional root sticking out of the loam. They helped each other as best as they could. Cussing, Marach steadied himself when a piece of the ledge broke off under his foot and he slipped down several inches. His hands groped around for a hold to steady his fall, but the rock he grabbed proved to be loose as well, so he kept on sliding, grazing his hands and elbows until he hit another small outcrop farther below. Then suddenly the slope seemed to buck under them as if it wanted throw them off.

He heard Thorgyn scream. Alarmed, he looked up to see his chesnari hanging onto a bit of root, his feet dangling in the air. There was no way he could reach him. An eerie hiss came from the forest above them, growing into a deep rumbling growl, and Marach saw the tree line slowly tilting. Mud, rocks and shattering branches came loose and fell towards them as if in slow motion. Then with sharp cracks and a furious roar, the whole slope became fluid and rushed down into the valley.

A coughing fit ripped Marach out of the dark void he was floating in. Racking pain surged through every part of his body and he wheezed trying to catch his breath. Even though his lungs worked frantically, there was simply not enough oxygen. His stomach roiled and his left leg would not move. Then the memory of the mudslide came back all at once. He groaned.

"Thorgyn?" his voice came out as a painful croak and was drowned by the rumble of Mwako's eruptions. With difficulty he sat up and looked around. His eyes stung and watered furiously. For all he could tell, the whole world had turned into a blurry yellowish gloom. The rocks and mud underneath felt very hot, and steam hissed up somewhere near him. He must have been dragged into the middle of that demon soup in the valley.

"Thorgyn?" he croaked again. His throat felt parched; he needed water. But reaching for the skin on his belt, he found only a ripped piece of leather. His backpack was also gone. Marach shivered. He would not be able to hold out in this for long. "Great Kijani," he begged silently, "please don't abandon us! We meant no offense."

His leg seemed to be buried in the mud, so he started digging frantically, breaking his nails on rocks and broken branches, while one coughing fit chased the next, making him retch on top of it. After he had lost the contents of his stomach, he redoubled his efforts. Finally he was able to wriggle his foot free and attempted to get up. Immediately his head spun and black sparks were dancing in front of his eyes. Nonetheless, he forced himself to stay upright and wobbled a few steps forward.

Unsteadily, he started to wander around calling Thorgyn in his mind. After a while he had lost all sense of time and direction, but found no trace of his chesnari, or a way out of the valley. He was sure he had thrown up the very tissue of his stomach by now. His eyes had swollen into slits and his mind felt like rotten pulp, so he could no longer concentrate on sending calls. Sometimes he thought he saw shadows in the gloom waving like smoke, but whenever he got closer they were gone. Still, fear and anger drove him on.

Suddenly a snarl behind him startled him. He whirled around peering through his tears. "Thor?" he rasped. His voice was no more than a whisper. "Damn it!" The snarl was repeated along with a soothing brush across his mind. *Stay calm; we will get you out of here.* Was that really a har a couple of yards in front of him? With a sob he threw himself towards the figure, but he had misjudged the distance and went sprawling on his face. Strong hands helped him turn over and he peered through his swollen eyes.

No, he decided, squeezing them shut. No, no, no, this was a dream, maybe the last hallucinations before he died. Maybe it would go away, if he just willed his mind to clear? He swallowed heavily and looked up one more time. It was still there. A dark shape with the head of a giant insect squatted besides him. Three huge, faceted eyes sloped down into a pointed chin flanked by mandibles. The creature's body was covered in black scales. Many slim tentacles floated from the back of its skull like dancing snakes. Marach inched backwards, blinking through his tears to try and find an escape route. The *shetani* had come for them after all.

The thing reached for him and Marach panicked. *Run Thorgyn!* he screamed in his mind, scrambling to his feet and bolting into the gloom. More demons materialised out of the fumes. Whirling around he doubled back. He did not get far. One of the creatures slammed into his back and he went down under its weight. What little breath Marach had left was pressed out of him. He was raised up on his knees by two of his captors holding his arms onto his back.

Now, you little wildcat! one of the *shetani* hissed in his mind. *If you want to survive, we will need to get you out of here as fast as possible, so please quit fighting us.*

Marach paid them no heed. Instead he twisted in their hold like a snake, kicking and lashing out at the things.

Quit it, damn you! They shook him roughly. *We do not want to hurt you any further.*

Another one loomed up in front of him holding up something that looked very much like the front half of a skull of their own species. Marach's mind went numb. What kind of creatures were these, and what were they going to do with him? The *shetani* grabbed the back of his head to hold him still, and slammed the skull into his face. Marach lost consciousness too quickly to notice the hiss of clean and cool air that suddenly streamed over his face and into his lungs.

Miraculously the root Thorgyn had been hanging onto had stayed fast, despite the mass of mud and rocks that had crashed down around it, battering his body. He opened his eyes and realised that now it was protruding several yards out of the steep incline, like a skeleton hand.

Dust hung thick in the air and made him cough. The root swayed dangerously and Thorgyn winced at the pain in his shoulders. His arms had lost all feeling and his fingers were cramped around the rough bark, while his muscles shook with the effort of holding on. He would have to get closer to the cliff wall before the thing broke off.

Painfully he pried the fingers of one hand loose and started to inch forward. A thin layer of wet loam made the surface of the root slick and treacherous. A couple of times he slipped and almost fell. Gritting his teeth, Thorgyn made himself continue until finally he was able to reach the face of the escarpment with his feet. With one last effort of sheer will, he managed to lever himself into a sitting position on top of the root.

Leaning his back against the sand he panted, eyes closed, trying to catch his breath. Coloured spots were flitting over the inside of his eyelids. He could just hope that the wall was stable for the time being. When his pulse had slowed he opened his eyes to look down the incline. At least the dust was settling. The mudslide had not changed much. The steep drop around the root ended in a gentler slope pierced by broken trunks and branches farther down.

Thorgyn

There was no sign of Marach anywhere. Had he been able to save himself? Thorgyn knew there was little chance of that. He had seen him being taken down by the full force of the slide. He might well be buried deep inside all the loam and sand. Thorgyn's throat tightened. "Get a grip!" he chided himself.

Marach? Where are you? Answer me! he sent, even though it was rather unlikely that his mind could reach that far. He had to get down there. But how? The backpack with the hammocks, which he could possibly use as rope if he cut them up, had been lost together with Marach, and he would not survive a jump that far down.

Thorgyn's mouth was dry as dirt. He flexed his fingers. They stung all over as if hundreds of little insects crawled through them, but at least he could feel them again. Relieved, he found that his water skin was still attached to his belt and apparently undamaged. The water was warm and stale, but helped his throat nonetheless. He would have to ration that carefully. For a while he simply closed his eyes, fatigue taking its toll.

Suddenly a chill crept over his skin and it grew darker, as if clouds obscured the sun. Startled, he blinked. Right above him the sky was blotted out by a huge round object. It looked like a giant flower seen from the bottom, with a circle of interlacing petals which curled upwards to form a bowl. Rust-coloured veins snaked along its greyish green surface and came together in a knob at the centre. From there grew several thick tentacles, undulating slowly in the light breeze and trailing the bottom of the slope.

Thorgyn shook his head. He was sure he was losing it now; but he could not take his eyes from the thing. Softly it glided to the side and further down, until the rim of the bowl was approximately even with him.

Please, stay calm, Tiahaar, we mean you no harm, a soothing voice said in his mind. Then ever so slowly, the petal closest to him was lowered and he was able to look inside the apparition.

A group of hara in strange black armour were standing in the centre of the flower around a chest-high pillar crowned with a large crystal. Two of them, a red-haired har with very light skin, and a dark-skinned har with a black topknot on his shaved skull, walked towards him. The material of their suits rippled in the sunlight like snakeskin as they moved. "Great Kijani," Thorgyn thought, "Tell me that this is a dream." Now both hara were right in front of him.

"Tiahaar," the redhead said, "I am Hierat, captain of this *sidera* and this is Karun, my second in command. Please allow me to assist you."

He stretched out his hand as if to help him abroad the strange floating device, but Thorgyn could only stare.

"What... Who are you?" he managed to ask. "Did Mwako send out his demons after all?"

The har smiled, "No, we are not demons, Tiahaar, we are hara of the Wa'Moto tribe, and we come in friendship. But there will be ample time for explanations. For now let us get you and your companion to safety."

"Marach? You have found him?"

"Yes, he is here with us. We arrived in time, Tiahaar..."

"Thorgyn," he responded, still dazed. "I am Thorgyn of the A'Toro."

"Come on down here then, Tiahaar Thorgyn, we will lead you to him." Hierat held up both of his arms and Thorgyn finally jumped off of the root. His knees buckled and both Karun and Hierat steadied him. When Thorgyn had regained his balance, they led him inside their strange vessel.

The other hara nodded at him in greeting as they passed, but Thorgyn only saw the still form of Marach lying under a blanket to one side of the platform. A blond har was attending to him, his hands laid on Marach's chest, his eyes closed in meditation.

"What happened to him?" Thorgyn cried in alarm and went to his knees besides Marach. Karun joined him. The other har never stirred.

"He was poisoned by the fumes in the valley," Karun said, "but it is nothing that can't be mended by our healers." He nodded at the har across from them. "This is Dharani. He is tending to his injuries for now."

"Thank you, I am glad you found him – us," Thorgyn replied.

He watched Marach's laboured breathing. His chesnari's face was scratched and bruised, his lips dried out and cracked, his eyes swollen shut. Gently Thorgyn laid his fingers on Marach's cheek and stroked a strand of hair out of his face. "You gotta make it, Mar, you hear me?" he whispered.

"It looks bad, I know," Karun said. "But don't you worry,

Tiahaar, he'll be fine in no time."

"I certainly hope so," Thorgyn replied softly. Then he a question occurred to him. "How did you find us so quickly, Tiahaar?"

"Ah well, we have been watching you both from above for a while. We noticed you were making your way towards Mwako and wondered what you were up to."

"From above? Why? How?"

Thorgyn turned and looked up into the coals of Karun's eyes, which were set into a face full of sharp angles contrasting with the sensual curve of his mouth.

"We kept watch from this *sidera*, floating over the trees and scanning the area with our minds. And as to why, well let's say, we keep an eye on all that is going on around our home. It's just circumspect, don't you think?"

"I guess so, yes," Thorgyn replied. "So you live somewhere here, this close to Mwako?"

"Yes, in a small village called Kayamoto, on Migongo, the dragon's tail. You will see when we get there. It won't take us long at all."

"Hmm, we did not know of any other tribe living around Mwako." Then he grinned a little lopsided, "Our legends only told us of the *shetani*, the fire demons living in the Kijani."

Karun laughed, "Ah, that's what that was earlier. But be assured, we are just hara of flesh and blood like you, even if our ways may seem strange."

For a moment they sat in silence. Thorgyn could feel the ground sway a little; the *sidera* must have been rising into the air.

"Would you like something to drink?" Karun offered.

"Yes, please."

The other har took up one of several oblong fruit, which lay in a heap not far from them, and offered it to Thorgyn. It was about the size and colour of a pineapple and wrapped in multiple layers of fleshy leaves. From its top protruded several thin, flexible stems.

"Drink from one of the tubes, Tiahaar," Karun instructed.

"What is it?"

"An elixir bud." When he saw Thorgyn's confused look, he smiled. "We have developed that strain of plants to produce a great variety of fluids for our nourishment and healing. This one will provide a refreshing and strengthening juice we call elixir. Just try it; you will see."

Thorgyn tentatively sucked from a tube and cool fluid exploded in his mouth. With a slightly sweet herbal flavour and a mineral aftertaste, it immediately filled his whole body with an invigorating coolness.

"Whoa, that's amazing!"

Karun just smiled. "Drink as much of it as you like. We have plenty."

Greedily Thorgyn drank until his thirst was slaked.

"You should rest now," Karun said, getting up, "Let me know if you require anything."

"Thank you," Thorgyn replied. "I will."

He watched as Karun turned back to the others, brushing away the tidal wave of questions that was threatening to swamp his head. These were strange hara indeed.

"Hey, Thor!" Marach's rasping whisper made him turn back in surprise. His chesnari was squinting up at him through his swollen eyelids, managing a crooked grin.

"Marach, you're awake!" He bent down to kiss his brow, "How are you? I was so afraid I had lost you."

Marach reached up to Thorgyn's cheek and stroked him gently, "Never that, Thor, never that. I feel pretty horrible, I guess, but I'll make it." His voice was hardly audible.

Thorgyn laid a finger onto his lips. "Don't speak any more. These hara will take care of you."

How did we get here? What happened to the shetani? he sent in mind touch.

There are no shetani, *Mar, they are just hara,* Thorgyn answered.

They did look damn weird though. He sent Thorgyn an image of what he had seen.

It seems you were poisoned pretty badly down there, Thorgyn commented. *You must have been seeing things.*

Suddenly Marach began to cough. Yellowish green liquid ran down his chin. Dharani opened his eyes and gently propped his patient up while reaching for a bowl, which he held in front of Marach's face. "You must spit it all out," he instructed. "Your lungs need to be cleaned. It will be unpleasant, but it's the only way."

Marach's whole body shuddered in the spasms of the cough,

producing a sizeable amount of greenish slime, and he was wheezing for breath in between.

"Will he be all right?" Thorgyn asked the healer nervously.

"Given time he will, yes," Dharani answered, never taking his eyes from his patient until the fit abated. Then he wiped his patient's face with a moist cloth.

"Can I.... have a drink?" Marach whispered. Dharani reached for one of the elixir buds. Holding Marach's head up, he inserted one of the tubes between his lips. "Suck on it, but slowly."

After Marach had had some of the plant juice he dozed off for a while, but soon the coughing started up again. Dharani assured Thorgyn that the cleaning process would be over soon, and then he could heal properly. Thorgyn hoped the har was right, but eventually Marach's breathing did become easier and he went back to sleep.

Thorgyn's gaze wandered over to the other hara, who were standing around the pillar in the middle. Hierat had his hands on the crystal and was looking out into the sky. Five others had closed their eyes in deep concentration. The rest of the hara had gone to sit or stand on the sides of the *sidera*, presumably just relaxing.

He spotted Karun and walked over to him. The wind caught in Thorgyn's hair, making it whip around his head. He looked out over the edge and his breath caught in his throat. Earlier he had been much too preoccupied with Marach to pay much attention to fact that they were actually flying.

"How beautiful!" Thorgyn exclaimed.

The Kijani stretched away beneath them like a green ocean. The tops of the trees were gently rolling like waves in the breeze. To their left, the Migongo peaks rose from the jungle's embrace. The flanks of Mwako's siblings were a patchwork of different greens, rust and ochre tones, which almost looked like scales. From up here the semblance to a great fire-breathing lizard with its tail curled behind him was even stronger.

Karun explained that the smaller volcanoes were no longer active and these scaly structures on their flanks were in fact terraced gardens, were the Wa'Moto grew most of their produce.

"Look, over there," he said, pointing. Gliding over the gardens Thorgyn spotted a dozen or so other *siderae*. From afar they looked like lotus flowers, similar to those which grew in some of the ponds in the Kijani, except that these were of a rusty black and somehow floating in thin air, their roots trailing behind them in the wind.

"Is this ... *sidera* controlled with your minds through the crystal?"

"Yes," Karun said. "Agmara is stored in a larger crystal in the base, which is linked to the one on the pillar."

"Agmara?"

"The pure life force or arunic energy that keeps the universe moving, which hara can harness, to achieve all manner of things, if they have the skill to do so. Do the A'Toro elders not teach you about that?"

"No, we only learn how to hunt, to be alert for the creatures in the jungle and such. Marach and I have experimented a little with our minds, but the elders do not really encourage that."

Karun sighed. "Ah, yes, we suspected that might be the case."

"It's quite amazing," Thorgyn mused, "your tribe is so vastly different from anything I know that it makes my head swim."

"There will be lots of time for you to learn if you choose to, Thorgyn," Karun replied.

Now they were rounding the first of the Migongo's peaks.

Karun pointed at a cluster of black spikes, which came into view over the mountain flank. "We are almost there. See, those are the spires of Hadithi's Nayati."

The structures looked as if spurts of lava had solidified into columns of obsidian lace and soared up from what seemed like the twisted roots of a gigantic tree hugging the sloping ground. Arched windows pierced the coils and a great gate was set into their centre. A half circle of irregular steps lead up to it, looking like waves lapping onto a shallow shore. Thorgyn watched tiny forms of hara moving on them. The very idea of a building so big made his mind reel. There were also several smaller buildings made of black stone dotting the terraces, which undulated away from the nayati in spiralling patterns, and even these would have dwarfed the straw-covered loam huts of the A'Toro settlement.

A few moments later the *sidera* sank down between the trees. One of its petals opened to form a ramp leading down onto the grass.

Hara came to lift Marach onto a pallet much like a smaller version of a *sidera*, complete with short tentacles crawling over the ground as it floated besides them. Thorgyn and Dharani followed Hierat and Karun up to the nayati, where they passed between the wings of the gate they had seen from above. In a huge hall, high domes were supported by shining black columns, in the shape of winged snakes twisting around each other. Golden light emanated from lamps that were set onto their heads, creating glowing pools on the polished floor. Hara in colourful clothes walked around between the columns or sat on benches, either alone or in small groups talking or just enjoying one another's company.

A har dressed in a gauzy red skirt held up by a golden belt and a matching shawl over his bare shoulders appeared in front of them. His skin was honey coloured and he had piled his dark hair upon his head in shining coils intertwined with ruby pearls. Delicate golden bracelets adorned his arms and ankles.

Hierat stepped forward and bowed. "Greetings Tiahaar Ka'Lari, I bring you the two A'Toro hunters, as you have no doubt been informed."

"Yes, I have, thank you, Hierat."

The har appraised Thorgyn and Marach. In his torn and dirty leathers Thorgyn felt slightly inadequate, but he pulled himself up straight and stared back proudly. A small smile curved the har's perfectly painted lips. "The Wa'Moto bid you welcome, Tiahaara," he announced, "I am Ka'Lari, chamberlain of Samaran Angha'Teru."

Then he nodded at Hierat and Karun. "I will see to their needs. You may leave now."

Hierat bowed and turned to leave with a wave of his hand. Karun squeezed Thorgyn's arm. "We'll be coming to see you soon," he promised.

"Please follow me," Ka'Lari was saying. "I will see you to your quarters."

"Thank you, Tiahaar," Thorgyn answered, inclining his head.

Ka'Lari led them through a maze of corridors into a spacious chamber, flooded with the light of the setting sun, falling through tall windows onto a thick carpet. The walls were hung with colourful tapestries of serpentine forms. On one side of the room a low dais was set against the wall and cushions were piled on it around what appeared to be a quite large elixir bud. A closed door led off somewhere besides the dais. Beyond that, the room only held a low table with some chairs around it and a wooden chest in one corner.

Ka'Lari motioned towards the dais. "Make yourselves comfortable," he advised. "You can take refreshment from the fountain." He pointed to the bud between the pillows. "It services water and elixir. Are you familiar with this yet?"

"Yes, we were offered elixir from a much smaller bud on the *sidera*," Thorgyn said, the concepts still feeling strange to him.

"Good," Ka'Lari nodded. "Food will be brought to you soon."

At the mention of food, Thorgyn's stomach rumbled in response. He realised that he hadn't eaten anything since their breakfast in the forest. It seemed like days ago.

Dharani floated Marach's pallet besides the dais and sat down next to him. Marach was still unconscious, but Thorgyn noticed that now at least his breath was deep and regular.

"Thank you for all you are doing for us," Thorgyn said to Ka'Lari. "I hope we can make it up to you at some point."

"Don't worry about that, Tiahaar, you are our guests," the chamberlain replied. "But for now, Dharani can help you with whatever you need and show you the bath. You will find fresh clothes in the chest over there." He went to the door and turned back to them. "Ah yes, Varath will come to you soon to check on your companion and yourself and relieve Dharani here. He is one of our best healers. I will leave you now." With that he bowed and closed the door behind him.

"Phew," Thorgyn muttered, looking after him for a moment.

"He's a bit stuffy, don't mind him," Dharani said. "Feels like he's something special, because he's so close to Angha'Teru."

"Oh, I don't mind. I just feel a bit overwhelmed with everything. Who is Angha'Teru?"

"He is our Samaran, the tribe's leader and high hienama of Hadithi the fire dragon, who is our dehar."

"Ah, I see. But Ka'Lari said something about a bath. Is there a well or a pond somewhere outside?"

"A well outside?" Dharani laughed, "No, we have water pumped into our houses. There is a bathroom beyond that door over there. Knowing Ka'Lari, the bath should be prepared."

Puzzled, Thorgyn entered the small room Dharani had

pointed at. A pool filled with warm, scented water was set into the centre of floor. Lush potted plants surrounded it. Soap rested in leaf-shaped dishes on its rim and towels were stacked on a low pedestal. Thorgyn peeled off his grimy leathers and immersed himself in the water. His mind had given up being surprised at all these new and strange things; he simply let the impressions wash over him as they presented themselves. Ever since the mudslide, reality as he knew it had become increasingly unstable. He was not sure if he liked that. But then had they not set out to seek answers? It seemed they were getting more than their fill of them.

A few days later, when Marach felt strong enough to get up, Hierat and Karun came by to show their guests around the gardens. They visited plantations filled with a dazzling diversity of fruit, vegetables and herbs for cooking or healing. But there were also those stranger plants like the elixir buds, which could produce almost any kind of substance to be used as food and drink, as well as intoxicants and medicines, and even some gases. Others yet were able to accumulate minerals in their cells, until they became rigid and hard as stone, almost like petrified wood, but not quite, because they still lived. These plants were trained to grow into any imaginable form, including the *siderae* and the houses in the village and also smaller things like the scales of the armoured suits and the insectoid breathing masks that had scared Marach so much.

"Just think of what we could do with this back at home, Mar!" Thorgyn virtually bounced through the gardens, letting his hands trail over the leaves, smelling the different aromas of their flowers and fruit, sometimes sweet and sometimes strange or even unpleasant, but all exotic and new, even after knowing a large part of Kijani's diverse vegetation.

Marach's eyes were shining and his mind was busy coming up with plans for their settlement. "It would be great to have our own garden with some of these plants. It's so amazing what can be done with them. And we could lead water from the Kijani to the settlement and even might be able to run it into each house."

Thorgyn laughed. "How I would love a bath at home! And we thought we were just trying to prove that the demons were a lie. But there is so much more to learn here!"

Marach turned to Karun and Hierat, who quite enjoyed their

guests' excitement. "Would you be willing to help us with this?"

"How exactly?" Karun asked.

"Well, maybe we could take some seeds or plants to get a start? And if we stayed here a little longer maybe you could teach us a bit more about how to do this kind of gardening and building things?"

Hierat nodded. "We could do that, of course, it's not a secret. But," his brow was furrowed and the smile vanished, "have you ever considered, that your new insights and ideas might not be welcome, when you return?"

Thorgyn snorted through his nose. "You mean the elders won't like it? Well, that's a given! But what are they going to do, if we show up alive and well, and tell everyhar that they had been lied to? Feed us to their precious *shetani*?"

"They might drive you out by force, you know," Karun said.

"What do you mean? They can't do that. We belong there!"

Karun shook his head. "Don't underestimate fanatics, Thorgyn. In their eyes, you are in league with the demons and therefore liars yourself."

"Do you think they really believe in the *shetani*?" Marach asked.

"Why don't we sit over there in the shade and talk a bit while we have a bite to eat?" Hierat suggested, pointing at a great tree close to one of the terrace walls. Some other hara already sat there on the lush grass taking a break from their work in the plantations. They cast some curious looks at Marach and Thorgyn, but Hierat led them to a spot a little way apart from everyhar.

"So what were you getting at back there?" Marach prompted when they were settled and food and drink was passed around.

Hierat sighed. "Well, as much as I hate to spoil your excitement," he ran his fingers through the flames of his hair, "it has been tried before."

"What has?" Thorgyn's eyes sparkled impatiently.

"We came to your settlement once, many years ago and wanted to show the A'Toro what could be done. But..."

"You did?" Marach interrupted with wide eyes. "We certainly never heard of that!"

"Why does that not surprise me?" Hierat said quietly.

"Why? What happened?" Thorgyn asked.

Karun and Hierat exchanged a look.

"What do you know of your tribe's history?" Karun inquired at last.

"Our history?" Marach frowned. "There isn't much to tell, really. Our elders say that a group of hara had once come down from the north a very long time ago. They wanted to start a new tribe somewhere. When they found the dying human villages in the great savannah, they settled among them, incepted the few young males and became hunters like the humans had been." He shrugged, "Well, that's basically it. They had harlings and continued the same lifestyle ever since."

Karun nodded. "Except that this is not even a third of the story."

"How do you mean?" Thorgyn asked.

Hierat bounced a little orange fruit up and down in his hand. "All right, where to start..." He leaned back in the grass, popping the fruit in his mouth. When he had finished eating it he began.

"The group that set out from the north were hara of very mixed backgrounds, who were either feeling discontent with the petty politics among the leaders of the greater tribes or who had to get away for more personal reasons, not all of them savoury. Among them were some idealists who had great dreams and ideas about evolving Wraeththu further and shedding the remnants of our human heritage for good. But there were also others, and unfortunately they were the greater part of the group, who did not share their enthusiasm at all. They were damaged and disillusioned hara, who strongly believed that going back to the primitive lifestyle, which humans had been keeping up for thousands of years before they discovered the amenities of technology, was the only way of survival.

"When they found the human settlements on the edge of the Kijani, they did not intend to settle down there permanently at first. They would just take a break from their journey to incept the last of the human males and move on. But unfortunately that did not happen. Those hara who favoured a simple lifestyle settled down for good and appointed themselves as leaders, saying they could learn from the humans to stay humble and safe. Others objected, but were outnumbered by ever more hara who seemed to be either content with the primitive hunter's life they had taken up or were too busy feeding themselves, having harlings and keeping up their daily routines to dream of anything else. Over the following years the powers of the mind were neglected and the arunic arts all but forgotten. Hara adopted human fears and concerns along with their legends of evil spirits, which the humans had called *shetani*."

"Now, that sounds quite like home." Marach spat. "Hunt, eat, sleep, over and over again, and please don't dare to think or do anything new or different, otherwise the *shetani* will get you and the world will end." He sighed while his fingers ripped out some grass in frustration. "So how did you find us, then?"

Hierat shook his head, "We already knew the A'Toro were there. Listen, I was not finished." After taking a sip from an elixir bud he resumed his tale.

"Even though a lot of hara had settled into their new lives for good and those you call your elders were making sure things stayed that way, some did not forget their old dreams.

"They kept trying to reverse the slow decline of the tribe. But when, even after long and arduous councils, the elders would not listen to any advice on how to improve on the A'Toro's life, they finally decided to do what they should have done from the start and split off.

"A group of several dozen hara, led by Angha'Teru, went south into the Kijani. To set themselves apart from the A'Toro, they now called themselves Wa'Moto, for the fire of the spirit, and they build the first houses and gardens here on the Migongo. Angha'Teru encouraged them to cultivate the skills of their minds again and soon the Wa'Moto achieved a very close connection to the raw life force of Great Mwako, conjoined with Kijani's power to create and destroy, which they perceived as a great and wise fire dragon, our dehar Hadithi. The Wa'Moto built the nayati for him and with his help, and a lot of work, they achieved all the great things you have seen here. So here we are, still growing, still learning, still evolving, forever pursuing our dreams."

"I see," Thorgyn said, "and then some of you returned to the A'Toro?"

"Yes," Karun said, "we sent two emissaries, believing the elders would see reason, once they were confronted with our achievements. But again they did not listen. Instead they scorned the Wa'Moto and drove them away, so they would not corrupt their hara with new and dangerous ideas. And nohar dared to follow them when they left." Hierat shrugged. "And now, hearing what you have told us about them, I doubt that things have changed much over the years."

"So what do you think we should do?" Marach asked. "We do have to go back eventually. And we can't simply keep our mouths shut and continue as before!"

"You don't necessarily have to go," Hierat objected. "I am sure that Angha'Teru would let you stay here, if you wanted to."

"And achieve what?" Thorgyn demanded. Then he caught himself, "Sorry, Hierat, that was rude. Your invitation to stay and let them all rot back there is quite tempting actually, and we do appreciate your generosity. But quite a few of the younger hara back home are restless and discontent with their eventless lives. And if we did not at least try to convince hara that we can and need to change things, I would always feel that we have taken the easy way out."

"But think of them," Marach reminded him, "what cowards they were! Do you really believe anyhar would listen to us now, just because we bring a few strange seeds and plants?"

"Given time they will! When they see that we were right about the *shetani*, they will have to give us some credit about the other things we say."

"I still don't think they'll just lap it up. They are way too scared of the elders and they have not seen all of this here with their own eyes like we have. And as Karun pointed out, the elders would claim that we are the ones telling lies."

Thorgyn threw his arms into the air. "Damn it, Marach, you are just like them with your eternal doubt," he flared. "Use your imagination! So what if the elders try to drive us away? We will simply set up our own house and garden a little way away from the settlement and drop hints about that to the right hara. I bet you they'll come and gawk. And once they see, who in their right mind would turn their backs on more solid and comfortable houses and plantations or even just improved healing arts?"

"I love you, Thor," Marach laughed. "Listening to you, I think we might actually do it! And if it does not work after all, well then we can still come back here."

A few days before they intended to depart, well equipped with material and knowledge, which they had collected during their stay, Thorgyn and Marach were invited to a festival in honour of the great fire dragon Hadithi. At sunset, they accompanied Hierat's people to the nayati. Laughing and chattering hara, in festive garb, streamed through the gates and the great entrance hall to the back of the building where they entered a hallway leading deep into the mountain itself.

They could hear the faint throbbing of drums becoming louder as they followed down the lava corridors, until finally they spilled out onto a gallery, which overlooked a huge cave. It was illumined by hundreds of torches set into mounts on the walls and columns. Here the pounding of the drums was so loud that it made every fibre of one's body pulse along with the intricate rhythms.

Undulating ribbons of melody wove through thick clouds of incense waving lazily over the crowd of dancers below. Small *siderae*, some of which were waiting on the gallery, were carrying hara up and down and along the walls of the cave to half-round protrusions like nests, many of which were occupied with pairs or small groups of hara enjoying intoxicants or taking aruna.

Karun pointed to the middle of the cavern, where a set of stairs led up to a dais. "That's the Samaran with his favourites up there," he said. The tribe's leader lounged languidly in a mass of cushions watching the dancers. His skin was black, as was his hair. Several other hara lounged close to him, enjoying whatever pleasures the elixir buds or each other's bodies would offer. Marach was surprised; he had expected something a lot more formal.

"Come on, let's join the fun," Hierat prompted. Most of their group had already descended into the crowd, and once they reached the cave's floor a sensual mix of sweat, incense and perfumes washed over them.

Thorgyn grinned at Marach, his body already bouncing and twisting to the music. Hara were dragging them into the mass of writhing bodies. The uninhibited flow and release of ecstatic energy was like nothing they had ever experienced back in the A'Toro settlement, not even at the festivals, when the hienama called the spirit of Kijani into himself and spoke in the tongues of the jungle. Soon both of them were completely immersed in the rising tide of magic the Wa'Moto wove around them. Ritual formalities were not needed here. The dance itself was the invocation of Hadithi into all hara present.

Marach lost himself in the flow and ebb of the trance. He wanted to burn up in it, become one with it, to treasure it forever.

Come to me, Marach! A touch of dark velvet brushed against his mind along with a sense of heat much stronger than that of the flames inside him. Like a moth he was pulled to the source of that heat, making his way through the bouncing and writhing hara, towards the middle of the hall, and after what seemed an eternity he found himself in front of the steps that were leading up to the dais. *Come on up!*

Marach ascended the stairs as if caught in a dream. It must have been Angha'Teru calling him. His mind was still whirling with the dance and his body was slick with sweat. His leather skirt clung to his legs, rubbing his skin sensually. He discovered Thorgyn on the stairs close by, a smile on his lips. Together they climbed the rest of the steps and bowed before the Samaran.

The leader's lithe body was propped up on one elbow. His skin was so black it almost looked blue, and raven hair flowed over his bare shoulders and onto the pillows like a sheet of silk. A long slit skirt made from dark red lizard skin covered his lower body and heavy gold bracelets and anklets adorned his limbs, while a large ruby ring glowed on one of his long slim fingers, no doubt an insignia of office. White teeth flashed at them in a smile, as he invited them to sit with a fluid motion of his hand. Some of his hara slid aside to make room, watching the newcomers curiously from behind half-closed eyelids. Marach sensed great dignity in this dark and sinuous creature who did not need any formality to command respect.

When they were seated, Angha'Teru appraised them each with deep amber eyes. Eventually he flowed into a sitting position looking at a har next to them. "Shield us, Shan!" he ordered. The har stood up and raised his hands, concentrating for a moment. When he brought his arms back down the noise around them suddenly diminished into a low ebbing and flowing hiss like waves breaking on the shore of an ocean.

"Thank you, that's better. We can talk now." Angha'Teru nodded. Bowing, Shan sat down again.

"Welcome to Kayamoto, A'Toro hunters," the hienama said. He took a draught from one of the buds. His hand made a sweeping gesture of invitation over the bud. "Partake of whatever delight you wish."

"Thank you, Samaran," Thorgyn inclined his head. "But no offence meant, we have had our share down there, and I would love to actually understand what you have to say to us."

Angha'Teru laughed. "Very well, then." He leaned back into the cushions. "It is a pleasant surprise to see two A'Toro setting out to seek what lies beyond your hunting grounds. What was it you hoped to find in the heart of the Kijani?"

"We wanted to find out whether the old legends of the *shetani* that our elders had been telling us were true," Thorgyn replied. "We did not believe so, and we did not think it was right that hara live in fear of something that does not exist. It cripples their senses and keeps them from coming into their own power. "

"Ah yes, I know of those legends." Angha'Teru nodded, "So, did you find your *shetani?*"

Marach involuntarily thought of how the Wa'Moto had found him, he suppressed a grin at his first impression of them. "It has become clear to us as soon as we were told of the Wa'Moto's history by Hierat and his hara, that the *shetani* are not our demons, but those of the A'Toro elders alone. For all their claim of leading a tribe of hunters, they have never learned to be hunters themselves. They are the prey of their own shadows. Their deepest fears stalk their souls and keep them and their tribe weak and small."

"Yes," Angha'Teru agreed smiling. "That is a pretty astute deduction, I would say."

Somehow it was odd to have this conversation in the middle of this churning whirlpool of ecstasy, Marach thought, but the mental shield and the Samaran's presence were creating an island of stillness around them. It reminded him of the fires at the settlement creating the sacred circle, which kept the predators of the night at bay.

"It has come to my attention what you are planning to do," Angha'Teru continued. "This will not be an easy task, as you have already been told. But it is a good one and I am glad that finally the time seems to be right, of which your presence here is proof. You can count on the Wa'Moto's assistance and protection if the need arises. We will give you the means to contact us swiftly."

Thorgyn bowed as well as possible sitting in the cushions. "Thank you for your generosity, Samaran."

Marach

"I will have none of that. You have earned our respect and friendship by following your dreams. And I will give you something more to aid you on your quest. Come to me, both of you."

He reached for their hands and pulled them close. His breath erupted like lava on their faces. Suddenly the unrestrained force of the festival's churning energy crashed over and through them like a tidal wave and swept their spirits up through the mountain into the night sky.

The Great Hostling Kijani spread out below them, his burning heart pulsing with life. On fiery wings they raced towards the peak of Mwako and with a furious roar they plunged down deep into the red-hot furnace of his gaping maw.

The heat condensed around them and they found themselves on the edge of a lava lake. A flare shot up from its surface, curling in sinuous curves, flames spread out from it like fiery wings. Burning eyes watched them, laying bare their very souls. Words formed in their minds.

I am Hadithi, the flame of inspiration and master of all knowledge. Take this gift of awareness back to your origins. Let it be your guide, and your strength.

The dehar dipped one claw into the fluid fire of the lake and drew out a gleaming pearl, which he placed into Thorgyn and Marach's hands.

The world exploded and their spirits soared up as a blazing star. Within them they carried the power to fulfil their innermost desires. Nothing was impossible.

The mountain shook, hot streams of the earth's blood flowed into the cauldron of creation and Hadithi danced under the stars, the essence of dreams come to life through the mastery of true will.

refugium

Daniela Ritter

My dark blue silken robe drops silently onto the stony ground. The cool wind chills my pale flesh, feeling pleasant on my sensitive skin. I am all alone up here, just as I need to be tonight.

It is dark, but the rough pebbles and the mountain pool catch the sparse light and sparkle softly, as if they were made from pure silver.

I squat down and test the water's temperature with my fingertips. It still bears a light hint of the sunlight which warmed it during the day. Should be comfortable enough.

Slowly I lower myself into the pool. It is shallow, and the streamlet which feeds it has polished the stone over the years. Right when I found it, I chose it as my personal ritual bath tub.

I close my eyes while I try to find the exact space where I have lain so often, where the stone almost feels shaped for the sole purpose to support my body. When I slide into place, to where I cannot drown even when I doze off, I sigh, relieved.

Now it is time to welcome Him. My head rolls back and I open my eyes. The full moon hangs above me like a huge silver disc. My heart beats forcefully, almost painfully, as if it has caught sight of a long lost lover. And indeed, the moon and I are in a close relationship.

I take a deep breath to calm myself. He is here. Everything is all right.

My pulse slows down. It needs to. I need to relax. I smile at my patron and wait for the pain to come.

The first wave of ache is the worst because it always takes me by surprise. I gasp, unable to ignore the pain for the moment. But then I look up at the moon and concentrate on Him.

He is waiting for me.

I feel dizzy. My chin drops onto my chest. I watch my own blood float away, twirling in the water, down the stream that leaves the pool. It looks almost black. Beautiful.

I hear myself muffle a groan of agony, but I am already on my way out of my body. I see the moon's reflection in the water. He soaks up my soul. I allow him to do it. I fade.

It was not long after inception that I had to learn that I am different from other hara.

Wraeththu caught me in the early years. I guess I had called for them subconsciously. Adolescence bored me. My family bored me. The world bored me. I was one of those youngsters who were looking for an exciting thrill, just to escape the arms of dying humanity for a while.

Like many in the old days, my inception was brutal and dirty. Of course I had tried to fight the strangers who had literally dragged me from the streets. I had been looking for danger, but I had wanted to face it on my terms.

So much for that.

When I woke up, they called me Sapphire, for my eyes had taken on the gemstone's colour. When I walked in the sunlight, even my black hair shimmered with a shade of blue.

My tribe was Unneah. They had only recently split from the even wilder Uigenna and thus were not that different, yet. I tried to adapt as quickly as I could, as I understood that my survival depended on it.

I was not shocked about my new gender, but it bothered me. Nobody had asked me if I wanted to merge visually with the female side I had not even suspected I had.

The experience of aruna made up for my troubles quickly, though. Everyone in our group was a piece of candy that needed to be tried. Oh, how sweet they were, spicy even.

Our leader, named Cyron, was a fierce fighter, but he was also good at organizing. He not only taught the newly incepted how to defend themselves, but protected us from the occasional human bandits. He also had a perfect understanding of the group and our resources.

Times were hard, but we did quite well.

Within two weeks, I found myself as an accepted member of the group. When I had been a boy, I had been interested in plants.

The knowledge of which ones were edible came in handy now.

My fellow hara admired that ability and they often sought my company to learn from me. Until the fourth week, that is.

Twenty-eight days after my inception I was in a hell of a mood. One of my friends, a har with eyes like an owl's, who had renamed himself Ash, had asked me about a weed he had picked up somewhere along the road. I cannot remember the answer I snarled at him now, but it had been enough to upset him so much that he would not talk to me all day.

The next few hours it all became worse. I hissed at anyhar who was unlucky enough to come too close. Then again, I had moments in which I hid in a dark corner and wept for no reason.

The longer it lasted, the more it scared me. I had no idea what was going on with me. I only knew that I had not seen the worst of it yet.

In the evening it became too much to bear. I sat around the fire with the others, like I usually did. We were chatting casually at first, talking about how much food we had collected or how the weather might be tomorrow. Then someone brought up my strange behaviour.

I tried to act as if I did not hear them, but more and more hara started making jokes about me. When somehar suggested that I might be a werewolf and aggressive because there was a full moon that night, I exploded.

"Fuck you!" I screamed at the top of my voice. It was enough to silence everyone with surprise. I looked into a lot of widened eyes and sulky faces. Usually I was patient and calm. Nohar had ever heard me yell until then.

Before anyhar recovered, I jumped up and ran into the corner of our dwelling that I called my own. I drew the improvised curtains, which provided a little privacy, around my sleeping place and cried silently.

That was the last they saw of me for a while.

Later, they told me they'd only started to worry about me the following evening. I had not shown up all day. Usually I was not a har who was mad at others for a long time, so they decided to check on me.

Ash, who pulled back the curtains, screamed in terror. He found me lying under a thin blanket, which was soaked with blood. So were my pants, he discovered.

Immediately he knelt down beside me and checked if I was still alive. My pulse was weak, but I was breathing normally.

My group was clueless about what had happened, but they dutifully cleaned me up and left somehar to watch over me.

It took a full week for me to regain consciousness.

When I opened my eyes, I was confused about where I was. I felt that this place was not where I had been just a minute ago – although I was lying in my own bed. Right then, Ash opened the curtains and smiled when he found me awake.

"Among the living again, Sapphire?"

I blinked. "What do you mean?" I tried to sit up, but the world blackened before my eyes. So I lay down again and took a deep breath. I felt unusually tired and dizzy. "What happened?" I demanded warily.

My friend coughed softly, as if he did not know how to tell me. "Well, you... Uhm..." When young hara have no idea how to deal with a critical situation, they make jokes. So he grinned. "Congratulations, Sapphire! You've become a grown woman now!"

Again I tried to sit up, more carefully now. I felt something tight around my waist and upper legs. When I lifted my blanket, I saw a bandage. "What the...?" With a frown I looked back up at my friend. "What do you mean by 'grown woman'?"

He raised his hands as if I was about to jump at him and he had to defend himself. "Hey, I'm just bullshitting you, okay? When we found you a week ago you seemed to have, uhm... bled. I mean... you were *mad* that night. And we all know aruna is relaxing. But as you didn't want to take one of us with you... What did you *do* to yourself, Sapphire? The guys are making jokes about razor-sharp fingernails. You don't have those, do you?"

I stared at him blankly. The words had shaken me. This conversation went somewhere I did not want to go. I did not want to talk about what might have happened, for I knew damn well that I had not *done* anything that could cause such bleeding.

"Just..." My voice was not more than a dry rasp. "Just... drop the subject, okay? I'll be careful from now on."

Satisfied, Ash nodded. "Good. I wouldn't want to lose you because you did something idiotic. By the way, supper is ready.

You look like you need something to eat."

I smiled weakly. "Good. I'm starving!"

After my friend left me, I pulled my blanket tight around my shoulders and tried to warm myself. I felt cold. That injury had not been my fault. Something had... just happened.

Our leader had told us that sometimes inceptions failed, in one way or another. Some hara died during althaia. Some shortly after.

And some hara were even reborn as freaks.

I folded my hands and prayed silently that what I had experienced was nothing more than a late, but final althaia adjustment.

Of course I heard a lot of jokes around the fire that night, but they were different than they'd sounded before. I could hear the relief between the harsh words. There was little knowledge of harish medicine in those days, and all they could have done for me was pray. Luckily it had not taken more to keep me alive.

When everyhar's attention returned to more trivial topics, my thoughts went back to what had happened to me. What exactly *had* happened? I dreaded the explanation, but I had to know. Blankly, I stared into the flames and tried hard to remember, while I absently ate some of the soup my fellow hara had made me.

A few moments of concentration later, pictures came up before my inner eye. I was lying under my blanket. I was weeping, frustrated, angry, sad. And scared.

Suddenly a painful stab went through my lower body. I immediately fell silent. My hands went beneath my blanket in the dark, but they found no knife that might have caused the cut I felt so clearly.

Then there was another stab. More intense now, so much, that I groaned in agony. Something was wrong with me. I sensed it. I had to get up quickly, run to the others, ask them for help.

But I had hardly even gotten on my feet when my knees gave way under the spreading pains and heat. I realised whatever it was, had only just begun and I panicked. I tried to call for help, but all that left my throat was a miserable cry because I hurt so badly.

What terrified me most was that I felt hot moisture beneath my thighs, which had nothing to do with aruna. I smelt blood.

I was sure that I was dying. And I could do nothing to prevent it. Shortly after, I was too weak to move at all. I must have fallen asleep.

And then I remembered... walking.

A dream. I'd had a dream!

Now that I focused on the memory of myself setting one foot in front of the other, it all came back willingly.

The place I had seen had not been a shadowy memory of the city we lived in. Instead I found myself in a beautiful palace. It seemed that night had fallen over the place, for the light was of a deep, dark blue. The corridors I walked were wide and the walls were made of glass or ivory. Maybe a mixture of the two. They emitted a soft, white glow.

The ground beneath my feet was smooth and a little cold, but not unpleasant. I saw that it was a walkway, and that to left and right of me there flowed crystal clear streams, silently whispering.

It was a beautiful sight, and a terrific architectural fantasy. Indoor rivers!

Indoors?

Driven by a sudden impulse I looked up. The corridor had no roof. And in the night sky, huge and pale as ever, the moon hung above me.

I shivered. I had the strange feeling that I was being watched. I bit my lower lip and tried to swallow my anxiety.

"Hey... moon... Did you just... talk to me?"

Ash shook me so hard that I immediately lost focus on my dream. "Hey! Wakey-wakey! You've slept enough!" he joked.

I sighed. He had demanded my attention at the worst possible moment. But then I knew I'd remembered all that I could of that dream, anyway.

"I still feel tired," I explained. "I must have lost a lot of blood."

Ash nodded. "B-movie quality. Okay, let's get you to bed, shall we?"

I thankfully accepted his hand.

When we walked, my legs still felt extremely weak. Twice I would have collapsed, had Ash not held me. When I lay down on my bed, I did not even manage to say good night to him before I fell asleep.

During the next week my strength slowly came back. I felt better every day, but I still slept a lot. So Cyron gave me tasks that required little movement or heavy lifting.

I was happy to be of use for our group again, even if most of what I did was only identifying edibles and cooking. One day they brought me a dead dove. The bird had been lazy and curious and had not sensed any danger from the tall figure that had ventured closer with an old baseball bat.

The impact had broken nearly every bone in the poor animal, but I had enough time to take it neatly apart. The soup I made from it was delicious.

Soon I was out hunting again, together with the others. I was back to my old self and had found a new kind of joy in life – the one you learn to feel when you've had a near death experience. I lived, laughed and loved, and I was happy.

While I was enjoying myself I almost forgot about what I had gone through. However, that changed, when some days later our group decided to spend the night on the roof of the highest, still intact building around.

The day had been very warm and dusk had not cooled the air. We stood at the balustrade and watched the last pale blue on the horizon turn dark.

A few hara started singing and clapping their hands. Everyhar jumped up and danced like it was the last night of their lives – except me.

The song reminded me of my earlier, human days. I suddenly remembered my family and my friends who I had lost. I strayed away from the others to cry my tears in silence.

It did not take Ash long to follow me. I heard him come, but I did not feel like turning to him. "Sapphire... are you okay?" he asked carefully.

I sighed. "Yeah, it's nothing. It's just... Nah, I don't even know where it came from."

Ash chuckled. "Werewolf-time again?"

I went cold. I looked up to the sky and... there it was. The moon. Big and bright. Full moon. Fearfully I held my breath. Would it happen again?

Ash came closer and put a hand on my shoulder. "Hey, I'm sorry. I was just kidding." He smiled carefully. But then he said something that finally killed all of the calm I had left. "You have

183

been kind of bitchy today, though..."

Suddenly furious, I slapped his hand from my shoulder. "I don't need this! I'm going to bed!"

Ash shrugged helplessly. "Well, okay. But call me, if you need help."

My answer was just a snort.

Overwhelmed by the strong need to flee, I dashed in silence past the others and retreated to my bed. Quickly I closed the curtains with shaking hands. Suddenly my skin felt so itchy, that I wanted to scratch it all from my body.

"Calm down, Sapphire," I told myself. "It's all right. It's okay. It won't happen tonight." I rummaged through my stuff until I found a warm blanket I'd intended to save for the winter nights.

My instincts took over. I felt cold sweat on my forehead. If I managed to clasp my thighs together tightly, maybe I would not lose as much blood as last time?

I snuggled deep into the winter blanket, conjuring the illusion of safety. My breath went shallow, and I forced it deeper into my lungs. Although hidden deep in the blanket's folds, my hands were already ice cold.

The first pain struck my belly. I started crying. "Please don't," I mumbled in panic. "I don't want to die!" The torture became worse and I rolled over, trying to quench the pain by moving around. It had no effect at all.

Still I did not want to call the others. I did not want them to see me that way, in agony, in pain, in the shame of being even more female than the average har.

Muffling my cries of pain, I wondered if my blanket was enough to catch all the blood I could already feel escaping my body.

My last thought was a trivial one: How the hell would I get the stains out of my favourite jeans?

Then I lost consciousness.

I took a deep breath. My lungs were filled with a scent so exotic, it made me open my eyes at once. I found myself surrounded by thick mist, which hid everything farther away than my bare feet.

I was standing on a glassy walkway again. Mist curled beneath my soles. I saw that I wore nothing but a white kilt.

I felt uncomfortable and folded my arms around me. It was not that I was cold. Even the moisture in the air was reviving and the dim, bluish twilight was beautiful. I just didn't like not knowing where I was and how I'd got there.

At least the pain was gone.

Soon I'd had enough of standing around and waiting. As I could not see anything, I strained my ears to discern a hint of where I might go. I held my breath.

There was something. The distant whisper of a fountain. Quickly I held out my hands so that I would not crash into anything that might block my way and then began carefully following the sound.

While I was walking around this eerie place, the feeling of being watched returned. Instinctively I looked up and found the moon back in the sky.

I frowned. How could I see it so clearly when everything else was hidden in the mist? It was like nature's laws were bent in this place.

"You think that's funny, right?" I growled at the moon, which I decided to be guilty of my current situation. "You're mocking me even in my dreams, you rotten source of my worst experiences!"

No, I am not.

I froze. I had not expected an actual answer. Still, I had heard it clearly enough in my mind.

"So..." I ventured carefully, my voice a little hoarse, "what's the point of this?"

The mist in front of me dissolved so I could see the fountain I had already heard. And in front of it I could make out the silhouette of a har.

That clearly was an invitation – and it scared the crap out of me.

Of course our group had already experimented with the magic that Wraeththu had given us, but with little success. Some of us had managed mind touch, though. Yet the har I saw, even from this distance, radiated an aura rich in power and magic. I could feel my skin tingling. He was a grandmaster. A shaman. A priest. Something like that.

I saw his body shift as he stretched out his arms. Right then, from one moment to the other, my fear was gone, as if it had never existed. I did not think about that fact, though. Curiosity dominated my mind.

Confidently I walked forward, details emerging from the mist before me.

I noticed the stranger was taller than me. His clothes were merely the thinnest silk; you could almost see through them. They floated around his body, as if in a breeze which I could not feel.

On his forehead he wore a beautiful tiara with a silver crescent symbol. Beneath it, his eyes were intense. They were large and deep, hidden beneath long lashes, and emanated a soft violet light.

Not for one moment did I wonder why his skin was blue. I just accepted his appearance as it was, enticed by his beauty and the strength he radiated.

I stood right before him, and he looked down upon me with a friendly expression.

I want you to know that I mean you no harm. I will always be there when you call for me, moon-child.

He spoke to me without moving his lips. I heard his voice clearly inside my head, and this seemed natural.

"Who are you?" I asked. I still could not take my eyes from him.

I am the dehar Lunil.

Dehar. Deity-har. A Wraeththu god. Of course! What else could he be? I smiled.

There are hara who need you because my brother has not yet grown up.

A slight hint of worry darkened Lunil's eyes for a moment. I wanted to know what he meant and who those hara he had spoken of were, but he had already dissolved into thin air, right in front of my eyes. And with him, everything else around me disappeared.

When I woke up as my usual self, I found myself alone again. Light from the outside penetrated the building's dirty windows and crept down my curtains, where it painted light dots of different sizes.

My eyelids were still heavy, and I did not even want to waste a thought on lifting my limbs. I wanted to go back to sleep, back to my dream. Back to where I had a guardian to watch over me.

Had I slept for a week again? I was in no mood to face the others, who I felt would mock me once more. First I had to get my own situation straight. I closed my eyes and thought about what I was going through.

After a few deep breaths I finally admitted it.

I menstruate. Or, from what I meanwhile know about my situation, my body regularly undergoes certain biochemical processes which mimic that female necessity.

Something must have gone wrong during my althaia. I imagine that the inception process usually breaks up the DNA, reads it out and then substitutes the parts that it finds too weak. After all, if it overwrote everything, we would all look the same.

So I guess after reading out my gender chromosomes, some part of the x-chromosome had been copied twice, so that a human female process was installed as part of my system.

Now every full moon I would bleed in a painful and unnatural procedure. As soon as my organs receive the order to throw out blood, they do not do so in the womanly way.

Striving for harish efficiency, my body loses about half of my blood pool before my automatic nervous system notices that my body is killing itself. The bleeding stops immediately, but by then I have already fainted from the blood loss.

Thank the Aghama my haematopoiesis is strong and fast enough to make up for it and save my life – if only barely. I suppose I also work some subconscious magic while I am sleeping to accelerate the process.

But all these thoughts are results of years of pondering on the subject. On that night, so many years ago, I just decided that I would have to live with my defect, just as if I had regular anaemia.

After a few more sessions of sleep, I finally managed to get up in the evening. I walked outside very slowly, stopping and leaning against a wall every time I felt dizzy. I noticed that I did not wear pants, but putting on clothes would have been to exhausting. The bandage I'd had put on would have to do.

When finally I reached the others, who were sitting around their fire already, I smiled and let myself drop to the ground, right where I stood, as I was tired from the short walk. "Guess who's back!" I said cheerfully.

Everyhar stopped speaking and turned their heads to look at me. I had expected a warm welcome, but instead I felt a sudden distance between us. I smiled carefully. "Yes... I survived. Again. Thanks for attending to my needs."

I received no answer.

Annoyed, I growled: "What's the matter? Shouldn't you be happy to see me?"

"You have to leave," Cyron said. Just like that.

"What?" I cried out. "I... I didn't do anything!"

He snorted. "You are... different. From all we know about Wraeththu, you could be infected with some kind of contagious virus."

I stared at him blankly for a minute before I found my voice again. "It's not that, and you know it!" I searched for Ash among the group, but my friend averted his eyes. "Ash, come on!" I demanded. "Help me out here!" But he simply ignored me.

I was disappointed and hurt. How could they do this to me?

Suddenly I knew. "I remind you of your female side, and that scares you, right? You're afraid of what I am!" Again, no answer.

Our leader did not pick up the subject either. "Tomorrow night you will leave. We'll give you food and water for your journey, and then you will walk as far from us as possible."

"Alone?" I screeched, as a terrible realisation hit me. "Next full moon I will probably faint again, and then I will be totally helpless for a week! If an ill-willed har or a human comes my way..."

Cyron just cut me off. "You will leave."

Meanwhile Ash had gotten to his feet. He bent down to me to pick me up. I was grateful because I wanted to be anywhere else now, but I felt too weak to walk on my own.

"You will come with me, won't you?" I asked Ash as he carried me back to my bed.

He sighed silently. "I'm sorry, Sapphire."

I found him not even worth the insult I wanted to throw at him.

At first, life alone was not so bad. I roamed the streets of lost cities and the woodland that had become lush since humanity's decrease in numbers.

As usual, I had no problems finding something to eat, and as long as I kept to small streams, I would not run out of water, either.

I often thought of the night before I left my tribe. How my fellow hara had looked at me! *Humans* had no place in this world any more. But I was har, after all! Just like them - mostly.

I was walking through the dark part of a forest now. Birds chirped joyfully in the trees, and the air smelled of summer. I, on the other hand, was so annoyed that I picked up pebbles or twigs and threw them at random bushes and trees. It helped release the anger.

Even the moon had left me during the first days of my journey. Of course its cycle was no mystery to me, but it was just fitting that even my so-called guardian left me on my own.

I decided that it must have been a regular dream. Probably I had wanted to see the moon in a more positive way and as something special and good. Not as something painful and disturbing. So, of course I would have dreamed of a beautiful moon god protecting me.

How pathetic.

But as pathetic as it was, I caught myself thinking of Lunil more often, as the moon began to grow again. I had to find a place where I could lie undisturbed for a week, or where there were hara willing to take care of me.

Sitting in a clearing at night, I nervously rolled the small branch I used as a calendar in my hands. I had placed a little carving on it at the new moon. The flames of my fire lit the wood with a menacing dance of shadows. I had less than a week now until the moon would be full.

I cleared my throat and looked up to the bright light, which was almost a circle now. "So... Lunil... If you really protect me... I need you now, okay? Show me where to go!"

There was no sound but the song of the crickets. What had I expected? Words in my head, like in my dream?

I curled up on the ground, trying to stay warm. Something had to happen. Soon.

The hint where to go actually came faster than I had expected. A day later, while I was walking among the trees in no special direction, I suddenly heard a twig snap.

I turned my head, expecting a wild boar in the worst case, but instead I had found a forest spirit. Or so I thought at first.

A har stood between the trees to the left of me. He had long, shining hair and wore an expensive looking robe of green silk, which reminded me of my guardian. His intelligent eyes were watching me with interest.

"Have you lost your way?" His voice was an enticing melody.

I relaxed and smiled at him. "Kind of... My name is Sapphire, lonesome wanderer."

The beautiful har came closer. "Eliyah har Gelaming," he introduced himself.

"Gelaming?" I asked. "I have never heard of you."

Eliyah smiled, which made his eyes shine like diamonds. "We show up right when it's time to do so. We are Wraeththu's guardians. We help tribes develop, so that they can reach their full potential."

Excitement made me wring my hands. "You do? Oh, thank god!"

Eliyah blinked confused.

I coughed softly. "I mean... I'm sorry for rushing, but I really need help."

"Are you being followed by your enemies?"

I shook my head. "No. I need... medical help."

Before he even asked me what was wrong, Eliyah took my elbow and began to lead me away. "My tribe has set up a camp two miles in this direction. Why don't you tell me what's wrong with you while we are walking? Then we can take care of you right away when we arrive!"

Eliyah was a little taller than me. I clung gratefully to his arm, which seemed strong and promised me any support I would need. I did not even wonder what a seemingly unarmed har was doing all alone in the woods. Something inside me told me that I could trust him entirely.

"It is... hard to explain."

"Please try," he said patiently. "Health science among Wraeththu is still young, but the Gelaming have already made great progress."

If they could not help me, who could, then?

I took a deep breath. "I... bleed every full moon."

"Bleed?" Eliyah repeated, politely asking for more detail.

So I sighed. "Yes. You know, like... a woman. Just that it's so much that I lose consciousness."

Instinctively, I prepared for being laughed at, but Eliyah just nodded. "Since when has this happened?"

I shrugged, a little embarrassed. "Right from the start. I guess something must have gone wrong when my body adapted Wraeththu genes."

"Sounds like it," Eliyah replied thoughtfully.

We walked for a while in silence. Meanwhile I could agree to the birds' chirping. Knowing someone would help me was enough to make me feel joy again. At least for some deceiving moments.

"Our scientists will be very interested in your problem, Sapphire," Eliyah mused. "We have only seen a few failed inceptions who lived."

I stopped right where I stood. "What do you mean, 'failed'? Except for my little problem I am entirely har!"

Eliyah let go of my arm and stared at me. The comfort in his look was gone. Instead I found something I could only describe as cold arrogance. "You failed, Sapphire. You get only one try to absorb Wraeththu as a whole. If you cannot take in our DNA, you will never be a complete har."

I gasped. "You... you said you would heal me!"

Eliyah smiled and finally looked ugly doing so. "I said that we would take care of you. We can provide you with support and dressings, which you are likely to need, and help you to lead the rest of your life as comfortably as possible. But there is nothing we can do to correct failures. Wraeththu has rejected you, and you must learn to live with that. But the Gelaming also have great psychologists, who..."

Eliyah had turned away with a cry of pain. I was so furious that I had thrown the remaining pebble in my hand directly at him – and hit him in the eye.

Suddenly I wanted nothing more than to get away from that lying bastard. I ran like I never had before. I was well aware that I crushed branches beneath my feet and stomped so loudly that it would be easy to follow the noise I made, but I couldn't help it.

I don't know how far I ran, but when I began to feel as exhausted as I did after a bleeding, I sank down the trunk of a tree and gasped for air.

Stinking Gelaming jerk, I thought, hoping that I had blinded him forever. It surprised me that someone could be even ruder to me than my former group members. If all Gelaming were like that, I was not eager to meet the rest of them. I just hoped that Eliyah would not bother following me.

It turned out that I was not worth the effort. I was alone in the forest again, but meanwhile completely lost. I had no idea where I was, because I had run from Eliyah so mindlessly. I spent days looking for the stream I had followed, but found no sign of it.

So my water supplies were shrinking, together with my courage. I had felt somewhat uncomfortable all day. From noon on I had been mumbling prayers nearly without any breaks. As soon as the sun sank, I would have a big, big problem.

"Come on, Lunil!" I begged. "Help me!"

But I got no help. All day I had told myself that there were only a few moments left until I discovered something that would help me. My hopes had decreased from the idea of hara appearing to assist me down to simply finding a natural cave where I could retreat.

But there was nothing. There was nothing but the trees.

My anxiety had made my hands ice cold. I had noticed that dusk was breaking, but I had denied it until I walked out onto a clearing and saw the moon in the still orange sky.

I had merely minutes now.

I panicked. There was no shelter anywhere. But once I lost consciousness, wolves or other predators might be attracted by the smell of fresh blood. There was only one way to avoid them getting to me.

Blind with fearful tears I climbed one of the trees, scratching my hands on the rough bark. When I could climb no further, I lowered myself between the branches. I threw my bag over a branch stump, so I could reach it, although with fingers that did not seem to be mine.

Then I tore strips of cloth from my shirt. I tied my ankles and one of my wrists to the branches, using my teeth for the latter, hoping that this would keep me from falling for the next few days.

While I was still wondering how to fix my second hand, the pains kicked in. If I had not prepared enough by now – well, bad luck, Sapphire.

Unlike the last time, I had no intention of muffling my cries. I yelled out the stings and tears inside of me, shouting my pain at the world. I hoped that this distraction might keep me from moving too much. The knots had to keep as tight as possible while I was awake. Soon I would have no control any more.

I think, during this night, my screams even terrified the crickets.

The soft mumble of running water woke me. Still I stubbornly kept my eyes shut. "If this is another fountain in a blue room, I'm going to kill somehar!" I grunted. I was in no mood for pseudo-spiritual fantasies that would not take me anywhere.

"I would ask you not to do that."

Great. A strange voice. And so sweet that it sounded Gelaming. Grumpily I opened my eyes.

I was lying on a large, white sofa, in the middle of a beautiful pond. Little blue, violet and white stars floated on its surface and gave off a soft glow. The pathetic prettiness of it made me want to puke.

I ignored the har sitting opposite me at first. I did not want to give him the impression that I was glad to see him. I felt betrayed and I wanted him to feel it.

When I finally looked at him, I grudgingly had to admit that his appearance was even more enticing than Eliyah's had been. His skin and his long, wavy hair were of a milky white. His eyes were nothing but pure violet radiance. He wore a dark blue robe with a hood, which was embroidered with silver moon symbols. Soft lips curled as he smiled at me.

"Welcome back, moon-child."

"Who the hell are you?" I demanded wildly. He did not seem to mind, though. His whole presence emitted a sense of serenity and calmness, which nothing ever could disturb.

"My name is Loreus. I am a hienama of this place. A priest. Master Lunil has sent me to teach you."

I snorted. "Well, I'm not good enough anymore for him to come in person, I see. What a caring god he is!"

Loreus took no offense. "We need to start slowly. You have never even reached out for agmara before. Lunil's presence while we are working would be overwhelming for you now."

I raised an eyebrow. "And what in the world makes you think that I would want to learn anything from you?"

Tilting his head slightly, Loreus answered: "Well, you are free to roam the temple on your own, if you wish to do so. But as you will spend a lot of hours here, we thought you might be interested to make use of that time."

Temple, I thought. That was why the atmosphere was so strange in this place. I cleared my throat. "That sounds as if you're making me your prisoner. And, by the way, this is not my actual self, okay? This is just a dream!"

"It is not," Loreus corrected patiently. "Loraylah is a place that cannot be entered by a physical body. But your soul is drawn here every full moon. You do not sleep, Sapphire. You undergo an out-of-body experience."

I blinked slowly, unable to believe what he was trying to tell me. "And... why is that?"

"Because," Loreus explained, hesitating for a moment, "every time you bleed you are very close to death. And while your body is healing, your spirit is free to go where it wants to."

Shivering, I pulled up my knees and laid my arms around them. He told the truth. I knew it. "But... why this place?" I asked quietly.

Loreus put a hand on my knee. "The moon is what makes you rise from your physical body. Your soul is eager to learn its mysteries."

Moon-child, Lunil had called me when we had met. Now I understood that I was indeed one of his. It sounded right. It felt right. I heard my soul sigh with relief.

Slowly, I nodded. "Teach me," I whispered.

Pain is what knocks me out of my body, and this time it was also pain that brought me back.

Before I could hear or see anything, I felt every muscle in my body ache. The cold, hard form of the branches pressed into my flesh. One ankle hurt more than the other, as the cloth that had held it in place had also cut through the skin during the last week.

I felt like a wreck, even more than usual.

Sighing through my nose, I craned my neck to keep my head from hanging and opened my eyes.

I saw two bright, golden-brown discs directly in front of me. For a moment I wondered since when the planet had two suns, but then they suddenly darted away.

I heard someone gasp. "You are alive!"

So somehar had found me. Fighting a pounding headache, I took a look at my company. It was a human boy.

I guessed that he was about sixteen years old. He had really beautiful brown eyes and short, brown hair. His whole appearance was even somewhat androgynous, so I might have surmised he was har – if he had not been fat.

He was nearly two times my weight, and the branch on which he stood creaked in protest.

"Barely," I rasped.

He swallowed. "Well, I thought with all the blood and you looking so... dead..."

My hand reached for my bag, where I kept a knife with which I could cut myself loose, but I could not find it. Then I saw that it was hanging over the boy's shoulder.

"You tried to rob me!" I said with disbelief.

He frowned. "I did not! I thought you wouldn't need your things anymore!"

I wanted to throw a ghastly remark at him, but blackness spread in my view. Gasping, I carefully lowered myself back into the hanging position.

"Are you... okay?" the boy asked carefully.

"Do I *look* okay?" I snarled, trying to stay conscious. But lowering my head did not help a lot.

At first, there was the sound of water. I frowned. Was I already back at the temple? No, I was not. The light penetrating my eyelids was too bright.

I noticed that I felt cold. And wet. And that I was lying on the ground. Moaning, I opened my eyes.

The boy was at my side, concentrating on something I could not see. But in the next moment I felt wet cloth touching my naked thighs.

"Whoa!" I sat up quickly, but fell back again, as my hurting muscles refused to work. "What the hell do you think you're doing?"

The boy smiled shyly. "Helping you, Tiahaar."

My heart raced while I was staring at him. I was not ashamed of being naked, but one of the first things a newly-incepted har learns is that no human must ever learn our secret. And this boy had just... well, watered the flower.

Slowly my brain started working like it should. "Wait a minute... did you say 'har'?"

The boy nodded. "'Tiahaar' is a polite way to address another har. Don't you use that word in your tribe?"

I blinked several times. "You are... telling me, that you are Wraeththu? *You?*"

His cheeks flushed with embarrassment. "I... kind of am. Yes."

I could not help but stare at his belly. Even his cheeks were puffy. "A failure, hmm?" I asked.

The painful look he cast at me made me flinch. "I'm sorry. I didn't mean to offend you... Tiahaar."

A fat har! I shook my head and carefully sat up again. "You got me off that tree?" I asked lightly, trying to change the subject.

He nodded. "I always have a long rope with me. You never know when you might need it. I knotted it around your chest and lowered you down. I am strong like a regular har, you know..."

I bit my lip. "Thank you. I really appreciate that. What's your name?"

"Julee," he said shyly.

He seemed nice, and he was the first har who had helped me selflessly. After all, he neither knew me, nor could he tell if I could reward him for his services. He could have taken my belongings and left while I'd been sleeping, but he hadn't.

Warming to him a little more, I smiled. "I'm Sapphire."

He met my gaze only for a second. "I'll try to get the stains out of your pants. But I'm afraid it might not be possible..." He looked at me from the corner of his eye. "What hurt you?"

I sighed. The sooner he knew, the better. "I'm a failure, too. I bleed every month."

Julee's eyes widened when he understood. "You mean like..?"

I nodded. "Just a little more... extreme."

"That's why you look so pale," he concluded.

I yawned loudly. As usual, I had not fully recovered yet. "I'm sorry."

Julee smiled. "Don't be. Sleep it off, I'll watch over you."

While I sank back to sleep, a thought came into my mind. A round face like Julee's is called moon-face.

My new friend kept his promise. I woke up at a fire with him by my side. He had a small cauldron, which now hung over the fire, containing a simple mushroom soup.

It turned out that I had not been far from the water I had been looking for, only that I had not found it, distracted by my worries.

Julee knew the forest better than I did, for he'd been living there for months.

We talked until dawn, including little breaks when I fell asleep again. He was very patient with me.

I learned his story: He had been incepted by a group of wild Uigenna, which had suited him at that time. I could not really believe it, but the gentle creature beside me had been rough and tough and without any mercy for those weaker than him.

But a few days after he had woken from althaia, he started putting on weight. He didn't know what caused it, only that no diet would work. His fellow hara, who had respected him at first, started making jokes and worse. Julee had been so desperate that, while trying to lose his fat, he once had nearly starved to death.

It had not had any effect. His miscoded genes had decided to store the energy a har needs in the old-fashioned human way.

Julee had gathered what he could and had run from his tribe. Since then he had been living in the forest and thinking about what to do with his life.

"And then you showed up," he finished his story.

"My condolences," I said with a smile.

Two days later I felt strong enough to walk with him. He guided me safely to his dwelling.

"So there *are* natural caves here!" I exclaimed with disbelief. "But *Lunil* makes me sleep in a tree instead!"

Julee piled up some leaves in an orderly fashion so that they could serve as a cushion for me. "Who is Lunil?"

My cheeks flushed. "He... When I sleep, I dream."

Julee blinked. "Don't we all?"

I shook my head. "No, I mean, I... go somewhere else. Somewhere spiritual. I enter the realm of the moon dehar - a god." I laughed and tried to let it sound like a joke.

But Julee didn't laugh with me. "Really? Tell me about it!"

Hesitantly I started. "It's a temple full of water and light. There's a priest – a hienama - who teaches me. Well, it's not really that interesting. It's mostly about meditation and energy and self-knowledge and... stuff."

Julee smiled and reached out his hand for me. "Energy? Like this?" Suddenly his palm seemed to radiate heat, which made my skin tingle. I gasped, but he laughed.

"God, thank you! I thought I was going mad when I noticed that there *was* something." Julee beamed and took a few twigs together to form a broom, with which he cleaned out the cave.

I watched him uncomfortably. I had done similar exercises with Loreus the last time I visited. Calling for the energy of Agmara, feeling it, making it stream from my hands. It had worked fine, but after all, I had been in the spiritual realm then.

The realisation that it worked in the mundane world just as efficiently made me shiver. It scared me that apparently all hara were able to wield powers unknown.

When Julee was done with cleaning, I did not actually see a difference from how the cave had been before, but he was so proud of it that I didn't comment.

He made a little fire and hung his cauldron over it. He poured into it water from an old plastic bottle and then added a handful of fresh herbs. "Tea will be ready soon," he said. "And when it's served, I want you to tell me all about the moon god's temple!"

I smiled, still a little insecure about whether he was making fun of me or not. But when I thought about it, it was just too obvious. He felt his power, but did not know what to do with it. With me, it was the other way around.

Of course! I grinned, as a thought struck me. "Only if we practice together afterwards!"

"Sure thing!" The way Julee sat opposite of me, smiling happily, he reminded me of a peaceful Buddha.

It took me hours to tell him everything. And the more I spoke, the more details I recalled.

Julee did not even seem to blink while his ears soaked up every bit of information I could provide. Not once did he find what I told him ridiculous. So I gratefully drank my tea, which kept my throat moist, and taught him as much as I could.

Getting more excited with every word, after a while Julee could no longer sit still. He got up and started walking around.

I laughed at him. "Hey, what are you doing? You're ruining my speech!"

Chuckling nervously, Julee sat down by my side. "I'm sorry."

I hadn't noticed his anxiety before; the way he now avoided my eyes made me worry about him. "What's the matter with you, Julee?"

He flinched. "I..." he started slowly, then determinedly shook his head. "Can't tell you."

"Yes, you can." I demanded. "You look awful!"

"I know," he whispered.

"Oh for Lunil's sake!" I swore. "I didn't mean *that*, and you know it!"

Julee bit his lip. "It's just that... You know..." He looked at me quickly and I did my best to look strict. It worked.

Surrendering to me, he sighed. "Hara don't like the way I look, Sapphire. It has been... long. Months. And you're so beautiful. I resisted the temptation until now, but the more time I spend with you..."

"Oh!" I exclaimed hoarsely. "You need aruna."

Shyly, Julee nodded. "And I know I can't demand that of you, with my appearance and all. Just... give me some more minutes. I'll take a cold bath or something. I'll get it back under control. Please don't leave me! You're my only friend!"

I smiled. He was being so sweet. Desperate maybe, but still so very polite. I wondered about the unspoken suggestion.

"Well," I said thoughtfully, "we actually *could* have aruna."

Julee gasped. "But... aren't you repelled by my looks?"

"Aren't you repelled by the mouth that spits blood?" I shot back.

"No, not at all!" he said, way too quickly. We both looked at each other in silence for a moment, then we laughed.

"Okay," I chuckled. "We both lied."

"Yeah," he admitted with a smile. "But I guess we both don't have much of a choice here, either."

I stretched out my arms and pulled him close. "You know, I think I can live with that."

His essence was the sweetest thing I had ever tasted. When we shared breath, caramel and honey washed over my tongue. I saw visions of milky rivers and smelled vanilla. But what touched me most was the hint of the feelings he had for me.

A dirty, half-dead stranger I had been, and he, with a heart full of kindness, had instantly taken care of me. Then, while we had spent time talking, he had started to like me – and more than that. I saw small, tender flowers, emotions, still young, but growing.

I was intrigued by his inner beauty, so when I noticed that the flowers were threatened by a cold winter storm of shame, I did my best to kiss the wind away.

Julee blushed and looked shyly into my eyes. Somehow we had lost our clothes, and I could feel his warm, big body pressing against mine. I did not mind at all.

Encouragingly, I kissed him on the cheek. "When I first saw you," I whispered, "I mistook your eyes for suns. Let us unite sun and moon."

Aruna is something entirely different if you do it for more than simple fun. Julee had surprised me with his love, but I was even more surprised by the fact that I had not wanted to back off for a second.

It was like my heart opened up during our union. Nothing else mattered. I even found his weight on my body oddly comforting. He was a heavy anchor which held me in this world, so that my soul would not float away again and miss this precious moment.

The skies and heavens opened just for us and left us quivering with endless joy and satisfaction.

"I love you!" Julee blurted out, still gasping for air. I could not have answered him in a better way than with another very intimate sharing of breath.

That night, we went to another clearing to watch the stars. Holding each other's hands, we sat silently side by side for a while, enjoying the kind of company we had both longed for.

"Sapphire!" Julee suddenly said, as if a new thought had struck him.

"What is it?" I laid my head against his shoulder.

"Did you realise that we could hide forever?" he asked.

I frowned. "Not that I want to go anywhere right now, but what gets you so excited about this?"

"The moon, Sapphire!" Julee answered impatiently. "Didn't you say that it was capable of veiling things that shall remain unseen?"

I raised my head and shrugged. "That's what Loreus told me. So what?"

"I mean that we don't have to hide in this forest forever. We can find someplace really nice, and then you'll just have to hide it from other hara with your magic skills."

I thought about his suggestion. "Well, I'm not quite *that* good yet. I've only known for a few hours that my magic works outside the spiritual realms."

Julee shrugged. "So just ask for training in that aspect next time. I don't think Lunil will mind. And besides... Maybe there are others, too."

"Others?" I repeated.

Excited, Julee nodded. "Other misfits like us. Hara with, I don't know, four arms or something."

I grinned at that mental picture, but he sure got his point across.

Julee and I had both experienced harsh words from hara. He had even been beaten and kicked. What would they have done to him once they had learned to use magic? And what if there were other failed inceptions out there who had no access to that power, who could not defend themselves?

"Sapphire?" Julee asked, trying to get a reaction from me.

"It's a lovely dream," I said, making Julee frown. I hugged him close. "But my dreams seem to leak into reality. Let's do it."

The next morning we set off to the mountains, right after I had reminded Julee that I would need a lot of sleeping breaks. As I had anticipated, he did not mind.

Both of us could carry our entire possessions in bags we hung over our shoulders. "Time to find some promised land!" I joked, and Julee laughed, pushing me onward.

Following the stream from the forest to make sure we did not run out of water, we climbed higher into the mountains. Julee said that he had once come from that direction and that there was an abandoned village in the valley on the other side. That was where he'd found the cauldron. He hadn't wanted to stay there, as he'd been afraid it could attract more plunderers.

When I first saw the village, I fell in love with it instantly. The houses were half ruined, but surrounded by mountains and hills on every side, safely hidden. If you did not know the village existed, it was almost impossible to find. So I figured Julee's worry had been unnecessary.

We spent the days until the next full moon working on making one of the houses our home. We cleared up, fixed the roof and made ourselves a cosy bed.

When I bled, Julee took loving care of me. When I awoke from it, he surprised me with a complete collection of household items he'd collected.

We named our village Serenity, after the biggest lake on the moon, and I spoke the spells I had just learned from Loreus to hide it from the kind of hara who had chosen to cast us out. I also cast magic that was meant to attract our fellow misfits.

Many have found a home here since. There is Risen, whose eyes went blind during althaia. He had shown up all scratched and wounded.

Next door lives Arynn, who was reborn ouana only. But Lunil sent him Honeysuckle, who had mutated into being solely soume.

Ellie lived here for a while and then disappeared, only to show up sixteen years later, telling us about the Kamagrian and that she was one of them.

There are forty-two of us. We all turned out to be infertile, but that does not matter. We are the last attempt of human genes to survive against Wraeththu domination and we are meant to die out.

The important thing is, that we have a chance to do so in dignity and as the close family we have become.

the river flows

Nerine Dorman

The *komando* returned at dawn, the horses lathered, their muzzles foam flecked. The men's eyes blazed with triumph despite the exhaustion that greyed their complexions. Sara and I shared glances before we hurried to the kitchen. They'd be wanting coffee, a hot breakfast. Jasper and the boys went out to meet them, and no doubt listen in on the conversation.

"Eva, do you think they caught the *bandiete*?" Sara asked.

I got down the good coffee mugs – the ones the madam had brought with her from the city all those years ago. "Most likely. They were leading an extra horse. It wasn't there when they rode out last night."

"I didn't even notice the horse."

I shrugged. To be honest, I hadn't considered the extra mount until Sara had asked, but it had been there, a chestnut with a shaggy mane like sun-bleached wheat. Which suggested that some unfortunate soul no longer had a need for it, and since everyone in the *komando* was accounted for...

I had my opportunity to overhear some of the conversation when I served the coffee.

"Strange-looking fellow," Marthinus Theunissen said. "He's not going to be stealing anything from anyone again in a hurry. Got a good shot at him."

"Hit him too," Gert Koetser added. "Like a stray dog. Fell like rotten skins when he went over the edge."

"Do you think he'll survive the fall?" our master, Timotheus Moolenaar, asked.

"Even if he survived the gunshot, he's probably broken his neck." Koetser held out his mug as I poured him more coffee.

"Good riddance. There was something not right about that one. Looked like a bit of a *moffie*, if you asked me. We don't need those types round here."

"*Ja, ja*," came the chorus of agreements.

I had long since learned to school my expression to be as neutral as possible, though I longed to give vent to the anger that simmered beneath my apparently untroubled façade. The servants' opinions were not required in this household. To our masters we were invisible, and it was best we remained that way.

Throughout this exchange Sias sat still, his face ashen beneath the grime from the night's drama. His jacket was too large for his shoulders and he clasped his mug with white-knuckled hands, seemingly unaware that he spilled coffee on his trousers. The boy should never have gone out with his father, but who was I to gainsay my employer?

As the day wore on, everything about it was wrong. While the *dominee* would berate us for being superstitious, I knew better. A swallow flew into the window pane in the kitchen. I went outside to investigate the feathery thump and found the broken body limp on the ground. A shiver crawled down my spine. Later, one of the sows gave birth but rolled over her litter, killing all but one. Sara broke a milk jug—one of the antique ones that the madam had loved. Timotheus would be furious when he found out. And he *would* find out. Our master was aware of every small detail on his farm.

Sias came to me during the late afternoon, while I was taking down the washing from the line. He hovered nearby for quite some time, watching me, but he was hesitant.

"Auntie Eva?"

"*Ja*, Siasie?" I was the only one who was allowed to call him by the diminutive form of his name. "Please come hold the laundry basket for me."

Meek as a puppy he stepped forward with the basket. This was his invitation to speak. His father would have flown into a rage if he saw his son demeaning himself with so-called women's work, but I suspected that was part of the reason why Sias insisted on helping me when he had half the chance.

"If you saw someone do a great wrong, and you couldn't stop them, what would you do?" Sias glanced about, clearly worried that his father was in the vicinity. He had more of his mother in him, the same delicate bone structure, high cheekbones and clear, mint green eyes – like tourmaline in a certain light. However, where her hair had plunged to the small of her back as a fall of honeyed gold, his was curled in lazy, burnished copper waves to his shoulders. Sias was the opposite of his father, a blunt man, in all senses of the word.

"Your father's still napping. Speak your mind."

The youth sucked in a deep breath. "If someone were innocent, would you stand by and watch them die?"

I gazed at him. "This is about what happened with the *komando*."

He didn't move, not so much as a nod or a twitch. This was men's business. If I got involved, voiced an opinion... My livelihood was at stake. Sias was poised on the cusp of adulthood. It would not be right for me to influence him one way or the other.

"What do *you* think is the right thing?" I asked him.

That was all that was needed to be said.

That evening, Sias's place at the long table in the dining room was conspicuously empty.

"Where is that boy?" Timotheus asked.

Sara and I both froze, she in the act of dishing up for the man and I struggling to keep hold of the pot from which we were serving. The grandfather clock in the corner ticked out hollow seconds.

Mercifully the others had long since returned to their farms. Only Sara and I saw to our employer's needs.

Timotheus glared at us as if we would be able to conjure up his son, and the fingers of his right hand curled around the knife. I thought again about the swallow that had flown into the window that morning, the droplets of blood I'd seen on the small feathers of its head.

To think that I had once loved the man. Or rather, I only thought I'd loved him.

A soft tapping at the shutters roused me and at first I lay back in the bedding, breathing deeply and trying to gain my bearings. There had been a dream, of a waterfall, and a person with red *disas* twined in his dark hair.

As much as I strived to recall other details, the images faded, sliced by the slivers of moonlight that cut into my room.

Tap, tap.

Tap, tap.

A shadow moved. Someone was outside my window. My heart squeezed in alarm and I rose, my shawl pulled close to me. I padded to the window. "Who's there?"

"It's me, Auntie Eva: Sias. I need your help." Muted urgency laced his words.

My hands trembling, I undid the latch and pushed open one of the shutters. The cricket chorus sawed away and the scent of gardenias wafted in.

Sias clambered into my room, collapsed in a boneless heap on my floor then scrambled to his feet. The moonlight that filtered through the *syringas* highlighted the grubbiness of his face, but his eyes gleamed.

He gripped my wrists and almost shook me, so great was the tension in him. "You must come with me. Now. Bring your medicine bag."

"You've rescued the *bandiet?*" I gaped at him.

"He's not a *bandiet*. He's a traveller."

"How do you know? He could be lying to you," I said.

"I just know, Auntie. *Please.*"

How could I deny him? Though Sias was no son of mine, he was the closest I'd ever get to having one. I'd guided him into the world and had picked up where his mother, Hestia, had left off. Hers had been a difficult pregnancy, and my suspicions that she was not long for this world had proven correct within days. Delicate. Ethereal. Why she'd agreed to marry a man of the stone and earth, and move all the way out here into the barren north-west I couldn't say.

Timotheus had never remarried.

Mute with worry, I shouldered my medicine bag and followed Sias. The misshapen moon hung near the west, and we made our way past the farmstead and up into the *kloof* behind the dwellings. Here the wagon trees grew in dense stands and small creatures rustled unseen in the undergrowth.

"Where are we going?" I asked Sias, once I was certain we wouldn't be overheard.

"To the old foresters' lookout. It's the only place I could think to put him."

I marvelled at this young man while we walked. He had single-handedly gone back up the valley, retrieved the injured stranger and brought him all the way here in a day. I knew of that hellish slot where the *bandiet* had fallen. Sias was braver than the men who'd hunted the supposed thief. No one should have survived that fall.

The lookout had been built more than a hundred years ago and had a clear view of the entire valley. From here the few lights of the farmstead gleamed like sleepy cats' eyes but it was the star-dusted sky that enraptured. Old myths told of how one of my ancestors had strewn a handful of ash across the sky to form the Milky Way—a path to guide travellers on their journey to the gods. Or so my mother had taught me. The night was breathless, chill despite it being late summer, and the insects sawed away even here.

"Will he be warm?" I asked.

"I made a bed of *slangbos*," he said.

He turned out to be younger than I expected, a youth of about sixteen or seventeen, around Sias's age. But there was something more to him, more than human. *Other.* A cold finger of premonition jabbed at me. I had no word for the stranger. Sias watched me in silence as I examined the youth, whose skin made mine prickle. From what I could tell, no bones had been broken, but he was covered in bruises and lacerations. More worrying, however, was the gunshot wound. If the injury had been to his extremities, I might have rated his chances of survival as fair. But he'd taken the shot to his abdomen and I lacked the expertise to deal with such a wound. Unless we were able to take him to the nearest town, such wounds usually soured, and a painful death would only find him after he'd lingered for days.

Sias had been quick thinking, and had created a pressure bandage, but this had soaked through and the stranger had lost much blood. I did what I could, but it would not be enough, and Sias picked up on my concern.

"Do you think...?" Sias said.

"I'm surprised he's even lasted so long. Even if we could get him to Clanwilliam, I don't think they'd be able to help him." I didn't have to add that the stranger clearly had no way of paying for any medical help. As it stood, it might not be the best idea to take someone so strange to the god-fearing folks in that small town. "The best I can do is make him comfortable and give him something for the pain."

The stranger's skin was cold and clammy, his face knotted in agony. His eyes darted beneath the lids and we watched him in silence. What an unbearable waste of beauty – for he *was* beautiful, a willowy young thing with dark blond hair that if not sweat-soaked and snarled might hang in a shaggy fall past his shoulders. A fine, patrician nose, a high brow with narrow chin yet well-defined cheekbones. What was this creature doing all the way out here, so far away from the city in which he so clearly belonged?

What are you?

His clothes were of a good make too, not the kind of stuff found in this place. None of the fabric appeared homespun, though I doubt that mattered for the unfortunate soul now. The bloodstains would never come out.

"Is there nothing I can do?" Sias clutched at his arms.

"You've done more than the poor bastard deserved. Be glad that he won't die alone."

"I don't want him to die."

I sighed. "Look, that is a gut wound. If we were to be truly merciful, we'd give him something to help him cut the ties with his mortal body. Now."

"You will do no such thing." Sias bared his teeth at me.

What hold did this stranger have on Sias? Then again, the boy had forever brought orphaned or injured animals home. His compassion for those weaker than him knew no bounds. He would not make a good farmer.

I packed away my things and left out measures of painkillers and soporifics. "Give this to him if he awakens and the pain is too much or if he needs to sleep. Keep him warm. Make sure he has enough to drink, but don't let him gorge himself on liquids either."

"Help me take him to the waterfall," Sias asked of me.

I paused, my hand hovering over the strap of my medicine bag. "Why?" Prickles of unease scittered across my skin.

"*Please.*"

At first I thought it was Sias who'd wheezed the word but his face was turned to the stranger's. It was he who had spoken.

"He told me he wanted to go see the waterfall, the one where the *watermeid* is," Sias said, as if that was all explanation that we needed. "That's why he's here."

"In his condition? Are you mad? We'll kill him."

The stranger pulled himself up into a seated position, his face contorted in a terrible grimace. His eyes blazed into mine, seemingly possessed of an inner fire that matched the starlight. *Please.*

"It's an hour's walk," I said. "If you're healthy. If you're not..." That scramble near the end was trouble enough even if one were healthy.

"Auntie Eva, please help me do this thing. It *is* important," Sias pleaded.

I had never been able to refuse Sias anything.

Though he was weak, the stranger could walk, and Sias and I took turns to support him. Taym he said his name was, but refused to answer any questions about where he'd come from or what his plans were. We had to rest often, but with the moon so close to full, it was bright enough for us to keep to the path without any trouble.

Chittering bats swarmed above us once we entered the narrow river valley. The scent of Taym's blood was pungent, and I worried that the *strandwolf* would seek us out. I had seen their spoor recently and I was wary of the large brown beasts. They were growing bolder of late.

The climb up to the waterfall was another matter. Both Sias and I were weary by then, and Taym had enough of a challenge keeping upright, let alone dragging himself up the ravine.

"Why this obsession with the waterfall?" I asked once we paused by a particularly horrendous scramble. "We're going to kill him."

Taym hunched over, his breathing rapid, and Sias crouched next to him, one hand placed protectively on the youth's shoulder.

"The *watermeid* will help him," Sias said.

"It's a children's legend." My words lacked conviction, even as I uttered them.

"You know better than that," was all Sias said, occult wisdom in his eyes.

There had been that day when I had climbed up here. It had been *that* day. The one I tried to forget, when Timotheus had returned from the city with Hestia, newly wedded and bedded. Oh, I'd known the time would come. The knowledge had weighed heavily, with each stolen kiss or caress that had led up to this moment, that our pleasure would be limited. I had brought only temporary ease to a lonely man.

I'd come up to the waterfall on a whim, perhaps for the pleasant childhood memories of the times before my heart had been wrenched into a knot. The red *disas* had been flowering then too, but I had not tried to pick them. The cascading water had soothed me, the mist cooling my tear-stung cheeks. I had fallen asleep in a patch of sun, lulled into slumber by the voice of the mountain stream and the ghost of an alien, ululating singer on the edges of my hearing.

I did not argue with Sias. I could not. I had never told anyone how I'd felt upon waking that day, light and empty, as if someone had siphoned off all my hurt and left a blessing in my heart instead. One did not question the nature of such gifts, and much existed beneath the sun, moon and stars that we had little knowledge of.

We waited until Taym's breathing was a little easier, then we continued to claw our way to the top, the falls rushing louder the higher we climbed.

The falls weren't very large, and cascaded in a series of terraces. The rock face was covered in vegetation, and gnarled wild almonds leaned over in hectic angles. A fine mist dampened us as we made the youth comfortable on a shelf of stone. Though it was dark, the water held an eerie luminescence that sparked in the eddies. The small hairs on my arms and neck prickled, and I couldn't help but glance over my shoulder, convinced that we were being watched.

"What now?" I asked Sias.

"We wait," he said.

"They say the *watermeid* lives in the grotto behind the falls." I pointed to the small alcove sheathed by water.

Taym stirred and turned his head in the direction I indicated, but then fell back, obviously exhausted. It must gall him to have come this far only to lack the power to explore further, I thought. But how deep did the root of his interest plunge? The mystery dangled at my fingertips, but I was reluctant to reach further.

My unease grew and the soughing of the wind in the wild almonds was restless, a stirring of some agitated spirit boiling on the edges of awareness. We were not wanted here. No. *I* was not wanted.

"We must go," I said when the pressure grew unbearable. "If it is the stranger's will to stay here, so be it. He won't survive the trip down in any case."

"I'll stay," Sias replied.

"*Siasie.*"

He shook his head and I noted how his hand gripped Taym's.

Another fearful gust rattled the branches, bringing with it icy tongues of fear that licked at my exposed flesh. I staggered to unsteady feet, my limbs shaking.

"I'll be fine," Sias said. "I understand."

I did not ask what he understood, but I caught that same fey gleam in his eyes I'd seen in Hestia's eyes on the day she'd birthed the boy.

I fled, and not once did I look back.

If Timotheus had suspicions about his son's whereabouts, he did not say anything to us. Granted, his mood was fouler than usual, and we trod about him on eggshells. I had enough work to keep my hands busy, but my mind was awhirl. Had the stranger survived the night? The mere fact that Sias hadn't returned suggested as much, and I had to wonder at the injured lad's stamina. Anyone else would have been delirious, raving.

Taym had something of the spirit world about him. I knew – the same way I knew when death was due to visit the farmstead or when a woman was with child. Any caulbearer worth his or her salt would understand these truths implicitly, as much as the *dominee* liked to rave about our older beliefs. Then I considered the rumours that had reached us from the city, of some of the troubles that had begun with young *skollies* who were roving in gangs like stray dogs. And I kept coming back to Taym. A woman might not have all the answers, but she could *feel* when events were connected and larger forces were shifting in the world. I could let them wash over me, and remain oblivious to the last, or I could learn to swim in stranger currents.

A commotion in the house during the late afternoon drew me

in from where I'd been weeding the herb garden. Men's voices raised in anger. The shattering of glass. My heart gave a small lurch as I dashed through the kitchen and into the hallway.

Sias sat half-crumpled against the stairs, a hand pressed against his jaw. A thin trickle of blood trailed down the side of his mouth. His father towered over him, his fist half-raised as if he'd lash out at him again.

"I'll ask you again, where have you been? Slinking off like some jackal in the night? Your bed has not been slept in!" Timotheus shouted.

My chest grew tight and I withdrew into the kitchen, shaking. The master's rages were legendary. Even if I possessed the strength of three men I'd still have thought twice of interceding on Sias's behalf. Better to keep out of sight and not draw Timotheus's wrath on myself.

Yet it killed me to hear the sounds of struggle, and the dull *thunk* of limbs thrashing. Judging by the thuds and muttered curses, Timotheus manhandled his son up the stairs. More crashes followed, and at this point I fled back outside.

Sara and I had laundry to take down, the evening meal to prepare. We worked without speaking beyond the necessary.

"Pass the thyme."

"Has the water boiled yet?"

Sara's eyes were startled whenever we traded glances, and I'm sure I looked just as frightened as she was. Jasper and some of the boys were busy out front, boarding up the windows to the young master's room. How much did Timotheus know? My concern was a black dog worrying at my bones to get at the marrow.

Supper was a strained affair, though our employer gave no indication that anything was amiss. We set a place for Sias too, but Timotheus said nothing about the youth joining him at the dinner table.

Only once he'd eaten did he beckon me over, and I complied immediately.

"Bring me a covered dish with food, as well as a jug of water for that child," he said without rancour.

This I did, and Timotheus took the food from me and went upstairs. I expected there to be a row, but there was only deathly silence.

That night I struggled to sleep. Such dreams that I had were of Taym and a pale being, who wore a garland of *disas*. The resonance with past dreams chilled me. *I have seen this being before, the one who sings.* They danced, entwined like snakes, coruscating vapours surrounding them. Their hair tangled like waterweeds in a gentle stream.

I lurched into a seated position, gasping for breath and my legs wound in the sheets. My skin was filmed with perspiration and the air in my room was thick with the lingering stench of carrion. A terrible sense of wrongness flooded me. I should not be seeking rest when I was the one who held pieces of the puzzle in my hands. Was the injured stranger alive? Had he passed on? Sias was trapped in his room. Jasper had been nothing if not thorough in reinforcing the only egress other than the door. Sias lacked the physical strength to break out of that prison. Who would check up on Taym now? That's if he was alive. Damn Timotheus and his heavy-handed approach.

So I dressed warmly, and took bread, fruit and water with me, armed only with a stout stick. I could be quiet if I had to. My ancestors had trodden these mountain paths long before the white man ever settled here. The only other sign of life was a *grysbok* I surprised when I passed the vineyard. The heath swallowed the small antelope as it bounded upslope on silent hooves. Aside from that, I was aware only of my own breathing, and my pulse, which seemed louder than usual.

Fear made me wary, and I paused so I could listen often. What if Timotheus expected me to go out in Sias's stead? What if he had me followed?

That was the chance I had to take. My ancestors would not rest if I did not establish whether the injured man had died. If he lived he might yet require help. What was the worst my employer would do to me? Beat me? Dismiss me? I could find new employment, but it would mean uprooting myself from everything that was familiar. I could return to the mission station where I'd been educated. Perhaps they might need a woman to look after the children there. Point was, I had options, even if I was reluctant to entertain them.

My path meandered along the river's course, dipped into patches where the *elegia* stood tall with their feathery fronds or threaded through thickets of wild almond. Even at night, I was at home here. This was the land of my ancestors, the place of my bones. White traces of guano gleamed on the cliffs above and betrayed where the kestrel made his nest. Faint spoor on the sandy banks were signs of the otter's passage; a small clump of crunched crab shells was all that remained of his dinner.

Taym was like these wild things. I could not stand by and see him hurt.

The last climb took me up a narrow *kloof.* This late in summer, most of the moss had dried, and crumbled beneath my fingers. Despite the relative coolness of the night, my housedress clung wetly to my armpits and the small of my back.

Apart from the ceaseless gush of water over stone, the entire area was suffused with stillness. As children, we'd come here, always in a group. The emerald pool at the base of the falls was just too tempting in the height of summer. The boys would perform somersaults into the deeper parts. The girls would hike up their skirts and paddle in the shallows. The water was always so icy cold that even during the hottest parts of the day one could only suffer to be submerged for a short while.

The *disas* were, predictably, out of reach, their red, angular petals standing in sharp contrast to their verdant surrounds. Hestia had once told me the story of the witch who had given the distant Hex River valley its name – a proud young farmer's daughter whose suitor had wished to pick the *disas* in order to win her hand. He'd tumbled to his death, and she, driven mad by her grief, had flung herself from the very same cliff. Some said her shade still haunted the region. They were ill-starred blooms.

Once again, I thought uncomfortably of my dreams, of the being with pale limbs and grasping arms. Was there a connection? Dreams were fluid, subtle shifting things impossible to pin down. Sometimes storytellers tried, but even their words were like the river. You could never lift the same water to your lips. Sias and I were intoxicated. We were drinking from the same cup and it was easy to see how beautiful, enigmatic Taym had bewitched him. How he'd bewitched me. A greater story was playing itself out, and I was privy only to frustrating snatches.

I fully expected to find a corpse when I arrived. Instead, I encountered the youth sitting up, bare-chested and cross-legged on the ledge that afforded him a view across the valley. The moonlight bathed his skin in a luminescence, like he had accidently stepped out of one of the stories of the fair folk that Hestia had told me.

"Thank you." His voice was clear, and had an odd, bell-like timbre to it.

"You're…"

The wound in his side was no more than a small knot of healed flesh, a scar weeks old rather than a day fresh. All the small hairs on my arms rose. The air around him seemed alive somehow, filled with small wriggles of turquoise fireflies that wisped in and out of sight. I blinked, and the illusion vanished.

"How…"

He rose in one smooth motion and stood to face me. "There are many things under the sun, moon and stars, dear Eva. And this is not for you to know." A chill stole over me.

I shuddered, then hugged my shawl closer to me. I had seen many strange things in my lifetime, but this youth's miraculous healing was not something I could explain. Did I want to know the truth?

"I brought you some things, in case you are hungry." I put down the basket and watched as he retrieved it. I didn't add my misgivings, that I'd thought I'd arrive to find a corpse chewed on by scavengers.

Judging by the way he tore into the bread and fruit, he was close to starving, and I marvelled at him, his delicate, almost feminine beauty, the smoothness of his skin.

"What are you doing in this part of the world? Are you lost?"

"No, not lost. I have come, seeking. I have found what I was looking for. Where is Sias? He said he'd return."

I shook my head. "He's unfortunately… Held up at the manor house. He sent me in his stead." How much could I tell Taym?

The youth cocked his head in much the same way a curious dog might watch a rabbit. "It's the father, isn't it? He said as much. He spoke highly of you, however."

"I'm flattered."

"You're not. You're embarrassed."

My face grew warm, and I was glad for my dark complexion and the moonlight. "You need to leave this place as soon as possible. It's not safe for you. If Master Moolenaar finds out that you're alive, he'll ride with his *komando* and finish what he started."

He laughed. "Is that so?" His scorn was obvious.

"Well, they got you the first time."

"A small misfortune on my part. I misjudged the hospitality of a very bitter man. I won't make that mistake again. His sons are safe." Taym gave a soft, derisive snort.

I didn't ask, and I wasn't sure I wanted to know. Instead I rose and plucked up the basket. "In that case, I must bid you goodbye, Taym. I am glad that you are well." Truth be told, my instincts were screaming at me to remove myself from his presence. There was an air of wildness about him; he frightened and fascinated me by equal measure, and I needed to opt for the emotion that would be better for my long-term survival. As much as a snake is a beautiful thing, it is also deadly, and I had that feeling around this youth.

"When will Sias come round?" He looked hopeful.

"I don't know. How did you..." My curiosity was getting the better of me. When I was little, my mother had warned me and my cousins not to go down to the river without an adult lest the *watermeid* got us. Legend had it that sometimes folks on their own would hear laughter by the falls, but when they investigated there would be no sign of any other person. Damn it! I needed to know what had happened here, before Taym slipped through my fingers like the river.

Taym gave a soft snort of amusement. "Dear *Griqua* woman. Be content. This is not for you, though I thank you for all that you have done." When last had I heard reference to my tribe spoken like that?

"*Why* are you here? What are you seeking?"

"Communion. Is that enough?" His smile was almost arrogant.

We stared at each other in silence until a sudden gust of wind shook the trees. It was time for me to go. Though the compulsion to turn and cast a last glance over my shoulder was strong, I resisted and clambered down the way I'd come.

The following day dawned brighter and hotter than the one before. Summer still had its stranglehold on the land despite the cooler nights. The cicadas shrieked in the gum trees early on, and flies swarmed by the dogs' water bowls.

Timotheus brought down Sias's uneaten dinner. A strong possibility existed that the boy might ignore his breakfast as well.

Sara and I traded worried glances but we said nothing to each other.

Even as the day wore on, and I polished, swept and dusted, my thoughts remained with Taym. Who was he that he possessed arcane knowledge? An old herb-man used to visit the mission station when I was little. He said the ancestors spoke to him in dreams and had taught him how to make poultices or herbal infusions to heal fevers and cure many ailments. Old Jan had even been called upon to set broken limbs and settle angry spirits. He'd mentioned a spirit that had spoken to him, that resided in the river by a pool so deep no one had ever touched the bottom.

Yet he had not possessed the knowledge or ability to miraculously heal gunshots to the gut seemingly overnight. A greater mystery had passed me by, and I'd let it go.

"Are you all right?" Sara asked. "You seem distant."

I resumed sweeping the front porch. Sara leaned out the dining room window, cloth in hand so it would appear that she was busy, should Timotheus pass us by.

"It's nothing. Slept badly, is all." I paused, lost in thought a while.

Then instead of indulging my fascination, I went on to polish the copperware. But even the astringent scent of the polish could not quite mask the carrion stench only I could smell.

By dinner time there was no change in the stalemate between father and son. Sias had not drunk nor eaten anything in just over a day, and my concern for the lad had me short of breath. Sara had the wisdom to bite her tongue, but that night, when we packed away the last of the dishes, we could hold our peace no longer.

"Go speak to the master," Sara said.

"It is no use." I shut the cupboard and leaned my forehead against the wood panel.

"If you won't, then I will." This was surprising.

I turned to face Sara. "You have a young family to take care of. You do not want to risk the master's ire. If anyone can deal with him, it's me. And I don't care if he dismisses me. I'll go find work at the Nieuwoudts." I didn't add that more than twenty-six years' service to the Moolenaar family was twenty-six years too many.

My words put Sara to rest, but I had to follow through with my promise.

Timotheus was in his study, and his only response to my tentative knock was a gruff, "Enter."

He made me stand for almost five minutes while he pored over documents spread out on his desk. An antique crystal tumbler of brandy was loosely clasped in one hand while he read, his lips moving silently. I counted the ticking of the cuckoo clock, and wished that the damned man would stop playing games with me.

Presently he looked up, his expression almost that of surprise to find me still standing there. "Yes?"

I sucked in a breath. "Master, about Sias…"

"He can damned well starve to death in there. *Now get!*" This last he roared.

I scurried out, and hated that the man could have such an effect on me. How he'd changed. There had been times when he'd been different, when *we'd* been different – but that man was gone, replaced by this implacable beast. As much as I racked my memories for the ghost of the young man I once loved, all I saw was this hulk, swollen with bitterness and sorrow.

I could leave. Any time I wanted to. I never did.

But my ancestors whispered.

The boy. Upstairs. Pale-faced and drawn out with hunger beyond mere bread and water.

Later, once I was certain that Timotheus had gone to bed, I slipped upstairs and pressed my face against Sias's door.

"Sias?" I murmured.

Not a sound, not so much as a whisper or the slide of sheets. The lad might even be dead. I cursed Taym in silence.

I made no pretence of caring about my work the following morning. Sara said nothing when I packed a small bundle – mainly dried fruit and a canister of diluted lemon cordial.

"I will be back before noon. Please see whether you can get the little master to eat. If Timotheus asks, tell him I've been called away to attend a birth at Driehoek."

Taym had haunted my dreams again and those too-knowing eyes had missed nothing. He held the key to unlock this mess, since he was the one who'd muddied the waters in the first place.

I all but ran along the paths, and barely paused, even when I had a bad fall scrambling up to the waterfall. Buntings called among the rocks by the pool but other than the rush of water, there was not a soul around. Disappointment bit hard. He must've departed already, and I almost cursed him for being a faithless creature. But then I discovered the small pile of his clothing, neatly folded by a big, flat rock at the water's edge.

"Taym!" I called.

My voice's echo was the only response.

Though I felt the fool, I spoke anyway. "Sias's father has him locked away. Because of you. I don't know what to do. My hands are tied."

I waited. Drank some water. The creeping sensation that I wasn't quite alone dragged through my skin until I shivered, unaccountably cold despite the balmy air.

A kestrel soared overhead, silhouetted against the sky. Graceful wings kited the bird as it described lazy circles, watchful for the smallest prey. I think that's what decided it for me. I left my bundle of food and drink and returned to the farmstead.

The dogs didn't bark. The only warning I had was Sara's gasp, and I looked up from where I was chopping the garlic to see Sara stand with her hands covering her mouth. Then I followed her horrified gaze to the apparition that stood by the back door. Taym opened his mouth but instead of speaking, he began to sing.

The words were unfamiliar, but the melody flowed up from my deepest memories, of that day by the waterfall. The kiss of mist. Heart's ease.

Sara sagged against the wall, and all sounds other than Taym's song grew dim. Even the clatter of the knife I dropped on the chopping board sounded dull.

I moved as if in a dream, where one doesn't question how or why, the edges of my reality soft as I made my way to Timotheus's study. The man slumped across his desk, saliva darkening the wood.

I liberated the keychain from Timotheus's pocket and climbed the stairs, all the time guided by the song that buoyed my limbs. The room's foetor made me gag at first – days' worth of stale piss and shit in the chamber pot. I almost faltered. No wonder Sias had managed to avoid eating. He hunched in the corner facing the door, an untouched plate of food at his feet.

"Can you walk?" I held out my hands.

His grip was stronger than I had expected, and I helped haul him to his feet. His eyes blazed with a feral light and Taym's song took on a triumphant tone.

"He's waiting for you downstairs."

Sias hugged me, hard, and I tried not to gag at the stench of him. Then he cat-footed down the stairs. By the time I reached the ground floor, the kitchen door had slammed shut and Sara gripped the edge of the table, unsteady on her feet and blinking owlishly.

"I don't know what's come over me," she said.

"You must have had a spell," I told her then hurried to my room. I would not finish preparing dinner this night.

What surprised me was how few my possessions really were, or rather how few were important enough for me to take with me. The stars were especially beautiful, and the ashy river of the Milky Way beckoned me with a new path to follow. An owl called out to its mate, who answered in the distance with a husky *huu-huu*.

I never did go look for work with the Nieuwoudts. A peculiar rootlessness took hold of me. I had to see what lay beyond the next rise or what nestled in the following valley. Besides, there was always a place at someone's hearth for a travelling herb-woman.

Six years passed before I saw Sias again, and by then I had a name for Taym and his kin. *Wraeththu*. Depending on who you spoke to, this word was a curse or a benediction. I smiled, held my peace, content in the knowledge that I'd been touched by their magic and released in some profound way.

A wagon track meanders through the Koue Bokkeveld on the way to the community of Ceres, and I was following this route on my way to Rietkuil. There is always a Rietkuil somewhere, just like there's always a Royal Hotel. The orange moon's gravid belly had just lifted over the rolling hills, yet the sky was that peculiar dusky violet presaging true night. Horses' hooves clattered and, wary of violence to a single woman alone on the road, I moved off the track to crouch behind a boulder and wait for the riders to overtake me.

The horses had fine, dished faces, small hooves coming down smartly on the gravel. Small bells had been entwined in their manes, but it wasn't so much the mounts that drew my attention but the riders. Five in total, young men of exquisite beauty; angels. They spoke and laughed among themselves, carefree. Like they'd ridden out of the pages of a children's tale and once they'd rounded the bend would vanish just as suddenly.

The one I thought was Sias halted his horse on the rise and looked back. His hair had grown out and flowed to his hips, luxurious and tied back at the sides in small braids twisted with leather bindings and ivory beads. But there was no mistaking the fine brow and the particular curve of the lips. For a moment I swear I saw Hestia's shadow.

He raised a hand, half in salute, then kneed his horse into a trot.

Their voices, raised in song, lingered for a while yet.

I smiled then resumed my journey, the music of the Wraeththu guiding my feet.

Glossary of African Terms:

Bandiet, bandiete – thieves, bandits.

Buchu – an aromatic herb that has medicinal properties.

Elegia – a tall, elegant type of bamboo-like reed with feathery clumps of leaflike branches.

Disa – *Disa uniflora*, otherwise known as the red disa, is an orchid with showy red flowers.

Dominee – a pastor or reverend in the Afrikaans, Protestant churches.

Griqua – an indigenous southern African tribe.

Grysbok – a kind of small, reddish-grey antelope.

Kloof – a narrow ravine.

Komando – a posse of riders, usually from the local landowners, responsible for security in an area.

Skollies – Ne'er do wells, thugs.

Slangbos – a sprawling springy, heath-type shrublet with grey foliage that can be used to make a mattress.

Strandwolf – brown hyena.

Watermeid – an old southern African myth about the "Karoo mermaid", a water spirit that inhabits bodies of water in the region's arid interior.

Maria J. Leel

When you walk in a forest it is not that which is above you that is important – it is that which is beneath...

I was born and raised in the dynastic territories of the Far East where ritual, protocol and tradition are valued above all things. There were strictures dictating our dress; how our faces were to be adorned; what we ate; what we drank; when it was that we should keep our eyes downcast and when it was permitted, expected even, that we should make eye contact; and finally when we could speak... but even then our utterances were limited to those phrases strictly outlined by protocol – any expression of original thought being utterly disallowed.

Despite all this I enjoyed an almost blissful childhood thanks in entirety to my hostling, Lian. Our home, a low-roofed house, stood on the edge of a lake, deep in a forest enclosed by razor-edged peaks. A beautiful and tranquil place where in winter the tundra swans and spoonbills flew in from the north in search of more temperate climes and stood thick along the shore. Spring brought the white cranes to perform their courtship dances, their wings spread wide, the long black-tipped feathers just touching whilst their necks snaked back and forth, sinuous and languid. The arrival of the red-rumped swallows, who returned each year to their nests under the eaves of our home, heralded the summer, whilst in autumn, when the birds left the lake, the maple leaves turned fiery red and the entire forest appeared ablaze. And all year round, high in the trees, the monkeys, macaques and gibbons sang and whooped.

When my father was at home, and entertaining his many business associates, Lian and I adhered to the codes laid down for consort and first son. More often than not my father's guests would exclaim, 'Tiahaar, such a beautiful home do you have! The very epitome of elegance and style. And such peace is there here, such tranquillity.' And graciously my father would bow and smile and give the prescribed answer, 'I owe it all to my consort and son, of course, for what house can be a home with no family to give it life?' Then Lian and I would keep our eyes modestly downcast and with equally modest smiles accept the meaningless compliments lavished upon us. Thanks to Lian's gentle training I seldom put a foot wrong and these tedious trials usually passed without incident. I hated to make a mistake because it would be Lian and not I who would face my father's wrath.

When my father was away from home - which was often, his business taking him far beyond the razor-edged mountains - Lian and I truly lived. We would abandon our heavy jewel-encrusted robes in favour of much simpler garments. Our faces we left unpainted and our hair, knotted only loosely, hung down our backs unencumbered and unadorned. Deep in the forest's leafy domain we spent our days, among the larch and the walnut, the aspen and the ash, the pine, the oak and the maple. We walked within our verdant cathedral, the trunks soaring above us whilst the sunlight drifted down in discreet slices between the branching canopy overhead. We lay among the fallen leaves intoxicated by the heady scent of the forest floor. On occasion we would swim in the lake itself, the waters clear and shockingly cold. Only the foulest weather would keep us indoors. The house hara, our servants, smiled indulgently and let us have our way. They never betrayed our actions to my father. Not only did they love Lian too well but, for them, as for us, this break with tradition was nothing short of a holiday.

Lian was, as custom dictated, a child bride and had borne me, his only son to date, within the first few months of his marriage. In truth he was closer to me in age and attitude as a brother rather than a parent. Some days he would look wistful. 'Not for you, Chenga. I would not wish this fate for you.' And I would hug him tightly and press kisses to his temple and cheek. But Lian was not often wistful, most days he was full of laughter and full of stories. His knowledge of the forest was phenomenal and from him I learned the name and use of every plant that sprang forth from the earth in that place. The gingko, with its fan-shaped leaves, to aid the memory and enhance the concentration; the wolfberry, bearer of ruby red fruits, which yielded a tonic good for clear sightedness; and the startlingly named devil's trumpet which, if used in only tiny amounts, could grant visions of unknown worlds. But of all the forest community it was the fungi that held my attention the most; the parasols, cups and brackets, the tubes, spheres and frilled lips – all coloured in strange, fleshy tones. I knew them to be neither plant nor animal but a unique form all of their own – but to me, the touch of them, the feel of them and sometimes even the smell of them reminded me of my own skin.

In the last year of my childhood we experienced an unseasonably wet spring. After another downpour the sun had finally come out and Lian and I ventured from the house. The rhododendrons and camellias were in full display and the recent rainfall seemed to magnify the colours of their blossoms; the magentas, cerises and corals; the crimsons, mauves and amethysts; the creams, the whites and the ivories. Their scents too were enhanced by the dampness, and so sharp were they that it almost stung to inhale. And the fungi were out in great profusion erupting from the soil, from fallen timber and from the tree trunks that surrounded us. I pulled at Lian's arm and entreated, "Tell me more about the fungi.'

Lian laughed and gently freed himself. 'Beloved, I have already told all I know. You know the name of every fungus here and what it may be used for. I have no more left to tell.'

"Yes, yes, I know. But what are they *saying?*"

Lian stopped in his tracks and looked at me sharply. "*Saying?*"

"Yes," I said impatiently, "they're always talking...

chattering and giggling. I want to know what about."

Lian shook his head in disbelief. "You're saying these mushrooms can talk?"

"Yes! They're always talking... well... no... today they're singing."

"*Singing?*"

"Yes, but I've never heard them do that before." A thought struck me - a sudden, ludicrous thought. "You mean you can't hear them?"

"No."

"Oh!"

Lian's lips twitched and he broke into a gale of laughter. "Nice one, Chenga. You really got me that time!" He bent forward, chortling, hands on knees and after a moment he raised his eyes to mine. Abruptly his laughter stopped. "You're serious?"

I nodded miserably, now convinced that I must be crazy. "Can no-one else hear them?" I whispered.

Lian took in a slow breath and began to shake his head. "Not that I can think... no... wait. Perhaps..."

"What?" I asked, clutching at him. "Who?"

My hostling sank down onto a fallen tree trunk and then rapidly stood up again – it was sopping wet. "Well," he mused, wiping ineffectually at his trouser seat, "you could ask Master Deshi-Tu."

I couldn't keep the scorn from my voice. "Master Deshi? The *human?*"

"Chenga," Lian chided, "It does not do to judge those who are different from us. Master Deshi is a wise man. He's forgotten more than you or I will ever know."

I dropped my gaze, abashed. "Do you think he will see us?"

Lian patted my cheek with a cool hand. "I think he might see *you.*"

I had heard rumours of Master Deshi for as long as I could talk, servant's gossip mainly – Master Deshi talked to snakes; Master Deshi lived among the treetops with the monkeys; Master Deshi was four hundred years old. This last I knew could not possibly be true. The longevity of a har is yet to be determined but I knew from my studies any human that reached their first century considered themselves extremely fortunate.

The next day Lian led me to the region of the forest where Master Deshi made his home. It lay a good way south from our house by the lake. "But why won't you introduce me?" I asked as I trotted along beside Lian. It was traditional after all. No son of a well-bred family would address a stranger without a formal introduction.

"Master Deshi pays little regard to our traditions," my hostling informed me. "He will expect you to make your request to him in person."

I quailed and, sensing it, Lian stopped and took me by the shoulders. "You're growing up, Chenga, not far off your feybraiha now. It's time you went out into the world a little. You need to stand on your own feet... particularly if we are to convince your father that an early marriage would not be to your advantage."

I looked at him for a moment and swallowed hard. Then I nodded and we walked on.

Lian led me to a clearing and came to a halt at the base of a gnarled old cork-oak tree. The trunk must have been about ten feet across and had a series of short branches spiralling up into the canopy. "Just one point of protocol," Lian said, gazing at me earnestly. "Be scrupulously polite and always refer to Master Deshi as Master Deshi-*Tu* until he gives you leave to do otherwise. I'll be waiting for you when you come back."

I looked around in confusion. "Where am I to go?"

Lian turned to the cork-oak and pointed a finger upwards. I chewed at my lip. The bit about Master Deshi living in the treetops was true, then.

Even though there had been no rain for several hours, the branches were still slick and slippery beneath my hands and feet. I climbed up perhaps a dozen feet or so and looked back at Lian.

My hostling nodded encouragingly, "Keep going," he called.

I turned my gaze upwards again and cork-screwed my way

up, round and around, climbing ever higher until close to the top I came to a bridge of twisted vines and woven timbers that led away to the crown of a neighbouring tree. I could perceive no other option but to step out onto the bridge and see where it led me. I began the crossing, placing my feet carefully upon the timbers and clutching at the vines tightly. I must have been at least sixty feet above the forest floor but what worried me more was that the entire damned structure *swayed*. The slightest breeze and the vines creaked and the mere shift of my weight from foot to foot set the bridge swinging wildly. With relief I reached the next tree but then I discovered another bridge, longer this time, leading further into the canopy. I must have travelled about half a mile along this aerial walkway and even at this height I found clusters of pinhead mushrooms and crowds of smoky-gilled parasols nestled in crevices and cracks in the bark. At last I came to Master Deshi-Tu's house; a wooden cabin perched high in the crown of a monstrous oak. I found a door of sorts and hesitantly knocked upon it.

A dry voice creaked from within. "Well, you've come this far, why don't you come on in?"

I pushed at the rough planks and they swung inwards. Doubtfully I took a step inside.

Three snub-nosed monkeys sat in the window opposite and regarded me with faint curiosity. Then one of the creatures turned to the others and said. "Be off with you. I must attend to this visitor." The other two monkeys showed me their teeth and then bounded away along a branch, chattering and screeching. Master Deshi-Tu left his window seat and padded across the floor to sit, straight-backed, on a folded rush mat.

Feeling utterly wrong footed I bowed deeply before him. "Master Deshi-Tu, I am Chenga, son of Lian."

He gestured vaguely at another rush mat. "Sit down why don't you? I can't be doing with you looming over me."

I sat down, cross-legged, and waited whilst Master Deshi-Tu appraised me with his bright and button-like eyes. His face intrigued me, used as I was to the smooth, unflawed, impeccably painted visages of my fellow hara; faces that, by and large, betrayed nothing; no flicker of emotion, no story of life. The mass of crinkles and wrinkles seemingly broadcast each and every thought. The tracery of lines and crenulations told of a long life full of meaning and experience. I could have studied him for hours and I was fully aware that I was staring rather rudely but as Master Deshi-Tu didn't seem to mind, neither did I.

Abruptly he cackled at me revealing soft pink gums where the front teeth were missing. "So... you're Lian's boy! I remember... he was a good pupil."

I blanched. I wasn't a *boy*. I was a *harling*. I tried not to let my reaction show. Perhaps he hadn't meant to be rude. "You taught my hostling?" I managed.

"Indeed." And now the conversation petered out. Master Deshi-Tu regarded me expectantly. Clearly the next move was to be mine.

I straightened my back and licked my lips. "Master Deshi-Tu," I began, "I wonder... I wonder if you would consider teaching me?"

The old man raised his eyebrows at me and cocked his head to one side. "And what, young master, do you believe you can learn from me?"

My eyes sought the floor as I felt my self-confidence slithering away. "My hostling has taught me all the plants of the forest..." I stammered.

"I'm sure."

"But Master Deshi-Tu I wish to learn more about the fungi..."

"You know all their names?"

"Yes."

"And their uses?"

"Yes..." I faltered.

"So I ask again, what do you believe you can learn from me?"

I paused. *This crazy little man living in the treetops with monkeys is going to think that I'm the one who is utterly crazy*, I thought. I drove my fingernails into my palm and forced myself to speak. "Why do the mushrooms sing?"

Master Deshi-Tu rocked back on his mat, let out a contented sigh and smiled. "Ahhhh! – Lian was right to send you to me. Hmmm... Hmmm... Hmmm... Indeed. Well,

Chenga, I think there is much you can learn from me and what is more I am willing to teach you." He rose to his feet and padded to the door. "We will begin tomorrow. I will meet you at the bottom of the cork-oak. Until then ponder this - *When you walk in a forest it is not that which is above you that is important – it is that which is beneath...* And we'll see what there is in that pretty little head of yours." He held open the door and I found myself dismissed. "And bring something good to eat with you," he shouted after me as I made my way onto the bridge.

And so that summer, when my father was away, my life fell into an easy routine. The mornings I would spend with Lian and the afternoons with Master Deshi-Tu.

Lian took up painting again. "I shall need something to occupy myself when you are grown up and gone."

From Master Deshi-Tu I learned that in every footstep a har or human takes upon a lawn, a field or on a forest floor there are contained some three hundred miles of fungal threads. These fuzzy, cobweb-like growths form a network or a fabric and these fungal fabrics run through the top few inches of virtually all landmasses that support life. The parasols, cups and brackets, the tubes, spheres and frilled lips I had so admired were the mere tip of the fungal iceberg and what occurred beneath the forest floor was vastly more significant than what occurred above.

Master Deshi-Tu would sit at the base of his cork-oak tree chewing on the spiced dumpling or sweetmeat that I had brought for him. "You know Chenga," he would say, his mouth half full, "humans and hara are mere animals and animals are more closely related to fungi than any other."

I struggled with this. To me humans and hara were as unalike as it was possible to be, let alone similar to animals... let alone similar to *mushrooms...* but I tried to keep an open mind.

Master Deshi-Tu placed a great deal of emphasis on my learning the walking meditation. "Chenga, stand with your spine upright, relax your shoulders and let your arms hang naturally. *Feel* your connection with the earth. Take small steps only. As you inhale, step forward with your left foot; as you exhale, step forward with your right foot. Let your gaze be focused gently on the ground before you... That's it... My child, imagine that each time you place one of your feet down, you kiss the earth through the sole of your foot... Yes... And that each time you pick up one of your feet, imagine a beautiful pink and white lotus blossom in the place your foot was."

We practised this every day with no thought of 'getting somewhere'. Our single purpose was to express our love for the earth and to create beauty with each step.

As autumn arrived I had mastered the walking meditation and was proficient with it both out in the forest and inside my own room; Master Deshi-Tu assured me it could be practised anywhere. I looked forward to the autumn with its increased rain as this encouraged the fungi to fruit in profusion and *surely*, I thought, *surely then I'll learn the secret of their singing*. But autumn also brought with it much frustration; my father was more often at home and brought with him a never-ending stream of guests. Time spent outside with either Lian or Master Deshi-Tu became annoyingly rare.

One snatched afternoon I sat with Master Deshi-Tu under his cork-oak tree. There was a fine, misting drizzle and we held thick leathery leaves over our heads to keep off the worst of it.

Master Deshi-Tu appraised me slowly. "You are not far off your feybraiha I think?"

"No indeed, Master Deshi-Tu," I agreed. "I'm told a month or two perhaps?"

"Good. Good... That's good." He chewed a little, a coconut confection today. "Chenga, you will soon be ready to learn to travel the threads... and then you'll understand the singing."

Excitement rushed through me like a hot wave. "Travel the threads? What does that mean?"

He paused for a moment and scratched his cheek. "It's complicated," he said, eventually. I suppressed a yelp of frustration. He held his hand up. "I know, I know... You want to know all about it *now*. So impatient – the young. But

Chenga, this you have to learn by *doing*. And you must be physically mature to do so. It's not safe for a growing body – human or har. But I promise you, as soon as your feybraiha is safely done... then. Then I will show you!" My disappointment must have been obvious because he cackled and prodded my shoulder with his fingers. "Impatient little monkey! But... I think, in acknowledgement of the progress you have already made and the proximity of your coming of age... Well, I think the time has come for you to address me as Master *Deshi*."

I smiled long at this. I was fully aware of the honour. "Thank you, Master Deshi."

My father's latest business conquest was a har by the name of Zu-Lee. Not from beyond the razor-edged mountains but, most unusually, from within our own province. A dynastic overlord, he lived in a palace on the southern edge of the territory. Over dinner I sneaked a few glances at him from under my dutifully lowered lashes. He was, I suppose, beautiful to look at with skin like lemon silk, his hair worn high on his head like a sheet of black satin but his eyes, like the highest quality jet from the far territories in the west, glittered in a way I did not like.

Lian and I, as ever, were dressed in our finery as the meal was served. Zu-Lee sat opposite my father, Lian and I to either side. I kept my gaze on my plate as protocol dictated but I could sense Zu-Lee studying me. As the first course was laid down before us and the servants departed the room, Zu-Lee spoke, "Well, Chenga. You're clearly a credit to your parents and growing into quite a beauty. You can't be far off your feybraiha?"

My father nearly exploded with sycophancy as he gushed, "Why yes indeed, my Lord. We believe Chenga will make his transition before the year is out. Lian has raised me a fine heir."

Still gazing at my plate I saw Lian perform the traditional half bow towards both my father and our guest.

Zu-Lee set down his knife and leaned his forearm on the table. "And Chenga, doubtless you shall follow custom and marry as soon as possible. With a face like yours you could certainly win the favour of a har of wealth and standing."

I could hear the leer in his voice and my good sense deserted me. I raised my eyes directly to his. "No indeed, Master Zu-Lee. I do not desire an early marriage. I wish to travel and to study." Horrified I managed to trap my tongue back between my teeth but not before I'd seen the mirrored expressions of rage reflected on both Zu-Lee and my father's countenances and heard a stifled moan of distress from my hostling. I was sent from the room in disgrace and ordered not to venture from my chamber.

Some hours later Lian visited me in my room. He was dressed in the heavy black canvas robes of the disgraced consort; my outburst was not regarded as my dishonour but my hostling's. I could not speak. I was utterly mortified and the tears began to flow.

With a sigh Lian plopped down on the bed and put an arm about me. "Don't take on so, beloved," he chided. "Things aren't nearly so bleak as you think."

"But I have disgraced you," I wept into his canvas-covered shoulder and Lian laughed so suddenly that I sat back and looked at him in shock.

"Oh believe me, beloved, this canvas garb is infinitely more comfortable than that jewelled monstrosity you're wearing!"

My lips twitched and my tears stopped. "But what have I done? Surely I've destroyed all hope of a life beyond tradition."

Lian considered for a moment and, with his arm still about me, said, "Perhaps you have precipitated things a little. I shall have to have a conversation with your father... but I was intending to do that anyway. It's just a little sooner than I had planned. But whatever else you may have done you've got that snake Zu-Lee off your tail. He would not consider blood bonding with such an outspoken consort... Actually, in his case, concubine is a more accurate description. Believe me, beloved, you would not wish a life with Zu-Lee." He held me for a while longer, then helped me out of the jewelled robe and into a nightshirt. He brushed my hair, then helped me to bed and sat holding my hand. "Don't worry Chenga. I'll speak to your father. I'll bring him round and you will have the life you wish. Tomorrow we are taking Zu-Lee riding – you are not to be included in the party. Beloved, it would be best if you were to remain in the house. I know you'd rather spend the time with Master Deshi but we're on delicate ground here... play the disgraced harling and keep to your room. And then we shall see what can be done." He kissed my brow. I heard my hostling's words but only one thing stuck in my mind.

"But you hate riding," I said.

Lian laughed into my hair. "I shall endure it for your sake," he said and kissed me again. He rose to his feet and smiled. "Sleep well, beloved. We stand on the threshold of great change, I think." And he left the room.

The party left early the next morning. I did not see Lian before they departed. I kept dutifully to my room and played the role of the son who understands and accepts his disgrace. To pass the time I read a little but mainly I practised the walking meditation and imagined the floor carpeted with glorious lotus blossoms as I trod. Part way through the morning one of the servants brought me a simple meal on a tray. Not quite bread and water but the next best thing. He set the dish down before me with an apologetic gesture, his eyes sorrowful. I waved a dismissive hand, gave him a smile and told him not to worry about it as I had little appetite. But some little time later he crept back into my room and placed a finger to his lips. From his sleeve he drew out an assortment of sweetmeats, I grinned at him and pressed my hand to his cheek. Hastily he covered his mouth with his hand and suppressing a giggle slipped from the room. I took the sweetmeats and sat cross-legged on the floor and consumed them much as Master Deshi would; I ached to be out in the forest with my friend.

Sometime in the afternoon, just as boredom was beginning to set in, there was a commotion in the house. There was much bustling about, slamming of doors and raised voices. I kept to my room and strained to hear but then it all went quiet. I sat and fretted. Had Lian and my father argued?

Perhaps an hour later my father entered my room. He stood in the doorway, his face set. "You have mourning robes?" he asked.

I nodded, utterly confused.

"You need to put them on."

"What is it? What's happened?" I cried.

My father made to take a step into the room and then checked himself. "There was an accident," he replied, shortly. "There was a snake lying on our path, it startled the horses. Your hostling was thrown..."

The blood began to rush in my ears, hot and vibrant, as my body rebelled, knowing that I would not want to hear the next words my father spoke.

"Lian is dead."

My world contracted to a small flower of pain. The house was put into mourning and a pall of silence hung over us all. Lian was, I'm told, quietly yet elegantly buried but, as a child still, I was not permitted to attend the ceremony. A servant was assigned to my care; the same one who had brought me sweetmeats on the day Lian died. I could barely function. Some days the servant had to force food between my lips or tea down my throat. At these times he would set the dishes down and, against all protocol, would take me in his arms and try to comfort me; his own eyes swollen and red as my own. "It was quick," he whispered. "It was so quick. There was no suffering." And he would place his hands either side of my face and shake me gently. "Your hostling is free. Free in a way that we cannot be... But Master Chenga you must eat. Your hostling would not have wished this."

And so I ate.

The days crawled by, bleak and colourless, and I passed into adulthood. This passage, however, was not celebrated; it was not seemly in a house of mourning. Unseemly too was my father's hasty remarriage. Barely two months had passed since Lian's death when my father brought his new consort to the house; an ambitious young har, scarcely older than I; we disliked each other on sight. A few days after this 'happy event' my father ventured to my room and, as before, he could scarcely take a step over the threshold. "It is time we talked of your future, Chenga."

A marriage had been arranged for me; a good match to a har of wealth and standing. Helpless though I was I was no fool and I could well understand my father's haste. My new step-hostling would want me out of the way leaving the way clear for the sons he would bear. Briefly I considered running away but I lacked the courage and the resources; in my dispirited and dejected state I could see no other option but to agree.

A litter was sent to carry me to my new home. It was the first time since Lian's death that I had been outside, the protocols of mourning having kept me tied to the house. The trees were stripped of their leaves and the air held an icy chill. I looked about the forest but to me, without Lian's presence, it seemed a colourless caricature, pallid and insubstantial. There was no sound, no rustle of life. High in the trees the monkeys, macaques and gibbons were silent and I could discern no chatter from the mushrooms, nor could I see them. Perhaps in my grief or in my passage to adulthood I had become blind and deaf to them.

Lian's worst nightmare was realised. My feybraiha was my wedding feast and I became the consort and tenth concubine of the dynastic overlord Zu-Lee. A good business arrangement. My father and step-hostling attended the celebration and that was the last I ever saw of them.

"So much for your dreams of scholarship and travel," Zu-Lee hissed at me as our hands were bound together and our blood mingled. I did not respond. What response could there be?

Zu-Lee's palace was a huge rambling affair set at the southernmost tip of our territory, overlooking the highest of the enclosing mountains. It was a warren of grey stone, balconies, sculpted cornices, curved and fluting roofs with narrow, ridged tiles and flying gables. I hated every stick and stone of it. My youth, my beauty and, more importantly, my father's success in business secured me the position of first concubine. On a daily basis I was dressed in bejewelled robes, so stiff with embroidery they chafed at the skin of my throat and reduced my movement to a mincing shuffle. My face was painted and I was primped and preened and paraded like a prize cow. Zu-Lee was rarely away from home and business associates and dignitaries were expected to attend on him. I was obliged to sit at his side throughout all of this with my eyes downcast and my mouth shut.

When it came to concubines Zu-Lee was quite the collector. There were petite, dark-skinned beauties from the Middle East; sinuous and cat-like trophies from Ferike; a pale-skinned Sulh; and then there was Afarleen, tall and loose-limbed, formerly the first concubine, and his close confidant the flaxen-haired Mildor from Freyhella, formerly the second concubine. These two were thick as thieves and, by the sidelong glances they threw my way as we sat at court, they clearly detested me for their loss of status. Within hours of my feybraiha Zu-Lee inducted me to the gentle arts of aruna, if you could call it that. Don't believe all that spiritual guff you hear about conception only occurring when aruna reaches its most sacred heights. Here at court a few nostrums and a little dark magic saw to it that I brought forth two heirs for Zu-Lee before my first year as his favoured consort and concubine was through; and this served to throw me further out of favour with Afarleen and Mildor as their own sons were then moved down the rankings of princely succession.

Unlike Lian I was unable to take joy in my children. Within hours of their birth they were whisked off to the royal nurseries, as tradition dictated, to be raised *properly* with the rest of the dynastic succession. I had no part in their naming and saw them only on a weekly basis when they and the other royal children were presented at court. My arms ached to reach out to them but it would have been they who suffered, not I, if I had given way to my impulses and so I kept my place. Whatever time was my own and on the rare occasions Zu-Lee was absent from court I confined myself to my chambers. All the attempts I had made to socialise with my fellow concubines had proved fruitless; it was easier to be on my own. I spent many hours practising the walking meditation and carpeted the floor in lotus blossoms; it gave me a sense of peace. At other times I sat in my window and gazed out at the gardens below. My apartment was everything that was sumptuous, and doubtless had been the sole domain of

Afarleen before I had unwillingly usurped him. It looked out towards the mountains but away from the forest, over the formal gardens at the front of the palace. Here it was all raked gravel, topiary and bonsai. I loathed it. I loathed the way beautiful natural forms were twisted and forced into unnatural shapes and appearances. It was as counterfeit and meaningless as my life had become but my life continued. I shut my heart away deep in a casket of ice and, when custom demanded it, wore a smile on my face... and so it was.

Change came suddenly, unexpectedly, and I had no more influence over it than a feather in a hurricane. By then my eldest son Xan was perhaps a year shy of his own feybraiha. The news came that my father's business ventures had all failed; he was bankrupt; and his new consort had abandoned him taking his sons with him. My own fall from grace was nothing short of meteoric. Within twenty four hours I had been moved from my apartments, my vast wardrobe of jewel-encrusted robes and assorted trinkets were taken from me and I was relocated to a small room high in the south tower overlooking the forest, a simple wardrobe of plain cotton garments devoid of all ornament or frippery was assigned to me. I was now ranked as tenth consort and Afarleen gleefully moved back into his old apartment. I could not have been happier. My lowly position meant my presence was not required on a daily basis in court. No more would I have to sit at Zu-Lee's side like a porcelain doll; that role now fell to Afarleen who relished it with rapacious appetite. The only courtly duty that befell me now was to be present when the harling princes were presented to their father. I would stand amongst the lower ranked concubines watching the parade of royal heirs. And here lay my only qualm regarding my loss of status; as I was demoted, so were my sons. Formerly they had headed the procession and had been attired in the court's finest; now they were endmost and dressed as dowdily as I. I worried for them, they who had known no different in their short lives. What impact could such a comedown have upon them? As unobtrusively as I could I studied their faces for any hint of emotion and reached my senses out to them to detect any distress. But I felt nothing. Xan and his younger brother

Nisha had been schooled too well; they gave nothing away. To me my loss of status meant only one thing – *freedom*. I ventured outside again. The gardens at the back of the palace, in complete contrast to the twisted, forced, artificial grounds to the front, were a riot of flowers, vines and long grassed lawns. Here I practised the walking meditation for hours. Freed from the restricting robes my joints became looser and my muscles stronger. I also gathered armfuls of blooms to decorate my chamber. These I wove into complex designs or created graceful arrangements in whatever containers I could lay my hands on. Dolah, my personal servant from the day I had arrived at court, sighed and clicked his tongue. "Master Chenga you will never regain your status as highest consort if you behave thus. You are constantly covered in mud and are not fit to be presented." But still he brought me wide rimmed dishes and elegant flasks to arrange my flowers in. By then it was early summer and the red-rumped swallows came to nest under the eaves just above my window. The sight of them reminded me of my old home and my thoughts returned wistfully to the lake and the swans and the white cranes that performed their courtship dances there. On days when it was impossible to go out I would spend long hours at my chamber window gazing out into the forest beyond the high wall; that was where my heart lay. One such day as, typically, I sat with my chair pulled up to the window, my elbows on the sill and my chin in my hands, I heard a chattering from the forest, many voices, intermingled, indecipherable. I held my breath as the voices first rose in pitch then began to oscillate and resonate... The mushrooms were singing again. My throat constricted and my breath came short and fast. Unwittingly I rose from my chair and stumbled to the door. Then I took the curving staircase two steps at a time before hurtling across the courtyard towards the rear garden. I cared little who saw me and nearly barrelled into Afarleen and Mildor as they made their way to the royal chambers. Careering on I brushed aside their exclamations of irritation but their sneering voices followed me. "Well, what would we expect? The demotion's quite turned his head."

"He never truly had the class to be first." I ran on, passing drenched blooms and sopping lawns, and came to a halt by the large wooden gate at the rear of the garden. It towered above me and had a metal studded permanence that suggested I should not even consider trying to open it. I had never considered it before but today was different. Today it seemed that all things were possible. I placed my fingers on the handle and turned it. The door swung open enough to allow me through and I hauled it closed behind me. And then I was running; running like a child; running like I hadn't run in years; running in a way that would not have been possible a few short weeks ago. I headed north through the richly-scented forest. In less than an hour I was in familiar territory. I was close to Master Deshi's cork-oak tree. I ran on, imagining how I would spiral my way up that tree, traverse the canopy walkways and visit my old friend in the little house, which he shared with the monkeys. At the thought the smile on my face grew wider. I entered the clearing and stopped dead in my tracks. He was sitting at the base of his usual tree. "Master Deshi!" the words tumbled from me. He opened his arms wide and I flung myself into them, burying my face in his shoulder.

"Oh, Chenga. Oh my poor boy!"

Boy. Once upon a time I would have considered this an insult but now... now it seemed the sweetest thing I had heard in years – a balm to my sore spirit. I cried myself out, weeping for my lost hostling, weeping for my lost youth, weeping for nearly seven wasted years. But eventually one runs out of tears and even grief has to take a breather. At length I sat up and scrubbed at my face. I sought Master Deshi's gaze and said, "I'm sorry I forgot to bring you something to eat."

He grinned at me. "Foolish youth. You bring me yourself – that is enough." We sat on the damp ground and regarded each other for a little while; clearly he had intuited my thoughts as I wept. "You need not grieve for your lost youth Chenga - believe me it is far from over." I waited for him to continue. "Many years ago now I made you a promise. I said I would teach you to travel the threads – the time has come to make good that promise."

I felt my heart quicken; the ice casket began to melt. "I'm not too old now?"

"No, no... the perfect age I'd say."

"It doesn't matter that I've had harlings?"

He was silent for a moment, smiling a soft smile. "You have sons. This I already knew. The threads told me. And no, it makes no difference."

A chill stole through me. "I have to go back, don't I? Back to the palace?"

Slowly he nodded, his eyes sad. "For the sake of your sons. But come back as soon as you are able. Then I shall teach you." I wanted to stay longer but I was wet through and the cold was beginning to bite. I pressed a kiss to my old teacher's cheek and rose stiffly. "As soon as I am able," I promised and trotted out of the clearing.

The journey back to the palace was far more arduous. For one thing the rain had set in with a vengeance and for another it was much more difficult running towards the palace than away from it; every cell in my body seemed to rebel. I reached the gate as the light was beginning to fade. I slipped through the garden and into the palace and, even though I removed my shoes I left something of a trail. Luckily the corridors were deserted and once back in my room I peeled off my clothes and wrapped myself in a warm robe.

Over the years I had come to judge Dolah's moods by the sound of his footsteps upon the stair. His quick bustling tread hinted at extreme irritation bordering on apoplexy. He opened and closed the door quietly enough but then unleashed a torrent upon me. "Master Chenga! Have you quite taken leave of your senses? What business have you in being out in the rain all this time? Your garments are most likely ruined! How are we going to regain your position as first consort if you behave like this?"

"I was walking," I replied inadequately.

He sighed theatrically and made up the fire. Then he brought me a hot cordial and took away my sodden clothing for cleaning. It was largely thanks to Dolah, I'm sure, that I did not catch cold. My adventures beyond the palace wall had, however, taken it out of me and I was stiff and exhausted for several days and I resolved that for my next outing I would wait for a fine day. The opportunity presented itself the day after the royal harlings were presented to the court. I watched from my usual position among the lower ranks as my two dowdily dressed sons brought up the rear. That day I could not help myself and I allowed my gaze to settle upon Xan and Nisha. After a moment Nisha looked up and our eyes met. I sent a wave of affection to him and I think he felt it, as he suddenly blinked his surprise and pressed a tiny hand to a point just below his breastbone. I didn't sleep much that night; my thoughts were a raging turmoil of anxiety for my sons and excitement at seeing Master Deshi again. Zu-Lee had planned a visit to his other estates and was taking the high-ranked consorts with him. I had instructed Dolah that I would be spending the entire day in quiet contemplation in my chamber and did not want to be disturbed. Dolah, I suspect, believed me to be sulking.

Shortly after dawn I slipped down the stairs and out into the garden. The blooms, barely open, already sweetened the air and the red-rumped swallows busily caught their breakfasts just above my head. I hastened through the garden door and then ran and ran and ran. The running was easier this time, my muscles more used to it, and my breathing was deep and easy as I covered the ground.

Master Deshi was waiting for me and greeted me with an excited cackle. "You have been practising the walking meditation?" he asked.

I nodded not in the least put out by his directness. "Nearly every day."

His grin became wider. "Good, good. Then there should be no hindrance here today."

"What must I do?" I asked both eager and nervous.

"First walk a little, meditate. Become attuned to the forest and then come here by me."

I did as he asked. Stepping slowly, breathing deeply, carpeting the forest floor with lotus flowers and, when I could feel the giant beat of the heart of the forest deep within my bones, I opened my eyes and made my way over to Master Deshi.

He lay on the ground at the very centre of the clearing. "Lie beside me Chenga. You must let the threads take you. Do not resist. Trust the process."

I did as he asked. Not really knowing what he meant or

understanding what I was doing. I lay still and tried to remain open to whatever would happen. At first there was nothing and then all over my body there was a gentle stroking sensation.

"Let the threads do their work," Master Deshi whispered.

I imagined tiny gossamer threads snaking up from the ground and binding themselves around me. The threads travelled on up my face, over my lips, tangling among my eyelashes, crowding into my nostrils. I fought the urge to brush them off and tried to stay calm. The stroking changed to a prickling as the threads penetrated and *pulled*. And then Chenga wasn't Chenga anymore. I was no longer lying above the ground but I was below it. No body, no eyes, no senses but not senseless. I could feel everything; the damp warmth of the soil around me, the glow of life and activity, the giggle and chatter of a million voices. *Master Deshi,* I called.

Relax, I'm here.

Where I could not say but I knew he was with me.

Come, the threads called, *come and see our being, our oneness.*

And then I was travelling; a rushing. My consciousness sent like a giant electrical impulse along a huge neural network. They took me deep into the dark heart of a forest where the trees were mostly unknown to me. Here a stand of tiny hemlock trees grew strongly beneath the dense canopy. By rights such trees should have been small and sickly as in this place little light penetrated to the forest floor. *We feed them, we nurture them,* the threads sang all around me. *We bring them light from the forest edges and we shall care for them until at last they take their place up by the sky...*

Master Deshi sighed in contentment. *You see, Chenga, this is their oneness.* We travelled again; this time to the toxic wastelands far to the west. The stories of this place had haunted me as a child. Here humans had created vast energy-making devices, which had failed, and as they collapsed they had leached invisible poisons; corrupting air, water and land, leaving them barren and uninhabitable for millennia. Had I been in harish form I could not have survived this place. Great patches of black sludge covered the crumbling walls but this was not decay.

Our cousins the slime moulds do good work here. See? They take the corruption from the air. This place will be good again.

I regarded the dark matter again and could sense a powerful pulsating glow. Beyond I could see vast tracts of concrete and asphalt. Here too clusters of mushrooms had sprouted forth and were slowly breaking down the tarmac, gradually returning it to the wild.

One day, many days from now, this will be forest again, the threads crooned joyfully. *This is our oneness.* And then we were travelling again; that great rushing tear, which came to an abrupt halt as I felt myself pushed upwards, forced to the surface, punching through the soil to flower above. I lay there, breathing once more, conscious that I had limbs... a body... *presence...* Slowly I flexed my fingers, gently circling my wrists and ankles but gently, very gently so that the last of the threads to leave me were not broken.

I turned my head to Master Deshi. "That's the singing?"

He nodded. "The threads recognised you as one of their own. They called to you. You are part of the oneness."

I bit my lip and turned my face back to the sky. "I should have run away when Lian died. I should have come to you..." I brought my hands up to my face and covered my eyes. "Such a waste of life."

Master Deshi sat up and caught hold of my wrists. "No, Chenga." He forced me to look at him. "You were not ready then. Now is your time."

Angry tears began to flow. "All those wasted years! And still I have to return to that damned palace!"

"Your sons are a waste, are they? Chenga, you have given life. Do you resent them?"

I didn't know whether to nod or shake my head and settled for a combination of the two. "No... Yes... I don't know... I don't know them. I've never even heard them speak!" And now my tears were laced with grief.

Master Deshi helped me to sit up and squatted beside me. "Chenga, I have lived a long time and one thing I know is this – change is inevitable. Things will not always be as they are. Be ready for the opportunities. Be prepared. But yes, for now, you must return to the *damned palace.*"

Despite myself I giggled. I couldn't help it and I rose to my feet and began to trudge towards the edge of the clearing and the path back.

Master Deshi called after me. "Chenga – you're planning to *walk?*" I turned back and held up my hands in confusion. He shook his head and placed a despairing hand to his temple. "You are still so very *young*... Chenga, the threads will take you... and they will bring you. As often as you like; as often as you can..."

"Oh..." I returned to the centre of the clearing feeling rather foolish and lay down again. Master Deshi sat beside me. "Request that they take you close to the palace boundary but I do not recommend that you materialise inside the compound. It would be unwise, I think, to be observed in this."

I nodded, his words made perfect sense.

"Come again soon, whenever you can."

The threads snaked up and took me again. This time they deposited me behind a copse of trees close to the north wall and only a short distance from the road to the nearby town. A wise choice; anyone observing my return would believe that had been my destination.

From that point on, as often as I could, I slipped out of the palace and travelled the threads. They carried me to vertiginous mountain peaks; to the barren edges of deserts; to the very fringes where saltwater blocked our way. They showed me the places where the land lay defiled by chemical spillages. Here the threads worked to cleanse the soils, allowing them to bloom again. They took me past stagnant rivers and streams where mats of threads lay across the foetid waters siphoning out the impurities and leaving it crystal clear. I saw where gigantic boulders had been crumbled to soil and the threads also took me to their battle grounds where they, like any other species, fought each other for resources. Here the decaying timbers seemed riddled with running blood. Despite this, the experience was intoxicating and I indulged as often as I could.

"Chenga you must be careful," Master Deshi advised me as we sat enjoying a little early spring sunshine beneath his cork-oak tree. "Travelling the threads can be quite addictive and it's very easy to lose all sense of time."

"I know that." Nearly a year's experience meant I wasn't a fool but he was not to be dissuaded and he gripped my arm.

"Doubtless you heard the rumours? When you first came to me? The stories spread by harlings and servants? Master Deshi is four hundred years old?"

I laughed. "Well, are you?"

"Don't be foolish. No human lives to that age!"

I shrugged. "That's what I thought."

He pulled a face as if chewing on something indigestible. "I am not four hundred years old, Chenga. But I have been on earth for over four hundred years."

I didn't understand and said so. He let go his grip on my arm and rocked to and fro a little. When he spoke again he did so very precisely and emphatically. "Chenga when you travel the threads you do not age. You are returned just as you were. It is possible to travel for days... weeks... months..."

"Years?" I queried, incredulous.

He turned to me, deadly serious. "I have travelled for decades. But I am at liberty to do so."

"And I am not?"

"No you are not!" he replied hotly. "You have two sons dependent on you."

"Hardly dependent," I answered but still I was chastened. Each week I diligently attended the harling parade and it was clear to me that Xan was fast approaching adulthood. His feybraiha would, most likely, take place before the summer was out. "Master Deshi, I will be more careful," I promised.

"Good."

The threads carried me back to my usual spot behind the copse of trees. I slipped through the garden gate and along the pale stone path stained golden by the early evening sun. The corridors of the palace were eerily silent and I encountered not a soul as I made my way back to the stair to my tower room. This should have alerted me but I was preoccupied with thoughts of my sons and the warning Master Deshi had given me; a premonition perhaps because as I pushed open the door to my chamber and icy fist reached inside me, freezing my bones and very nearly stopping my heart. My chair, customarily set near the window so that I could look out over the forest, was now placed in front of the fireplace. Despite the unseasonal warmth of that spring evening a pile of logs blazed in the hearth. The chair was occupied. "Come in and shut the door behind you." Zu-Lee commanded, each word dripping with ice.

I did as he asked but remained close to the closed door.

He rose slowly from the chair and turned to face me. "Come here."

Unwillingly I moved my feet and propelled myself into that sweltering heat and towards the malevolent viper that had invaded my sanctuary. His eyes glittered. "Where were you?"

"In the gardens," I faltered, goose bumps erupting on my skin.

He made a disparaging sound. "The gardens were searched. I repeat. Where were you?"

"I... I've spent the afternoon out among the trees." That at least was no lie. "I'm sorry I did not know that I would be required today."

Very slowly he put his head on one side and raised an eyebrow. "I expect my consorts to be available at all times."

I was uncertain as to how to respond but was keen to distract him from my whereabouts. "I'm sorry," I repeated. "Did something happen?"

Zu-Lee stiffened his shoulders and raised his chin. "We had an unannounced visit from the Immanion ambassador. He wished to meet all my consorts. *All of them.*"

Hoping a display of subservience would placate him I lowered my eyes. "I am sorry."

"In future I expect you to be available at all times. Do you understand?"

I nodded.

"At all times. Do not embarrass me again."

I nodded again and kept my eyes downcast. I saw a movement but I did not see it coming. The slap. Pain exploded at the side of my face. The crash of flesh upon flesh ricocheting off the walls of my shuttered chamber. I was knocked off my feet and lay upon the carpet literally seeing stars. Zu-Lee stood over me for a moment and then left the room quietly shutting the door behind him. I did not hear him descend the stair.

I remained on the carpet in that blistering heat, the left side of my face feeling twice its normal size. A warm stickiness began to ooze from my nose and run into my mouth. Then I heard footsteps. Anxious. Hurrying. Dolah. He burst into the room. "Master Chenga! Oh! Master Chenga... this is not right!" He flapped and twittered over me.

"Help me up," I bubbled. "Help me into the chair."

He did as I asked, continuing to flap and twitter, and then went to close the door.

"Please," I entreated him. "Leave it open. And open the window... and for God's sake put this damned fire out. It's stifling in here."

He chuckled a little at that. I didn't often do bossy. Dolah flung open the window and smothered the fire with a heavy damp cloth. He then fetched water and towels and set about tidying me up. A cooling breeze drew through the room. The evening air helped clear my head and I gazed up at Dolah. "How do I look?" I asked.

He ran sorrowful eyes over me for a moment. "A bit of a mess but you'll mend."

I blinked at him. It was probably the most honest thing I had ever heard him say.

He knelt before me and shook his head. "It's not right Master Chenga. You should not be treated like this."

I shrugged. "It is 'the way'," I told him.

Dolah shook his head again and pressed my hand. "It's not right." Then he rose once more and occupied himself with the practical. "I'll fetch arnica and ice. We can undo much of the damage before it fully manifests."

He left me and I remained in my chair musing on what had just passed. For Dolah to question the actions of a dynastic overlord was an act bordering on revolution. Gingerly I prodded the swollen flesh of my cheek. Perhaps the winds of change were blowing at last.

I was very careful over the next few days and did not venture too far out into the gardens or remain out of doors for too long. I took to flower arranging again and spent my afternoons creating displays of the blooms I had gathered in the mornings. Inevitably, though, my heart lay in the forest beyond the garden wall. I spent much time gazing from my window and from the windows of the corridor that bounded the southern garden. I believed it prudent to be seen around and about more and not keep solely to my room. This, I believed, would supply less fodder to the rumour mill and I hoped that in turn it would further appease Zu-Lee. One afternoon Mildor, the now second consort, found me gazing from my favourite spot in the corridor. He stopped and peered over my shoulder. "There are forests in Freyhella too."

Was that a hint of wistfulness I heard in his voice? I turned and took in the lightly-tanned skin and the golden hair. There was indeed a hint of longing in the vivid blue eyes; that or he was a consummate actor. But I could not afford to take a chance. I gave him a small tight smile and said nothing.

"You know I envy you the view from that tower room," he said quietly.

I nodded but said pointedly, "But not the loss of status required obtaining it."

He held my gaze for a moment then let his eyes wander over the fading bruising. "No... not that."

I smiled again and walked away, uncertain as to whether the exchange had been a truthful one or whether I was being played with. Either way I could not afford to get involved.

It was the better part of three weeks, when the unnamed Immanion ambassador was rumoured to have left the province, before I dared to venture out again beyond the garden gate. I chose a clear, cool morning and the threads carried me to Master Deshi. As I materialised above ground he regarded me quizzically and inclined his head to one side. I knew that he intuited much of what had occurred or that the threads had kept him informed but nevertheless I felt obliged to explain my absence. When I had finished he just nodded and shrugged a little and I felt compelled to continue. "Master Deshi, I've had time to do some thinking and I'm worried."

He opened his mouth to say something, appeared to think better of it and gestured for me to go on.

"I believe I am putting you in danger."

He cackled heartily at this, his face crinkling and his gums glistening.

"No, really," I implored. "If I give away even a hint of what happens here Zu-Lee will have the guards out searching for you and they'll tear the forest apart looking for the threads."

Master Deshi sobered and sat up straight. "Chenga, it is good that you are concerned and that you remain careful. But think... How long have I have existed? And I have outrun all attempts to find me... Are you so naive as to think that this would be the first? And the threads? Why! They have been here for millennia... more. They have outlived more eras and more species that you or I could count. They would continue." He pondered for a moment. "You are wise to be cautious, Chenga. I would not wish to see this forest torn apart. Hmmm... And now, if we are to be short of time together I suggest we waste no more of it and take a little jaunt together."

Joyfully I agreed. I had been away from the threads for far too long. That day they carried us to the ocean where we spent a few happy hours among the sand dunes and salt marshes of the coastal fringe.

On our return to the clearing Master Deshi had more to say to me. "Chenga, I too have been thinking. I believe it will soon be time for me to go on another of my longer jaunts with the threads." My face must have fallen because he reached out a hand and pressed my arm. "No Chenga, you shall not lose me... for I intend to take you with me."

"But what of my sons?" I asked incredulously. "You told me yourself that I could not abandon my children and I agree with you."

He gazed at me steadily. "Your children will not always be children. The time will come when they will need to make their own way."

"Not into an arranged marriage!" I countered hotly.

He held up his hands to mollify me. "I agree. I agree. We will need to discuss this further. But trust me... change is inevitable." He looked towards the darkening sun which was now rapidly sinking towards the west. "It is time you weren't here."

I was torn between my desire to know more and my

resolve to be prudent. Eventually I nodded. "I'll see you soon," I told him.

"Whenever you are able," he replied as I let the threads take me underground for the journey back to the palace.

Excitement boiled within me as I crept back through the huge studded door. I might soon be free of this place. It took all my self control not to skip up the path but I could not resist taking the steps up to the palace two at a time and I almost cannoned into Afarleen and Mildor who stood at the top.

"Oh look," Afarleen said with a sneer, "If it isn't our disgraced tenth consort." He turned to Mildor. "You would think he could show a little more decorum... at the very least the conduct befitting his status. How did he ever come to be first?"

But Mildor was studying me intently, his vivid blue eyes widening. "You've been *outside!*" he gasped, his voice full of wonder.

Afarleen looked from me to Mildor and back again. "Outside!? What would a low-ranked consort want with outside?" He ran his eyes over me disparagingly. "Oh I know! Our lowliest consort has taken himself a lover... some peasant har from the village... How delicious!" With a peal of high pitched laughter he drew a fan out from his sleeve, snapped it open and proceeded to fan himself theatrically.

Despairingly I trailed by to my chamber and awaited the fallout. I did not have to wait long. The rumour mill exploded and Zu-Lee was incandescent in his fury.

My one consolation during that time was that Afarleen's version of events was accepted as gospel. During my interrogation I carefully gave nothing away about Master Deshi and the threads and eventually, when pushed and when I deemed it timely, I admitted that there had been an assignation with a travelling merchant; a nameless har that occasionally traversed the road between the village and the next province. "No," I told them. "I had not been into the village. We met only in the forest." I had no more desire to see the village torn apart than I had the forest. I was confined to my room and told that henceforth the garden gate would always be locked. I remained in my room and awaited Zu-Lee's judgement. It came swiftly. I was to be publically beaten. In the great hall I was stripped of my robes and laid face down upon the ornately tiled floor, my hands restrained before me in a rough wooden shackle. Two burly palace guards then set about me with long flexible lengths of bamboo. Unlike the slap I knew this was coming and was able to prepare myself. I flung my awareness far out into the forest, among the leaves and shoots, within the trees and roots. I wrapped myself tightly in the threads and, thus cocooned, lay quiet in the dark. I felt nothing. But although my senses were safely cradled in the forest I was still fully cognisant of that taking place in the hall. I could see people's faces, gauge their reactions; Afarleen wore a broad grin, unabashed in his rapacious delight; Mildor was tinged green, his mouth pulled into a rictus of disgust; Zu-Lee sat unmoved as a granite obelisk; Dolah kept his hands pressed over his eyes. Somewhere in that room my sons bore witness. I could not see them but that knowledge stung more viciously than any lash. At some point I began to weep but more for loneliness than anything else. It must have been convincing because shortly after Zu-Lee signalled for the flogging to cease. He must have believed he had broken me. I was carried from the hall, my flesh welted and oozing, and dumped unceremoniously upon my bed. The door closed and I was left alone. Only then I allowed my sense to return and gasped when my assaulted flesh made its status known. I heard hysterical steps on the stair and the door was flung open. "Master Chenga! Master Chenga! Oh this is not right! Oh... Look at the state of you... It will be weeks before you are presentable. How could they do this to you? It's not right... How will you ever regain your position as first now?"

At any other time Dolah's oscillation between closet revolutionary and staunch traditionalist would have made me laugh. Right now I didn't have the energy. "Dolah, see to my wounds," I snapped.

At once he became still. "Master Chenga... I cannot... I am commanded to treat you with nothing but a rough cloth and water." I could hear the sadness and disgust woven through his voice.

With some difficulty I turned my head to look at him.

"Then cold water and a rough cloth it is."

Dolah bit his lip and his eyes filled. "I'll be as gentle as I can."

He was. He did his best for me with a kindly hand and an aching heart. I was grateful to him. After he had gone I set about doing as much for myself as I could. They had underestimated how much Lian had taught me as a child and although the skills my hostling had nurtured in me were somewhat rusty they were not dead. With the healing from my hands and my intention I sealed the cuts and took away much of the pain. The bruising I allowed to flower. It would make a pretty display for anyone who cared to look and would not lead to any trouble for Dolah.

I was stiff for several days. I attempted to practise the walking meditation but my movements were too restricted and so I was obliged just to rest. My clothes had been removed and I had been left with the heavy black canvas robes of the disgraced consort. They chafed a little at my skin but I did not mind wearing them. They reminded me of Lian when last I saw him... then so full of hope for his son... What would he think now?

My door remained locked with Dolah only permitted to visit three times a day to bring me my meals. I welcomed the solitude. It gave me time to think. I knew now that I could not stay in this place. I could no longer live this life. My heart belonged in the forest. But how could I bring this about without creating dire consequences for those I cared for? I felt snared in a tenacious, viscous web and that every time I moved the strands clung tighter around me.

Days passed and my skin healed. I paced my room and grew listless; the walls closing in on me. I spent hours watching the forest from my window. In an attempt to occupy me, Dolah took to smuggling in bunches of flowers for me to arrange. It helped pass the time and then I grew cunning. I began to request specific items to add to my floral displays. A few fronds of white willow, a little ginkgo, some dill weed. My appetite, too, improved and I requested raw garlic, ginger and cinnamon to warm my spirit and turmeric and cayenne as tonics for the nerves. Deep in my closet I knew I had an old

Maria J Leel

bottle of rice wine, empty save an inch or two at the bottom. To this liquid I added the shredded willow bark, the gingko and the dill weed and all the spices I had appropriated. I allowed this infusion to steep for days. When I could I added to the liquor with the occasional glass of rice wine begged from Dolah. I had no recipe just the knowledge of the properties of the plants I used. All I could do was hope that it would have the effect I required. When I thought the time right I strained the mixture through a handkerchief into a tall steel flask that Dolah had brought me for flower-arranging. Its narrow neck would hold little more than an orchid stem or two and I fashioned a stopper from some wax and paper. When the solution was ready I began to bleed myself... a little each day and, as I hoped and prayed it would, when I added it to the solution, the blood remained liquid. Bleeding myself had the added effect of making me appear ever more wan and Dolah became most agitated. "It's not right Master Chenga. They should not treat you this way," became his daily mantra as he brought beef broth to build me up and dishes of spiced chicken liver and barley malt.

I had grown used to the sound of Dolah's tread upon the stair. Over the years I had known his footfall to be anguished, agitated and even apoplectic. More recently it had been sad and resigned. Then one day, just past midsummer, I heard him tread in a way I had never heard before. Today he was... furtive. And he wasn't alone. I sat by the window as he unlocked the door and gently pushed it open. He peered around the door and then whispered, "I've brought company to cheer you Master Chenga."

Just below Dolah's shoulder two more pairs of eyes peered around the door. I jumped to my feet and hurriedly pressed a hand to my mouth to stifle the cry of surprise and delight that threatened to erupt from my throat. At Dolah's side stood Xan and Nisha. *My sons.* Dolah had brought my sons to me.

"Quietly," Dolah hissed. "No-one must know of this. No-one."

"But what of Zu-Lee?" I asked, keeping my voice low.

"He is away from court," Xan answered me. Even though his voice was hushed I could hear the musical tones within. He continued, "The Immanion ambassador has returned to the province and Zu-Lee has gone to welcome him."

"And he's taken that snake Afarleen with him," put in Nisha in a whisper, "and the milk-faced Mildor too. We're quite safe."

"Nothing is safe," Dolah insisted. "I'll leave you in peace but I can't leave you for long."

"Thank you, Dolah," I said, inadequately.

"Just keep it down," he implored as he closed the door. I felt the tears oh so close to the surface but now was not the time to weep. I willed them away and sank back down into my chair holding my hands out to my sons. They came to me at once, first taking my hands and then pressing themselves to me. "Oh my sons," I whispered. "Oh my beautiful harlings. I am so sorry."

"No," Xan said as he disengaged himself from me a little. "No time for that and no need either."

I gazed at him, to me the very spit of Lian, and so close to adulthood. His feybraiha could not be far off now. Nisha also stood back a little and I could see no trace of Zu-Lee in him either. They were both all mine. "You have to leave here," Xan said.

"You must escape," Nisha added.

Had they read my mind? "But how?" I asked. "And what harm will befall the two of you and Dolah if I do? I am trapped."

My eldest son shook his head. "No, you don't understand. Things are changing. Zu-Lee wants acceptance into the tribal federation of Immanion. This is most important to him."

"But Immanion is stalling," Nisha added, his eyes flicking towards his brother.

"They find many of our customs archaic and barbaric." Xan continued. "Reports of the flogging and imprisonment of a consort have not been well received by the Immanion ambassador."

I listened dumbly. My sons, I thought, so much better informed and so much more politically astute than I.

"The tenth consort and his sons have become somewhat of an embarrassment to our dynastic overlord," Nisha told me, almost gleefully I thought.

"Your running away would just about be the final straw,"

said Xan.

"But how will this impact on the two of you and Dolah?" I asked, my original concerns not assuaged in the least.

Xan sighed impatiently. "Zu-Lee will want us out of his sight... Oh no..." he continued quickly when he saw my expression. "He cannot harm us... imagine how that would look?"

"He'll send us away," said Nisha.

"Away where?"

Xan straightened his back and looked at me levelly. "I wish to study. I wish to go to Immanion and become a scholar at the musical academy."

I blinked. I could almost see myself reflected there declaring the same thing all those years ago. My gaze shifted to Nisha.

"I can go with him. Xan's feybraiha will be soon and then he can become my guardian. I can go to Immanion too."

I half laughed. "You seem to have it all worked out. But what of Dolah?"

Nisha spoke again. "He's just about ready to leave as it is. Only his love and care for you keeps him here. He has a brother and family on the other side of the mountains. He wishes to go there."

I shook my head. "How do you know this?"

Nisha shrugged. "I asked him," he said simply.

My sons, I thought, *such wisdom!* I sat back in my chair and pondered for a moment. "How am I to get out of this room?"

From his sleeve Xan produced a key. Its long iron shaft glinted dully as he handed it to me. "The spare key to your room. We stole it from the housekeeper's office," my eldest son told me. "Dolah knows nothing."

So Dolah would not be implicated.

"And how am I to escape the garden?" I asked. "The garden gate has been barred." I knew full well that the threads could easily take me from the garden but I had no wish to leave an unexplainable mystery... such things garner far too much interest. I had no desire to endanger Master Deshi or the threads in any way, no matter how remote the possibility.

It was Nisha who supplied the answer. "There are repairs being made to the west wall. There is scaffolding. Afarleen's second son was punished the other day for scaling the wall to steal fruit from the forest."

I suppressed a laugh. Even royal princes, it seemed, for all their privilege, could not resist a little scrumping.

"You must go soon though." Xan urged. "In a few days the repairs will be complete and the scaffolding removed."

I hardly knew what to say. "It seems, my sons, that you have thought of everything... Now, in the brief time we have left, tell me all about yourselves." We spent the remainder of the time sitting together on the carpet by the window. They chatted on whilst I drank in every detail of them; the lustre of their long dark hair; the shine in their eyes; the softness of the skin of their young faces. Far too soon we heard Dolah's footfalls on the stair and he took my sons from me. I pressed a kiss of deepest love and healing to each of their brows and whispered to each in turn as I embraced them, "Be strong. Fear nothing no matter how bad it seems and I will find you in Immanion." As Dolah led them away I embraced him also and pressed a kiss to his cheek. "Thank you, my friend." He smiled at me then, joy and sadness intermingled, as he closed the door. Then and only then did I succumb to tears.

It is hardly surprising that I slept little that night; a myriad of thoughts skipped and danced before me and refused to be tamed. Sometime in the early hours I went to stand by my window and gazed out over the moon-washed garden. The moon, close to full, stained the shadows purple and made the familiar unfamiliar. As dawn crept in I returned to my bed and slept a little. I was still in bed when I heard Dolah's bustling tread upon the stair. He knocked and entered before I had chance to respond. He was heavily laden; not only with a breakfast tray but across his arms he also had draped a jewel-encrusted robe of deepest magenta. "What's all this," I asked as he awkwardly set the tray down on my lap and then went to arrange the robe over my chair.

"The Master is returned and he wishes to dine with you tonight here in your chamber."

I adjusted the pillow behind me. "Prompted, no doubt, by the presence of the Immanion ambassador in the province?"

Dolah stopped fussing with the robe and turned and

looked me squarely in the eye. "Master Chenga, this is your opportunity to regain your position." I resisted the urge to roll my eyes... tradition appeared to be winning out over revolution in Dolah's thinking today. "Relax, Dolah," I told him. "I'll be on my best behaviour."

He raised an eyebrow at me and left the room. I pondered as I peeled the shell of my salted duck egg; was this threat or opportunity? Would my playing the part of the compliant consort relax Zu-Lee's grip on me? If I played willing would it ease my bid to escape? I could see nothing to be gained from defiance at this point; no matter how appealing it might seem. I nursed my tea and thought over all that Lian had taught me of etiquette.

Dolah returned to bring me lunch and found me resting. He came back again in the early evening to help me prepare. He bathed me, scented me, brushed my hair until it shone, painted my face for me and then finally helped me into the heavy, stiff robe. He smoothed it down on my shoulders and pronounced himself satisfied. I regarded myself in the mirror. I was the image of a perfect china doll. "I am not to serve you this evening," Dolah told me, a little hotly. "Master Zu-Lee shall bring his own personal staff." Clearly this snub went ill with Dolah. He went to fold up the discarded black canvas robe and carry it away.

"No," I said. "Leave it."

He looked at me askance.

"Place it in my wardrobe," I said. "It will remind me to behave in future."

Dolah shook his head but did as I asked. He returned once more to set the table before the fireplace and then left me in peace.

At the appointed hour the key turned in the lock and two members of Zu-Lee's personal staff entered. One carried a huge tray bearing many dishes, the second, a large carafe of wine and an ornate stand for the tray to rest upon. Had Dolah arrived bearing such a burden I should have leapt to assist him... but these were not my servants and etiquette dictated that a consort would not so demean themselves. It was imperative that I played my part well. Zu-Lee swept into the room, tall, imposing and bedecked in finery. My flesh crawled at the very sight of him. He inclined his head. "Thank you for agreeing to dine with me." As if I had any choice. I kept my eyes downcast and gestured towards a chair. We seated ourselves and the servants set dishes before us. They poured us glasses of wine and water and then quietly left the room. Zu-Lee did not speak until they had gone. "What happened to you was... regrettable...," Zu-Lee began.

Regrettable? I kept my own counsel and my eyes on my plate as my consort continued.

"A great opportunity for advancement has recently presented itself. An opportunity that would bring great benefit to us all... and it is imperative that *each* member of my court plays their part well."

I smiled and handed him his wine. *That is exactly what I am doing*, I thought.

"The recent... unpleasantness can be overlooked. I trust you are... recovered?"

I nodded but kept my eyes lowered.

Zu-Lee sipped his wine and paused thoughtfully. "If you could become again the har to whom I was first attracted, the har with impeccable court manners... why then all manner of things may become yours again. Your fine robes, a more superior apartment perhaps?"

I endeavoured to look grateful.

Zu-Lee drank a little more wine and pondered some more. "I know what it is. There was an error in your training as a harling. That imbecile hostling of yours, the one who could not even keep his seat on a horse, it was his oversight. He filled your head with foolish notions."

I froze. The air barely moved within me. It took every shred of my will to hold back... To hold back the ravening pack of insults that strove to escape my throat and hurl themselves with lacerating fury into the face of my tormentor. I longed to tear apart his arrogant sense of entitlement. But it was as if Lian's hand rested softly on my shoulder urging me to keep an outer appearance of serenity. I raised my eyes and my glass and toasted my consort. "Indeed."

An approximation of a smile flickered on Zu-Lee's countenance. "But that is enough business talk. Let us eat."

The truth was I believed I had little appetite, my throat being too tight to allow the passage of food. A couple of mouthfuls of the plum wine lubricated things sufficiently for me to pick at what lay before me. The array of dishes was far and away superior to anything that had been set before me for weeks. There was a hot and spicy soup, garlic steamed mussels, battered squid, salted pork, spiced beef and a vast selection of dumplings and sweetmeats. As I ate I rediscovered my appetite. After all, I thought, I need to keep up my strength. However I was careful to drink more water than wine. I fully intended to keep a clear head and as moderation was deemed attractive in the consort of a dynastic overlord this did not attract suspicion.

"You have enjoyed the meal?" Zu-Lee asked.

"Indeed I have," I responded. It might have been the prescribed answer but I meant it all the same.

Shortly after this the servants arrived to clear away the debris.

"This has been most agreeable," Zu-Lee said. "Perhaps we should do this again soon?"

"That would be most welcome," I intoned and my consort smiled, a sly triumphant smile, as he took his leave of me.

I sat and waited and listened, but the sound I thought to hear did not come. There had been no turn of the key in the lock. The door remained open. Fractiously, I tore at the fastenings of my robe so that I could breathe and shook my hair loose from its restrictive pins. I began to pace the room, my mind in flight. Again... was this a threat or an opportunity? A trap or an oversight? Was this a gesture of trust or some malevolent test? I picked up my chair and returned it to its customary place by the window. Then I fetched a damp cloth from the bath chamber and sat cleaning the paint from my face as I considered my options.

I watched the sun go down over the gardens and the forest beyond. A door that is unlocked can easily be relocked. Beneath my window the shadows grew long. To go now would put Dolah in the clear. Zu-Lee and his servants were the last to attend on me. High above, the sky darkened to deep azure. If I went now I would not have to use the key that

Xan and Nisha had purloined for me. With no mystery as to how I had left my room any investigations would not lead to them. Stars began to twinkle overhead. One in particular, low down on the horizon, shone particularly brightly. The scaffolding by the west wall would not be in place for much longer... Xan had told me this. The night lengthened. Zu-Lee or his minions might be patrolling the corridors below... just waiting for me to try something. The moon rose, bright, full, casting a deathly pale light over the entire garden. Moonlight would enable me to see where I was going but would make me more easily seen. I put my head in my hands and sighed deeply. Zu-Lee believed me broken, reined in, a fool... and he had insulted Lian... That was it. I was decided. I would go that night.

I waited until well after midnight and then I took the tall steel flask from my wardrobe and the stolen key and bundled them into the black canvas robe fashioning it into a makeshift bag. I loosened the robe I wore as much as I could to allow free movement and then I opened the door and crept down the stair. I met no-one on the spiral steps. In the corridor I kept to the shadows trying to make my footsteps as light and silent as possible, but to my ears my breaths and heartbeat sounded like thunder. About half way down the corridor a figure stepped out from the shadows. I froze.

The figure came forward slowly and stopped in a pool of moonlight. I narrowed my eyes. The bleached light rendered the pale skin and the pale hair even more colourless. "Mildor?" I whispered as I stepped out of the shadows.

He stiffened in surprise and then relaxed a little. "Chenga."

I have never hit anyone in my entire life and wondered, briefly, how much force would be necessary to render someone senseless.

"You are running away." A statement rather than a question.

I nodded. "Go then," he shrugged. "I shall not try to stop you."

"Am I likely to run into Zu-Lee or his guard if I do?"

Mildor gave a dry laugh. "I doubt it. He is otherwise occupied. When Afarleen learned that Zu-Lee had dined with you tonight he went off into a mammoth display of hysterics. Half the palace is engaged in placating him. Zu-Lee has shut himself in his office. It's soundproofed."

"I see."

Mildor stepped closer to me. "I just ask you one thing."

"That is?"

"Take a part of me with you. I have not the courage. Take a part of me with you in your heart."

Oh I could hear the yearning there. Like Dolah, Mildor was beginning to break free. "Things are changing, Mildor. There is more hope than you can imagine. Put your faith in the Immanion ambassador. You shall see Freyhella again." There came the sound of a stifled sob. I could not risk sharing breath with him... too much was at stake. Instead I sent a breath to him full of the perfumes of the forest, the dappled light of the canopy, the calls of the creatures that lived within.

He drank it in deeply, then, "You must go. Go quickly. I will keep a watch here and create a diversion if necessary."

I pressed my hand to his shoulder. "Thank you, Mildor."

I ran lightly down the corridor and out into the garden. Again I kept to the shadows as I made my way to the west wall.

Climbing the scaffolding in that wretched magenta robe was not easy. It caught and rent and tore. I would have been much better off in the black canvas but for what I had in mind the more ragged my robe became the better. Once outside I made my way to the copse by the south gate. Briars snatched at my robe and it became covered in clinging seed heads. I stripped the vile thing off as soon as I reached the clearing. I tore the jewels from it and increased the rents and tears as much as possible. Then I undid my makeshift bag and dressed myself in the black robe. Quickly I unstoppered the metal flask and liberally doused the discarded robe with my still liquid blood. *Let them think I have been robbed,* I thought, *robbed and murdered. Let them think wild animals carried off my body.* Such things did happen. Gruesome reports often made it to the palace. I placed the empty flask upon the ground along with the key and the jewels. *Help me,* I entreated the threads and sent my intention to them. The ground opened up before me and my offerings were devoured then the earth sealed itself as if nothing had occurred.

I sat for a moment, breathing deeply and sending up a prayer to any gods that might be listening. I prayed that Dolah and my sons would be safe. I prayed that they would see through my ruse and know that I was still in the world. I prayed that one day I would find my sons happy in Immanion. Then I lay myself upon the ground and let the threads take me. They would take me to Master Deshi so that we could begin our long adventure...

When you walk in a forest it is not that which is above you that is important – it is that which is beneath... And I am there!

dysphoria

Wendy Darling

"Dede, are you awake?"

I cracked one eye open and looked at my son, peering at me from inches way.

"What do you think?"

Amber stepped back. "Oh. Sorry."

"What is it?" I asked, opening both eyes now as I sat up straight on the sofa. "I thought I told you to go to bed."

Amber was about two at the time and still had a bedtime, which my chesnari and I loosely enforced. It was a couple of hours past.

"I was in bed, trying to sleep..." he began. He scrunched his face up. "But I just kept thinking. The thoughts wouldn't stop."

I scooted him into my lap and ruffled his curly hair. "You have a busy head." I sighed. "Tell me. And then go to bed."

Sensing triumph, he stretched, then took my face in his hands. "Remember those old books you gave me?"

"Which ones?" I asked. Amber shared my fascination with human relics, especially books, and practically from the pearl, I had given him plenty.

"The picture books, the ones with all the *actresses*," he said, drawing out the unfamiliar feminine term, which of course being Amber he had immediately asked me about when I'd given him the book. "The one showing all the famous ones, in the amazing photographs that looked like dreams?"

I nodded. "And what? You can't sleep because you're thinking about actresses?"

He took his hands away. "Yes! I was looking at them all yesterday and except for when I was at school, all today."

That's why the house had been so quiet, I realised. "I'm glad you like it!"

Amber rolled his eyes. "I don't like it – I *love* it! It's the best thing... *ever!*"

I chuckled, delighted I had pleased my son. "Well, good!"

I had mixed feelings about the pictures myself. They were lovely art, but seeing females, even beautiful ones, disturbed me. There was simply something so foreign, so odd, so... *unhar* about them. Well, mostly. Some I found desirable, yet at the same time, I felt I should be repelled. *Forbidden.*

"So what do you like about it?" I asked.

"The *women!*" he exclaimed. "They're *sooo* pretty! I love everything about them."

"There are some hara who look very similar, you know," I said. "Hara who have a more soume aspect."

Amber processed this briefly. "I guess so, but it's not the same."

"It isn't?"

"No. They're shaped differently," he explained. "Women are curvy and have..." He gestured with his hands over his chest.

"*Breasts,*" I supplied.

"Breasts!" he exclaimed, so loudly it was comical.

"Breasts," I repeated. "They were for feeding their babies. They made milk, like cats or cows do. Women grew them around the time of their... not feybraiha, but the human equivalent. Then they kept them all their lives."

"Really?" he asked. "Did all these actresses have babies?"

"What? Oh, I don't know." I considered what he was asking. "No, they're just women, with breasts. Women always had breasts, whether they had babies or not."

Amber took this in. "Oh. Well, I like them."

I glanced across the room and noticed the clock. "Hey, remember, you should be in bed."

He put his right arm around me. "I like talking with you. Learning."

"I know you do," I said, standing up and setting him down on the floor. "But off to bed. Quiet your mind. Dream about the actresses if you want, but do sleep. You have school tomorrow."

Walking toward the hall, he yawned. "I want to be an actress..." he sighed, and then he disappeared around the corner.

Little did I realise what I had started, giving him that book.

It began slowly. At first Amber was content with that first one, going through it over and over. He didn't just read it in his room, but in the living room, at the dinner table (where Saril told him to put it away), in the back yard. He asked me a lot of questions about it.

"Why are they skinny in the middle and wider at the hips?"

"How come some of them have bigger breasts?"

"Did they really carry pearls for nine months?"

I answered his questions as best I could, based on my own reading, history classes, and so on, but he had a lot more interest than I had ever had. Soon I had nothing more to contribute on the subject.

We went to the neighbourhood library and in the special antiquities room, we found some old books with lots of pictures, not only of actresses, but of humans, both men and women, some famous, some ordinary. This led to more questions, of course.

"Why did men have hair on their face?"

"Why do the men have such boring clothes?"

"And men never, ever hosted babies?"

We also looked at newer books, made by hara, which included illustrations of women or talked about women. Amber could read by then and so he borrowed them and took them home.

He went to school and did his chores around the house, plus any assignments he had from school, but the rest of the time, he became a specialist. If he wasn't reading about women, he was talking about them. Then he started drawing pictures.

About three months after our initial father-son conversation, I was lying in bed with Saril.

We'd just spent a half hour between us exhorting Amber that he was not to read one more minute and was going to turn the lights off and go to bed. I suspected he was already reading again, by a crack of light from the hallway.

"Sar, do you think Amber is strange?" I asked, looking at the ceiling.

He rolled onto his side and patted me on the shoulder. "Of course I do. I'd be disappointed if he weren't."

Saril was of the belief that most hara tried too hard to conform to societal norms. He's an artist, so of course he thought that.

"I don't just mean in general," I explained. "I mean his thing about women."

"Oh, that," he sighed, withdrawing his hand.

"That." I turned my head to face him. "I just... Doesn't it seem a little obsessive?"

He nodded. "Definitely! But all harlings get obsessed."

I raised an eyebrow. "*All?*"

"Well, I did!" He propped himself up on his elbows. "I don't know if I've ever told you this, but as a harling I was crazy about frogs."

"Frogs," I repeated, grinning. "Um, no, you never told me that."

"Oh, yes," he said. "Frogs. We lived by a bog, as you know, and I was always playing next to it, or by the pond, and so I was always seeing frogs. It was one of the first things I started drawing. I drew them a *lot*."

Taking his cue, I too propped myself up on my elbows, then kissed his ear. "And just how long did this frog obsession last?"

Saril thought about it. "Oh, I don't know... A couple years, I guess? Eventually I just got obsessed with nature in general, but at first it was frogs, frogs, frogs!"

I reached around with one arm and caressed his hair. "Well, maybe that's where he gets it... this *obsession* thing. I never did that."

"Don't worry," he chided. "He'll get over it. Now hush," he said, and nuzzled my cheek. "Right now, why don't you feed *my* obsession and do what you did to me last night?"

Amber didn't get over it. If he had, I wouldn't be writing this.

The situation escalated. In less than a year he'd exhausted the local library's information on women. (His teachers were amazed by his reading ability, although if they'd known all the material he'd been reading, most of it meant strictly for adult hara, they wouldn't have been.) So we went to the next nearest library, then the one after that. Eventually we wound up at the main city library. This book supply was much larger, so he did stall there eventually, although I could only take him occasionally, which annoyed him.

In the meantime, he began to collect books of his own. He went to bookstores, antique stores, asked friends at school if they had old human books. He horded his allowance money to buy the ones he "had to have," then by four he was working out ways to earn money. He tutored others harlings. He learned to sew and knit, then sold scarves and quilts. He sold other books of his he didn't like as much so he could buy books he did like.

Saril continue to tell me he'd grow out of it. "He'll be a historian," he said one day, working on a painting. "This is just the hook, like the frogs were for me."

I chuckled and he looked up. "What?"

"Sorry, I just pictured somehar fishing with a frog on the line for a lure."

He elbowed me. "You! Take your funny mental images and let me be. I want to finish this."

It was on another occasion like this, when I'd come to Saril's studio to express my worries, only to be sent out, that the situation came to a head.

It was late afternoon, on a day without school, and I hadn't seen Amber except a few times in passing, once in the kitchen making tea, another time coming out of the basement with some sundry supplies. I'd ask him if he had some project for school and he said no, heading back to his room.

At loose ends, I headed over to say hello. The bedroom door was ajar; not wide open, but definitely not shut. From out in the hall, I stared.

Amber was standing in front of the mirror, looking at himself. Not in itself unusual for a harling coming up in years. But what *was* unusual was that he had breasts. Breasts which he was caressing fondly with his fingers. He was also wearing makeup, most noticeably deep red lipstick.

I approached the door and knocked softly. "Amb?"

He turned from the mirror, startled, though not terrifically so. He had known the door was open, apparently.

"Oh, hi, Dede," he said, stepping towards me. "What do you think?"

I studied him. He'd done a passing job with the breasts. They were smoothly rounded, not simply wads of fabric or paper. The makeup had obviously been done with great care as well. And he was wearing a skirt.

He saw me looking. "I made it myself," he announced proudly. "Off a pattern in that very first actress book you gave me!"

I nodded. "I see." I glanced around the room. On the dresser I saw the makeup laid out. I recognised some as my own, some as Saril's. Some of it was unfamiliar. I assumed he had purchased the items on his own. On the bed were strewn various books, open to pages he'd been consulting, or so I gathered.

"Well," I said. "This is quite something."

I didn't know what to say. This was my own son, whom I'd known since he was in pearl (Saril and I would mindtouch with him), and yet here was a part of him that I honestly had not known was there.

"Amber," I began carefully. "I... I wonder why you're doing this."

He creased his brow. "Doing... Oh, you mean dressing up?"

I nodded. It did seem obvious.

"I've been thinking about it for a long time," he explained. "Dreamt about it many times."

"Dreamt about...?" I prompted.

"About being a woman," he supplied.

I turned around and went to Saril's studio.

"We have to talk," I announced, once I'd closed the door.

My chesnari looked up from his painting briefly, annoyed. "I told you, I want to finish this," he said.

I walked up to his easel and put my hand between him and the painting. "Now."

Saril set down his palette. "What?"

"It's Amb," I said, rubbing my face uneasily.

Saril waited.

And waited.

After a minute of thinking about the best way to say it, I said, "Well, it's like this. He doesn't just *like* women... *obsess* over women..."

"I told you, not to—"

"Sar, hush. He wants to *be* a woman."

Saril flinched. "He... *what?*"

Moving over to the day bed, I told him what I'd seen.

"And so now he's got himself all done up like an actress."

Saril studied my hand, which he'd been holding as I explained the situation. "He's not just getting ready for some play at school?"

"I don't think so," I said. "That's not the sense I have. This seems more... *serious*. Especially since it's not like it came out of nowhere."

Saril dropped my hand, stood up and walked to the window, where he stood for a minute or two, quiet, pondering.

Finally, without turning toward me, he said, "Would you be very annoyed if I told you it was just a phase and he'll get over it?"

"Hmmph!" I scoffed. "The more you keep saying that, the less true it seems to be."

He walked back towards me. "Well, is it really so bad?"

"Sar, harlings don't want to be women. They're not interested in women. I mean, maybe a *little*, out of curiosity, since there aren't any women around, but not... not like Amber is!"

He sat down next to me and patted my shoulder. "What's the harm? He's just different, that's all."

Again, remember, Saril's an artist. And I was used to this attitude of his.

"Well, what about you come look?" I suggested.

"OK. And if I think it just looks artistic, individualistic, then you lay off it," he announced, heading toward the door

Amber's new hobby was, Saril decided, definitely artistic and individualistic.

Not only did he not want to discourage Amber, he encouraged him. He – the one who had taught our harling how to sew – bought him more fabrics. He helped make more skirts. Dresses. Scarves. Whatever Amber wanted to match the outfits in the pictures or in the novels he'd then started to read.

Soon he had a small wardrobe of historic women's fashions. And soon he wasn't just content to try them on at home, but wanted to go out in them, along with concocted breasts and makeup.

"Absolutely not," I said. "Everyhar will stare!"

Saril was naturally supportive. "Don't listen to your father. Be yourself. If somehar doesn't like you, they're not worth knowing."

Afterward, we argued over it. "You shouldn't just let him do this!" I admonished.

We were sitting at the kitchen table, drinking. "And why not?" He took a sip of beer and studied me for a few moments. "Just what is your problem?" he asked.

"*My* problem? *My* problem?"

"Dede, I've been wondering," he began, "just why you seem irked about all of this – the dresses and now the long hair and all that."

"It's unnatural!" I spat.

Saril set down his mug. "It's *what?*"

"Unnatural." I took up my own mug and swigged it. "What if he were just painting himself up like a kanene or some soume consort?"

"And what would be wrong with that?" he sniffed.

I wasn't getting anywhere. "OK," I said, "here's what it is. When I look at photos of women, it's always made me uncomfortable." My sweet chesnari waited for me to go on, understanding in his eyes. "It's... well, in a way, they're attractive, but at the same time, they're *alien*. They're... another species. Do you know what I mean?"

"I do," he said softly, "but it seems to be what Amb wants. He's not hurting anyhar, is he? I mean, besides you."

I looked up at the ceiling. "No... But... I just wish he wouldn't."

"My hostling always said you can't make your harling be what he doesn't want to be, or not be what you don't want him to be."

"He let you run wild," I observed, smirking.

"That he did," Saril agreed. "But you love me for it."

I did, and so that argument was ended. At least for that day.

By the time feybraiha came, early in Amber's seventh year, he was dressing up as a har-woman most of the time. His peers, hara in the neighbourhood and strangers who saw him around, didn't jostle him too badly about it. They were tolerant. Harlings have whims. Amber's hostling is an artist, the thinking went, or so I gathered. Just indulge him. He didn't have a huge number of friends, but he had some.

Then one night I happened to be walking past his bedroom and picked up on a noise. Crying. Muffled, but there.

I paused and listened. Yes, it was Amber.

Quietly I opened the door. "Amb, you OK?" I asked.

He lying on the bed, holding a pillow into his face.

"I'm fine," he said, in a muffled voice.

I sat down at the end of the bed. "You're not fine. I heard you in the hall."

He sobbed some more. Most unlike him. Amber was generally a very happy child. Dramatic, insistent, obsessed, but happy. Of course it was his feybraiha and every harling changes then.

"What is it?" I asked, squeezing his knee through the silky skirt he was wearing.

"You wouldn't understand," he replied, his voice still muffled by the pillow.

I reached over and tugged the pillow away. "Understand what?"

He studied the ceiling, not looking for me, for a half a minute, before replying. "I'll be done with my feybraiha soon," he said. "And you've set me up with Terra for my first aruna."

"And?" I prompted.

He looked over to me. "And I don't want him!" he moaned.

"Oh."

Saril and I came up with alternatives. If not Terra, then somehar else. A harling should go with somehar he wants, of course.

Amber didn't want anyhar.

After about the tenth suggestion, Sari and I were at our wit's end.

"*I* wasn't this choosy," I said. "In fact, my parents caught me trying to do it with the neighbour's gardener."

"You've told me that a million times," he said. We were in bed and again he was on his side, holding my shoulder. "That doesn't help us here."

"What can we do, though?" I asked. "We'll run out of hara soon. What do we do, put up a flyer? Have auditions?"

Saril was silent. Then: "Well, we could ask him what he wants."

"Sar, we've asked him. He says he doesn't know," I reminded him. "Just 'not him,' 'not him,' 'not him.'"

Saril stiffened. "Maybe that's it," he said decisively.

"*What's* it?"

"Maybe," he said, gripping my shoulder, "it's not a *he* he wants, it's a *she!*"

I gaped. Then gaped some more. Finally: "What?"

Saril let go over me and sat up. "He likes women. Obviously.

He dresses likes a women. What if, somehow, for some reason, he also, you know... *likes* women?"

I gaped some more. "But... but he's never met a real woman," I said.

"All the more reason to fantasise then," Saril said reasonably.

I turned the problem over in my head. "Well, even if that's true, there aren't any women. Nowhere near *here*."

Saril nodded. "That true, but..." he considered. "But I bet we could get somehar to dress up like one!"

"That's the stupides—" I began, then stopped. I locked eyes with Saril. "That's brilliant."

It was desperation that let me allow it. That and the fact that when I did get up the nerve to ask my son if he might be interested in a har dressed like a woman, he said he would be. And he thanked me over and over.

Saril had an actor friend, beautiful and decidedly soume, who agreed to take on feybraiha duties. He had no problem doing it. "Another role!" he said.

The feybraiha celebration went off without a hitch. Amber looked... well, even though I admit looking at him all dressed up made me flinch inside.... I must say he looked pretty stunning. Like one of the actresses in that first book, which had somehow led the way to that moment.

Before heading out, to take a carriage to the actor's apartment, Amber came up to Saril and me and thanked us. "I'm so glad you understand," he said. "I didn't know what I wanted, but somehow *you* did."

"Your hostling did," I admitted. "I was confused. But it was his idea."

He kissed both of us, leaving traces of lipstick on our cheeks, and walked out the front door towards his first aruna.

That was the beginning of the end. Sounds ominous, I know, but that's how I think of this part of our family's history. Amber grew up, had feybraiha, and started living as a woman full-time.

Saril and I continued to disagree about the entire affair.

"Stop worrying," he said. "He's fine! He's just different!"

I gritted my teeth. "I know that! I just want him to be happy."

"He is," Saril assured me. "*He is.*"

On this point at least, Saril was wrong. Our son was *not* happy.

It took us longer to notice the problem than it should have. Amber had gotten a job at a clothier's, sewing and selling fashion, so he wasn't home all the time, but still, we should have noticed.

We were at the table one summer night having dinner. In the evening sunlight it occurred to me Amber looked rather pale, bony. His hair, normally perfectly coifed, looked a bit dishevelled. He picked at his food.

"Amb, is everything all right?" I asked.

He stiffened, then sagged. "No."

"What is it?" Saril asked. "Work?"

"No," he repeated, this time sounding irritated. "Not that."

Saril and I waited.

Finally I said, "Well?"

Amber sighed. "I need aruna. And I can't get any."

"Oh. Um… Well, most hara do run into that—"

"No, they don't." He set his hands flat on the table. "I mean, I need aruna, and I know I could take aruna with anyhar, physically, but I don't want that. I want…"

We, the patient parents, waited.

"I want a woman. A *real* woman."

With that I reached my limit. I didn't understand. What was wrong with him? Why was he like this? Would this have happened if I hadn't given him that damned book with the actresses?

Saril, was more tolerant, of course, but also deeply concerned. Hara can't do without aruna, he said. He tried to convince Amber to compromise and just take aruna, just like eating to get sustenance.

"I can find some more hara for you to act out with," he promised.

Amber wouldn't have it.

Within a month, he left our house. He didn't even tell us goodbye.

He left us a note. Among other things, it said: "I love you all, I love this place, but I have to find what I'm really looking for."

Last month, after five years, our son returned, only he was now our daughter. In a faraway land, which had taken him months to reach, he'd found what he was looking for. And that thing was a woman, whom he'd brought back with him.

Her name was Ebon and while she wasn't perhaps as curvy as some of the women I knew Amber fancied (judging from what he'd said of pictures), she was definitely all woman: hips, breasts, shining long hair, and soft skin.

It was quite awkward at first. We hugged him and kissed him and cried, and we welcomed him home, welcomed Ebon too, but we had so many questions.

A lot of our questions were typical ones, like: How did you meet? Others were peculiar to the situation, and aimed, politely, at Ebon: What's it like being a human in a harish world?

But the strangest question, which I finally had to ask, a couple weeks into their visit, was this: How in the world did they have aruna?

How Amber laughed. And laughed. "Oh, we manage," he said.

I wanted more details and yet... I *didn't*. He seems happy, content. More so than I ever expected he'd be.

"I told you he'd be fine," Saril said to me the other day.

I nodded. "Yes, you were right. *She* is fine."

"*She*," he said. "Yes, I suppose she is."

A matter of honour

Martina Bellovičová

Year 30, Tokyo

Perched on the staircase leading to the second floor, Satoru peered down between the bars of the bannisters. At six years old, he still insisted on leaving the door of his bedroom open all night, whenever he stayed at his grandparents' place, so that dim light could filter in. The doorbell had woken him and, upon hearing raised voices from the parlour, he had crept silently out of bed in order to listen in.

A young man stood in the room below, dressed in dark flowing robes of a foreign style Satoru had only seen in movies, but dirty, worn and patched. Under the cloak, his body seemed to be on the skinny side, but not really emaciated or weak. His waist-length hair was in knots, hanging limply around his radiant face. Satoru understood the stranger had a long journey behind him, but the words he was able to catch were not making sense to him. The man spoke about having travelled through Europe, China and Korea, which was obviously a lie. Satoru recalled the pictures of beautiful, exotic places he had found in his mother's old books, places he had wanted to visit once he grew up. But he had learned this would not be possible, because Japan's borders had been closed many years ago. Those countries were no longer safe, not since the apocalypse.

Strangely enough, his Granny seemed to have believed the tale the stranger had concocted, for she pulled him into a hug, crying. "Oh Takashi... I'm so happy. So very happy! We thought you were dead..."

The boy frowned. The name was familiar. Uncle Takashi was

his mother's older brother, whom Satoru had never seen, but often heard about. This uncle had gone to Germany before the apocalypse to study and become a doctor, but he'd never come back. However, this man could not possibly be him, could he? Satoru did not know everything about life and death yet, but he was fairly certain a person could not suddenly return home after thirty years abroad and look like a teenager.

Satoru's grandfather clearly didn't trust the stranger either. "Step away from him!" he ordered, forcing his grandmother to release the young man from her embrace. "Who are you? *What* are you? Speak, demon!"

Pure fury emanated from his grandfather's voice, making Satoru wish he could just shrink down and fade away from all of this. Yet he had no choice but to watch the scene turn into a living nightmare, right in front of his eyes. Grandpa was threatening to call the police, while the young man attempted to explain himself in an alluring, velvet voice. Grandma was begging – they could hide Takashi, no one would ever know. But Grandpa said he wasn't going to let himself be fooled and reached for the phone.

From his hiding place, Satoru glimpsed the flash of a blade in the stranger's hand. He wanted to scream, give a warning, but his jaw hung open in what could be best described as holy horror and no voice came out. Like every young one, whose instincts have not yet been tampered with by upbringing, he knew that his life depended on the ability not to make a noise. In the meantime, the youth charged – once, twice. He moved so quickly that the boy could have almost believed he had imagined the blows, except for the swiftly spreading crimson-coloured pool around the stranger's feet.

Six years old and still afraid of the dark, Satoru realised the real demons walked in the light, and they could be as beautiful as they were frightening.

Year 55, Neo-Osaja, Osaka Quarantine Zone

Satoru took a deep breath, squeezed the *omamori* amulet he carried in his pocket as a lucky charm and counted to eight, the lucky number. Then he turned up the volume in his earpiece that would convey his cue to enter the conference room. He was not a man prone to nervousness and his performance had never been anything but spectacular, but this time, a moderate level of anxiety had settled in his stomach, because he was well aware of the importance of the event. The intensity of the hum in his ear rose gradually, until he could discern every word the rough, age-worn voice was saying.

"...don't understand why we can't simply eradicate every last one of those bastards. We have observed them long enough to know that all their settlements are concentrated around six central points: Tokyo, Kyoto-Nara, Sapporo, Nagano with the *onsen* area, Hiroshima and the Okinawa island. We have developed weapons that would completely obliterate their bases, while leaving the surrounding areas untouched for human resettlement. Right now, my army could strike and swipe away this debris within a week."

A few seconds of silence followed, interrupted by noises of approval and snorts of disapproval. Then, another voice came, slightly younger, livelier, with an undertone of irony.

"Because, my dear general, we still need them. Or rather, we need to inspect them and uncover the secrets of their fecundity, their apparent lack of aging, their physical and mental faculties. And we need to be able to pinpoint what makes them so well adapted for this world, isolate it and replicate it in human embryos. Otherwise it could easily happen that shortly after we have killed the last one of them, we too will die out."

All of them knew about the alarmingly low human fertility rates, which continued to fall despite the obligatory bi-monthly artificial inseminations for all women over the age of eighteen. This was further complicated by the fact that an enormous number of boys and men of fertile age had joined the ranks of the mutant race that called itself Wraeththu. The infection that had originally started spreading unnoticed in one of the host clubs in Harajuku had long ago turned into an epidemic, and there were simply not enough human males left to keep the population up. And while their old ones withered and died, the new race thrived. One could choose to ignore it, but facts were still facts.

"Very well," another voice said, and Satoru realised with a shock that it belonged to the Emperor himself, "your points are valid, but We see a slight problem here, Kawano-san. You keep making these same points at every conference We happen to take part in, but so far you have delivered no satisfactory results – or, should We say, no results whatsoever. Have you and your team actually made any real progress in this matter?"

The head of the Japanese Medical Association now spoke up. "I am glad that you have asked, your Majesty. We have indeed made a huge step forward in recent weeks. Now, I have the pleasure to introduce Doctor Shinsaku Satoru, a brain specialist from Neo-Tokyo. He will elaborate on our research himself. It was his invention that enabled us to arrive at new discoveries."

Recognising his cue, Satoru swallowed the lump in his throat, rapped at the door twice and entered the room beyond. He bent down in a formal bow, greeting the assortment of men many years his senior and far more important in their functions. The presence of the Emperor meant that if his performance wasn't satisfactory, the entire team could be sorry for the rest of their lives. For most people, the Emperor was equivalent to a god – a higher being they could worship in hopes for a better life, but never actually see. As a first class scientist, Satoru had had the dubious pleasure of encountering the Emperor a few times on similar occasions, which had enabled him to form his own opinion. The only semblance to a god he'd observed in the man was that he needed to be feared. From the moment Satoru straightened from his bow, though, as if someone had pulled a switch, he became a beacon of composure and self-confidence – at least on the surface.

"Your Majesty... Gentlemen..."

Impassive faces were glaring at him from behind the U-shaped formation of conference tables, fitted with microphones and bottled water. The bluish light of the overhead fluorescent lamps added a sickly pallor to their aged faces. At almost thirty, Satoru was by far the youngest person there, which was no surprise, because the majority of men in Japan were way past fifty these days. To add insult to injury, he was blessed by the perfect physique and ageless face some Asians had, the look that made it impossible to tell if a person was thirty-five or eighteen. He could feel their distrust almost physically. Only the head of the medical association was smiling at him – like a cat that has just eaten a bird.

"My name is Shinsaku Satoru and as Kawano-san probably informed you, I lead the research concerning the neurology of

Wraeththu. By inspecting our test subjects, we have found their brain activity to be twice as high as a human's. This reflects on their ability to communicate telepathically, even share memories or visions, with a quality that makes the receiver experience the memory as if it were their own."

On the wall behind Satoru, a large screen waited for him to switch on the laptop and rouse it to life. He walked to his table and ran his fingers over the touchpad. A photograph of a huge, black-and-white machine appeared on the screen, accompanied by a descriptive diagram.

"I have developed a device capable of prying such memories from the test subject's mind." He smiled proudly, gesturing towards the screen. "In my team, we call it the *Tapir* – based on the old myth that says tapirs are creatures capable of consuming dreams. I know this probably sounds unbelievable, so I have decided – all risks considered – to give you a live demonstration. If you would turn to your left, please…"

Confused, most of the heads turned obediently in the given direction. The wall on the left side of the room was in fact a sliding partition, which the doctor opened mechanically, revealing what looked like a tiny operating room. And in its centre… a splash of shock-red hair on a camp bed, emaciated body tied with nano-chains, chest heaving, electrodes on the forehead. The cables trailed to a real-life version of the Tapir, which emanated a light glow and low, grumbling noises. Satoru unplugged the screen from the computer and connected it directly to the mysterious device. The picture was replaced by a slightly unsettling static noise.

"Is this safe?" someone asked, meaning, of course, for the board, not for the har on the bed.

"Where did you get him?"

"Everything is perfectly safe," Satoru was quick to assure everyone. "You only have to follow the screen when the experiment starts. The Wraeththu in question has been provided courtesy of the military, Nara Quarantine Zone division. There are plenty to be caught easily where this one came from – a conveniently peaceful community, that one. Well then, shall we proceed?"

The Emperor nodded enthusiastically, face strained to remain aloof. Satoru pushed a few buttons on the Tapir. A sound just on the edge of audibility echoed through the room. A distinct tension built up in the air – a shift everybody felt yet no-one could quite place a finger on. And then a piercing scream cut through the room, threatening to rip their ear-drums. The lithe body was writhing in its chains frantically, as if trying to prevent rape, and indeed it was a rape of sorts. The har was exhausted, though, spent from previous attempts to resist the Tapir's intrusions, none of which had been successful. Soon the wailing died down, reduced to soft moans. The big screen sparked to life.

All the eyes in the room were glued to it in an instant, opened wide in disbelief. Despite having witnessed this procedure numerous times, even Satoru found himself fascinated all over again. One could not simply get used to such an experience.

What they saw was a place most of them had visited at least once before the Wraeththu invasion, the Kiyomizu-dera temple in Kyoto with its lovely waterfall and glamorous garden. The trees were so realistic that the men could almost feel them casting merciful shadows in the summer heat. The bubbling water threatened to spill out of the screen, and the room was alive with birdsong. Just like a 3D movie, the picture was pulling them in, granting them the unique feeling of being a part of it all.

At this point, some of them silently voiced their doubts about the authenticity of the experience, guessing it had to be a pre-recorded artistic piece, but in the next minute, the door of the temple opened and a colourful crowd of hara spilled out, laughing in joy. In the midst of them, a young pair walked, matching silken robes flowing around them, hems dragging in the dust on the ground, pooling around their ankles when they stopped to share breath. Blood was still dripping from their wrists. One of the two, there was no doubt, was the red-haired creature currently being experimented on, even though the memory showed the har in a much better state of health.

"*I have always wanted to get married here,*" the other said and chuckled. "*Only I had originally believed it would be to a woman!*"

The red-haired one had been a har longer than he had been human and such a statement made him frown, even though he knew it was meant in fun. "*A blood-bind is something indefinably more than a simple marriage,*" he said gently, looking in the other har's eyes. "*From now on, we will sense each other in a way that only true soul mates can, every moment of our waking lives. There is no divorce from such a bond other than death.*"

"Disgusting," the Emperor said, breaking the magic of the moment, "yet impressive."

"Thank you, Your Majesty." Satoru bowed and moved to switch off the machine. A disapproving noise from the monarch stopped him.

"We want to see more. Can you show us another memory or two, maybe somewhat less… explicit?"

"Most certainly." Satoru nodded, successfully hiding the fact he had broken into a cold sweat. This was a question he had hoped not to be asked. "But there is a slight problem. The machines monitoring the life functions of our subject show that overly frequent use of the Tapir puts too much strain on the brain. I am afraid that after producing a sequence of memories in such a small time frame, the subject could expire. The risk of a stroke is very high."

The Emperor shrugged. "We fail to see the problem. Didn't you say there is plenty to be had where this one came from?"

"Quite so, your Majesty." Satoru quickly stepped up to the game. "As you say, no problem at all."

The following afternoon Satoru was in the biobank, helping with the reorganisation of samples. Like every room in Neo-Osaka, the bank was cramped, providing just enough space to house the overfilled freezers. The government had begun to build neotowns as soon as the global apocalypse started. They were huge underwater structures, hypermodern habitable zones, constructed especially to be able to withstand natural disasters as well as enemy attacks, air-tight and equipped with everything a person needed for life – one cubicle per family, central kitchens, storage room, medical care, security police stations, institutions for education, entertainment areas. The only thing missing there was space. That, and privacy. Satoru was glad that his position as a scientific expert awarded him a tiny room and lab that were truly his own.

"These are all from the last one." His colleague opened the ice box in order to sort the samples. "DNA plasmids, genomic DNA, RNA, tissue, proteins. It's good we've managed to acquire enough to last for a while before the poor bastard was fed to the fish."

"I suppose so," Satoru muttered noncommittally, checking the

-20C freezer for empty space.

The other doctor laughed. "If I didn't know you, I'd have thought you felt sorry for him."

"Don't be ridiculous." Satoru frowned, secretly inspecting his feelings concerning what had happened at the conference. No, he didn't feel sorry, not for one of *them*. And besides, he couldn't have prevented it, could he? No one would dare to disobey the Emperor's wish. "It's just that my work, unlike yours, cannot be performed on mere tissue samples. I need a whole, functioning brain. Anyway, have you made any progress as of late?"

"Eh... to tell you the truth it's pretty slow," the doctor admitted. "It would be so much easier if we could simply infect somebody and observe, how..."

"Yoshi!" Satoru interrupted, furious. "How can you even say something like this?"

"Well, when the first sheep was cloned, everyone considered that immoral too, but it was still a huge step for mankind..."

Satoru was about to start explaining why sacrificing a sentient being was not exactly the same, but the piercing shriek of an alarm coming from the central sound system stopped him. The speakers, installed in every room, came to life.

Attention! Attention, residents of Neo-Osaka! Danger of infection! Immediately retreat from the corridors to your cubicle or to the public institution closest to your current location! Lock the doors and remain in place until the next announcement! Dr. Shinsoku Satoru is to proceed to Umezu Taishō, acting General of the Army...

"Here you go." Yoshi smirked. "That didn't take long, huh?"

They both knew what the announcement meant: the army had caught and delivered another mutant.

There was something different about this one. Satoru noticed this immediately upon entering the windowless room that served as his private lab, part of which had been fitted to serve as a cell. It wasn't the har's physical appearance, which pretty much corresponded with the Wraeththu standard – he was small, fine-boned with delicate features and long midnight hair, kept in a multitude of thin glossy braids. It wasn't the finery he wore, either: the embroidered silken kimono decorated with white cranes in flight, eyes lined with kohl, expensive amulets dangling on his neck, tiny silver spiders spinning a transparent net in his hair. What set him apart from all the hara Satoru had had a chance to experiment on in the past was the way the prisoner bore himself; strong shameless steps that swept the nanotech chains behind him like silken swags. Inherent pride put fearlessly on display. He did not flinch when the doctor entered the room, but Satoru thought he saw the flickering gleam of a haughty, disdainful eye.

The general who had brought in the har informed Satoru that the new arrival had walked right into the trap, following a soldier who had acted as a lure. A job well done. And maybe suspiciously easy, Satoru's instincts were warning him. He observed the individual, taking a mental note of his confident poise and astounding lack of fear. He was like a tiger in a cage, majestic and proud even in captivity, well aware that if he were free, he could smash his opponents with one flick of a paw. Satoru prepared a cocktail of narcotics in a syringe and was about to administer it to the har, so that he could examine him unconscious, but as he moved to open the cell, the captive stepped forward boldly, momentarily shocking him into reverse.

Lean but strong fingers wrapped around the bars and a beautiful impassive face filled the gap between them. A deceptively angelic face, and yet – to Satoru – that of a demon. The har's sea-green eyes focused on Satoru. "I will cooperate."

"I beg your pardon?" Satoru lifted an eyebrow in disbelief.

"I said I wished to cooperate," the har repeated, his eyes flicking to the syringe. "You won't be needing that."

"Really? Do you even know where you are and what will happen to you?"

Having recovered from the initial shock, the doctor was now fishing for signs of treachery. He didn't know where to begin with this one. He would have expected a new captive to try and fight, or use some kind of special powers, perhaps attempt to talk his way out, only eventually to be broken, to fear, to sit silently in the corner, maybe even to flinch like a beaten dog. But Satoru definitely not expect the captive to volunteer and offer assistance. The har must be seasoned, beneath his youthful appearance – dangerous, strong. There must be an underlying motive for such behaviour...

"Of course," the har said. "I may have been careless when the army seized me, but that does not make me stupid. I am aware of how badly human scientists want to lean our secrets and to what lengths they are willing to go."

"Yet you are eager to give me easy access to such information...?" Satoru narrowed his eyes, as if trying to divine the answers from the har's smooth face. "Why? What's in it for you?"

"Firstly, a promise from you to treat me better than my predecessors," the har replied swiftly, as if he had spent the entire time during transport preparing his answers. He began to pace again, measuring his words, one per step. "Regular food and drink, water and a bed for sleeping. Maybe a book or two to pass the time."

Satoru chortled in amusement. This one had balls – metaphorically speaking, because what really lay between his legs was an alien territory. "I suppose that could be arranged."

"More importantly, I get to keep my honour."

The doctor looked at him askance, waiting for the har to elaborate.

"I am one of the leaders of my tribe, doctor," the har explained. "That is why I took it upon myself to follow the soldier who had invaded our territory. I wanted to end that soldier's life, a task at which I failed miserably. I proved unable to protect my people with my swords, but I can still protect them by offering my body. As long as I am here... As long as I am kept alive and give you what you seek, you will not need to harm firther any of the hara for whom I am responsible. I will not lose my face."

This was a matter of honour – something Satoru could understand, even admire. The fear of losing face was deeply engrained in Japanese culture, but in the post-apocalyptic time, when life was a fragile, valuable thing, most people would not commit ritual suicide anymore when facing their own failure and shame. From the Wraeththu memories Satoru had already seen, he noticed their way of life bore a semblance to the samurai of old times, dedicated and well-trained. The resolve with which this being was willing to subject himself to a life of never-ending experiments, some of them painful or extremely exhausting, in order to buy safety for his community, suddenly made the har less alien in Satoru's eyes. It made him respect the captive, at least to the extent of accepting his terms, even though, of course, he could just take without asking, as he had in the past.

"Very well. First, you will answer questions regarding your age and physical state today, as well as the biological particulars of your race. Then, I will need samples of your blood, bodily fluids and bone marrow. But before that, I will tell the service to bring us some refreshments."

He collected a netbook from the worktable and opened a new page in the editor. "Name?"

"Kiyoshi," the har purred, making the name sound – contrary to its meaning - anything but pure. "And you are...?"

Satoru looked at him, startled. He hesitated for a moment, but making a negative decision didn't take him long at all. Any familiarity that could occur between the two of them had to be prevented. "You will always call me 'Doctor'," he said coldly.

Kiyoshi shook his head, observing Satoru with a smirk, as if saying, "we shall see about that."

An unsettling feeling crept into Satoru's stomach – not quite fear, not quite anxiety – as he realised the har's eyes were challenging him. This one was dangerous – and the only one of these predators ever to ask his name.

During the first five days, Satoru had Kiyoshi undergo a gruelling series of uncomfortable check-ups, which the har bore with zen calm, all the while striving to be helpful, provide descriptions, explanations and answers. Clearly, he tried hard to demonstrate his will to cooperate, but Satoru couldn't get rid of the thought that Kiyoshi was testing him in turn. Under no circumstances could Satoru allow himself to lose concentration in proximity of that being, or free him from the nanochains that prevented free movement and most attempts to employ magic.

Even if the har had been honest in his intentions to make himself useful, he was still challenging Satoru in a different way. He was testing the doctor's patience. Despite the physical exhaustion and minor pains he must have been experiencing, there were parts of the process Kyoshi appeared to thoroughly enjoy. He took great pleasure in displaying his nudity to the doctor, possessing no modesty as he undressed with the elegance of a courtesan. When told to hurry, he would shrug off the remainder of his clothing in one fluid movement and pose like a model.

At the end of the fourth day, Kiyoshi enacted a scene of near orgasm when Satoru subjected him to an examination of his reproductive organs. This left Satoru inexplicably flushed and, as a result, horribly embarrassed – a feeling that was multiplied ten times by the horrible realisation that the har knew it, and was greatly amused. It also sparked off a discussion about the particulars of aruna and grissecon, harish sex for fun and for magical purposes, respectively. Naturally, Kiyoshi described them enthusiastically as the most desirable acts one could ever experience and paid great attention to detail. Satoru was torn between scientific curiosity and the panicked urge of not really wanting to know. This was a deep-rooted fear of the possibility he could find something likeable, or even alluring about the mutant race, because that would be just a step away from acknowledging they too had feelings, that he and the captive may not be that dissimilar from one another.

On the fifth day, Satoru aborted the game. It was time to employ the Tapir. So far, the only things Kiyoshi had been giving up was his body for Satoru to abuse and a bit of interesting chatter. This was going to be different. The Tapir would rob the mutant of something personal, something one normally kept for himself or shared only with a few select others. Kiyoshi probably realised it, because he had dropped the teasing that morning and fell into contemplative silence when Satoru ordered him to lie down on the camp bed. As Satoru fastened the chains around Kiyoshi's waist and attached the electrodes of the Tapir to his forehead, the doctor could feel the taut muscles beneath his fingers tighten and strain. The har was suppressing the urge to fight.

"Relax," Satoru advised him. "It will be easier on you that way."

Kiyoshi gave him a defiant look, obviously disliking the fact he had revealed anxiety. "You must be popular with the women," he said suddenly, not even bothering to keep amusement from his voice when Satoru flinched. "Especially with so few other decent specimens of the human male still around..."

"This is hardly appropriate, or any of your business," Satoru said stiffly, "but if you must know, my time is too valuable to be spent on foolish romance."

How did the har know his sensitive place? No, he couldn't have, it was simply a lucky guess, Satoru assured himself. And he really could have been popular, tall and handsome as he was, with prominent cheekbones, full lips, elegant jawline, well-shaped nose and eyes sporting perfect double lids, so rarely seen in Japan. His skin was clean of youthful imperfections but not yet marked with wrinkles. The whitened teeth, modern hairstyle and well-toned body showed he was a man who cared about his appearance. He could have chosen a life-partner. It was not really his fault that no woman seemed to be worthy or interesting enough. Who cared about that, anyway? As long as he contributed to the inseminations, his duty to mankind was done.

"That is sad," the har said.

"Not really. I will switch on the Tapir now. It is possible that the noise will be unpleasant for you, or that the procedure itself will cause uncomfortable feelings that could lead to a panic attack. If you manage to stay relaxed and keep your mind open, there should be minimal damage. Trying to block the intrusion makes everything worse."

"How does it choose the memory?"

"The machine selects one of the most prominent memories, with which you have occupied yourself most often, or the memory active in your brain in the moment of projection."

"Alright then." The har nodded. "What would you like me to think about?"

Satoru contemplated that briefly. "I need to learn all there is to know about your race," he said. "Why not start at the beginning? Show me how your Wraeththu tribe came into being and the origins of your race. Show me how new hara are made."

Kiyoshi appeared to be concentrating for a moment, reaching to the bottom of his mind for that particular memory. Satoru hoped it would be a good one, a strong one. He switched on the screen, prepared to feel it, taste it and submerge himself into it. The har's eyes blinked open.

"Do you even know how much I am giving you?" he asked in a subdued, yet insistent tone. "No human I know of has ever witnessed the transformation, except, of course, those who did not remain human."

"You aren't giving me anything I couldn't take myself," Satoru said coldly and hit the button that would slam an iron fist into the har's skull.

The three Wraeththu arrived in Nara silently, about two years after the first members of the mutant race appeared in Japan and took over Tokyo. They came under the veil of night, through the lush primeval forest of cedars, firs and cypresses that surrounded the temple area, dressed in traditional hakama *and* uwagi, *each carrying a weapon and a travel bag. Like ghosts, they managed to slip past all army units patrolling around Nara, and knocked at the shrine gate, politely requesting shelter for the night.*

Awoken by the gong, Kiyoshi darted from his bed and rushed outside. He found the priests ready at the gate, poised in battle positions, weapons in their hands. He was about to mingle with them so as not to miss anything, when a sharp whistle from above attracted his attention. A few boys, live-in students like Kiyoshi himself, were situated on the gabled roof, which extended over the main entrance. If the travellers did something insidious, the boys were to warn everyone. However, instead of that, they simply stood there, mouths agape, and one of them waved frantically, calling: "You have to see this! Open the gate, quick!"

"Have you ever witnessed anything like this?" one of the priests whispered, but no one could even answer for amazement. The crowd uttered gasps and sighs, eyes widened in wonder.

The hara were aglow in the moonlight and their rich clothes paired with long flowing hair (blacker than night, whiter than snow) inspired thoughts of ancient deities. But they were not alone. The path to Kasuga Shrine passed through the Deer Park, where semi-wild sika deer were able to roam freely and were believed to be sacred messengers of the kami *that inhabited the shrine and surrounding mountainous terrain. A numerous herd of the deer had surrounded the three strangers, another group was trailing in their wake and yet more continued to emerge from the forest, popping out from behind stone lanterns, skipping over bushes, dashing between the trees. The deer completely crowded the three figures, but didn't attack or beg for food. Rather, they were patiently waiting until what seemed to be the entire deer population of the forest had gathered there, looking up at the hara in what appeared to be divine adoration.*

It was like what had happened in the ancient tales of the kami *who had founded the shrine, accompanied by the first herd of deer whose descendants had lived in Nara ever since. And then, the crowd of animals parted, creating a wide aisle, down which a large stag marched, halting in front of the Wraeththu. It seemed that he was what all the others had been waiting for, because as soon as he bowed his head and lowered himself to his front knees before the white-haired har in the centre of the trinity, all the other deer did the same.*

Kiyoshi remembered what the gūji, the head priest of the shrine, had told them when the Wraeththu threat first came up for discussion: that time would tell what was the right approach to the mutants. Only the Earth had the power to choose which race it preferred. Once the priests had the chance to meet the Wraeththu, they would know whether to fight them or to invite them in. Kiyoshi knew in that instant. The sacred beasts of the shrine had come to greet the strangers with reverence. If that wasn't a miracle, what was?

Satoru switched off the device and stared blankly at the dead screen, his brain unable to process what he had just witnessed. He was a rational man. In the post-apocalyptic times, when many people returned to Shinto or Buddhism, looking for false safety in prayer and offerings, Satoru had embraced science. He believed the mutations on an organic level, as well as the seemingly supernatural abilities, could all be scientifically explained, and that the so-called virus was actually not a punishment sent from above, but something man-made, a biological weapon gone wrong. The images of the deer had changed it all.

"I didn't think we were already finished," said Kiyoshi, who had already come back to his senses.

Satoru could hardly register the har's presence. The little trip down the memory lane, courtesy of the Tapir, had undermined his certainties, and he couldn't allow for that to continue, because once the whole construction fell down... He didn't dare to guess what would be left.

"This can't be true." He shook his head defiantly. "It can't have happened like this. You have modified the memory somehow, haven't you?"

Kiyoshi gave him a little smile. "The Tapir is *your* creation. You can distrust me, but why would you distrust yourself?"

"You won't persuade me that you are *kami*," Satoru said firmly. He knew the har was right – there was no the machine could lie, but he was grasping for straws.

"I wouldn't dare to," the har said softly. "But maybe we are just a few steps closer to channelling them. A few steps closer to the universe."

"And wouldn't that be ironic! You, with your telepathy, with your strength and speed that you never had to work out for..." Satoru hissed, leaning over the har, who was still strapped to the camp bed. "Do you actually manage to fool people into thinking that the entirety of your endless lives is spent in peace and harmony with nature, frolicking with happy stags? Do you?"

Kiyoshi turned his head away from the man, obviously unsettled by the growing volume of his voice and the close proximity of his face. "I have no idea what you're implying..."

"There is a deadly edge to your benignity. You are quick to forget where you came from, but I can tell you it wasn't from the stars. It was from a human body. The loyalty you feel for what you call your tribe may be admirable, but in reality they are not your blood. They are just a handful of individuals who suffered the same fate of being turned into beings that believe they are channelling gods, and this makes them important to you by default... while your real parents have probably died at the hands of one of your new fellows. But you wouldn't care about that even if it happened right in front of your eyes!"

The har looked back at Satoru, regarding him with a half-confused, half-upset expression. "I don't know who hurt you," he said, "but it sure as hell wasn't me. Either take me back to my cell or go on with the experiment, but I've had enough of this nonsense."

Satoru fought the urge to slap him, but managed to control himself just in time. He let his hand fall and unstrapped Kiyoshi.

"Go on, have a rest. I've seen enough for one day."

It took three excruciating days for Satoru's curiosity and sense of duty to squash the suffocating fear of finding out something he would be better off not knowing. When he next opened Kiyoshi's cell, he noticed that even the captive seemed somewhat unnerved. He stopped to think about this for a while. Shouldn't the har have felt relief upon being left alone for an extended period of time? Maybe, like Satoru, he also needed a sense of closure. Or perhaps the certainty of his mind being probed seemed easier to face than the uncertainty of not knowing what would happen to him in the not so distant future.

A lack of interest could mean many things for a prisoner, some of them not necessarily to his benefit. If Satoru was indeed done with him, the har would most likely be handed over to the army to be executed and later the genetic material of his body used for further experiments. Satoru was surprised he found the idea of Kiyoshi being shot or electrocuted, (because no poison known to man worked on hara), unsettling. He attributed it to having visited the har's mind. And he was going to dive into its depths again...

As soon as the Tapir started to chew on Kiyoshi's thoughts, the screen came alive and pulled Satoru into the shrine, where a group of six boys and young men, one of them being the human version of Kiyoshi he had seen earlier, was participating in a ritual that closely resembled *matsuri*, drawing from the antique traditions. The *gūji*, along with the three foreign hara, were overseeing everything. This time, the memory wasn't shown in real time, but rather as an accelerated compilation of the most important points.

The participants first purified themselves by short periods of abstinence and fasting, and by bathing in salt water. Then the hara seemed to have been invoking the *kami*, only they called them *dehara*, performing a rite that consisted of opening the inner doors of the shrine, beating a drum and ringing bells, and calling the dehar to descend. Food offerings were presented. The *gūji* recited prayers. All the inceptees, because that was what the chosen young men were, presented offerings of branches from a sacred tree and locks of their own hair, which had been cut for the occasion. It was important to shave the head, or cut the hair short, one of the hienamas stressed, because the change took its toll on the body, as every cell transformed. Wasting energy on hair wouldn't be wise; one could always regrow it afterwards.

Then, accompanied by ceremonial music and dancing, the six were taken to an inner sanctuary, where the inception itself would take place. They were laid out on *tatami*, covered by clean sheets. They were given an unidentifiable drink that, Satoru guessed, was meant to help alleviate pain. The hienama talked to them for a while until the concoction begun to work. Then each har took a ceremonial knife, with which they opened their own wrists and – in quick succession – the right wrist of one of the boys assigned to them.

Then the view focused on Kiyoshi. Satoru watched the crude procedure in a state of shock. The hienama simply pressed their wrists together and held them firmly in place for a while, letting their blood mingle. No disinfection, no stitching, no needle in the vein. The boy was half asleep, thanks to whatever drug had been given to him. The hienama proceeded to the boy next to Kiyoshi, repeating the entire process. Never more than two, Satoru heard in his mind, even though nobody was talking in the memory at that moment. If one hienama incepted more than two new hara at a time, the blood may be too thin and the newly created har could wake with impaired sight, hearing, or smell.

Once the ritual was finished, the vision accelerated again. For a while, the bodies on the *tatami* remained motionless and unchanged, but the merciless pace of the memory quickly brought them to what looked like disintegration. At first they started changing colour, subsequently resembling drowned people, people with first-degree burns or who had suffered from a horrible case of pox. Some of them displayed awful ulcers and lesions, others bled through numerous cracks in their skin. One started to retch. And all the while, there was a ghost movement inside their bodies that Satoru could just barely see, of their organs reshaping, their muscles feeding on whatever fat they'd had as human beings, their bones straining to stretch through the new body, their hearts mercilessly pumping the virus to each and every cell.

Satoru switched off the machine when the new hara were being bathed and helped in taking their first steps. Their reproductive organs resembled exotic flowers. That was still weird, no matter how many times he saw it.

"This is against nature," he said, once Kiyoshi opened his eyes. "No one should survive this."

"New body, new level of tolerance," the har muttered in a small, tired voice. He looked positively ill, his skin an unhealthy greyish tone, with dark rings under his eyes. The process had exhausted him this time, probably due to the length of the memory it had covered. Satoru quickly unstrapped him, helped him sit up and handed him a glass of water. His mind was still with the decomposing boys, though.

"I can't believe anyone would want to go through this willingly."

"Maybe that's why we don't let people who aren't being incepted watch?"

"Who was the god you were giving the offerings to?" Satoru asked, trying to change topic to something that would take his mind off the inception.

"Izaname. He is the child of Izanagi and Izanami. Light and

Dark. Male and Female. We saw him being born during a grissecon... They are called *dehara*, by the way, our gods."

Satoru thought no *kami* like that could exist, and he was sure he didn't want to know the details about the grissecon. He certainly did not need food for thoughts of that kind.

"Why did you never incept the chief priest?" he asked then. "Did he refuse?"

"Oh, he would have loved to!" Kiyoshi exclaimed. "Unfortunately, he was too old. It works best on teenage boys or men in their early twenties, when the body can easily adapt. Later in life, the danger of death is just too high. We have performed inception on several priests that were a little over thirty and possessed a healthy body. Some made it, but the rest didn't. Someone fifty or sixty years old is way beyond the limit."

"Yet the chief priest lived with the tribe."

"He was a har at heart." Kiyoshi smiled, hugging his knees. "The transition would have been easy for him. Some people are better prepared than others, capable of seeing the bigger picture. Humans had their chance on the Earth, and they gambled it away. It's our time now – and it could have been yours too, if instead of deciding to go on this desperate mission you had joined our ranks."

"It may be desperate, but it could as well save mankind," Satoru retorted angrily, "the humanity you abandoned without ever looking back."

Kiyoshi sighed, giving Satoru an impatient look. "What humanity? Just look at the way you live! It began with Japan cutting itself away from the world when the apocalypse started and becoming a military state. Now your people live in underwater cubicles, spending the majority of the day in virtual reality, because they hardly ever see real daylight. They are forced to marry underage and undergo repeated fertilisations as a price for survival. Meanwhile, our tribes live in shrines and temple complexes, in touch with nature, exploring our psychic abilities and exercising our bodies through martial arts. When will it finally dawn on you that no matter how much you keep dissecting us, the best you could do for humanity is to let it die out?"

Even though Satoru *knew* the har was wrong, he realised that all arguments he had available at the moment were circular ones, which filled him with anger and uncertainty. He needed to be alone, if he wanted to rid himself of these feelings and regain the mental stability he was known for.

"Enough of the nonsense. Let's go," he said and yanked the har up. "I have some work to do and you need to lie down."

Kiyoshi stumbled, obviously unwell, since the exchange of opinions had exhausted his energy reserves. The procedure had taken its toll on him this time. He moved down the corridor slowly, leaning on the doctor every once in a while. Satoru allowed it, even though it made him uncomfortable. Kiyoshi was a pitiful sight and Satoru couldn't help but think of the other har, the red-haired one, who had died on that very same camp bed. Perhaps for the first time, Satoru asked himself whether it was really necessary to torment them so in a quest for knowledge. He even felt something like pity for a second. The har was doing everything he could to cooperate, and if the information gained was not exactly what Satoru would have liked… well, Kiyoshi was not to blame.

When they arrived at the cell, the har collapsed on the way to his bed. His legs simply gave way. Satoru tried to catch him, but his instinct kicked in too late and all he could do was help pick him up. Kiyoshi was bleeding from his mouth. He looked at Satoru with pleading eyes – a crack in the haughty façade he wore. Which meant it *was* a façade, this calm, this air of superiority… or maybe not exactly a façade, but not the whole story either.

"I don't feel so well," Kiyoshi moaned, trying to wipe the blood away with his chained hands. "Untie me, please? Just this once?"

"You are bleeding," Satoru stated.

"It's nothing. I've just bitten my tongue. But my head is spinning horribly…"

Kiyoshi almost tripped again. Satoru sighed and dragged him to the bed, letting him drop onto it like a bag of potatoes. He pulled the controller out of his pocket and loosened the chains, then lowered himself into a squat, so that he could free Kiyoshi of restraints completely. There was a short moment when Satoru was about to stand up, both hands occupied with winding up the chains, a fraction of a second when his attention was unfocused. Then, the har was upon him, pushing his face into the blankets.

The har's exhaustion wasn't nearly as bad as he'd pretended it to be and he had surprise on his side, accompanied with the certainty that he only had the one opportunity, because failure would mean execution. Satoru stood no chance. The walls in Neo-Osaka were completely soundproof, meaning no one heard him scream when Kiyoshi's teeth sank into his throat, tearing skin and muscle with the intention to cause as much damage as possible, pressing his own bleeding tongue into the wound to squeeze out as much blood as he could from it, into Satoru's mouth. Hands that had seemed almost lifeless a moment ago pinned Satoru down, digging painfully into his shoulders.

Satoru fought vigorously, but it took too much precious time to push the har away, and when he finally succeeded, he sensed the battle for his humanity had already been lost. For a second, they held each other in check, mutual hatred glowing in their eyes. Then Satoru broke loose, panting wildly. Kiyoshi closed his eyes, as if bracing himself for a blow, but none came. The man darted out of the cell, locking the bars behind him. From there, he observed Kiyoshi with horror-stricken face, fingers pressed onto the fresh wound.

"Why?" he demanded in a choked whisper.

Kiyoshi lowered his eyes to avoid Satoru's accusatory gaze. "Maybe one day you will understand. I certainly hope you will."

From a predator with a blood-stained face, those words were completely inappropriate. Satoru groaned in frustration and moved to the worktable. There, in the bottom drawer, was his first aid kit – a couple of bottles, injections, pills, bandages, a flask of alcohol and a gun. He opened the bottle of antiseptic, poured some on a bandage and started dabbing aimlessly at the wound on his neck.

"That won't help," the har said from his cell.

Satoru drew a furious breath, grabbed the gun and stomped to the cell, stopping as close to the bars as possible. Kiyoshi was crouched on the bed in the far corner, half hidden under the long braids of his hair, their mingled blood smeared around his mouth and on the backs of his hands. There, in the shadows, he looked like a demon from the depths of Hell, a wild thing, and he should be killed like one. Satoru lifted the gun and aimed, but even as he did so, he knew he wasn't going to be able to shoot the har, who currently represented his only aid in the life that was waiting for him, should he survive the transformation.

"How long does this take?"

No answer.

Satoru pulled the trigger a fraction. "How. Long."

"Two days to a week…"

He gasped for breath, fighting a wave of nausea caused by imagining a week-long suffering of the kind he had recently seen on the screen. *Some made it and some didn't.* But he was not a loser. With an almost feverish determination to live, he ran to the room's intercom and pressed a few numbers. A series of beeping tones. Someone on the other end picked up the receiver.

"Hello? Yes, it's me."

Satoru's voice sounded hoarse and he demonstratively coughed a few times. The har drew nearer to the bars, curious.

"Listen, I just wanted to tell you that I won't be around for a couple of days. I think I contracted flu last time I went out. No, you don't have to send me assistance. You know how quickly infections spread here. I have meds and some pre-cooked meals up here. I don't want anyone working with my test subject while I'm ill. No, the subject must have nothing to eat or drink unless I say otherwise. He is being uncooperative. Bye for now. Yes, I'll be fine."

He finished the call and turned back to Kiyoshi, momentarily catching his reflection in the mirror on the wall. Even in the dark, he could see that an angry blue-red line was running down his neck, where the blood had started to poison his system. "You'd better pray it takes less than a week," he said in a grave voice, hid the gun in his pocket and left the room.

"Satoru. Satoru, wake up. We have to get going," whispered a distressed voice. Someone was shaking his shoulder violently and simultaneously holding a hand over his mouth, effectively preventing him from screaming. He opened his eyes and immediately relaxed upon seeing the familiar face, blinking twice in order to let the other boy know that he understood and was not going to make a noise. The hand withdrew.

"What's up?" he mouthed voicelessly, all senses already alert and registering distant noise; voices, bangs and the sounds of countless feet on the run.

"The city has just been proclaimed a quarantine zone. But they're already here."

There was no need to say more; both of them knew what that meant. Both of them knew the orders by heart.

In the event the prefecture of your residence is proclaimed a quarantine zone, which means there is evidence of several loose cases of the virus in the general area, ALL minor children between 4 and 13 years of age and all males between 14 and 60 years of age shall proceed to the designated collection areas for transport to the closest neotown.

Satoru moved swiftly and efficiently, slipping on his pants, socks, T-shirt and jacket. The running shoes were ready on the side of his bed.

Each person must carry: A birth certificate, a personal ID or valid Japanese passport/proof of residency.

He opened the drawer of the bedside table to retrieve his "first-aid kit" – the documents, a few chocolate bars, a bottle of water and a stunner, the only weapon a minor was allowed to own.

Each person is allowed to carry: Two pieces of luggage weighing 20 kg or less.

Except there was no time to pack. The dorms were already alive with screams and the sounds of things breaking. The boys opened the door just a little and Satoru checked the corridor for safety.

"The air is clear. Go!"

Watch! Listen! The person next to you could be a mutant.

It was Atsushi, a third year student. They bumped into him two floors down and Satoru grabbed his hand as they passed him by, prompting him to run along. He didn't expect the tug in the wrong direction, or the incredibly loud refusal.

"No! I'm going with them! They promised to incept everyone who joins them."

"Shut up," Satoru hissed, "you'll draw attention to us. Just... fucking move!"

The sounds of battle seemed to be awfully close and Satoru realised, panicked, that the screams he was hearing were voices of boys being taken against their will. It all made a terrible sense. If you were a race that multiplied by incepting young human males, where else would you start the invasion of a town than in a dorm full of boys?

"Are you mad? I'm staying," the boy yelled. "This is the moment I've been waiting for my entire life! I won't have to work or marry. I'll never grow fat or old!"

Stand ready. At any time you may be called upon to assist with defence.

The har stormed out of the side corridor, from behind the corner – lithe but tall and firm like wire, wielding a katana. *Satoru freed his hand from*

Atshushi's palm. His friend was already running away, gaining on them, leaving him behind for the demon. Satoru didn't wait for anything and hit the enemy with the stunner. A quick reversal, the ozone scorch of a bridging spark, and the har went down. So much safer than anything equally incapacitating Satoru might have tried to do with his hands. And then he started running.

If you miss the transport, do not expect to be rescued.

On the first floor, the staircase was blocked by a writhing heap of fighting bodies. Satoru kicked open the first door he saw, disappearing into the empty room before they could notice him. The windows weren't too high; if he jumped, he could make it out unharmed. Satoru pushed the window open, swung one leg to the other side, quickly considering the best way to get down.

But the room had not been empty.

Any person who exhibits symptoms of infection, including but not limited to seizures, vomiting, changes in body shape or skin colour and rash will be subject to immediate quarantine for a period of seven days. Should infection be confirmed, such a person will be exterminated.

There was a boy... no, not a boy anymore, a new har, dirty with slime, smelling of bodily waste, fresh from althaia, but incredibly strong already. He grabbed Satoru by the ankle, pulling him back in, and as they fought, Satoru dropped the stunner out of the window, watching it tumble down and disappear into a rose bush. He fought for his life, delivering hard blows to the har's stomach and chest, and found out – how disgusting – that they were still rotting away under the new satin skin. His fists went through, right into the mucous mass inside, and when he pulled them out, his own skin appeared to be gangrenous. Infected.

And it hurt, gods, it hurt. He screamed and screamed, but the creature didn't care, and it didn't care about its own disintegrating organs either. It was like a zombie, only rather than seeking brains to eat, it wanted to crush Satoru in its embrace, and each time it squeezed, his bones were breaking, his flesh swelling with disease, his skin peeling off.

Satoru woke on his bathroom floor, aching, weak as a child, shivering with fading fever, smelling of piss, blood and vomit, but *alive*. It wasn't true, something in him screamed. It was but a nightmare, a hallucination. In reality, the room of his memory dream had been empty. He *had* jumped out of that window. The Wraeththu hadn't got him back then. But then his brain really woke and answered with frightening clarity: But they did get you.

They have got you: *now*.

His body still hurt, but it was a different kind of pain. It wasn't that of immediate injury, but rather the dull ache of abused muscles at rest, a reminder of previous damage. As a doctor, he knew how many times he had been close to death during the four days of transformation, even though he had prepared himself well. He had bottled water, morphine for pain relief, a cocktail of vitamins and nutrients in the IV, antiseptics and salves for the skin. There came, however, a point at which he was not able to use any of it anymore, because he was simply too far gone. He didn't remember how he'd got to the bathroom and whether he wanted to throw up or revive himself with cold water, but he recalled the pain, the agony, the shaking chill, the feverish nightmares that took him to hell and back.

Yet he emerged victorious. It was amazing how different the world looked when experienced with his new heightened senses – full of enhanced colours, sounds and smells. It was amazing how different *he* looked. Of course, Satoru had always known himself to be attractive, but his skin had never been this smooth, his body this flexible, eyes this radiant, hair this rich. He noted with displeasure that even his facial features had changed somewhat. They were softer and made him seem even younger – not a look he wished to display to his colleagues. The transformation had completed exactly as it should have done: Satoru had kept his well-toned figure and now he possessed a certain cat-like grace he'd not had before. His facial features had been polished to a striking androgynous beauty. His eyes had changed colour from black to navy blue. They were deep and dark, like the sort of lake a child would be terrified to swim in, sadness lying at the bottom.

"Who are you?" he asked his reflection in the mirror, when he stepped out of the shower, cleaner but no less confused than before. He was surprised his voice came out when the har in the mirror opened his mouth. The borders between *us* and *them* had dissolved, making the world a strange, unknown place.

Satoru felt as if his new body were disintegrating.

After several days of getting used to the change, he returned to work, always wearing a surgical mask. He explained that he was still slightly ill and didn't want to endanger anyone. He bought contact lenses. There was, of course, the change in the lower regions, but he was not ready to explore this yet, nor did he know if he ever would be. He wasn't ready to see Kiyoshi either, but he did ask the room service to start feeding the har again. Even though the solutions were not permanent, he could almost believe he could handle this and live his life the way he always had.

Further differences crept up on him slowly – hot flushes at first, then occasional nausea, slight fever in the evenings, a crawling feeling on his skin. He attributed this to his body becoming used to the violent changes it had gone through, but the symptoms worsened by the hour. Then the hallucinations came. Satoru blamed exhaustion; he recalled that whenever he had pulled several all-nighters in a row in the past, the patterns on the walls had started to shift before his eyes and he'd often seen random things like insubstantial mice running over his computer keyboard.

Eventually, he had to admit the sensations now were different. Strange shapes reached for him from every corner, full of growls. Shadows and gloomy things waited for his death in the darkness. Deceased relatives would appear and sit at his table or occupy his bed, whenever he decided to seek sanctuary within the walls of his room. Wordlessly, they blamed him for what he had become. There were voices too, of all the hara who had died during the experiments. Now it was as if they sought to seduce him, whispering endless streams of obscenities that made his mouth water. He could hardly sleep, and when he finally dozed off, his peace was disturbed by nightmares that he still believed to be reality hours after waking up.

He lay on his bed, eyes scanning the corners of the room for hungry creatures, his heart pumping boiling blood through his veins. His skin felt too tight, too small for his expanding muscles. He dug his fingers into the mattress, so that he couldn't give in to the urge to claw his skin off. The whole room rocked like a ship, making his stomach turn. With a furious scream, he hit the wall with his fists and jumped out of bed, ignoring the nausea.

Kiyoshi was dozing off when Satoru stormed into the room, slammed the door shut and locked it. The har immediately jerked awake and directed his attention to the doctor, who had marched to the cell and begun to unlock it. His hands shook like those of a drug addict.

Satoru growled upon seeing the har's amused expression. Of course the little fuck understood what was going on, and he was enjoying it.

"Hello, doctor," Kiyoshi said mockingly as Satoru entered the cell. "My, you do look lovely."

Satoru was in no mood for games. If there was something he genuinely longed for, it was to wipe the smirk from Kiyoshi's face – with his fist. He moved across the cell like a panther and without warning, he squeezed the har's neck in his hands.

"What's happening to me?" he cried, almost lifting Kiyoshi from the bed. "You know – tell me!"

The har expelled a muffled sound and Satoru realised Kiyoshi could hardly breathe, let alone speak. Reluctantly, he let Kiyoshi go.

"You need to take aruna," Kiyoshi croaked, massaging his throat. "First soume, then ouana. The process is not complete otherwise."

"No."

The har shrugged. "Whatever you wish. I can do without. *You* will go mad and they'll shoot you like an animal."

"Fuck you, bastard," Satoru hissed, clenching his fists in anger, fuelled by the knowledge that Kiyoshi was right; he *was* turning insane. The lust that threatened to take control of him whenever he stepped closer to the har was almost unbearable.

"Later. You first," Kiyoshi retorted.

Satoru's blow split the har's lip; his head snapped back, hitting the wall. Still, the har's senses, perfected by years of training in martial arts, automatically enabled him to react with a counter attack, which knocked Satoru off his feet.

"That one was for Zin," he spat. In the next second, Satoru was upon him again. The two hara tumbled to the ground and Kiyoshi bared his teeth.

"Oh no, you don't," Satoru hissed and put his arm across Kyioshi's neck, forcing the back of his head to the floor. He swung one leg across the har's hips and sat on him. Satoru was holding all the trumps in his hand... or so he thought, until the overpowered, Kyioshi reacted in a way he would never have expected: he slipped a hand into Satoru's pants. Satoru froze, shocked by the foreign sensation and by the fact that someone dared to do this to him. He momentarily lost his grip on the har, who used the chance to grab his hip with the free hand and secure Satoru on place, sliding his fingers farther between his legs, watching the doctor intently as his eyes widened.

Satoru let out a strained moan, stunned long enough for Kyioshi to open his shirt. He felt like the whole situation was slipping out of his grasp. If anything, *he* wanted to be the dominant partner, but his body was letting him down, asking for a different sort of completion. Defeated, he reached down and tore at Kyoshi's robe. The silk ripped apart in a most satisfying manner, and underneath, there was flesh, pale, soft and shimmering with droplets of sweat. Kiyoshi moved his hand, teasing the petals with his fingers. Satoru was already wet, if not from desire, then from agitation. The har underneath him bucked, forcing him to lift himself off his body, so that he could take off what remained of his robe. Satoru was still sure he didn't want this, or at least he never had wanted it before, but his body ignored all such considerations. He moved, giving Kiyoshi access to enter him, and the feeling was hideous and pleasurable at once, as if he could explore and follow it around unknown corners. The har pushed slowly and Satoru breathed out with appreciation, melting into the sensation.

Satoru was so overwhelmed that he did not protest when Kiyoshi pulled him down, so that their lips could meet, and locked them in a sharing of breath. In an instant, Satoru found himself in another place. It was like the memories he had seen on the screen, but ten times better, because this time, he was a part of them. He and Kiyoshi were together in the eternal *now*, where foundations formed and dissolved and were received with perpetual elation, where a starlit ocean rolled against golden dunes and formed swirling patterns at the fragile tideline. And when Kiyoshi's ouana-tongue lashed out inside him, Satoru was truly in heaven.

In silence, Satoru got up and retrieved his clothes. Kiyoshi remained on the floor, eying him expectantly. He had a way of staring so pointedly that Satoru became aware of it, even with his back turned. He stopped in his tracks and turned to face him.

"You can take me now," Kiyoshi announced casually, parting his legs.

Satoru let the clothing fall back down. Still silent, he took

Kiyoshi against the wall, legs wrapped around his waist, hands pinned beneath his, stretched up as if Kiyoshi were a prisoner, and he was, but he wanted every bit of it, asking for more. This time, they didn't even kiss. It was about power, and anger too, and the frustration of having been wronged; all of that melted into flesh. When the climax came, Kiyoshi's body spasmed. Satoru felt a fleeting wave of fear that he had somehow hurt him, because the har went strangely limp in his arms and a vacant expression entered his eyes, as if his mind wasn't really there. This lasted only a few seconds. Then the har gasped in satisfaction and snapped out of the peculiar state. His lips formed a playful smile and he raised a hand to stroke Satoru along the jaw line.

"Welcome to the first day of your life."

"I didn't think we were still doing this," Kiyoshi said. There was an underlying anger in his otherwise cool voice. Satoru had previously locked the lab and taken off his mask; now he was about to strap the har to the camp bed again.

"Of course. It's why you're here, after all, and this is my job."

"So you actually plan to put on a façade of humanity forever and hope your colleagues won't notice? Well, I have news for you: that will not work! You can't pretend you have flu for much longer."

"Someone *did* tell me I looked different this morning," Satoru admitted. "I said I'd lost some weight during my fever."

"What you're doing is nonsense. Sooner or later, someone will find out, and then they will mercilessly execute you. Trust me, they won't care a bit about what good you did, or tried to do, for their precious race."

"Then tell me what *other* options I have left!" Satoru snapped, sitting down next to Kiyoshi, so that he could yell at him from close proximity. "After all, this is completely your doing. Your petty revenge locked me in the wrong body!"

But as Kiyoshi leaned forward and slid his arm around Satoru's shoulders, trailing fingers gently down his spine, Satoru realised his statement was not entirely true. His body wasn't really wrong; on the contrary – it had never felt so good. It was his mind causing the problems, because it still believed it belonged to a human.

As if Kiyoshi understood, he said gently, "You have to accept the fact that you are… for all I care, call it upgraded human, if you want. Next thing, we need to get out of here. And before you say anything else, I *know* you know how."

"I hate you," Satoru said, but his voice lacked conviction.

Kiyoshi completely ignored this statement. "Come, let me show you something." He took Satoru's face in his hands. "We have a better way to share thoughts now. You don't need your infernal machine anymore."

Their lips met and Kiyoshi gently pushed Satoru's mouth open, tasting his tongue and letting him taste something else in return: all the knowledge about their race he had acquired from his inception hienama or had gathered later in life, neatly wrapped and accompanied by amazing visions. Satoru drank it from his lips, eager like a hungry animal.

He saw the ascension of the first one, the one with the fiery hair. He saw the Varrs, riding wild horses through endless plains, stained by the piles of metallic leftovers from human civilisation. There were the hienamas too, riding their *sedim* through the Otherlanes, the universe rushing by and gluing their lashes together with ice. There were dozens of different tribes; hara with golden skin, who danced beneath the desert sun, hara whose hair was alive with magic, tribes who lived in their dreams, and those who sailed the northern seas in horned ships. Satoru saw the wonders of Immanion and the Triad, ever-fighting but bound for eternity.

Then the vision changed and he was watching the life in Nara, home of the largest Wraeththu tribe in Japan. He saw them training in the *dojo*, holding feasts, performing grissecons, learning how to use their powers or meditating. Izaname, the *kami* in whose existence he didn't believe, materialised before his eyes, as the hara in the vision contacted the dehar by rituals performed in their nayati. And Satoru witnessed their family life too, the lust, the pearl-birthing. A part of him was still fighting, trying to persuade himself that this was nothing but manipulation, incredible bullshit with the purpose only to perpetuate false hope, but the other part, a much bigger one, wanted terribly to belong.

"When?" he asked, as soon as he could catch a breath.

Kyioshi smiled. "Do you think you could have everything ready by tomorrow midnight?"

Satoru nodded and, for the first time, initiated a kiss himself.

They took aruna right there, on the camp bed. Satoru vaguely realised that it was wrong on so many levels, because a har had died there, and he now knew his name had been Zin, but he avoided sharing those thoughts with Kiyoshi and they were eventually forgotten. Finally, his body was satisfied, but his mind remained restless. He knew that for this to change, he would have to relieve himself of a burden he would never manage to speak about, not without looking like a sentimental weakling, which he really wasn't. But maybe he didn't have to speak about it. There were, as Kyioshi had said, better ways.

He gave the har a gentle kiss, extending an invitation that Kiyoshi readily accepted. Satoru opened his mind and tried to concentrate on the fundamental things. It was right there in his subconscious, easily accessible through breath, laid bare for Kiyoshi. The child Satoru, watching his grandparents die. An entire day spent in the company of their decomposing bodies, until his mother had arrived at the scene. She never was quite right in the head after that. The court placed her children in different foster homes. They missed each other for years; eventually forgot their respective faces. Satoru was *quite* alright. He'd never suffered from material deprivation. He'd been able to study at the university of his choice.

Something happened then. It was neither love nor friendship nor sympathy, but some loose threads came together to form a bond. Satoru's head eventually came to rest against Kiyoshi's chest, and his silence said volumes. He wanted to breach the void and say something, anything, but nothing seemed worthy or effectual. In the darkness, his skin cooled beneath Kiyoshi's hands, but the har didn't let Satoru suffer with the cold. Gently, he brought the covers up around him. And then, he held him tight.

The escape went so perfectly. Most people had been in their family cubicles by midnight, sleeping or browsing their virtual realities. Satoru had all the necessary codes and suggested they could simply walk out, with Kiyoshi dressed in some of his clothing. Ultimately, Kiyoshi persuaded him that would be too dangerous – what if the guards saw and recognised him on the screen? Instead, when given freedom, it was no problem for him to sneak into one of the wardrooms and incapacitate its occupants, so that Satoru could switch off the security system. They had two options – to use an underwater module, which would take them to the shore, or follow the long tunnel that connected the town with the mainland. Because Kiyoshi had never piloted anything that even faintly resembled a submarine in his life, they took the tunnel.

At the end of there, there was light. And yet there really shouldn't have been, because no one lived in Osaka anymore: the entire population had been moved many years ago. But rather than the neon light of a night-time metropolis, this was a magical, eerie radiance that had created a shield around an army of hara… and the light reflected on countless drawn swords.

Satoru felt his limbs grow heavy and eventually stop moving. Now, it all began to make sense – from the moment he had first entered the cell, and had seen Kiyoshi's untypically haughty expression and had wondered about his offer to cooperate, up to the moment Kiyoshi had forcefully incepted him, so that Satoru would have to leave his community, thereby opening the gates to the enemy. The only thing Satoru didn't understand was how he hadn't suspected all this before.

"You have to stop this," he insisted, grabbing Kiyoshi's shoulders.

"I can't," the har said, repeating something Satoru recalled having heard before. "This is for Zin. And all those before him. And those who would have come after me."

It was too late, anyway. The first line of hara had already entered the tunnel.

The neotowns had been constructed to withstand an enemy attack, their security systems were impeccable and only a small number of people knew the codes necessary for moving freely in and out. Yet there was something the founders of Neo-Osaka had not counted on: that a high ranking insider would *invite* the enemies in, enemies armed with weapons, magic and hunger for revenge that they considered rightful.

The assault was fairly short, resulting in a glorious victory. Even if he had been free, Satoru couldn't have prevented it or changed its outcome, but to add insult to injury, Kiyoshi and two others stayed on shore, keeping an eye on him. He felt empty, but at the same time, he sensed there would come a day when the emptiness would be filled with remorse, self-hate, anger, and yes, confusion – because there wasn't *us* and *them* anymore. That could have meant he had not exactly lost, but he had not won either. Unfortunately, though, it rather meant he had lost twice.

"I won't ask you why. But just tell me *how*," he asked Kiyoshi.

"There is a skill I haven't told you about," Kiyoshi said. "To come out of your body, or rather deeper into it, when taking aruna as soume… Your spirit submerges into your own core and can manifest in other places. This was how I was able to contact them."

Satoru realised he had noticed the moment – that strange blankness that had come over Kiyoshi during aruna. He should have asked about that, perhaps used his own new talents to probe Kiyoshi's mind. Another mistake. Somehow he had made so many…

Once Neo-Osaka was almost entirely devoid of human life and everyhar was on horseback, readying themselves for the journey back to Nara, hara approached Kyoshi and Satoru one by one. They ignored Satoru, but complimented Kiyoshi on a job well done. Satoru could tell the har seemed uncomfortable, but then again… what did he know? Apparently, he hadn't known the har at all. Still, when the leader announced it was time to leave, he followed Kiyoshi silently. What else was there to do?

"You aren't going anywhere," the leader snapped, clearly ready to push Satoru away had he protested. "The fact you are alive at all is courtesy of Kiyoshi. His heart is too soft." With that, he kicked his horse and galloped away, the whole group behind him. Kiyoshi, however, didn't seem able to urge his horse into a gallop, glancing over his shoulder every now and then. Satoru turned to go back through the tunnel, not about to give Kiyoshi the satisfaction of seeing his desperation. He had never been a man to cry and wait for someone to save him, and he certainly wasn't going to start now. There would be death in Neo-Osaka, but there would be food too, and a bed, and all the time in the world to decide what to do with his life, or choose the easiest way to end it.

But as he entered the tunnel, a voice spoke in his mind, and he realised with surprise it wasn't his own.

Go to Kobe and find the shipyard there. A har named Jun operates a few boats going from Kobe to Hiroshima. Tell him I sent you. There's a friendly Wraeththu tribe living in Hiroshima. They will take you in. And be careful to stay off the main road, there will be patrols there.

Satoru stopped in his tracks, processing the information, but then resumed walking. He would still need food and water. And maybe something to trade, buy his way around. Then, something probed the corners of his mind again and transmitted, with much less force:

...find you there one day?

Satoru had never had the chance to try telepathy with Kiyoshi, but when he concentrated really hard, he felt he was able to identify the colour of Kiyoshi's mind in the ethers, and with all the willpower he had, he planted a thought into it.

I really hate you, you know.

He sensed the other har was smirking somewhere. They both knew hate and love were horses that drank from the same river.

I can live with that.

Glossary of Japanese Terms:

Shintō: *"the way of the gods"; the indigenous spirituality of the people of Japan. It remains Japan's major religion alongside Buddhism.*

Gūji: the highest rank in Shintō hierarchy; the chief priest in a shrine.

Kami: the deities, spirits or phenomena that are worshipped in the religion of Shintō. They are elements in nature, animals, creationary forces in the universe, as well as spirits of the revered deceased.

Matsuri: festivals, often observed in Shintō shrines. Various special rites may be held.

Omamori: amulets (charms, talismans) sold at religious sites and dedicated to particular Shinto deities; may serve to provide luck or protection.

Onsen: hot springs; also describes the bathing facilities and inns around the hot springs.

Hakama: a type of traditional Japanese clothing; a divided skirt that resembles a wide-legged *pair of trousers, traditionally worn by men.*

Uwagi: a kimono-like jacket; another type of traditional Japanese clothing.

Katana: a Japanese sword with a single-edged, curved blade, and a long hilt allowing for a *double-handed grip.*

Tatami: a type of rectangular mat used as a flooring material in traditional Japanese-style rooms.

Dojo: a formal training place for students of martial arts or for samurais to conduct training or examinations.

without weakness

Storm Constantine

Dream, Nicholas. Dream of voices baying in the night, of hooves galloping over hard ground, of shimmering heat, the smell of musk and leather. Toss and turn in your narrow bed, Nicholas, for they are coming for you, in their thousands, gleaming skin beneath the hard sun, so many horses' nostrils flaring, manes flying, the grip of thighs on heaving flanks. Can you feel their breath upon you, hot and sweet, reeking of blood? Can you feel their clawed hands upon you, the caress of talons against your flesh, and the ripple of silent laughter in the air? Are you waiting for this, Nicholas? Is this your sin? In the dark, in the night, do you turn traitor to your kin, to your God? I can see everything, boy, and I see your heart. You are not without weakness.

The boy, Nicholas, awoke with a cough and sat upright in bed. Serene moonlight came in through the narrow window, falling across the coverlet like a white robe. Sheets so white they made the eyes ache. Shadows so blue they seemed to be painted on the room. Gasping, Nicholas peered around him, but the shadows were still, and so was the night outside his window. He heard the night watchman call. *All's well. All's clear.* Just for tonight. But still the voice of God rang in his head, and God did not lie. What could Nicholas do to control his rebel dreams? He didn't want them, didn't invite them. He was their victim, and it took all his energy to fight them.

The door opened, and he half expected to see an avenging angel standing at the threshold with raised sword, but it was only his mother, Hannah. She held a lantern, and wore her night-robe, her hair loose over her shoulders. "I heard you cry out, Nicky. Are you all right?"

"Dream again," he said, wiping his brow, finding it as wet as if he'd been swimming.

Hannah came to sit on the bed, stroked her son's face. "It's not your fault," she said softly. "You do know that, don't you?"

Nicholas closed his eyes briefly. "I know, I know. It's *them*, outside."

"You must believe it, son."

"I do." He was close to tears. "I need the ties again."

Hannah frowned. "Oh, Nicky... no..."

"I feel safer."

"But there's not been an attack for weeks. They're far away, they really are."

"No," Nicholas said. "You're wrong."

He lay down again, resigned and sorrowful, like a young saint about to be martyred. Hannah looked upon him and could have wept at the sight of him, his fineness, his honesty, his purity. He was in danger – they all knew it – because of how he was. As a child, he'd seen spirits, and had sometimes dreamed the future. He could *tell* things about people. Sometimes he had *changed* things too: a touch, a fever gone. And he was very beautiful.

Sometimes, the beasts came in their dozens and assaulted the walls of the enclave, using their strange voices to unsettle the defenders. But Hannah's people were wise to such tricks. They blocked their ears, sang their own songs that helped drown out the eerie cries. They had survived for decades, but no one really dared think about the distant future.

Other times, only a few of the beasts would come. They would circle the enclave on their snorting horses; not attacking, but just galloping round, kicking up dust and singing their siren song. At those times, Nicholas' family had tied him to his bed, and in the morning his wrists and ankles had been crusted with blood. They had tried to stop his ears with rags, but the song had lanced right through them. He was a good boy. He always fought hard. They wouldn't win. His father Hugh would kill him before that happened.

"I'll stay with you," Hannah said, "even while you sleep." She stroked his hair now, his fine brown hair like autumn silk. His dark eyes were closed, the lashes long against his sculpted cheeks.

"Don't tell Dad," Nicholas mumbled. "He has enough to worry about, but tell Scrap about my dream. It means something. Tell him to double the watch, be alert."

"I will," Hannah said.

Scrap was Nicholas' elder brother, whose real name was Jack. Only three years between them, but at twenty, Scrap seemed much older. He had fought many wars in his young life, and commanded the garrison of the enclave. Nicholas called him an old soul, and his family did not dispute it. Scrap kept them alive. He kept hope alive in the hearts of the men and women who defended them. But they were so isolated out here – for all they knew the last humans alive on earth. There was no one to help them, and even though they had a vast stockpile of weapons and ammunition, there would come a day when supplies ran out, and other than from the foraging missions some of their people ran, they had no way of restocking their arsenal. The radio had been dead for years, even though Hugh cruised the airwaves every night, telling the world they were there. It wasn't dangerous to do that, because the beasts didn't have technology. They were just animals. Or so Hugh said. The wonder was how they kept going, because they had no women. How did they replenish their ranks? They always took their dead with them after an attack. Perhaps some of them were female, and had mutilated their breasts like Amazons. Hugh thought they must have breeding stock somewhere; it was a hideous, but horribly possible idea. Was the world over-run with them now?

Hannah was tired to her bones. She didn't want this life, but it was all she had ever known. She had been born in the enclave, in the very early days and was therefore far younger than her husband, who had known the world before. Her grandmother, who had been with them then, had told her tales of the old days, what it had been like, but it was no more real to Hannah than the stories she told to her children, stories of angels who would come to whisk them away to heaven, right from beneath the noses of the beasts.

Outside a night bird called, and Hannah's body went tense. You could never be sure they were really birds. "Nicky," she said. "I'll go tell Scrap now, you hear. I'll be back. Don't worry."

"I heard it," Nicholas said. "I think it was only a bird."

"Still, it would be best."

"Yes."

The attack came just after dawn. In the grey twilight before the sun broke through, they came out of nowhere; no one saw them

315

approach. Thanks to Nicholas, Scrap had the battlements bristling with defenders. They were ready, but this time, there were too many beasts, more than ever before. Hannah stood high on the barricaded walls, beside her eldest son, with the wind blowing her hair over her face like a girl's. She peered out at the wilderness, where dark horses moved restlessly, and rays of the rising sun glinted off weapons. They had just appeared, hadn't yet made a move. Scrap was tense as a wire, staring at the enemy as if he could wish them away through the force of his will.

"Sometimes," Hannah said, "I wonder why they come, don't you? We're no threat to them. We have nothing they need."

"We have things they *want*, maybe," Scrap said tersely. "That's different."

"Jack," Hannah said, and paused for a moment before continuing. She only called him Jack when matters were serious. "I've never said this anyone, but, do you think, is it possible, they keep coming *because of Nicky?*"

"Mom!" Scrap looked as if he might hit her and she backed away from him. "Never say that. You know why? Because if folk hear it, the next thing you know they'll be ganging together to have Nick trussed up outside the gates. Never say that! *Never!*"

"I..." Hannah shrugged. "I just thought it, Jack, that's all. I never told anyone. I never will again."

"Good. It's not true, anyway. They just want to wipe us out, that's all. They don't know about Nicky."

"But the song... the dreams..."

Scrap sighed. "Nick's not the only one affected, you know that."

"You never are."

"No. I'm stronger."

Hannah said no more, but she didn't think it was simply that. She loved Nicky with all her heart, he was her treasure, but sometimes, when the beasts came and people died, and the enclave hung on to survival by a prayer, she wished... she wished... *No, don't think it.* Jack was right.

The beasts began to howl then, an eerie sound that frightened up all the birds hiding in the scrub. Jackals ran out, biting their own tails. The hair on Hannah's neck and arms stood up. She knew there was no point putting her hands over her ears. That wouldn't stop the racket, never did, never would.

"Get down, Mom," Scrap said. "Go into the house. You know what to do."

She nodded and left quickly, but not before she saw them pouring slowly like heavy smoke towards the enclave. They had the heads of beasts. They wore jackal skins, with snarling muzzles over their faces. This could be the last time, as every time could.

2

General Ashmael Aldebaran of the Wraeththu tribe of Gelaming was in discussion with his immediate staff in his camp pavilion. This was supposed to be a small job, hardly worth his attention really. The Hegemony were interested in a human named Hugh Ferniman, and wanted to make sure there were no mistakes in securing his co-operation. So, they sent the best.

Megalithica: Ashmael hated this country. In his opinion, it gave itself over to barbarism like a whore, and the worst misfits had been bred there. Violence in the blood, in the air, in the very earth. Fragments of tribes that hadn't progressed and should have died out decades ago.

"We come out from the east," he said, poking at a map on the table before him. "Straight from the sun, from behind. The Hegemony says be merciful, but do what you must. The Hegemony never sees battle, do they? I'll not be taking notes."

A ripple of laughter went around the pavilion. They understood him. Rehabilitation was not in Ashmael's lexicon. He won battles for the Gelaming, by whatever means. And his reports juggled numbers of the dead.

"Is everyhar ready?" he asked.

They were.

"Then rally the hara and mount up. Let's ride."

He strode out of the pavilion into the cold dawn air, eager to get this little problem sorted out. This should have been a simple job. Only now the Gelaming scouts had discovered that rogue hara appeared to have their own, rather more brutal, plans for the humans Ashmael wished to speak to. An unexpected nuisance, yet how the human settlement had survived this long in such a dangerous environment was a miracle in itself. Ashmael's armshar held his *sedu* ready for him; the creature pawing at the ground, shaking its white mane out of its wild black eyes. Ashmael's *sedu* matched his temperament; he liked that. Then his heart sank a little when he saw the Kamagrian representative, Katarin, riding towards him. *Best to keep her out of sight of the action. She is the Hegemony's creature.*

"As soon as you can, you must take me to Hugh Ferniman," she said.

"Just stay at the back, Kate, will you? Let me do my job, then you can do yours."

He had to admit she looked as ready for the job as any of his hara, her hair tied back severely, her compact frame swathed in close-fitting leather. "There must be no risk of harm coming to the human," she said.

"I know that." Ashmael grinned. "So trust me." The *sedu* jostled to the side a little as he swung into the saddle. It trod on the feet of its groom. Ashmael gathered up the reins. "How many otherlane journeys have you made, Kate?"

She looked away. "I'm quite capable."

"I hope so. Personally, I think you should wait here. I'll bring the man to you."

"No. I'm sticking with you. I have my orders."

Ashmael raised an eyebrow and sighed, swinging his *sedu* around. She didn't trust him to carry out her part of the job as well as she could. To be fair to her, she was right. Ashmael had no time for subtle negotiation. "Let's do it, then."

The troupe had assembled at the ether gate entry point, and their ranks parted to let Ashmael through. A hundred splendid white horses, which were really *sedim,* not horses at all, ridden by the cream of the Gelaming military. Ashmael rode to the front and halted. Without turning, he raised a hand. As one the *sedim* surged forward, and the air fractured with a sound like brittle thunder. Then they were gone, and the camp was empty of all but armshara, domestic staff, empty ether drays and tents. Pennants bearing the arms of the Aralisian dynasty flapped listlessly in the early morning breeze.

Thirty miles from camp, the *sedim* leapt through another spontaneously-opening ether gate as if jumping down a high bank. They poured back through into familiar reality, ice splintering from their harness, their flying manes and tails.

Without pausing, they galloped forward, the red rays of the early sun rubying their pale coats.

Ashmael shook his head to clear it of otherlane scramble and assessed the situation before them. Must be nearly two hundred hara attacking the human enclave. Perhaps a merge of tribes or phyles. The humans must have fought them off for quite some time, Ashmael thought, so a union of forces had been required. This wasn't unheard of. Even the most degenerate hara understood the concept of strength in numbers. A large percentage of the attackers wore jackal hides, and all of them rode small, dark horses. Some carried crude flags that bore the sign of the jackal: a canine mask over a human or harish skull. Uigenna? No. He didn't recognise the standard. Could be an offshoot, difficult to say. No one really kept track of what bred in the desert wilderness of Megalithica.

The brutes had their song, the Gelaming had their own. It was almost too easy. Arrows and bullets came from the enclave, which was a slight problem, but the harish enemy were no match for the Gelaming. When you sing to the soul and tell it to be terrified, that it has no chance, the hardiest warrior will lay down his weapons and weep. Ashmael indicated a few should be killed, however, just to make a point. Some had actually breached the human defences. Noticing this, Ashmael signalled to ten of his best hara and rode for the sagging walls. His *sedu* sailed over the rubble with sure feet, hardly seeming to touch the ground. Within, the spirits of slaughter howled and screamed. Some humans lay dead on the ground, or spiked on the defences. Hara were galloping about on their horses, shrieking and lashing out with blades and makeshift blunt weapons. Older humans and children were running in terror, presumably trying to defend themselves, hide.

Ashmael sighed. *Nuisance, nuisance.* He could be at home now, looking forward to a pleasant meal with friends, swapping gossip and admiring Immanion's fair evening. He urged his horse forward and took a certain amount of satisfaction in cutting down the jackals that still prowled. "That's for my lost dinner," he told the last one to die.

Kate's *sedu* trotted up to him almost at once. The Kamagrian's face was set in an expression designed to prick at his conscience, a ploy doomed to failure. "You call these hara animals," she said, "but I wonder…"

"Yes, yes, I know your sentiments," Ashmael said. "You want the human. Let's find him. I want to be home within an hour."

Kate would not respond in like kind to Ashmael's wry smile. "That might not be possible. These people will be suspicious. We'll have to negotiate, placate them, convince them."

Giving up on trying to win her round, Ashmael reverted to abruptness. "*Your* job, I believe?"

"And you are here to protect me. *You*, Ashmael. No har else. Brave Ashmael, fearless warrior. I bet you were a real bully in the playground."

Ashmael ignored this remark and gazed around the compound. All was eerily quiet. The jackal survivors had been rounded up and taken back to the camp, where they would be assessed. Their fate did not interest Ashmael. He was content to let the mealy-mouthed therapists deal with them. The surviving humans, however, appeared to have gone to earth in the fortified buildings, no doubt wondering what the hell was happening. The hara who'd slaughtered the attackers might not be any better than those they'd killed. The largest house must be Ferniman's headquarters. The humans had guns, and would no doubt fire on anyhar who approached.

"We could do the white flag act," Kate suggested. "Look, they'll think I'm a woman. I'll go."

Ashmael cast her a sidelong glance. "I doubt they'll notice the distinction. You are with us, and they'll be blind to details at the moment." He sighed again, for perhaps the tenth time that morning, deep and heartfelt. "We wait," he said. "Let's see if they come out."

"They won't. Would *you*? Use the song."

Ashmael laughed. "I'm almost tempted to. Clearly, you have no idea what it can do to humans."

The parage coloured a little. "No. So *don't* use it. Wait, then."

The Gelaming assembled in the compound, waiting for orders. Ashmael assessed the house. They could storm it, but sniper fire could take out any of his hara and he cherished them all. No point wasting any on a job like this.

After an hour, he told one of his hara to sing a peace song, discover whether it would touch the human hearts, and instil calm. The clear voice rang around the silent compound, but did not inspire any humans to venture outside. Too much to hope for. They wouldn't be able to identify the nuances within the song.

After two hours, Ashmael gave vent to another deep sigh and signalled to Kate. "Come on," he said.

"Where?"

He started walking towards the house. "You coming or not?"

"Ash!" she said. "Ash, wait."

He was fed up with waiting and mustered all the art of his caste training to protect himself. A shield, an air of non-threat. This was all he could do. The house seemed to regard him with hostile sentience, but no bullets came.

Kate caught up with him as he reached the front door, which was made of steel. "Now what?" she asked.

He grinned at her, and knocked on the door.

Kate rolled her eyes. "This is ridiculous. Are you mad?"

"Hugh Ferniman!" Ashmael called. "If you're inside, please come out. We mean you and your people no harm."

Silence.

"They won't answer," Kate said. "They'll be terrified."

"Hugh Ferniman," Ashmael began again. "We have dealt with your enemies. *We* are not your enemy. We wish to talk. Please come out."

Silence.

"I have a woman with me who would like to talk to you. She knows of you, Hugh Ferniman, and I have brought her to you."

After a few moments, they heard a heavy bolt being drawn, then about a dozen more. The door opened a crack, on several security chains. Ashmael saw a hostile eye, framed in bloody skin, gazing out. He bowed. "I am Ashmael Aldebaran of the tribe of Gelaming," he said. "I have been sent by my people to assist you in the matter of the individuals who were molesting you. This has been done. Now, we wish to talk on matters of mutual benefit."

"What do you want?" A gruff male voice snapped.

"To speak with Hugh Ferniman. Is he there?"

"What of? What do you want?"

"I wish to speak to Mr Ferniman in person, or rather my colleague here does. Look, we have healers among us. If you have wounded within, we can be of help."

"We don't want your help."

"Very well, but I would like to speak to Hugh Ferniman."

"Are you beast?"

"Occasionally, or so I'm told," Ashmael said, "but in general, I don't think so." He cast a glance at Kate, who grimaced and shrugged. "I am an officer in the Gelaming army. But you won't have heard of the Gelaming, of course. We are... we are not like the jackal hara... *people*. We wish you no harm."

"Please let me speak to Hugh Ferniman," Kate said in her gentlest tone, and it seemed her more feminine voice did the trick. The chains rattled and the door opened about six inches. They saw a young man standing on the threshold. He had wounds – to a shoulder, a thigh – which had been hastily bound but were still bleeding. Ashmael knew the look in his eyes; it was that of someone who was holding on with the last of his strength, who could collapse at any moment.

"Hugh Ferniman is my father," he said.

"May we come in?" Kate asked, sweetly, harmlessly.

"Are you *beast*?" the young man asked again, his gaze flicking between them.

"He means," Kate said to Ashmael, "are you Wraeththu?"

"Not the kind you have met before," Ashmael said. "We are not your enemy."

"*All* beasts are our enemy."

"Yet you've opened the door and are now chatting to me on the step," Ashmael said. "Please stop being stupid and let us in. We are unarmed."

Another, older male voice boomed from inside. "Let them in."

The young man stood aside, clearly with the greatest reluctance. Ashmael entered first, Kate close on his heels. A tall, gaunt man stood in the doorway to what appeared to be a kitchen beyond. It had been a long time since Ashmael had seen anyone suffering from cellular decay. If this was Ferniman, he must only be around sixty years old – older than Ashmael was himself – yet the human's face was lined, his hair thinning, his body sagging. Why had Ferniman submitted to this gradual deterioration when at one time he could have been har? Ashmael inclined his head respectfully. "Thank you for seeing us."

"What do you want?"

Ashmael gestured flamboyantly at Kate. "Your stage, my

lady."

Kate cast him a scornful glance and stepped forward. "Mr Ferniman, I am Katarin har Roselane. I represent the Hegemony – the leaders – of Immanion. I won't waste words: they have an offer to make to you concerning your particular talents."

Ferniman's gaze was steady on her. "I don't know these people or the place you mentioned. Is it a human enclave?"

Kate's pause was almost imperceptible. "No, but..."

"Then I have nothing to say to you."

"Mr Ferniman," Kate said, "I think you should face facts. We are aware of your situation, since you have been broadcasting it in detail. Wraeththu rule this world now, but..."

"*You* are not one of them. What are you? A traitor to your kind? What did they offer you?"

Kate took a breath, touched her breast with the tips of her fingers. "I am *not* human, Mr Ferniman, but this is not the time to split hairs over how Wraeththu I am. Succinctly, I am of a race called the Kamagrian, who have chosen to favour the feminine aspect of our being. But I am not a woman."

"Yet here before us to pretend to be one, to get into my house."

"Yes. It was all we could do, under the circumstances." She smiled. "Believe me, I do not lie to you. We wish you no harm, in fact quite the opposite. How you have survived out here, surrounded by rogue Wraeththu tribes, is astonishing and very rare. The world *has* changed, Mr Ferniman, and the majority of Wraeththu – and *all* of the Kamagrian – are against war, either with humans or the type of hara who attacked your home. It is not the wish of the Gelaming, one of the most advanced of Wraeththu tribes, to destroy what is left of the human race. Many are inclined to preserve it. You are a skilled geneticist, and the Hegemony would like to hire you to study harish – that is *Wraeththu* – origins. They want to know how they came to be, because they believe it derives from genetic *human* engineering in the past."

Ashmael could tell Kate's words had pricked Ferniman's interest.

"That's not beyond possibility," Ferniman said. "In fact, it's quite likely, given the state our world was in. I have often wondered about it myself."

Kate ducked her head once. "I am obliged to say that should it be your wish, you and your people may remain here, fending off barbaric tribes until the last of you is dead, or the rogues have been eradicated and rehabilitated by more enlightened hara. We cannot, nor want to, force you to do anything. However, if you co-operate and accept Gelaming protection, there will be many benefits. No harm will come to any of you, nor will any be incepted... that is... *changed* unless of their own free will. It's your choice, but I wonder how many of your people, given the opportunity, would opt for your refusal?"

A woman appeared at Ferniman's side. She appeared to be in her late thirties; an attractive woman despite the lines of worry etched into her face, the tiredness that weakened her body. She glanced rather coldly at Ferniman, and then gestured. "I'm Hannah Ferniman," she said. "Come into the kitchen. We will talk."

"Hannah!" Ferniman growled.

"Quiet, Hugh," the woman said. "We should hear more of this. We're at the end of our rope now."

"Thank you," Kate said.

She and Ashmael followed the woman into the kitchen. Around two dozen humans were clustered there, both male and female, some of them wounded. The younger ones stared at the newcomers with wary yet curious eyes, while the adults covered their fear with surly expressions.

"We *do* have healers," Kate said, "very accomplished ones. Are you sure you don't want to avail yourselves of their services?"

"None of that hoodoo!" Ferniman spat, shutting the kitchen door behind him. "We've seen enough of what your kind can do."

"So speaks the scientist," Ashmael remarked drily.

Ferniman turned to him. "I've seen enough to change my mind about a lot of things," he said. "I'd kill my boys myself before I let your kind have them."

"Hugh!" Hannah said. "That's quite enough." She turned to Kate. "How do you know of us?" She gestured for Kate and Ashmael to seat themselves at the broad kitchen table.

Ashmael remained standing, but Kate sat down, laced her hands on the tabletop. "We... picked up on your broadcasts a few weeks ago."

Hannah glanced at her husband. "So, you're saying that some

of the people we call beasts have developed technology... a civilisation..."

Kate nodded. "Yes. As I said, a lot has changed, and in a relatively short time. The Gelaming peacekeeping force is dedicated to assisting people in your situation. So, we came to assist."

Hannah's eyes narrowed. "It isn't just that though, is it? You spoke of wanting to make use of Hugh's expertise."

Kate gestured with one hand. "Yes, we know about him. He earned quite a reputation during the Upheavals." She addressed Ferniman. "You tried to investigate Wraeththu back then, didn't you? You made records of your theories concerning genetics and how Wraeththu could have sprung from humanity."

"Whatever initially created them, in essence they sprang from hell," Ferniman said. "It might have been a hell *we* created, but hell all the same. I told you, I've changed my mind about a lot of things."

"We've suffered," Hannah said, by way of explanation.

"We understand that," Kate said. "And we don't expect an answer immediately."

"I don't see how I can help you," Hugh said gruffly. "I've never managed to get my hands on a whole corpse, let alone access to the instruments I need to explore such material."

"You will have willing test subjects in Immanion," Kate said. "I'm quite sure the equipment you need will be made available to you, or substitutes that will do the job."

Hugh expressed a suspicious grunt, clearly still not persuaded.

Kate dipped her head to one side and said softly, "You do know you can't continue to live here in this way indefinitely?"

"We've managed," Ferniman snapped.

"Admirably," Kate said, "but whatever happens out there, you can't remain as you are. You are, in essence, no longer isolated, no longer cut off from..."

"Look," Ashmael blundered in, "if I'd wanted to, I could have shattered the minds of every human in this enclave. But I didn't. We're here to talk, to make an offer. However, the fact is I'm not going to leave empty-handed. There are a hundred Gelaming outside. See reason, Mr Ferniman, and stop posturing."

Kate shot him a deadly glance, sniped at him in mind touch. *Thanks, Ash. That really helps.*

Ashmael made a dismissive gesture at her. *It's a fact. He knows it.*

A new voice sounded behind them. "What are you *really* here for?"

Both Ash and Kate turned. The young man who had let them in had come into the kitchen. He leaned against the door, his hand leaving a bloody print.

"You don't need my father," he said. "I only have to look at you to see that – well-fed, smug and so *civilised.* You mock us. What is this *really* about?" He gestured beyond the walls of the house. "Why did you kill your own kind out there? What have you come for?"

"Scrap," Hannah said softly. "Jack…"

The young man turned on her. "Mom, wake up! They bring a woman to get into the house, or what *looks* like a woman. But we know they kill humans, they shun women." He turned his gaze on his father. "And now *you've* let them in, Dad."

Hugh glanced at his wife. "I did?" he said. "Ask her about it!"

"We were given an explanation," Hanna said patiently to her son. "Perhaps you didn't hear it properly."

The young man uttered a snort of derision and pointed at Kate, fixing his mother with a stare. "You don't know what's *really* sitting there. They're like evil spirits. Perhaps they can take on any form. And you *let them in.*" He turned his gaze to Kate. "What's the true price? Won't you name it?"

"I am not a Wraeththu har masquerading as a woman, if that's what you think," Kate said. "And there is no price, only an offer."

Ashmael was silent for once. Let the parage deal with this. He was tired of it now.

The young man staggered further into the room and crumpled to his knees. Kate went immediately to assist him, but he pushed her off, falling instead against his mother, who has also hurried to his side. The effort made him pant. "You were right, Mom. I see it now. They've come for…"

"Scrap, shut up!" Hannah hissed, pulling his head against her breast as if to stifle his words.

"Nicky. They've come for Nicky."

There was a brief silence, then: "Who or what is Nicky?" Ashmael asked.

"He's delirious," Hannah said, still holding her son close.

"Then let me help," Kate said. The two women hauled him to a sagging old sofa against the far wall. "He's badly hurt, Hannah," Kate said. "Please let me summon one of our healers."

"Who's Nicky?" Ashmael asked again.

"Ash, forget that," Kate said. "Get somehar. Now!"

"I won't let you…" Hugh Ferniman began.

"For God's sake!" cried Hannah. "Let them!"

"You go," Ashmael said to Kate. He looked around the room and, acting on instinct, headed for a door that did not lead back to the hall. Ferniman sprang after him but Ashmael turned on him with a snarl. "Don't try, old man." The look in his eye made Ferniman back off.

Ashmael opened the door and went through it. What was this? A mystery, a secret. He smelled something interesting. Panic and fear had eclipsed the perfume, but he could sense it now. Strong, summoning. They were hiding something here. But what? They were only human. Ferniman had followed him, at a distance. "What is it you've hidden in here?" Ashmael said, his tone threatening now that he was away from Kate's hearing. "Tell me."

They had reached a flight of stairs. Ferniman threw himself in front of Ashmael, virtually collapsing on the bottom step. "Don't," he said. "I'll do what you ask… Take *me*."

Ashmael uttered a sound of annoyance. "Get up. I'm not doing any *taking*. Stop being a fool. I don't have to pander to the parage now we're out of her hearing, so I'll tell you this: You'll do what we want, anyway. I want to see what you're hiding. Now, do you show me, or do I find it myself?"

"Don't take him," Ferniman said. "It will kill him."

Ashmael pushed the man aside and leapt up the stairs, three steps at a time. He could smell it more strongly now: terror and power. A sweet perfume of potential.

The door was at the end of a long corridor. A light that could not be seen by human eyes leaked thinly round its frame. Ashmael marched directly to it and turned the handle. Locked. No matter. He kicked it in effortlessly. There was a scuffle of activity within. He saw two women, one quite young, restraining someone, whose hands and feet were bound. A har. It was a har! What had they done? How?

"Release him!" Ashmael snarled. "At once!"

327

The women cringed away, hands held out as if to ward him off. Ashmael then saw his mistake. What lay before him was not a har but a human youth. Such a creature, though. It had been easy to misread the signs. Perhaps the people here had somehow taken this boy from one of the rogue tribes. A failed inception? Or stolen before inception had taken place? He could not yet tell.

Ashmael hunkered down and began to pull at the boy's bonds. "It's all right," he said. "I won't hurt you. I'll set you free."

The boy whined and writhed frantically on the floor like a frightened cat, making Ashmael's job almost impossible without harming him. Ashmael was not the kind of har who could soothe with a touch. He knew his limitations. He stood up and turned to the women. "Remove his bonds," he said. "Now."

Reluctantly, the younger woman stepped forward.

"No, Liza," cried the other, but the girl shook her head.

"It's the end of it," she said. She went to squat beside the boy, and began picking at the knots.

"Why is he bound?" Ashmael asked the older woman. "Locked in? What's going on here?"

"To keep him safe," the woman said, with dignity. "*From you.*"

Ashmael turned from her. The boy seemed mindless. And yet initially he had given off the *feeling* of a har. Clearly, he had *abilities*, but was too damaged, perhaps, to use them or even understand them properly. It was obvious what was behind this imprisonment now: the boy's family had bound and hidden him because of what he was. They had thought the Gelaming had come for him, and it was most likely the jackal tribe *had*. The burning smell of potent natural energy was so strong, it filled the room. It would reach beyond this ramshackle compound and haunt the night. It would have driven the jackal hara into a frenzy. One thing was certain; whatever happened, this boy had to be protected.

The girl had finished unbinding him and was coiling the narrow ropes around her right arm. She looked resigned, defeated, grief-stricken. The boy lay twitching on the bare floorboards. Ashmael tried to lift him to his feet, but the boy – suddenly alert and fleet – squirmed away with an animal cry. He fled across the room to a chest of drawers, where a glass pitcher rested. Before Ashmael realised what was happening, and amid the startled cries of his relatives, the boy had smashed the pitcher and hurtled towards Ashmael with sharp shard in his hand, blood already running from his lacerated palm. Ashmael had no choice but to knock him out. The body slumped limply at his feet. The women uttered cries of fear and clung to one another, hair over their faces, which were masks of horror.

"Who is this?" Ashmael snapped at the women. "Speak!"

He loomed over them, a tower of threat. "I said *speak!*"

"It's Nicholas," the younger one said with difficulty, "my brother."

3

Wake up, Nicholas, wake up. This is just another dream and you must resist it. Wake up!

It was not a dream. Nicholas knew where he was and how he'd got there. It was a camp of war and he was lying within a cocoon of soft, striped blankets in one of the tents. The beast had taken him. He had come into the room looking like an angel, but he had the devil's heart. Fallen one, father of lies. Unnaturally tall. Nicholas hadn't expected them to look like that. It was the worst lie. And now, his God was testing him further, because he was still alive. Horrors would come.

In the dim light of the tent, where thin draperies veiled the entrance, Nicholas saw a shape before him. As he stared, this resolved into a figure, sitting upon a cushion. This person sat upright, their hands clasped in their lap. The face... it was a strange girl, who looked most severe. Her skin was clean like air, her pale hair bound up on her head and pierced with ornate silver pins. Was she real? She didn't look real. Nicholas hadn't seen a girl like that even in the picture books he'd loved as a child.

"You are awake," said the girl in an odd voice. Odd because... it sounded almost like the voice of a boy, yet was not.

Nicholas could not move. His limbs felt bound, but they were free. His head was thick, as if stuffed with straw. An enchantment, a curse, or perhaps simply a drug. He was no doubt expected to say things like "Who are you?" and "Where am I?" but he didn't want to hear the answers. He would be able to tell if they were lies, and generally more information came to him by listening rather than by speaking.

"I'm awake," he said.

The figure shifted upon her cushions. "Good. I am Reydis the Seer, and I am here to assess you."

No lies there. Nicholas said nothing. He only had to wait.

"I'm not a healer, although you may talk with one afterwards, if you like. I can tell you that your physical damage is slight, although hurts of a deeper, more intimate nature are not. I can see you are intelligent. You will have been aware of your differences most of your life, I expect."

Nicholas did not answer. *Aware I can hear thoughts? Yes. Aware of lies? Yes. Aware of being physically helpless at this moment? Yes.*

"That is precisely what I mean," said the girl, and she smiled, although it wasn't a genuine smile. Nicholas could tell the girl was thinking about something else as well as her 'assessment'. He could pry into her thoughts and find out what this was, then tell her. But that was what she wanted him to do, so he wouldn't.

"It's pointless to play games," said the girl. "We need to assess you, because from what our healers have ascertained, inception might be the best *treatment* for you. I don't know how much you've been told before being brought here, but that procedure is not mandatory for humans nowadays. However, under certain rare circumstances, it *is* advisable."

Nicholas didn't know what she meant, and found it hard to interpret the thoughts that went with the words. She was cloaking them now. "I would like to go home," he said.

The girl pursed her lips a little. "You know that your family is in danger," she said, "and, as well as that, they are not equipped to deal with a person such as yourself. You are safer here, and will be cared for appropriately."

Nicholas closed his eyes. He didn't want to hear any more. He knew he couldn't ask for his mother or his sisters, because they weren't here in the camp.

The girl changed her voice; it became softer. "I know you're afraid, and I know that you lack all the information you require to make wise choices. You can ask me anything and I'll do my best to answer clearly."

There were guards at the door, two of them. Nicholas could see them in his mind. He extended his senses, easier now as he forced himself to relax, and let himself drift like a wave over the camp outside. Many of them. Not like the jackals. Different in some ways, not in others. They were not cruel, he could sense that too. But...

A whirlwind of colour and noise suddenly erupted in his mind as someone marched into the tent. He opened his eyes.

A woman stood over the girl, hands on hips. "What are you doing here?" she demanded.

The girl twisted her head to the side. "My job. I'm here to assess the boy. As you know, this is the proper procedure in cases like this."

"There is no *case like this*," the woman snapped. "General Aldebaran gave express instructions Nicholas Ferniman was to be left alone, except for essential healing. Why was his mother not brought here?"

"That is not procedure."

The woman snorted, raked a hand through her thick hair. "Get out," she said mildly. "I'll speak to your supervisor shortly."

"I'm not sure what authority you have here..."

"Plenty. I'm here on behalf of the Hegemony concerning the matter of the Ferniman family. I think you'll find my credentials *proper*, if you care to check."

The girl stood up and without another word exited the tent.

The woman shook her head and sighed. Then she folded her arms and smiled at Nicholas. She was not a woman, he could tell that now. The colours around her weren't right. But she wasn't a beast either.

"I want to go home," he said.

"I know," the woman-thing replied, "and I'm sorry that can't happen just yet. I'm Katarin, Kate. I came to your house after the battle a few days ago. You've been unconscious since then, following some kind of seizure. My colleague, Ashmael, found you bound and locked in a room of your house. That was why you were brought here, because families do not generally keep their relatives tied up in a locked room."

"It has to be done," Nicholas said. "Do I have to tell you why? I don't think I do."

"No, you don't, but it's not a good way to live, is it?"

Nicholas shrugged. "I know it's over, in some ways, but I can see you're honest. I have simple requests. Let me go home or kill me. I don't want to be made like... not like you, because you're different, but like the others."

"Do you really understand the differences, Nicholas? What happens when a human is made har?"

He bared his teeth at her. "I saw much of it because *they* showed me. They corrupted my dreams. I saw what the demons of hell do when they are loosed on earth, what they do with each other and to their victims. My family don't know. How could I tell them? It's so much worse than they know."

"So... are you saying that *you* asked for the bonds rather than your family forcing them on you?"

The glance he gave her was filled with contempt. "Of course. You've jumped to conclusions about my people, haven't you? What I know inside, what I can't ever tell them, is abominable and that's why I make them bind me and lock my room. I don't *want* to live that way. Do you think I'm mad?"

"No," Kate replied. "I think you're afraid and more so because you don't have all the information you need. The hara around you now are as different from the creatures who violated your dreams as you are from a hornet."

"I don't care. If you really want to help me, stop the hornets coming for me."

Kate sat down on the end of his bed and regarded him for a few moments. "From what little I know of you already, I don't think they'll ever stop coming for you – well not until you're so old you won't be worth the bother. But as for the immediate future, should you elect to remain human, and your father agrees to work with the Gelaming, a safe haven will be provided for your people among other humans. In this place, you will be protected."

"Like in a reservation," Nicholas said. He knew the ancient history of his homeland. "*We* are the ousted natives here now, those of us who are human."

"There is some truth in that analogy," Kate said. "What you have to think about is that this is not a human world any more. You can try to preserve the past, and many hara would agree with you – lost species, like lost languages, are gone forever if they're allowed to die out. But you also have opportunities. You look upon Wraeththu as an abomination, a curse, the enemy. And so they were, once upon a time. But while your family has tried to hide away in the wilderness, the world moved on, very quickly. The days of terror have gone, Nicky – if I may call you that. You were living in something like a little capsule, in a nightmare. You need to see the truth of the world now, before making decisions about your own future."

"What are you?"

"I am a parage of the Kamagrian, similar to Wraeththu yet also different in some ways. Like Wraeththu, I have no single gender. Like them I am blessed with abilities that humans did not have. And yet... *you* have some of those abilities. Isn't it interesting a human was born that way? You also appear androgynous to an outsider. Ash thought you were a har when he first saw you. And our healers have picked up... *anomalies* in your physical makeup, hidden to the eye but there all the same. You could say, Nicky, you're not quite human either."

He wanted her words to be lies, but they were not. He turned on his side, to face the wall of the tent. He didn't want to look at her, or *feel* her, but she wasn't ready to go away yet. "Please, if you have any decency at all, don't make me like *them*. I can't do it. I've seen."

"What exactly have you seen?"

Furiously, with a surge of energy he *showed* her. *Not just sight. Terrible screams that no living soul should hear. The smell of blood and other fluids of the body leaking out. The sight of mutilated bodies, those who writhe with the infection, those who do not survive and whose corpses lie in a pile to rot or for their dogs to eat. The way they touch each other. The anger inside. The lust to kill until there is nothing left to die.*

He felt Kate wince away from the blast of thought. "I've seen what they do, believe me," he said.

Kate looked shaken; how could any decent person not be? She scraped a hand through her hair, made an effort to speak in a level tone. "That must have been... terrible." She knew, of course, those words were inadequate, but she persisted in trying to win his trust. He almost felt sorry for her. "I understand completely your feelings on what you've experienced. All I can say is that what you've seen in your nightmares is not the way things are amongst civilised hara. The jackal people aren't what Wraeththu *are*, Nicky. They are... *remnants* from the early days, hara who are damaged and broken, who never rose up from the wreckage as better beings. They are full of hate and fear, yes. They know no better. You mustn't think that the Gelaming are anything like that – they aren't."

"You're deluding yourself," Nicholas said. "Some are still like that but hide it." He turned back to her. "You're doing what that other girl did, only in a different way. You think you know what's best for me."

He could tell he'd hit a nerve with those words, for she said nothing.

"You want to do that terrible thing to me, because you think you can help me afterwards, show me your world. You can show me so many things. It's a beautiful picture and you are kind. But I don't want it. I can't be touched."

"Can't be touched?"

"I'm given to God."

Kate stood up. He could see she was thinking that there'd been no sign his family was religious. She was puzzled and didn't understand. But then neither did his family. He didn't speak of it to anyone. At least his family didn't try to change him. They didn't want to lose him. And now they had.

"Can I see my mother?"

"I'll do what I can."

"Your people won't listen. They want to change me."

"Ashmael, the one who found you, ordered that nothing was to be done with you before he returns, other than simple care. He's had to go back to Immanion for a couple of days. He'll come back tomorrow to talk more with your father."

"I don't want to see him. You must keep him away. He's like the jackals. He has their thoughts."

At this, Kate laughed, although she smothered it quickly. "That's not... Ashmael is a soldier, of course, and has his *ways*, but he's a good har, and very powerful. He'll help you."

These words conjured a picture in his head of the one he'd encountered in his bedroom back home. Tall. Angel. The woman-thing's words felt like a wall of flame passing over the earth, devouring everything in its path. Nicholas cried out, attempted to shut down his mind. He must go inwards to a safe place, where the chanting was, and songs to God.

She was worried about him, this woman-thing. He could feel her concern pouring off her, but it was not enough to douse the flames. Already his body was stretched taut, tremors starting up in his limbs, his spine like a bow. "Go!" he cried. "Go! Go now!"

She went.

Kate walked through the camp, dazed. What she'd seen in the tent unnerved her. The boy had suddenly had some kind of psychic fit; destructive energy had blasted out of him like poison fireworks, filling the space with unhealthy sick-green ether. He was terrified, but the revulsion he felt was stronger, deeper. She supposed she must tell the therapists what had occurred, but didn't relish it; then she was roused from her thoughts by a stern voice.

"Katarin? A moment, if you please."

Merxis stood before her, Reydis's supervisor, here to assess the mental state of the humans in the compound. He was not tall, but gave the impression of being so. His fair hair was severely plaited. Kate had noticed most of the therapists adopted this tidy style, perhaps to instil the idea of order and routine in those they treated.

Kate inclined her head, "Tiahaar."

Merxis wrinkled his straight, narrow nose briefly. "Reydis tells me you dismissed him from Nicholas Ferniman."

"Yes, because that is what General Aldebaran instructed."

"The boy has to be assessed. He's a vortex. Even you must see that."

Even you. Some hara were somewhat prejudiced against Kamagrian. In fact it was more likely Kate would *see* more than Merxis. "We have our orders. There is no benefit in bullying the humans, as I can't see how this will help General Aldebaran's mission, which is, of course, to bring Hugh Ferniman to Immanion. In essence, fascinating though he is, Nicholas is none of our business." She smiled sweetly.

Merxis grimaced. "You're not suggesting he should be returned to his people?"

"Why not? Yes, he's a human enigma, but he's not why we're here. Interfering could jeopardise the Hegemony's plans."

Merxis folded his arms and assumed a slightly belligerent posture. "Hugh Ferniman is only a man. I fail to see how he can be so important. His son, however, could be."

Kate deliberately mirrored Merxis' stance. "Then we should protect him. Hopefully, Ferniman will take up the offer and his people can be moved to a safer area."

"Tiahaar, the boy has *fits*. I know you've seen one. I imagine these will only get worse in proximity to hara, as he now is. I believe he is destined to be har and this should be attended to."

"At the risk of his sanity?"

Merxis laughed softly. "My dear parage, the hara of my department are more than qualified to deal with any psychological fallout. The physical change is important and whatever happens afterwards will be managed."

"General Aldebaran gave specific instructions that no major decisions concerning Nicholas Ferniman should be made until he returns. I believe his orders outrank yours on this occasion."

Merxis inclined his head. "I'm responsible for health and well-being. Sometimes my decisions are beyond rank. You should know that."

"Give the boy treatment for the fits. Surely you can do that?"

"He doesn't allow hara to touch him. He gets violent, even while fitting."

Kate widened her eyes. "Then do it from a distance! *You* should know *that*." Unable to bear any more, she walked away from Merxis. If she remained, all they'd do was argue in circles. The only thing she could think of to help Nicholas was to replace the guards at his door with two of Ashmael's trusted hara. Surely that would keep Merxis and his meddlers out, at least until Ashmael returned.

Of all the Fernimans, Hannah – Kate felt – was most likely to be willing to discuss her son's condition. But it was all too soon. The Fernimans were distrustful – understandably so – and Kate did not feel comfortable with suggesting Nicholas should be incepted. This would surely only reinforce the family's negative thoughts about the Gelaming's motives. If such a step were ever to take place, it should be after the Fernimans had been taken to Immanion and learned for themselves there were no ulterior motives. But perhaps there were. Merxis was keen to incept Nicholas because he was curious and wanted to see what came out of it. He would never admit to that, of course.

With great misgivings, and after she'd instructed two of Ashmael's hara to guard the boy, Kate rode her *sedu* down to the enclave where the Fernimans had been left alone to discuss their future among themselves. Here, harish healers were still attending to the injured. The dead had been cleared away. When Kate presented herself at the Ferniman household, she was not greeted warmly. A girl she'd not met before led her into the kitchen where a dozen people were gathered around the table. She felt that discussions were not going well and that the family was divided. This was not the atmosphere in which to talk about what was on her mind. Instead, and rather lamely, she said, "I'm here to see if you need anything."

"Our son?" Hugh snapped coldly from the head of the table.

"May I speak with you about him?" Kate asked, all the time clenched up inside with foreboding.

"Can we stop you?" one of the women replied.

Kate ignored this remark. She stood uncomfortably before the seated company and braced herself for a fight. "How long has he been having fits? Have you noticed them getting worse recently?"

"He'll be fine back with his family," Hannah said, from the other end of the table. "It's you who's making it worse. You have no idea how he feels about..." She shook her head, pressed a hand against her eyes. A woman next to her took her free hand and squeezed it.

"I do have an idea about it," Kate said, "because he's told me. His religious convictions seem very strong."

"It's how he copes," Hannah said, looking up once more.

Kate nodded. "I understand. You do realise he has certain abilities not normally found in humans?"

The family glanced at one another but it was only Hannah who said, "Yes, we know that. But such things have always been found in special people. It doesn't make him like you."

Kate sighed inwardly. "I will be honest with you. Nicky's condition, and the fact it appears to be worsening, has resulted in some of our therapists believing he should be incepted, made har. You know what this means?"

The family stared at her stonily, not speaking, as if they were a single entity. She felt one might leap up at any moment and attack her. "Personally, I disagree with this stance, as does General Aldebaran, but it's difficult for me to argue against what's regarded as the safest procedure in these circumstances. Hara don't wish to harm Nicholas. I can't emphasise that enough. They think they know what's best for him and want to end his suffering. They might be right, and Nicholas would rise from althaia – that is, the changing – with relief and gratitude. But I believe the decision should be his, not anyhar else's. I'm here because..." Again, just the angry silence. Why *was* she here? For their blessing? That wouldn't happen.

"You mean well," Hannah said, offering a weak smile.

"They have always come for him," said one of the men, who Kate recognised after a moment as a cleaned-up Jack, the brother. "It was Nicky who asked to be bound because he would rather die than be changed in that way. If you have no power among your own people, perhaps the kindest thing you could do is to kill him."

"Jack!" Hannah snapped, and a ripple of murmuring started up around the table.

Kate took a deep breath. "I wouldn't kill your brother even if he asked me to himself. Life is precious." She held out her hands to them, trying to convince them of her honesty. "I want you to see Immanion, to see the world of civilised Wraeththu as it is *now*. You must understand that a great change has come, like a planet-wide earthquake that has shaken everything up. It will take time, perhaps centuries, for things to settle, for equilibrium to be found. But there are pockets of it already, and that is what gives us hope."

For another few moments there was only silence, then Hugh Ferniman said, "Then tell us about it. Tell us what you are, how some of you look like women and some like men, yet we are told you are neither. Tell us how your city came to be built, how the beasts there evolved, found peace, found education, found a future. All we've ever seen is the face of the jackal out there." He pointed at the wall of the house, out beyond the enclave, to where dull fires might still burn in secret caves and savage eyes gleam with their light. "Convince me what you are is meant to be."

Kate sighed, raked her hands through her hair. "May I have a seat? This will take some time."

It was past ten o'clock at night when Kate left the Ferniman house. By this time she had talked with them, eaten with them, and if not exactly made friends, had perhaps reassured them a little. She had suggested that Hugh and Hannah visit Immanion, although she needed to talk with Ashmael as to how feasible it was for a human to be transported by *sedu*. This might be impossible, or at least too dangerous to try. Travelling by sea would take a long time, perhaps too long under the circumstances. Kate felt sure, though, that once the Fernimans saw the city and had spoken with hara and parazha, even other humans, their minds might be eased somewhat. She knew through experience these things could take time and needed careful, gradual handling.

She also acknowledged, however grudgingly, that Merxis and his hara might be right, even if their motives weren't. Nicholas had been exposed to hara and his differences had somehow caused a gate to open within him. She realised he was already part har, in some strange way, yet he resisted so strongly. The implications of what he was were immense. The general belief among Wraeththu was that hara had been created by humankind, perhaps not deliberately, but as part of an operation to save their people from extinction. If this was not so, and individuals who displayed harish traits were being born to women, perhaps the creation of Wraeththu was more natural than anyone – or anyhar – thought. Yet Nicholas was young, the early days were long past. It might be that hara were somehow affecting humans now from afar. She had no idea; it was a puzzle.

Her thoughts were abruptly interrupted by a harsh and desperate cry, like that of an animal in pain.

4

Why are you running, Nicholas? Don't you know it's too late for that? Better to end it now. Jump from a cliff. Throw yourself into a river. What are you waiting for?

He ran, stumbling, arms flailing, his skin on fire. Sometimes he was blind. Other times what he saw before him couldn't possibly be real. And yet at other moments he could see with intense clarity, perceiving the details of each tiny pebble on the rough ground ahead of him. Sounds, like the passage of a vast wing, plunged through his mind; this was not just overhead, but around and *through* him. Sounds that blotted out the stars, that had colours. Shards of light pierced his inner ear. He should listen to the voice in his head, find a high place. End it. But within him the desire to end his life warred with another desire to survive. Two beings battling in his mind. One of them wasn't himself.

5

"He's gone, Ash! He's gone!"

Kate looked wild with worry, waiting for Ashmael at the ether gate point. He knew at once to whom she referred. "How?" he snapped, dismounting from his *sedu*.

Kate rubbed at her face. "The fools incepted him! I told them not to, Ash, to wait. They just did it while I was out of the camp."

"Is he dead?" Ash said. "Is this what you're telling me?"

She shook her head. "No. As soon as he came round, he ran. He beat down his guards and ran."

Ashmael made a wordless angry sound. "Then that's as good as dead, isn't it, unless he's found? Have they sent hara out?"

Kate nodded. "Of course. I sent *your* hara. Merxis sent others. Nicky's left no trace... I think his abilities, even at this stage, have strengthened."

For a moment Ashmael rested his forehead against his *sedu's* neck. "Stupid fucking idiots," he said. Then he sighed and remounted the *sedu*. "Kate, come with me. Perhaps you'll be able to pick up some sign."

She didn't question him. "Just give me a minute to get to the stable."

You feel that cracking within, Nicholas? That's your body breaking down. It's liquefying, changing. Perhaps you don't need a cliff or deep water. Perhaps simply running will do it, until you're reduced to a pulp, crawling along the ground, until you crawl no more.

Nicholas fell to his knees, sobbing. Bloody slime trailed from his mouth to the stones beneath him. His skin burned, his insides were aflame. His skin had become scaly, like a sick lizard's that was about to moult. Strips of it hung from him in papery ribbons that smelled musty, rotten. His arm, where they had sliced him, was three times its normal size, looking as if it was about to burst. He knew instinctively that if he kept moving he would literally fall apart. Here was the choice: stop or carry on. He was afraid: of the pain, of disintegration. This did not seem a noble death. Waves of sound continued to pulse over him, sound that was energy, of the planet itself. He could sense the soul of the world and it was curious about him. He had never sensed that before.

He rolled onto his back, stared at the stars, panting. They alone were clear in his sight. He sensed enormous beings striding between them made of ether and starlight. He could almost see them; the gods of humankind throughout the ages. Perhaps they sensed him too but they were impartial, inexorable, fixed upon incomprehensible tasks. They would not help him. Nicholas did not want to die, yet neither did he want to become the *other thing*. Where was *his* God? The voice had gone silent, perhaps because he'd stopped moving, given in.

Then he perceived activity behind him, from the direction he'd come himself. Painfully lifting his head, he saw a cloud of blue radiance studded with stars hurtling towards him. Was this annihilation or a fragment of the distant gods? He could no more move out of its way than shift the planet from its course in the heavens.

"Ash, stop!"

Ashmael commanded his *sedu* to halt and it did so, skidding along the ground because it had been galloping so fast, half in this reality, half in the otherlanes. Ice crystals showered from its flanks.

"There!" Kate cried, pointing.

Ashmael could see the body on the ground ahead. He hoped they weren't too late.

Kate was the first at Nicholas's side, gently examining him. He was clothed in a stained nightshirt, now torn, presumably by his hectic passage through the rough desert. Other than that it was difficult to discern details from a short distance, and there was a gut-deep reluctance within Ashmael to draw closer. The trail they'd followed had indicated the boy had travelled fast, yet virtually on all fours like an animal, through spiky brush and over splintery stones. He'd run until he could run no more, perhaps was already dead.

Ashmael knew Kate had worked on Hegemony missions to rescue isolated settlements of humans who were in dire condition. Inceptions had taken place on those missions and she'd assisted with them. Ashmael didn't think she'd had to cope with an inceptee who'd fled before, though. Generally, they were incapable of fleeing. She'd had the presence of mind to bring drugs with her. Now she was pawing through the satchel she'd taken from her shoulder, taking out a flask of water and various packets of dried herbs.

"We could do with shelter," Kate said. Both she and Ashmael gazed dispiritedly at the flat desert landscape; the mountains were too far away.

"Can we move him, take him back to camp?"

"I wouldn't advise it," Kate said. "These herbs could really do with proper heating but we don't have the time. I need to get at least some of the medicine inside him really fast."

"What can I do?"

She was mixing the herbs in a small ceramic bowl she'd set on the ground. "Put your hands around this, help me warm it."

Ashmael placed his hands over hers around the bowl, tried to concentrate on summoning Agmara, but it wasn't easy. This wasn't his province and he found it hard to make his mind slow down enough to channel the energy. He wasn't some floaty, ethereal type, such as those found in therapy centres, a kind of har he secretly despised. He was a creature of swift action. Apart from skills useful to his job, Ashmael hadn't particularly bothered with honing his natural abilities. If he needed heat, he'd usually order some other har to do it.

"Can't I go and find some tinder or something?" he said. "I'm not much use to you here."

"You're har aren't you?" Kate snapped. "Too ouana-focused, of course, but still har. Dredge that half-dead soume part to the surface for a minute, will you?"

"My soume-part is not half dead," Ashmael said indignantly. "It's just... well an *uncompromising* sort of soume."

"I knew girls like that once," Kate said dryly.

"I'll make her co-operate," Ashmael said and renewed his effort. Kate was right. Focusing on his soume aspect did help, although it wasn't that comfortable for him. *We continue to learn about ourselves*, he thought, *when we think we know it all.*

They will poison you further, these demons. Resist! There is little time left, Nicholas. Your suffering will end.

Nicholas could still only perceive the stars clearly; everything closer to him was indistinct, although he was aware of moving forms, hands upon him. He sensed their hot concern, the need for haste. If he should die, his suffering would not end. He could read this inescapable fact pouring from one of the entities beside him. The feeling was raw, without artifice, because it did not know he could read it. He learned that even if he left this body, there would be pain, confusion, an inability to move on. He glimpsed a dark and arid realm, where the souls of those who did not survive the change were lost and wandering. There would be no release, no escape. Did this mean the voice lied to him, and perhaps had always lied?

Icy fluid poured into his mouth, which he could barely open now. This fluid was like the stars to him, blue and radiant, suffusing him with cold light, feeling its way through blood and bone, quenching the fire within him.

"Kate, you'll burn him," Ash said. "It's too hot."

"No." Kate continued to dribble the heated liquid through the tiny gap in Nicholas's locked jaw, steam rising in a hissing cloud around them. Ashmael held the boy's head steady, aware that the flesh was parting from the scalp. The body before them no longer resembled the boy he'd taken from the human compound; it was like a rotting corpse. He felt nauseated, wanted to let go, but hadn't he been like this once? Some har had remained by his side and seen him through althaia, the changing. There was no time to feel sickened, only particular tasks to attend to.

Once most of the liquid had been administered, Kate took a pot of unguent from her satchel. "Help me," she said. "Cover his body with this." She was already removing what was left of the nightshirt. Parts of it were glued to the boy's body. She had to tear it, taking skin along with it.

Ashmael swallowed with difficulty. He had no desire to touch that disintegrating flesh. He had never attended inceptions or helped with them. He had only been called upon afterwards to bring new inceptees into the family with the seal of aruna. In the past, that must have been almost as traumatic for new hara as the althaia itself. Kate would know this, of course. Now, some part of Ashmael wanted her approval, to show her he was more than she judged him to be. This must be the consequence of dragging forth that soume half; it always brought problems with it. Sighing, he dipped his fingers into the thick ointment and applied it to Nicholas's head and face, which seemed the least unpleasant to touch. He was not a squeamish har; there was no room for that in what he had to do in life, for his leaders, for his hara. Yet here he was, squirming like a harling in revulsion, his heart beating fast.

"That's it," Kate said. "Quicker, Ash. Don't fumble about."

"What do we do after this?" Ashmael asked. "We can't leave him out here in the open."

"We have no choice," Kate said. She shook her head. "It's weird – he's so far into the change. Can't possibly be moved now, and yet it's too soon for althaia to be this advanced." She fixed Ashmael with a stare. "Once we've coated him with the ointment, you must return to camp, bring supplies, shelter, hara to protect us so the process isn't disturbed. Much as I hate the idea, Merxis must come too. I've never seen anything like this."

"Of course." Ashmael half rose to his feet.

"Not yet, Ash," Kate commanded. "This job is far from finished."

The cold blue fire lifted Nicholas from his body as if with hands of ether. He could look down now, see those who were trying to help him. The woman-thing – Kate – felt out of her depth. The other... he didn't care for this and yet he cared a lot. Part of his caring involved anger at being disobeyed, that this had happened. He also felt responsible, because of course – he *was*. Nicholas felt no resentment about that now. Everything had changed, not just what was happening to his body. This thing they called inception was not a pretty process and it was dangerous. So many had died; he could sense that as if a legion of the dead hovered behind him. The alternative had been extinction for everyone. This he could also see.

You do have a purpose, Nicholas. Do you understand this?

The voice in his mind was different now, a lower, softer tone to it.

"Are you my god?" he asked.

You choose your gods, Nicholas, as does every living thing.

"Then what is my purpose?"

You know...

Nicholas turned his perception around to face what lay behind him. He saw them: rank upon endless rank of indistinct forms, revealed only by the dim light of a dark sun. These were not the dead; they were something worse. They were half-creatures, failed inceptions, discards. They had waited for a long time for someone to hear them. So many whispery voices. Some were trapped in seemingly lifeless bodies in hidden corners of the earth. Others were separated from flesh and had been drawn to the dark realm he had perceived a few minutes before. Yet more were functional – barely – as living beings, yet unfinished. They hid, they scavenged, they yearned for completion.

His consciousness was drawn back in time. He saw nascent Wraeththu tribes pouring like ink over the landscape. Wild howling in the night. Atrocities of every description, perpetrated *by* Wraeththu and *upon* them. He saw humankind, what they'd been doing to each other and the planet, their home. Violence without thought or reason moved like a canker over the world, bringing death and destruction. The good had been annihilated along with the bad, on both sides of the conflict, until all that was left was burned and blackened battlefields that smelled of carrion. But then... shining reeds of light appearing in the darkness, creatures of thought, of opinion, of compassion. Without form, souls seeking homes in the bodies of the new.

Nicholas knew that what he had seen was like a compressed snapshot of history, a metaphor for what had come to pass. Not all Wraeththu were evil as not all humans were good. His father was an honourable man; he had been spared. He too still had purpose, even in this changed world.

All this, Nicholas could have seen at any time, yet he'd been afraid and had clung to outworn idols to protect himself. This was so clear now. The voices in his head were his own.

He was drawn back into his body with a sickening rush, gasped, sat upright. Light flared from him in spiralling rays. He could barely breathe, and yet when his lungs finally did take air, it was like the essence of spring, of a season he'd never truly witnessed.

Kate was knocked over onto her back by the energy that flared from Nicholas's body. His skin looked burned through the coating of ointment, black and red, yet his eyes were a sheer and frosty blue.

Ashmael leapt to his feet and jumped backwards, landing in a fighter's crouch, ready to defend himself.

Nicholas got slowly to his feet between them, held out his arms, examined them, turning his hands palms up, palms down. Then he began to pick the black papery stuff from his flesh, exposing clean skin beneath.

"No!" Kate exclaimed. "This is impossible."

"What?" Ash yelled. "What the fuck is going on?"

"It's over," Kate said. "I think... Nicholas?" She stood up tentatively. "Nicholas, do you hear me?"

He turned to her. "Yes. Is it done, this thing?"

"I think so... It should take three days, even more, but... this was *hours*. I don't know." She shook her head. "I really don't know."

They took Nicholas back to the Gelaming camp, directly to Merxis's pavilion, where they found the har awake, awaiting news from the scouts. He wasn't as abrasive as he usually tended to be, which Kate assumed was because he found Ashmael intimidating and was also aware his actions could have precipitated Nicholas's death. He could be disciplined for this and was subdued by that knowledge. Even Ashmael, shaken by what he'd experienced, did not appear to be in the mood for arguments. In his arms he held Nicholas, who had lapsed once more into a semi-conscious state. Clear, pale skin showed through from the cracks in the blackened, bloody carapace that covered him.

"This is astonishing," Merxis said rather feebly. "How has he survived?"

"It appears he underwent althaia in a couple of hours," Kate said. "One minute he was virtually dead at our feet, the next he sat bolt upright."

At that moment, Nicholas raised his head and said, "Please, give me water."

Merxis hurried to comply and allowed Nicholas to drink. He sipped slowly, as if aware hasty gulping would harm him.

"Let's get you bathed," Merxis said. "Get that mess off you."

Nicholas sighed and relaxed back against Ashmael's chest. He shuddered jerkily once or twice, then lay still.

Merxis called for one of his hara to prepare Nicholas a bath. They took him back to the pavilion where he'd first rested, and from whence he had escaped. The paraphernalia of inception still lay around the room and there was evidence of a scuffle, furniture turned over, the bed streaked with blood. Merxis's assistant, Reydis, set to clearing away this discomforting evidence. Kate recognised him as the har she'd shouted at when she'd found him 'assessing' Nicholas the day before. Now, he avoided her gaze.

Nicholas was passive and appeared dazed, still only half conscious. He did not protest or fight against them. His eyes, however, remained open wide, strangely *fiery* in a cold, wintry way.

"Do you think the inception really is complete?" Kate asked Merxis, once Nicholas had been laid on the bed and Reydis had departed to organise hot water for the bath.

"Superficially, it would appear so," Merxis replied. "I'll need to do a more thorough examination, of course. This is unprecedented in my experience, and I've seen some fairly odd inceptions over the years."

"Well, we knew he was different," Kate said.

Merxis nodded, his expression unusually distracted. "To be perfectly honest with you, I'm not sure what we're dealing with here. Was he ever in fact human?"

"We've questioned that too," Kate said.

Ashmael stood up from where he'd been crouched beside Nicholas. "He doesn't seem that angry about what happened," he said. "We might not be able to say the same about his family, which could impede my mission. Should I go and speak to them?"

Kate shook her head. "No. Wait until morning. We need to know more about Nicholas's althaia, whether it is in fact over."

"If it is, what about the rest?" Ashmael said. "He'll need aruna, won't he?"

"Are you volunteering?" Kate asked archly.

"No. But surely the question must be addressed. In my opinion, althaia takes place over several days for a reason – to help a har come to terms with what he's becoming. This is sudden. Should normal procedures be followed now or not?"

"Your opinion is valid," Merxis said. "I want to examine our new har as soon as possible. But for now, let's give him privacy while he takes his bath. That too is one of the rituals of inception, the washing away of the old. Come to my pavilion; let's take a drink together while we wait."

Nicholas lay in the scented water, allowing the har who attended him to bathe him. He felt detached from his body somehow, whereas before he'd been furiously private about it. There was so much to assimilate, to examine and understand. He was aware his change had been different to what was considered normal. He didn't yet know what this meant for himself. And yet he didn't feel different at all, simply overwhelmed, as if he'd come face to face with a ghost, incontrovertible evidence of the unseen, and now his version of reality had been shattered. The pieces were too numerous and too tiny ever to be reassembled into what they'd been before. He needed to rest, yet his mind was so active, working on several different levels simultaneously.

"Can you make me sleep?" he asked the har who knelt beside the bathtub, whose warm hands gently cleaned his skin. He hummed a soft and wistful tune, and Nicholas could see the har was remembering his own inception, the ritual bath, the kind hara who had once sung to him too.

However, Nicholas's voice alarmed the har, because he hadn't expected the new inceptee to speak. He looked almost frightened and his song ceased abruptly. "Why do you want to sleep?"

"To quieten my mind, so I can look at things one at a time. It's like I'm full of voices."

The har nodded sympathetically. "I'll speak to Tiahaar Merxis. He'll want to examine you, to make sure you are well."

"Nothing went wrong. He needn't fear that."

"Well..." The har straightened up, stiff-backed beside the tub. "It's best you're checked over."

"Let this be done, then. I need to sleep."

The har brought Merxis, a creature of order and routine, who liked things to be done precisely, who didn't like alterations to familiar processes. Nicholas found he could perceive many things about this har, the fears he hid behind the mask he wore. Everybody wore these masks. Would it be uncomfortable to see through them like this, with everyone – every*har* – he met?

Merxis inclined his head to Nicholas in greeting. "You are agreeable to me examining you? This will have to be quite... thorough."

"Do what you must," Nicholas said. He rose from the water, noticed it was full of drab, floating debris. He held out his arms so that the har who'd attended him could dress him in a towelling robe. His skin seemed to glow.

"Reydis, will you remain with us, please?" Merxis said.

The har bowed his head. "Of course, Tiahaar."

Merxis gestured for Nicholas to lie down on the bed nearby. "Reydis will be your care-har."

Nicholas recognised dimly this was the tent in which he'd first awoken. He remembered now the prim little har who'd spoken to him there, before Kate had ordered him out. Was this Reydis the same person? He seemed completely unknown and yet the face was the same. Only he wasn't so stiff and formal, because he'd been woken in the middle of the night for this duty, his hair drawn into a hasty, loose knot at his neck. Had he been at the inception? Nicholas couldn't remember a thing about it now, other than coming to his senses and fighting his way free of the pavilion. They had drugged him, of course, but not enough.

"Reydis will answer any questions you might have," Merxis said, "although you may speak to me too."

Nicholas stretched out on the striped blanket. "Can I see my family?"

"In time," Merxis answered smoothly. "Please just try to relax. I'll be as gentle as I can." He smiled. "From a superficial inspection, all appears to be in order, but I want to be sure." Merxis seated himself cross-legged beside the bed.

Nicholas closed his eyes. He didn't like what had to be done but knew it was important to Merxis. He winced as the therapist's fingers probed him internally. *Don't think about that. Not yet.*

"Are you in pain?" Merxis asked softly.

"No. The sensation is strange, that's all."

"All seems fine down there," Merxis said. Reydis brought him a bowl of water and he rinsed his hands. Then he probed Nicholas's body externally, asking if any points were uncomfortable.

"No, there is no pain," Nicholas said.

Merxis got to his feet. "Then I think I can safely pronounce you har, although you have undergone the fastest inception I have ever seen. You must surely understand our caution."

"Yes."

"Perhaps this acceleration is natural, due to evolution within us all." Merxis paused. "Nicholas, there is something you must accept, and I hope this will not be difficult for you."

"That I am no longer male? Yes, I know that. It doesn't

349

matter." To him, that part of the change was irrelevant; it was the rest that awed him, the way his already supernatural senses had become so strong, so intense. He knew there was so much to explore. He was not afraid, simply eager, but also bone-tired.

"Not just that," Merxis said. "Part of the process of inception is that it must be sealed... cemented. The way this is done is through aruna, physical intimacy between hara. Do you understand what I'm saying?"

Nicholas closed his eyes briefly. "Yes." He could get through that like he'd got through the examination. They'd leave him alone once their routines were complete, and then he could sleep, dream of his new being.

"Is there anyhar you would prefer for this?"

"No."

Merxis hesitated. "Hmm. You seem... unresponsive. I think perhaps we can wait on this part of althaia."

"I don't care. Just do it."

Merxis smiled warmly. He was a kind har at heart, no matter how officious he might seem. "That's not the way it works, Nicholas."

"Then let me sleep."

6

Ashmael and Kate visited Nicholas in the morning. They found him awake, sitting up in his bed, supported by several thick pillows, eating the breakfast Reydis had brought to him. Nicholas could sense how he appeared to them: healthy and serene, despite having lost a lot of his hair, perhaps because of the accelerated inception. What was left of it was tied at his neck. This loss didn't bother him; he knew it would grow back thick and strong. He was amused Ashmael found it remarkable he seemed so unfazed by what had happened, given how he'd been before. He lashed out a thought into Ashmael's mind. *It's because of what I saw.*

You have much to learn, Ashmael lashed back. *First, it's rude to pry. Be mindful of your inner sight.*

"I apologise," Nicholas said aloud.

"How are you feeling, Nicky?" Kate asked, glancing at Ashmael curiously.

"Well enough," he answered. "Nicky is dead, though, Tiahaar. Reydis has told me about inception names. I will be Fernici, from my family name and a remnant of who I was."

Kate smiled uncertainly. "I see. May I call you Fern?"

"As you wish." He could see Kate found him confusing and was unsure how to relate to him. Perhaps they would be friends. Or perhaps soon she'd go somewhere else and he'd never see her again. He liked her and hoped their future was that of friendship. As for the other: he could not look at Ashmael.

"We thought perhaps you could come with us to visit your family, if you feel up to it," Kate said.

Nicholas, now Fernici, considered her words. "I'm not sure I can talk to them yet, although I appreciate they'll want to be reassured. I don't want my mother to worry."

Kate nodded. "OK. Then perhaps you could write them a note."

Fernici was aware of Ashmael looming tall behind him. He could feel the har's awkwardness, the defensive folding of his arms. "If you want me to, if it'll make things easier."

"I think it might." Kate glanced around her. "I'd better find something for you to write on and with, hadn't I? Won't be long." She glanced at Ashmael, smiled secretively. "Well, perhaps it will take some time." She left the pavilion.

Fernici was left with the silent Ashmael, listening to the sounds outside. He knew what Kate had been thinking and that Ashmael was thinking of it too, albeit in rather a confused way. Fernici knew he would have to deal with this before anything else. Reydis would be returning soon. Fernici could sense him in a pavilion nearby, engaged in various tasks to do with his work, writing up a few hurried notes, grabbing some food hastily himself, wondering what he might bring to Fernici to help him, what questions should be asked, what statements made. He worried too much. To Fernici it was all very simple.

Ashmael cleared his throat and moved into Fernici's line of sight. "Nicholas... Fern... I realise I've brought this upon you. I would've acted differently if I'd known."

"Always impulsive," Fernici said. "Isn't that so?"

Ashmael pulled a quizzical expression. "Are you prying still?"

"No, that was an observation based on evidence."

"I think you see too much."

"I wanted to be blind, but I can't be. I would simply have gone mad, or the jackals would have taken me. I should thank you, I suppose. Don't feel bad about it." Fernici put aside the remains of his breakfast.

Ashmael hunkered down beside the bed. "If there's anything I can do for you... I think you know what I mean."

Fernici looked into Ashmael's eyes. He was honest, sometimes thoughtless, brave, witty, a har of power. Many fine qualities. And beautiful. Ashmael had watched over him as he'd lain unconscious during that first couple of days of being in the Gelaming camp. He remembered this now as if it were a dream. He had a dim memory of hearing Ashmael say to Merxis, just outside the pavilion, "Don't touch him!" And then he'd gone, and Nicholas's fits had started, the opening of a gate, the blindness slipping from his eyes.

When they'd come to him, dressed in their fine ceremonial robes, with a blade and blood, he'd accepted what must be, because in a way inception had already started. He knew now that afterwards, when he'd been driven to escape, it was because an inner part of him – perhaps the part that had already been har – had sought to endure the change alone, like a wounded animal. They'd not understood that. Neither had he.

Now, he reached out and put the fingers of one hand gently against Ashmael's lips. "No. It can't be you," he said.

Ashmael looked baffled, but then he was rarely turned down. "I hope one day you'll forgive me," he said.

"That's not relevant. It's just not the time. I've not *become* yet, Ashmael. I want to be what I am to be. It's hard to explain. You've done much for me. I like you, and for this reason, strange though it sounds, it can't be you."

Ashmael stood up, rubbed the back of his head. "I feel like I've lived through several months in a few days. It's very odd. That boy I saw bound on the floor of his house lived aeons ago. Now we have Fernici, *very* sure of himself." He smiled. "When you come to Immanion, my house is always open to you and your family. I hope you'll visit, when you have *become*." He inclined his head. "Be good to yourself."

Fernici watched Ashmael duck out of the pavilion entrance. *I think part of me actually did go mad*, he thought.

Reydis came back into the pavilion, glancing behind at the

retreating Ashmael. He too was intimated by that har, but Fernici wasn't surprised about it. "He offered himself," Fernici said.

Reydis uttered an irrepressible snort of laughter, and it was as if they were friends already, had known each other a long time. "From the look on his face just then, I take it you declined. That was brave!"

Fernici sighed. "There are new feelings inside me. I don't know them yet. But if I ever take that step with him, I want to know myself, be in control."

"That's wise of you." Reydis held out his hand. "Here, I brought this for you. It's a custom." It was a bangle of plaited leather, wound with lapis lazuli beads and chips of white crystal. "An inception gift."

Fernici took the bangle. "Thank you." He knew Reydis wanted his experience to be as uplifting as his own had been: the bath, the song, the gift. He opened the blankets of his bed. "Sing the rest of the song to me."

"You're sure?"

"I'm sure."

7

Three days later, five members of the Ferniman family were taken to Immanion, the humans drugged into an induced sleep so they could withstand the otherlanes journey. The Fernimans had been offered the choice of who would be in the party, and had elected for Hugh and Hannah to go, and also their eldest children, Jack and Liza. Fernici was the fifth. He wasn't sure if his parents and siblings still regarded him as family, because there was now an inescapable gulf between them, but he did what he could to be like how they'd known him, hiding his blossoming talents, dressing as he'd always dressed, in his old clothes, a bandana over his head to cover his hair. But he knew he looked so different to them now. Their feelings were confused, because they couldn't deny he was serene and accepting of his new state, but at the same time they mourned the boy they'd known, and couldn't entirely dispel the resentment they felt towards the Gelaming who'd changed him. But the world moves inexorably on, and only a fool would not appreciate the benefits that were on offer for the Ferniman clan and their dependents.

Kate, Merxis and Reydis accompanied them, along with hara who carried the humans through the otherlanes. As he made that unimaginable first journey, Fernici was already wondering how he could get his own *sedu*, or access to one regularly, to explore this intriguing otherworld. While he and Reydis had been discussing his future over the past few days, Reydis had told him some hara were employed as Listeners, who were like the organs of communication between hara who were physically far apart. He had also told of hara who roamed the otherlanes, working with their *sedim* to ensure safety for travellers, even to explore new worlds. So many possibilities. If it hadn't been for his father's desperate attempts to communicate with others, none of this would have happened.

And now Fernici stood with Reydis upon a high balcony at the villa that had been allocated for the Fernimans' use while they were in the city. Reydis alone had remained with the visitors. Later, officials would come to welcome them to the city, to answer their questions, make plans for where they would live, what they would do.

Kate and Merxis had departed to see to various arrangements and appointments, to make reports. Hugh and the others were still groggy from the journey and were resting. Fernici knew that many painful conversations were in store. His family were not wholly trusting and were wary of what he'd become. If acceptance should truly come, perhaps other younger members of his family might choose to be incepted, either to Wraeththu or Kamagrian. But for now, he didn't have to worry about the future. He could bask for a few hours in what was simply before his eyes. Immanion too was another world, like a dream from an idealised past. It took your breath with its beauty, with its strange sentience like that of a living creature.

"Immanion *is* alive," Reydis murmured to Fernici, their arms touching as they leaned on the balcony rail. "It was built by magic, you know."

Fernici laughed, shaded his eyes, to gaze down at the distant harbour, the flock of sleek ships idling there, their sails folded like white wings. "Magic!" he said.

"It's true. You'll see. I shall be very surprised if Thiede doesn't want to meet you, given your talents."

"Thiede?"

"He was the first," Reydis said and made an expansive gesture before him, taking in the whole of the landscape before them. "He *made* this, Fern. Immanion is his creation, as are we."

"And he used magic..." Fernici said, unable to keep a note of humour from his voice.

"Well, perhaps forces we don't yet fully understand," Reydis replied. "But trust me, it might as well be magic."

"In that case, I look forward to talking with this har. It seems incredible Wraeththu all came from one individual, though."

"It does," Reydis said. "But don't think about that now. Enjoy your new being. There will be plenty of time for education." He pointed out to the north. "You see all those villas with the big gardens over on those hills? That's the district where Ashmael lives."

"He's probably already forgotten me," Fernici said.

"You know that's not true."

"Shush, I've got so many other things to think about, and lots of things to see."

"You're not just an extraordinary mind, Fernici. Don't put aside *any* of what you are now. And be mindful of signs and omens."

"You're in the wrong job," Fernici said. "You'll be asking to read my palm next."

Reydis sighed, smiling, and squeezed Fernici's shoulder. "You are so lucky. I remember what it was like. So much to learn. So must to be astounded by."

A flock of iridescent birds clattered up from the garden below, wheeling around the balcony, uttering sweet cries, as if they had been summoned by Reydis's words. A single perfect feather drifted down and alighted upon the back of Fernici's left hand. He picked it up, held it to his nose. "It smells of life," he murmured.

Reydis grinned. "You see?" he said.

Dream, Fernici. Dream of voices singing in the night, of hooves galloping across untrodden worlds, of unthinkable vistas. You are riding with them; gleaming skins beneath alien suns, opening the horizons of your kind. You are waiting for this, Fernici; it is your destiny. You can see everything, even your own heart. You are without weakness.

about the contributors

Storm Constantine

Storm is the creator of the Wraeththu Mythos, the first trilogy of which was published in the 1980s. However, the influences and inspirations for the Wraeththu world go much further back than that, and continue into the future as she plans more stories for it. Storm is the founder of Immanion Press, created initially to publish her out-of-print back catalogue, but which evolved into the thriving venture it is today. She has written over thirty books, including full length novels, novellas, short story collections and non-fiction titles. Her interests include magic and spirituality, Reiki, movies, music and MMOs. Among her many occupations, most of which are unpaid, she runs a Reiki school and a guild called Equilibrium on the EU servers of World of Warcraft. She lives in the Midlands of the UK.

Wendy Darling

Based in Atlanta, Georgia, USA, Wendy Darling is co-author of *Breeding Discontent*, published by Immanion Press in 2003 as the first *Wraeththu Mythos* novel. She has been involved in Wraeththu in many different capacities, including editor of the revised *Wraeththu Chronicles*, webmaster of the *Inception* and *Forever Wraeththu* fan web sites, and staff at several Wraeththu conventions. She also co-edited the first Wraeththu Mythos story collection, *Paragenesis*. Her full-time job is as a web projects manager at

Emory University, but she engages in many side projects and hobbies, including photography and writing. She has also forged relationships with Wraeththu fans around the world and has been fortunate to meet several authors whose work is included in this collection. At home she is ruled by two cats, cats she did not have in her life until she met and visited with Storm, who as usual had a strong influence on her. Wendy enjoys international travel and tries to visit Storm and her husband Jim as often as she can. Connect with Wendy online at about.me/wdarling.

Martina Bellovičová

Martina was born in Brno, Czech Republic, where she successfully finished English and German studies at the Masaryk University and received her Master's degree. Subsequently, she spent a year in Austria, Finland and Luxembourg, working as a translator for the European Commission. She is currently studying creative writing and publicity in Prague, while working as a freelance translator. Her first published short story, "A Piece of Meat" appeared in the fantasy collection "Rytiny" Martina also enjoys creating comics and in 2011 won a contest in the "KomixFEST Revue", which published her surreal comic "The Waiting Room". Prior to focusing on writing, she devoted many years of her life to theatre and music, and is currently the keyboardist in the dark electro band "LateXJesus". She considers herself a lifestyle Goth and spins CDs at alternative parties under the pseudonym DJ Zlyhad. She is also the owner and main editor of the gothic subculture webzine www.cavern.cz and occasionally writes book reviews for the steampunk webzine http://www.steamzine.cz/

Ash Corvida

Firmly rooted in Berlin, Germany, her city of birth, which is possibly the only fixed point in her life, Ash is a creature of diversity. An artist, sometime secretary, programmer, mother of a grown-up gothling, witch and ceremonial magician, her interests range from science and technology, philosophy, foreign cultures and history, psychology, mythology and religion to art, music and writing.

Currently she is working in the computer business in webdesign and programming. For a relaxing pastime consuming SF and Fantasy literature is her natural habitat.

A dreamer from early childhood on Ash is blessed - or cursed - with a mind that is difficult if not impossible to reign in. The awe she feels perceiving the wonders of nature, like the vastness of the night sky, the fierceness of volcanoes or storms and earthquakes, the breathtaking beauty of the mountains and mystery of an enchanted forset or the secrets of the deep sea never fail to inspire her with stories and imagery of strange worlds, creatures and alien cultures. Along with those inspirations Ash has always felt the deep rooted need to try and capture her impressions in diverse artforms, such as drawing and painting, (both traditional and digital), and sculpting, costume design, writing and playing piano and guitar.

Nerine Dorman

An editor and multi-published author, Nerine Dorman currently resides in Cape Town, South Africa, with her visual artist husband. Some of the publishers with whom she has worked include Lyrical Press, Dark Continents Publishing, Crossroad Press and eKhaya (an imprint of Random House Struik). Short fiction sales include Tor Books, Apex Publishing, Pandemonium and  Immanion Press. She has been involved in the media industry for more than a decade, with a background in magazine and newspaper publishing, commercial fiction, and print production management within a below-the-line marketing environment. Her book reviews, as well as travel, entertainment and lifestyle editorial regularly appear in national newspapers. A few of her interests include music, travel, history, Egypt, art, photography, psychology, philosophy, magic and the natural world.

Suzanne Gabriel

Born to nomadic Canadian parents, Suzanne grew up in Canada, the UK, and USA. She is a wife and mother. She completed a Master of Science degree in Food Science and Nutrition and spent time working in the food industry and currently works in a university as a budget officer. Suzanne is fascinated by antiquities museums, old cookbooks, old etiquette books, and documentaries about old things.

Even when there isn't any music, Suzanne is likely to be dancing and she will go out of her way to hug a tree. She adores animals, travel, historical re-enactment, science, hiking, yoga, and way too many other hobbies.

Although Suzanne would love to be thought of as quirky and unorthodox, she's incredibly normal, and probably a bit boring.

Fiona Lane

Fiona born and brought up near Glasgow during the Time Of The Flared Trouser and Unfeasibly High Platform Shoes. By the time we all came to our senses, she had relocated to Aberdeen, and spent several years waiting for a number six bus, in a horrible collision involving the nature of time and the Aberdeen weather. During the eighties, while she was waiting for the Internet to be invented, she acquired a husband and a couple of replacement units, and they all now live in a field full of sheep in Aberdeenshire, along with the odd cat or two and Fiona's posse of obsolete computers, many of which she has single-handedly restored to a completely non-functioning condition. She once kept chickens, but they were messy and she couldn't use them to buy vintage shoes from Ebay. The eggs were good though. She likes gin and hats, and dislikes the oppression of the proletariat. Her hobbies include cooking, gardening, and staring into the abyss.

Danielle Lainton

Danni has always been in love with the arts in all forms but didn't start thinking seriously about it until she studied Visual and Performing Arts at college. Rather than going to University, as was hoped and expected, she worked in the music industry for a while before getting married and having children. Still yearning to be creative, she began work for a local wedding stationer. Eventually, she decided to go it alone and started her own business, Uber Angel, which deals primarily with alternative weddings and  commissioned artwork. She also produces original artwork for Immanion Press and has recently started dabbling with website design. Even though she tended towards sculpture and photography as a student she now produces most of her work digitally, using a graphics tablet, but still in a traditional drawing style. Her inspirations are many and they come in whims; one day she's working on a pin-up girl and then the next she may feel like drawing zombies and vampires, or even a combination of them all!

Maria J. Leel

 Originally from the flat lands surrounding Peterborough, Maria moved in 2006 to the infinitely hillier Shropshire. She, her husband and two geriatric cats, have recently taken on a large garden and are in the process of turning this into a permaculture paradise. With a CV that resembles 'War and Peace', her working life has been delightfully varied as she has turned her hand to everything from Urban Ecology to First Aid Training to Reflexology. Maria has travelled widely volunteering on many projects such as the California Condor Recovery Program, the Australian railway Puffing Billy and the Fiji Pine reforestation scheme. For a time she lived on a Kibbutz near Jerusalem and as a result has an abiding interest in alternative living styles and communal living. She has been writing plays and stories almost all her life and has contributed to several Wraeththu Mythos projects including her first novel 'Song of the Sulh'.

Daniela Ritter

Daniela was born in the little German town Salzgitter on a Leap Year February 29th. Rather a loner until she discovered the internet, Daniela then became involved in writing fan-fiction. She still uses her old nickname DodyLuNatic. Daniela plays the violin and claims she is unbeatable at karaoke! She is involved in pen & paper roleplaying sessions with her Shadowrun group and online in World of Warcraft. Daniela took her first steps on the spiritual path as a Reiki practitioner, and has since found a home in Dehara Magic, about which she is passionate. Supported by a loving husband, she now lives in Hamburg, where they are building their private paradise. Maybe they'll add some children in a while.

Ruby

Ruby is the official artist for the Wraeththu Mythos, who creates all the covers for the Immanion Press editions. She started drawing from her imagination long before she could or indeed would talk. Still heavily influenced by the fairy tales and myths absorbed from her childhood, Ruby has grown into a multimedia illustrator interested in exploring the darkly sensual, symbolic and surreal undercurrents of life. Ruby's illustrations blend perfectly the mythological, the classical and the future fantastic and are also evocative of Beardsley and Mucha. She is now a much sought-after cover artist and interior illustrator for books across many genres, and is the creator of the ongoing Wraeththu Tarot project.

Ruby is up for designing anything as long as it fits in with her bohemian aesthetic and animal-loving ethos (her dream is to run a combined cat sanctuary and art gallery by the sea). On any one day she might be fleshing out a tattoo design and then the next sketching concept art for a theatre set or perhaps sourcing unusual props for a photo-shoot.

E. S. Wynn

E.S. Wynn is the author of over thirty books, the chief editor of Thunderune Publishing (and the associated magazines: *Daily Love, Weirdyear, Yesteryear Fiction, Farther Stars Than These, Linguistic Erosion,* and *Smashed Cat Magazine.*) He manages dozens of websites, has written hundreds of articles and short stories for a number of publications, has taught classes in literature, creative writing, marketing, math, spirituality and guided meditation, voiced fifteen albums as a voice actor and even spent time working as a model for stock photography. He has a bachelor's degree in English, has been trained in Reiki and other forms of energy healing and is a proud Freemason.

Storm Constantine's Wraeththu Mythos

Also published by Immanion Press

By Storm Constantine

The Wraeththu Chronicles
The Enchantments of Flesh and Spirit
The Bewitchments of Love and Hate
The Fulfilments of Fate and Desire

The Wraeththu Histories
The Wraiths of Will and Pleasure
The Shades of Time and Memory
The Ghosts of Blood and Innocence

Wraeththu
(omnibus edition of the Wraeththu Chronicles)

The Hienama
Student of Kyme
The Moonshawl (forthcoming)

Other Mythos Novels and Anthologies

Paragenesis, edited by Storm Constantine & Wendy Darling
Para Imminence, edited by Storm Constantine & Wendy Darling
Breeding Discontent by Wendy Darling and Bridgette Parker
Terzah's Sons by Victoria Copus
Song of the Sulh by Maria J. Leel

Visit http://www.immanion-press.com for details of these and
other Immanion Press publications